Beelzebelle

Heide Goody & Iain Grant

Pigeon Park Press

Paperback ISBN: 978-0-9933655-0-8
Ebook ISBN: 978-0-9933655-1-5

Cover artwork and design copyright © Mike Watts 2016
(www.bigbeano.co.uk)

Published by Pigeon Park Press

www.pigeonparkpress.com
info@pigeonparkpress.com

No babies were harmed in the writing of this book.

Or monkeys.

Or dogs.

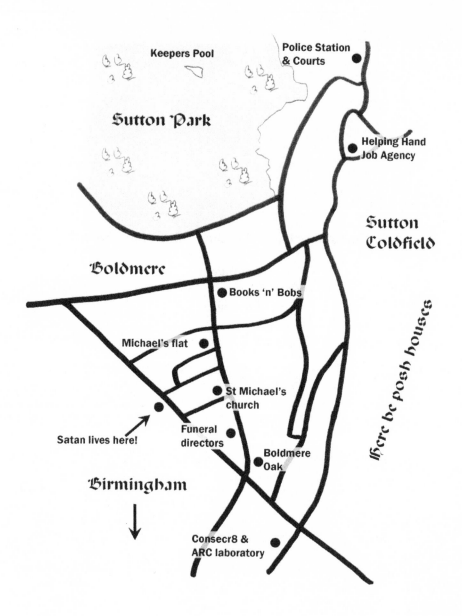

"Jeremy. I thought we said six o'clock," said Sandra.

"Running a little late. That's all," said Jeremy Clovenhoof.

"You could have phoned," she said.

Clovenhoof held up a Mars Bar.

"It seems to be out of charge."

"Well, you're here," she said testily, "and I am incredibly late. Good news is Jack-Jack is already in bed and fast asleep. Help yourself to anything you like in the house. I'll be back by eight, nine at the latest."

Sandra squeezed past him.

"Call me if there's any problem!"

Clovenhoof waved her off. He actually waved at a hedge, but didn't know because he was blind and had been blind all day long.

"Right, Gorky," he said, feeling his way into the house. "You heard the lady. We can help ourselves to anything in the house. Loose change, jewellery, portable valuables. Let's get to it."

Clovenhoof's capuchin monkey helper squeaked and set to work.

After much in the way of stumbling, tripping, and a painful encounter between a dining table and groin, Clovenhoof discovered this family household had nothing worth stealing.

Gorky screeched imploringly. Clovenhoof knew what he wanted.

"No, he's asleep," said Clovenhoof. "It would be nice, I know, but if having a child of my own has taught me anything, it would be that, well, if it taught me *anything*, it would be that the faces babies pull while pooping are just hilarious. But if it's taught me two things, the other would be that if a baby's asleep, you let it sleep."

Gorky humphed in his squeaky capuchin way.

"Cheer up, chimp," said Clovenhoof. "If we don't cock this up tonight, we'll get invited back another time. Play the long game."

Gorky muttered to himself.

"Well, life is tough. And short. And it's always unfair. Now, go and get me something to eat and drink."

Gorky hopped off.

Barely minutes later, Clovenhoof sniffed.

"Is something burning?" he called.

Gorky squawked from the kitchen.

"Are you sure?"

Gorky bustled through the doorway and placed a tray on Clovenhoof's lap.

"What's this?" said Clovenhoof.

Gorky guided his hands to a spoon and a hot bowl.

"But everything's okay in the kitchen?" said Clovenhoof. "Because I thought I could smell something."

Gorky lacked the vocal control to tut but gave Clovenhoof a simian equivalent.

"Well, I can smell soup *now*. I meant something else."

There came the piercing high-pitched whistle of a smoke detector upstairs.

"Like that!" snapped Clovenhoof.

He stood up quickly, the tray nonetheless held carefully in his hands.

"You left the cooker on!"

Gorky screeched angrily at him.

"If a monkey is clever enough to cook soup, he can remember to turn the bloody gas off!"

From the baby monitor came the murmurs and sniffs of a baby tossing unhappily in its sleep. Clovenhoof turned to the door.

"You find the smoke detector and take the batteries out, Gorky. *I* will deal with the kitchen."

Clovenhoof took one step and kicked something hard, round and plastic. It flew through the air, bounced off the wall, and then landed, playing a tinny nursery rhyme at high volume.

"Bloody toys!" snapped Clovenhoof, stepped forward, trod on the same object again, and slipped over onto his back. The soup hit him a moment later, but it seemed a very long moment, probably because he knew it was coming.

Steaming tomato soup splashed across his chest, its gooey heat seeping through his shirt almost instantly. Clovenhoof had endured and enjoyed the fires of Hell, but it was the surprise of the bubbling broth that made him leap up, screaming, and, in an instant, rip his scalding shirt from his torso.

The first hints of a cry warbled from the baby monitor.

"Gorky! Smoke alarm!" Clovenhoof yelled.

He hurried to the kitchen.

"Cooker," he said and felt his way along the surface.

By luck more than skill, his hands found the hob controls and managed to turn the gas off.

The smoke detector was still going.

"Damn it, Gorky," he said and turned.

At that point, his midriff nudged something metal and pokey. Before he had time to register it, Clovenhoof had tipped the pan of burning soup off the hob and over his crotch. Clovenhoof screamed again. Louder, naturally.

"Hot cock!" he yelled and, pained, stripped off his trousers and boxers to cool his tender parts. "You've melted my manhood, you maniac!" he cried. "Did no one ever tell you to always keep the pan handles turned in? You're a health and safety nightmare!"

The alarm still persisted. Clovenhoof could hear Jack-Jack crying.

Naked and lightly coated with slowly cooling soup, Clovenhoof scrambled blindly for the stairs. At the top, he could hear the alarm almost directly above him. He reached up, found the fast plastic disk of the alarm and ripped it from the wall. It continued to whistle in his hand, so he pounded it against the wall until it shut up.

He threw the defeated alarm down.

"Gorky!"

Clovenhoof heard a gurgle and laugh from along the landing. Coughing on the plaster dust, Clovenhoof entered the room. He could see nothing, of course, but he could hear Jack-Jack in his cot. He could, he was certain, also hear the sound of a disobedient capuchin playing peek-a-boo with the little boo.

"I told you to sort out the alarm," said Clovenhoof.

Gorky made a dismissive noise and then gave a curious grunt.

Clovenhoof gestured at his own naked, sticky body.

"This is your fault," he said. "All of this. And look what you did to my knob! I'm sure even you can see it's red-raw." He thought about that. "Redder than usual. I'm going to be dipping it in ice-cream for a week just to soothe my pain."

The thought of basting his genitals with ice-cream distracted Clovenhoof and his anger for a moment.

"Well, you're looking after young Giblet now. You keep him occupied while I find some fresh clothes."

He turned from the room and worked his way along the landing to another room. The plush carpet underfoot suggested a bedroom.

"Bathrobe," he said to himself, feeling around. "Trousers. Anything."

He found the door handles of a fitted wardrobe and opened it. He ran his grubby hands along the hanging clothes.

"Too frilly. Too thick. Corduroy? In the twenty-first century? Jesus! Ooh."

Clovenhoof pulled out something light and silky. It could have been a kimono or a dressing gown; he couldn't tell. He struggled with the fastenings, spun in circles while he struggled into it and then, huffing, pulled it down.

"A little snug in the chest, but not bad," he said. "Right, Gorky. I'm coming to take over."

He became disorientated in his manoeuvring and edged towards the nearest wall. His fingers found a door handle.

He opened it, slipped through, and, almost instantly, walked into something.

"What?"

Realisation dawned quickly. The iron railings to the front and side of him. The cool air wafting around his exposed legs. The bedroom had a balcony, one of those pathetically small British balconies that was barely deep enough for one person to stand on. It was ostentatious, and Clovenhoof was jealous. To be able to step out of one's bedroom and greet the morning, to feel the breeze rise up your skirts and soothe one's scalded nether regions...

The door behind Clovenhoof clicked shut. Clovenhoof could tell from the chunky nature of the sound that this was the click of something locking firmly into place, of a door rendering itself unopenable. Clovenhoof found and waggled the door handle. He was correct. The door was locked.

"Hmmm," he mused out loud. "Locked out on an upstairs balcony, covered in soup, and wearing nothing but what I now suspect is a woman's dress." He patted his pockets. "With no phone to call for help."

8

He felt beyond the edges of the balcony and found nothing to grasp onto, no neighbouring balcony to leap to, no drainpipe to shin down. He shrugged.

"I've been in worse situations," he said. "Probably. Gorky!"

The monkey screeched from the bathroom window. Something hard and plastic smacked Clovenhoof in the face. It was one of the household phones.

Clovenhoof felt for the buttons and attempted to dial Ben Kitchen's number. On the seventh attempt, Ben said, "Hello."

"Good. It's you," exclaimed Clovenhoof.

"Who else would it be?" said Ben.

"Well, so far it's been three angry old women, a tyre fitter, a pizza delivery place, and a man called Roy."

There was a pause.

"By any chance," said Ben slowly, "have your attempts at blind babysitting gone horribly wrong?"

Clovenhoof made a noise of disgust.

"Some people have no faith. You want me to fail in life, don't you? Just because a friend phones you up when they're locked out on a balcony in ladies clothes, doesn't mean things have gone 'horribly wrong'."

"What's happened?" said Ben wearily.

"Well..." said Clovenhoof.

Some weeks earlier...

Chapter 1 – In which Clovenhoof gets a baby and Nerys doesn't get a free holiday

Jeremy Clovenhoof regarded the cat on the counter. Its eyes were half-open and seemed to gaze through him.

"Don't give me that look," said Clovenhoof. "I bet your life didn't pan out the way you planned either. What? You think you're some sort of mighty jungle predator? I know you. You've spent your whole life lounging about in Mrs Tompkins' house. Rubbing yourself against her like some shameless hussy for turkey titbits, chasing shadows, doing recreational catnip from time to time. Hunting?" Clovenhoof spat and stamped his hooves. "Wander into the kitchen. Look for the pink food bowl. Dinner is served. Whoop-de-do." Clovenhoof gave the animal a bitter stare. "You can't judge me, *pussy!*"

The cat said nothing. It was a cat.

"Me?" said Clovenhoof. "I'm Satan, Lucifer, Angel of the Bottomless Pit. I've still got the moves. The horns, the hooves. The looks of a rock god. Maybe a rock god who's partied a little too hard, but a rock god nonetheless. Okay, I work in the back room of an undertaker's, grappling daily with coffin dodgers who failed the acid test. Yes. Yes, I know that The Royal Borough of Sutton Coldfield isn't exactly the kind of place people think of when they talk about the devil walking the earth but, I've got to tell you, you go down to the Boldmere Oak on Grab-a-Granny night and you'd be surprised ..."

The outer door chimed. Clovenhoof immediately swept the dead cat off the counter and out of sight, and began to whistle a nonchalant little tune that sounded anything other than innocent.

Spartacus Wilson, the ten-year-old bane of St Michael's Primary School, and the reason why the entirety of the 6th Boldmere Cubs were kicked out of the scouting movement and had to form their own unaffiliated breakaway group, backed into reception. Behind him a hulking contrivance of black shininess, pink folded material, and an almost infinite number of buttons, clips and levers came to a halt.

"What the Hell's that?" said Clovenhoof.

13

Spartacus looked at him like he was mentally deficient, but then he looked at most people that way. Having said that, Clovenhoof was surprised he didn't get stranger looks from people. He was, after all, a red devil with goat's legs and horns, and hardly anyone seemed to notice. Or maybe it was as Michael said: the British were just too polite to mention it.

"It's a pram," said Spartacus.

"For a baby?" He looked at the monstrosity. "One baby? I've seen emperors with less showy carriages."

"You chat a load of eggy guff," said Spartacus.

"And you're late," Clovenhoof replied. He slapped a wad of home-printed leaflets on the counter. "These aren't going to post themselves. There's a quid in it when you're done."

"I don't get out of bed for less than ten pounds," said Spartacus.

"Yeah, but you're already up. A hundred leaflets and there'll be two shiny pound coins for you."

"Eight quid and I don't care if it's covered in dog doo."

"A fiver," said Clovenhoof, exasperated.

"A fiver and you let me look at a dead body like you said you would."

"I'm not allowed," said the Angel of the Bottomless Pit. "I could get into trouble."

"And you're not going to be in trouble for advertising an illegal pet cremation service?"

"It's not illegal. It's just deeply unprofessional and very wrong."

"Particularly since you don't even bother cremating them. Just give them a pile of ashes in a tin trophy from Tony's Sports Emporium."

"I've had no complaints," said Clovenhoof. "And then I get to sell the furry stiffs to my mate next door, Ben, and he uses them for taxidermy."

Clovenhoof saw the question in Spartacus's eyes.

"He stuffs animals."

The look in the boy's eyes no longer contained a question.

"I heard about a man who did that with a horse and caught a bum disease that made him go blind."

"I mean he mounts them," scowled Clovenhoof.

"Whatever," said Spartacus. "Anyway, I've got to take Bea round to my gran's." Spartacus pointed at the pram. "Beatrice. My sister. Mum and her boyfriend, Animal Ed, had this bust up cos he was snogging a tart in the Boldmere Oak, so she's taking the tickets and his cash and going on holiday cos she's got post-traumatic thingy. I'm taking Bea to my gran's and I get to stay over at Herbie Gates' house for a few weeks while she's gone."

"Animal Ed? The guy with the exotic pet shop on Bush Road?"

"Yeah, loves animals. Mum reckons he was all over that woman because she was wearing a leopard-print dress."

"Nerys," said Clovenhoof, recognising the dress sense and modus operandi of his upstairs neighbour.

"Ed let me hold a tarantula once. Actually, Ed was probably one of the least crappy boyfriends my mum's had."

"And she's certainly had a lot."

Colour flared in the boy's cheeks.

"I'm just saying she's had a lot of men," said Clovenhoof. "Popular woman."

The thing in the pram made a burbling sound, and Spartacus automatically jiggled the pram by the handle until the noise subsided.

"You're a cock, Mr Clovenhoof."

Clovenhoof was happy to agree with that.

"Tell you what. Leave the baby here, tell your grandmother she can pick it up later, and you can do my leaflets in the meantime."

"You? Look after Bea? Have you ever looked after a baby before?"

"Sure. Feed them. Walk them. Throw a stick in the park. Child's play." Clovenhoof thrust a crumpled five pound note at the boy with one hand and his mobile phone with the other.

Spartacus snatched up the money but stared blankly at the chunky brick of a mobile phone.

"Seriously? I'm not touching your clockwork knob-phone." He pulled out a slim rectangle with a protective rubber cover featuring a T-Rex. "You should give that back to Queen Victoria before she notices it's missing."

Spartacus swiped and tapped his phone.

"Gran," he said loudly. "It's me. Mum's told me to bring Bea over but I'm leaving her at the funeral place. The funeral place. Buford's. I've got to deliver some flyers, but I've left Bea with Mr Clovenhoof for a bit and then I'm staying at Herbie's. No, she's not hungover. She's going to Kenya. On holiday. Look, I've got to go and deliver these things." Spartacus's voice dropped to a sudden whisper. "Love you too." He hung up.

"Right." Clovenhoof pushed the pile of leaflets towards Spartacus.

"And?" said the boy.

"What?"

"A dead body."

"Coming right up."

Clovenhoof bent down, hoiked the cat off the floor by the scruff of its neck and held it up for the boy to see.

"Spartacus, meet Snarf. Snarf, Spartacus."

"A real dead body!" said Spartacus.

"This is real. Deposited with me by Mrs Tompkins yesterday, who's expecting an urn of precious cat dust later this afternoon. Real body. Real dead. You didn't specify a species."

Spartacus snorted.

"You truly are a complete cock," he said, and left with the leaflets, slamming the door behind him.

"Wouldn't want to be half a cock, would I?" said Clovenhoof.

In response to the slamming of the door, the baby started to cry, a few tentative wails at first, a little limbering up exercise, and then a full-throated howl. Clovenhoof scooted round the counter, pushed back the pram hood, and looked at the creature for the first time. Clovenhoof had very little experience with babies, either in this life or his former existence as Prince of Hell.

There were no babies in Hell. In the Good Old Days, babies had been sent to the nothingness of Limbo and, later, in the namby-pamby restructuring following the Reformation, all were transferred to Heaven. Babies could never go to Hell; they were deemed incapable of sin. Sure, there were demons with baby faces. In fact, the screwed up little face in the pram, all red, furious and

16

open-mouthed, put Clovenhoof in mind of Beelzebub at the height of his demon wrath.

He'd had little need or reason to come into contact with babies on Earth. They didn't hang out in pubs. They didn't frequent the bookies. They had no money he could steal, borrow or con from them. They didn't know any juicy gossip or dirty jokes. They were clearly without use or value.

They weren't particularly attractive either. Their limbs were too pudgy and their heads were too big. This last attribute, Clovenhoof understood, was a deliberately cruel joke the Almighty had played on mothers in labour following that whole garden/apple/serpent business. He'd heard it said that all babies resembled Winston Churchill and Clovenhoof could see that, assuming that it referred to physical resemblance only and not, say, political opinions on Indian independence or the desire to carpet-bomb German cities.

The baby's cry was something quite impressive. The high notes were clear and piercing, like a needle to the brain. Below, the throaty roar wasn't particularly strong, but it had a tone of utter urgency to it that cried wordlessly, "Attend to me! Attend to me! The world is going to end if you don't attend to me!"

Clovenhoof could have listened to it forever, but it was the kind of noise that drew attention in the hushed confines of a funeral directors.

"You need to stop now," he told the baby.

The baby did no such thing.

"Right, listen. Bee... Beebee... Beelzebelle. You need to pipe down before someone comes in."

The baby wailed on.

"Fine," he said, pulled back the fleecy covers, dug his hands under her armpits, and lifted her out. She stopped crying immediately.

Baby Beelzebelle kicked and wriggled as he held her up.

"You're not even working with me," said Clovenhoof. "I'm putting all the effort in here."

As he drew her close, all warm and squidgy, the baby reached up and grabbed onto his horns. Clovenhoof froze and thought on the matter.

"Hmmmm. Endearing behaviour or gross invasion of private space?"

The baby popped her lips, blinked, and pulled on his left horn.

Clovenhoof growled. The baby smiled and burbled.

"Let's put you somewhere out of the way. I've got a cat cremation to fake before lunchtime."

Clovenhoof went into the viewing room next door, dragging the pram with him. An unoccupied coffin rested on the panelled table. Forcibly unpeeling Beelzebelle's grip on his horns, Clovenhoof laid her down in the cushioned satin interior.

He stepped back and looked at her. She looked at him.

"Can I get you anything while you wait?" he said. "Tea? Coffee?"

Beelzebelle gurgled and blew a spit bubble out of her mouth.

"Fine," said Clovenhoof.

Ash theft was a fine art. Buford's Funeral Directors had numerous clients' ashes on the premises for short periods of time. These would be the source of Clovenhoof's fake pet remains. He had weighed Snarf the cat and done his calculations, and planned to steal a teaspoonful from each urn, four and a half ounces of ash. This was a sneaky and laborious process and involved not only avoiding the attention of Manpreet Singh, his supervisor, but also humming his own 'secret mission' theme tune under his breath.

Mission completed, Clovenhoof returned to his back room and secured the ashes in a tin urn that had once been an under-13s netball trophy, just as the door chimed and a woman walked in. Clovenhoof looked her up and down, from her over-stretched lycra leggings to her gravity-defying hair. She peered at him with wide eyes, made all the wider by the thick eyeliner she wore and by the fact that she clearly needed glasses but was too vain to wear them.

"Over here, madam," he said, waving at her from a distance of six feet.

She gave Clovenhoof a look.

"My grandson said I should come here," she said. "That's right. Grandson. Don't look old enough, do I?"

She gave him a further look, an invitation to either agree or perhaps say something charming.

"Funeral plan, is it?" said Clovenhoof and pulled out a brochure from the rack.

"I don't need a funeral plan," she said.

"Ah, planning on being left out with the recycling, are you? Or doing a DIY job in the back garden? Very green."

"What?" she scowled. "I've no intention of dying yet. How old do you think I am?"

"Seventy-three?"

"Spartacus said something about posting leaflets and me needing to come down here."

Realisation dawned on Clovenhoof.

"Oh, Spartacus. Got ya." He swapped the funeral brochure for one of his far jollier and much more cheaply printed animal cremation leaflets. "Gerbil. Tortoise. Guinea pig. You bring 'em, we burn 'em. Got a special on dogs this week."

"I beg your pardon?" said the woman, her voice rising to a squeak.

"You do have pets, don't you?" said Clovenhoof.

"I have tropical fish."

"Hmmm. Never done fish before. They'd be quite soggy. Maybe if I batter them first..."

"Is this some kind of joke?"

"No, madam," he said. "This is the funeral industry. We're not allowed to make jokes. You take that and give me a call when little Nemo dies."

Spartacus's grandma took the leaflet hesitantly.

"But he told me I had to come here. Something about his mum."

"Yes," said Clovenhoof helpfully. "She's gone on holiday to Kenya because leopard print drives her boyfriend wild with desire."

"Yes. That sounds about right," said the woman faintly.

"Now, is there anything else I can help you with this morning?"

"Definitely not," said the woman and left.

Clovenhoof smiled broadly. He liked helping members of the public. He also liked not helping members of the public. Most of all he liked to confuse members of the public.

Clovenhoof went through to the viewing room and saw the baby asleep in the open coffin.

"Ah," he said.

In an upstairs flat on Bush Road, Nerys Thomas woke up in the tangled sheets of an otherwise empty double bed and stared at the ceiling.

Here we are again, she thought to herself. How many different bedroom ceilings had she stared up over the years, her hungover brain awash with both a sense of shame and of minor sordid triumph? She used to keep a tally. She actually used to keep a dossier, a scrapbook of her sexual conquests, but she was past that phase. She sometimes posted on the *Rate My Shag* website, but that was mainly to help others.

From elsewhere in the flat came the sounds of breakfast being cooked, and of at least three tropical birds hooting and squawking at each other. Nerys rolled naked off the bed and groaned as the blood and the full force of the hangover rushed to her head. Maybe a fry-up would do her some good. Subjecting herself to the menagerie of pets and exotic creatures Ed kept around the house definitely wouldn't.

"I'm getting too old for this." She stumbled over discarded stilettos and a pair of jeans and, in the closed-curtained gloom, checked herself in the mirror above the bedroom sink. She was nothing if not critical. "Still looking perky though."

She jiggled up and down and considered her best-loved attributes.

"Soon. Soon, I'll be too old for this."

Nerys heard a buzzing sound. She rooted through the debris on the bed, tossed aside tights, socks and bra, and found her mobile inside her screwed up leopard print dress.

"What do you want?" she said.

"How you doin'?" said Clovenhoof.

"I was fine until you rang," she said. "Does Satan do wake-up calls now?"

"People call me Jeremy," he said.

"People don't know the real you," she replied.

Nerys held the phone wedged between cheek and shoulder, and attempted to climb into her dress.

"Are you still at Animal Ed's?" he asked.

Nerys froze.

"How did you know that?"

"I have ways and means."

"I don't want to know."

"Wouldn't want to spoil the air of mystery?"

"No, just don't give a shit."

"You're such a flirt. I've got something you might be interested in."

"I've seen it before, Jeremy, and I wouldn't touch it even if you cleaned it in bleach."

"No. It's something every woman wants."

"What?"

There was a sharp knock, not at the door, but at the window – the first floor bedroom window. Frowning, Nerys adjusted her dress and pulled back the curtains. Clovenhoof grinned at her, his mobile phone to his ear.

She lifted the window sash.

"How the Hell...?"

She looked past him and down. Clovenhoof stood at the top of an extended ladder with its feet wedged into the gutter of Bush Road. Behind him, the slate-grey rooftops of suburban Sutton Coldfield stretched towards the distant motorway.

"Where did you get that from?"

"Number sixteen," he said, nodding up the road. "They're having new tiles."

"The roofer will be furious when he comes back and sees his ladder is gone."

"What do you mean 'comes back'? He's going nowhere. It'll be fine." Clovenhoof made to peer past her into the bedroom. "So, how was he? Animal by name, animal by nature?"

"It's not like that," Nerys replied.

"Oh?"

"Ed and I are going to go on holiday together. He suggested it last night. An all-expenses paid trip to Kenya. Flights leave this afternoon."

"And so last night was just to..." Clovenhoof attempted some vulgar hand actions but wobbled precariously and had to grab hold of the ladder once more. "... to cement the deal?"

"Exactly."

Clovenhoof nodded approvingly.

"A woman using her body to get material rewards."

"Hey. I'm not a prostitute," said Nerys.

"The word is entrepreneur," Clovenhoof corrected.

Nerys really wasn't sure if she should be offended.

"As an entrepreneur, you'll have an eye for a bargain," said Clovenhoof. "And have I got a bargain for you."

He gestured downwards. Nerys leaned out the window to look. A chunky pink baby carriage stood on the pavement.

"You've stolen a pram? Oh, that's low. Ladders is one thing but..." She fixed him with a glare. "Why would I want a pram? I don't have a baby."

"But that's the beauty of the deal I'm offering," said Clovenhoof. "Not only do you get the pram for the rock bottom price of five thousand pounds, but I'm also throwing in ..."

He was interrupted by a shout from within the flat.

"What?" yelled Ed. "You can't!"

Nerys looked the bedroom door and listened to her lover's frantic words from the kitchen.

"I paid for those tickets!" he shouted at whoever was on the other end of the telephone. "They are mine and this is theft!"

Nerys began to shake her head. This did not sound good.

"Jesus Christ, Toyah, what have I done to deserve this treatment?" There was a very long pause. "Well, yes, but apart from that?" said Ed.

"I would suggest that your holiday to Kenya might be off," said Clovenhoof cheerily. "No matter how much cementing of the deal you did last night."

"It's not my fault!" cried Ed. "She was wearing leopard print! Wait, Toyah! Wait!"

There was silence and then a stream of quiet swearing.

"Nerys?" called Ed. "Nerys, I've just got to pop out for a bit. You can let yourself out, can't you?"

Keys jangled, feet clattered on stairs, a door slammed, and then silence. Nerys stood, stunned, in the musty pet-shop and sweat stink of Ed's bedroom, wearing nothing but a tight dress and a gobsmacked expression.

"Now, about this pram..." said Clovenhoof.

Nerys whirled on him.

"Absolute bargain as I was saying," he said.

"Jeremy."

"Yes?"

"You can't die, can you? You can't even really be hurt."

"True," said Clovenhoof. "Those Heavenly gits fixed it that I couldn't get back to Hell by just killi..."

As the pavement rushed up to meet him, Clovenhoof couldn't help but admire the strength of a woman spurned.

Books 'n' Bobs, Ben Kitchen's second-hand bookshop on Boldmere High Street, was the kind of shop that had almost no customers and only survived because of low rent, low capital outlay, and an owner who was willing to live on beans on toast nine meals out of ten. Whole days went by without a single customer.

So it was that when the door chimed and Ben was forced to drag his attention away from a battered copy of *Christmas Stuffing: Make Your Own Nativity Scene From Roadkill,* it was with the air of one who has been rudely interrupted.

It was Jeremy Clovenhoof, sporting a livid graze on his face and wheeling a pink pram ahead of him. Ben grunted in greeting and flicked a pointing finger between Clovenhoof's face and his own.

"Snap."

Clovenhoof looked at the scratches that covered Ben's face.

"Head-butted a pavement. You?"

"You know those Canada geese in Sutton Park I was going to kill and mount?"

"Mmmm."

"Turns out that they have strong opinions on being picked up by amateur taxidermists. And did you know that webbed feet could have claws too? I did not know that either 'til today."

"Cheer up," said Clovenhoof, and pulled out a carrier bag and deposited it on the counter. "Brought you a little something."

Ben peered inside the bag.

"Cat. Neat. Thanks."

"Always happy to help a mate. That'll be twenty quid."

Ben grimaced and patted pretend pockets.

"Bit low on funds at the moment. Been trying to entice customers in with my new window display."

"Ah. The window display," said Clovenhoof.

Ben had decided to merge his new taxidermist interest with his work, and created a decorative diorama in the window. Stuffed stoats, squirrels, moles and a solitary badger were arranged in a homey little scene, several with tiny books in their paws.

"What's it supposed to be?" said Clovenhoof.

"What?" said Ben, surprised and somewhat offended. "They're all enjoying their books, aren't they? Perhaps they're on a picnic or a school outing. And all those little ones are listening to wise old badger read his stories."

"And why are their eyes pointing in different directions?"

"Eyes are difficult."

"And the badger with his mouth wide open?"

"He's reading. Quite a few of my customers look like that when they're reading."

"And that white stuff pouring out of his ears and nose?"

"Some of the tapioca stuffing has escaped. I'll clean it up."

Clovenhoof nodded.

"Because, to be honest – and I'm nothing but honest ..."

"Err, no."

"It looks like a bunch of riverbank crackheads trying to fund their habit by robbing a bookshop. Stoaty-boy there, high as a kite, is going to fence that copy of Barbara Cartland to buy his next fix."

"But look at all the little ones gathered round badger."

"Clearly, the Fagin figure," said Clovenhoof. "Except their poor old leader has found one of them ancient magical texts that drives you insane. All his brains are oozing out and, at any moment, he's going to go mad and eat all the tiny rodent junkies. It's smashing!"

"You're rude, Jeremy."

"I'm just speaking the truth as I find it. I think they could be of great use though, for frightening burglars away. I wouldn't want to break in here and find those things facing me." Clovenhoof looked round. "Not that there's anything worth stealing in here anyway."

"Taxidermy's a fine art."

"At least when you were painting tiny soldiers, none of them looked like they were tripping on acid."

"I'm just learning, Jeremy. Each one better than the last. Look at this."

Ben pulled out a white rabbit skin and placed it on the counter. He smoothed it out so it looked like it had been caught unawares by a steam roller.

"I think he's overdone the five-two diet," said Clovenhoof.

"It's a lovely pelt," said Ben. "So soft."

"It'd make a lovely pair of gloves. Or a muff."

Ben gave him an irritable look.

"I think this rabbit is going to have a very noble bearing. He'll be the Alexander the Great of stuffed animals."

"You've always pictured Alexander the Great as a white rabbit?"

"I think if I find the right pose and the right mounting materials, it could be something truly special."

"Special is the word that definitely springs to mind."

"I'm popping out to see what I can salvage from that skip on Beechmount Drive. Um." Ben pointed at the pram. "I couldn't help but notice..."

"Ah," said Clovenhoof. "Now, you're a man of the world, aren't you?"

Even Ben would be the first to admit that this was not true. Not unless the 'world' was limited to the confines of the city of Birmingham and that world was defined in terms of taxidermy, small scale table-top warfare, old books, and takeaway menus.

"Your wife, Jayne," said Clovenhoof, "is currently bumming her way around the world. Where is she now?"

"Tuvalu, I think," said Ben.

"But one day she'll come back for you and she'll want to settle down with you and have kids."

"Right..."

"Well, why not get ahead of the game?" said Clovenhoof, gesturing dramatically to the pram. "What a lovely surprise it will be for her. Yours for a pittance. Four thousand quid, from one friend to another."

Ben put on his stern face.

"Did you steal that, Jeremy?"

"It was given to me. I swear."

Ben shook his head.

"Then take it back," said Ben. "Do the right thing."

In their flat on Cofield Road, the Archangel Michael bent down, kissed the forehead of his sleeping love, and silently slipped out of the front door. The noonday sun brought a light to the world that matched the contentment in his soul, and he offered up a brief prayer of thanks to the Almighty before setting off down towards the busy Chester Road and work.

The last year and a bit had brought some monumental changes to his life. Yes, there had been the wholly traumatic transition from life in the Celestial City of Heaven to life in urban England. That had been deeply unpleasant, not least because he had been forced to take a flat in the same house as the Adversary, Satan himself. The following months of adapting to life as a mortal – oh, the gross *anatomical* processes of the human body, it had *way* too many orifices – had proved a true challenge to his resolve and his spirituality. But he had come through them all a stronger individual, with faith, purpose, and a totally kick-ass wardrobe.

These had now all been put into a deeper perspective by more recent changes. Three months previously, Michael had taken up a full-time job with ARC. A month after that, he had sold the rights to his self-coded G-Sez phone app to a Korean company and used the funds to put down a deposit on a flat for himself and Andy. He had moved from the House of the Devil into a world of gentle calm in the Kingsleigh flats on Cofield Road. It was still startling to *not* be disturbed by the drunken antics, the yapping of Nerys' rat-terrier, or the bamboozlingly frequent explosions in Clovenhoof's flat. Normality had come as a surprise, and a sweet one at that.

On Beechmount Drive, a pair of legs stuck out from a skip beside the new Consecr8 Church. There had been a lot of changes in the area recently. In an area previously dominated by old and tired-looking tower blocks, a new housing estate had sprung up with the Consecr8 Church at its heart. The pre-fab units of the ARC laboratory where Michael worked had been constructed even more recently. The hairy little legs in the skip were just the latest addition.

Michael crossed over to inspect them. They looked too thin to be real legs. Michael wondered if someone had dumped a shop mannequin, but the demand for mannequins with hairy legs was probably very niche. Up close, Michael not only saw that the legs were quite human, but also recognised the cheap trainers.

"Ben?"

"A little help, please," came the muffled reply.

Michael stood on an upturned paint pot. He took great care to ensure that his clean shirt and trousers did not touch the filthy skip, and angled Ben's legs round to the side so that he could sit up in the skip.

"Let me guess," said Michael. "You got drunk and this looked like the ideal place to sleep for the night."

"No," said Ben, pulling a piece of electrical cabling from his hair. "I was scavenging for some materials to help turn a rabbit into Alexander the Great and I over-reached."

Michael nodded.

"I would never have guessed that. Not in a thousand years."

Ben gasped uncomfortably and removed a piece of metal tubing from under himself.

"Exactly what I need. Not seen you in a while, Michael."

Michael shrugged charmingly.

"Keeping myself busy. Got the new job." He nodded down the road. "ARC Research Company."

"An IT job?"

"Genetics actually. Working with animal DNA."

"I didn't know you were a scientist."

Ben cast about himself, evidently trying to determine how best to climb out of the skip.

"I try to be all things to all men," said Michael.

Ben put his foot on the lip of the skip, put his weight on it, slipped, rolled off, and landed on the pavement like a very clumsy crab. Michael helped him up.

"So, Alexander the Great?"

"What? Oh. Yes, taxidermy. My new hobby."

Michael treated him to a condescending look.

"Not happy to make a mockery of God's creation of man with your little soldiers, you've moved onto making a mockery of his animal creations."

Ben brushed himself.

"Seriously, Michael?"

"You shall not make any graven images."

"And what does the Bible have to say about homosexuality, Michael?" Ben waggled his eyebrows.

"I see what you're doing," said Michael haughtily. "The Bible has nothing but praise for love expressed between one man and another."

"Yeah, but it's not so keen on the physical expression though, eh?"

Michael spluttered.

"I think it's quite, yes, quite naïve of you to think that love and ... certain acts are synony... Look. It's not like that. In this day and age ... Well, frankly, if lesbians get off scot free, I don't see why I, that is we, that is, you know ... men ..."

Ben slapped him affectionately on the upper arm.

"Just messing with you, Michael. So what do you reckon to this place?"

Ben jerked a thumb at the Consecr8 church behind them. The building had gone up rapidly over the past year and, although there were safety fences around parts of the site and several vehicles from *C. Malarkey Construction Ltd* still about the place, the church building was now complete.

"It's certainly an interesting building," said Michael diplomatically. "All this wood panelling construction makes it look quite... foresty."

28

"Like a log cabin," said Ben.

"Yes," said Michael. "I suppose. That's if log cabins were shaped like bowls. Badly made bowls." He gave up on being nice. "What is it with modern buildings these days? I'm sure buildings are meant to be bigger at the bottom than they are at the top. And what's with all those curved walls? It must have been a devil to carpet inside."

"I think it's funky," said Ben.

Michael made a disapproving noise.

"Funky is one thing but, if it's a church, where's the steeple? Where are the carvings of the saints? Where's the huge image of St Michael throwing down the Great Dragon, Satan? Um, for example."

Ben grinned.

"Your loyalty to St Michael's church would do Reverend Zack proud."

Michael smiled back awkwardly.

"Well, yes. Anyway, duty calls."

Michael headed off down the road towards the ARC module buildings and, once Ben was gone from sight, dusted down his sleeve where the grubby little man had touched him.

Clovenhoof was not a personal fan of manual exertion. Of course, he approved of it in *others*, particularly if it looked arduous and pointless. He went to watch the Birmingham half marathon each year, to point and to laugh and, if no one was looking, to throw things. But he did not enjoy having to do manual work himself.

The house on Chester Road in which he lived had three storeys. It would have been a generous family house a hundred years earlier, but was now divided into flats. Clovenhoof's was on the first floor. The pram carrying little Beelzebelle had many exciting levers and functions but, annoyingly, none of them enabled it to carry itself up stairs. Beelzebelle giggled while he rocked, huffed, and grunted his way up and backed into flat 2a.

"Welcome to *chez* Clovenhoof," he said to the baby, between wheezes. "Bathroom's there. Kitchen's there. Don't touch the Lambrini. That's mine." He lifted her out to give her the full tour.

"Sofa. Computer in case you want some porn. Skull collection, TV. Got a selection of DVDs. All of them about me. *Angel Heart. Devil's Advocate. Constantine. Bedazzled*, both versions."

The baby seemed unexcited, barely able to focus her attention beyond the end of her nose. Clovenhoof positioned her on his hip and steered her chin so she was facing him.

"Listen, chuckles. I'm not exactly happy about this either. No one wants to buy you. Charity shops won't take you. That's your fault for not bringing your A game. Now, I'm not interested in wee babyfolk myself. I'm a lone wolf and my life is all about me, myself, and I, and I don't need you cramping my style. Way I see it, I'm stuck with you until I can get an eBay listing up. In the meantime, you're going to behave yourself and earn your keep by helping me score dates with broody milfs."

Beelzebelle patted him on the nose and dribbled.

"Deal," said Clovenhoof. He propped her in the corner of the sofa and turned the TV on.

Beelzebelle immediately started to cry, an utterly unprovoked wail.

"What?" said Clovenhoof. "But it's *Bargain Hunt!*"

He passed her the remote control. She didn't even bother picking it up and just continued crying.

Beautifully discordant though it was, the crying was entertaining for approximately one minute. After that, Clovenhoof was by turns bored, irritated, and annoyed.

"Okay. Enough now," he said.

She didn't stop.

"No one's impressed."

Still she continued.

"I think this is just attention-seeking behaviour, Little Miss Beelzebelle, and you need to stop right now."

Clovenhoof re-evaluated his approach, went to his computer and googled 'why won't the bloody baby stop crying?'

"Ah-ha. Seven reasons why your baby might be crying," he read. "Just a process of elimination. Number one, hunger."

Clovenhoof went to the kitchen and came back with a bowl containing half a Findus Crispy Pancake, a packet of cheesy Wotsits and a jar of Marmite. He arranged them in front of Beelzebelle but she only paused in her crying long enough to inspect and reject each of them before setting up again.

"Here," said Clovenhoof and tried to push a Wotsit into her mouth. Beelzebelle recoiled and screamed.

Clovenhoof could see what the problem was.

"You've only got one tooth. Hell, girl, you've to cut down on the sugars or get yourself some dentures." He thought for a minute. "I could probably steal some gnashers for you from somewhere. But for now..."

Clovenhoof squished the Wotsits and crispy pancake with the palm of his hand until there was nothing but crumbs and mush.

"There."

And still the ungrateful little creature cried on. Clovenhoof went back to the computer.

"Oh. Milk. Breast milk." He smacked his own forehead. "You need a wet nurse."

He did a quick search for 'wet nurse' and, when the results were unhelpful, added 'tits for hire'. The resulting pages, though interesting, weren't what he was after right now. He bookmarked them for later viewing and searched on. All the while, Beelzebelle wailed.

"All right, all right," he hissed peevishly. "I'm doing my best. It's not like I can produce it myself."

He found the website and number of something called the Sutton Coldfield Union of Mums. The airy-fairy language on the webpage, all about 'bonding' and 'support networks', only confused Clovenhoof, but there was a picture of a smiling woman with a baby clasped leech-like to her breast, and that was good enough for him.

While the phone rang, Beelzebelle's crying got louder and louder.

"Sandra Millet-Walker," said the woman who answered.

"No, I'm Jeremy Clovenhoof. I need breast milk. Do you have any?"

"Pardon?" said the woman.

"Breast milk. Need now. Are you lactating?"

"Who is this?"

Clovenhoof put his finger in his free ear to block out the baby cries.

31

"I told you. I'm Jeremy Clovenhoof. I don't know who you are. Can you help me or not? I've got a baby crying so hard I think it might explode. This is a five boob emergency, woman."

"Mr Michaels," said a voice in Michael's ear.

Michael methodically and unhurriedly placed the pipettor onto the laboratory counter and tapped his earpiece.

"What is it, Freddy?"

"There is a lady here to see you," said Freddy in reception.

Michael looked at the clock. He then stripped off his latex gloves, took the phone from his lab coat pocket.

"Little A," he said aloud.

"Yes Michael," came the beautifully modulated tones of his beloved Andy from wall-mounted speakers.

It had, he had to say, been a stroke of genius to sample Andy's voice for the computer's speech synthesiser. His previous voice-activated AI, Little G, had been included in the deal when he sold his app, so he had built a second generation, which had the added bonus of bringing Andy's voice into the workplace. Michael found computer development ridiculously easy, given that it was simply a way of encoding his will upon a given environment. Such a well-defined and structured way to run things! Michael wished that humans could be more like computers.

"Do I have any appointments today?" asked Michael.

"No, Michael," said Little A.

Michael tapped his earpiece.

"I don't have any appointments, Freddy."

"She says she doesn't have an appointment."

There was a faint and tinny bark in Michael's ear.

"Does she have a stupidly tiny and rat-like dog?" he asked.

"She has an absolutely adorable Yorkshire Terrier called Twinkle," said Freddy.

"Didn't know you were a dog-lover, Freddy."

"There are many facets to Freddy."

Michael inspected the computer next to the sequencer. The latest batch would be running for nine hours at least.

"Tell her I'll be there in a minute," sighed Michael.

The sliding doors zushed open and Michael stepped into reception.

"Michael," Nerys said and, standing on tiptoes, put a kiss on his handsome cheek. "It's been a long time."

"Three weeks."

Twinkle growled at Michael's turn-ups.

"Are you keeping well?" asked Michael.

"Work's a bitch. My boss even more so. My life's a rollercoaster. More of a water ride really. You?"

"Life is beautiful and every day a gift."

He smiled but Nerys knew Michael's smiles – the fake ones, the smug ones, the impatient ones. They were all masks. He did have genuine smiles but hid them as soon as he saw anyone looking.

"So..." she said.

"So," he said.

Nerys tried a smile of her own

"Twinkle's happy to see you."

"What's he done now?" said Michael flatly.

"Twinkle?"

"Jeremy."

"Who says I was here to talk about Jeremy?" she said.

Michael turned to Freddy.

"I'm going out for a bit. Text me if there's an emergency. Fire. Flood. Some of the DNA samples spontaneously turn into dinosaurs and start eating people."

"Could that really happen?" said Nerys.

Michael took her by the elbow and steered her out.

"I think it's important you have a word with him," said Nerys, as they pootled along in Nerys's little car.

"I'm sorry, this is because you saw him with a pram?" said Michael.

"A pram today, a child tomorrow," said Nerys. "It's a slippery slope."

"Why would Jeremy want to steal a child?"

"I don't know," said Nerys. "Harvest their organs. Sell them to running shoe factories in the Far East. The man is the devil incarnate. I mean, literally. You know that. I know that."

"I think I preferred it when you didn't know that," said Michael.

"Doesn't matter," said Nerys. "I just used to think he was a disgusting and self-centred git, but now he's got a label. Anyway, you need to do something."

Nerys emphasised her point by revving the engine in frustration at the traffic lights.

"Why me?" said Michael. "He doesn't like me. He doesn't listen to me."

"You were once the Archangel Michael," said Nerys.

"I still am, dear woman," said Michael, a little wounded.

"Even better. It's like he's the criminal on parole and you're his probation officer."

"I was... demoted, Nerys. It's not my responsibility anymore."

"But you've had training. You've got the knowledge, the insight, the *cojones*."

"Actually, this particular archangel is still getting used to having *cojones*," said Michael. "Swapping my angelic powers for a wrinkly sack of tender things was hardly a step up."

"But can't we report him?" said Nerys.

"To who?"

Nerys gestured upwards.

"You know, God."

"Sure," said Michael. "Of course you can do that."

"How?"

Michael gave her a withering look and silently put his hands together as though for prayer.

"Oh," said Nerys and then, "I just don't know why he has to live *here*, with us."

"I am frankly surprised to hear you talk like that. He is your friend."

Nerys's face twitched irritably.

"I have an appalling taste in friends."

"And lovers," said Michael.

"Hey!"

34

"I was just agreeing with your assessment of your emotional and social intelligence. Point is, though, he is your friend. That he's even managed to make any friends is above and beyond any expectations I ever had."

"So?"

"So," said Michael, "he's happy. And he's going to be as happy here as he would be anywhere else."

Nerys made a doubtful noise.

"What?" said Michael.

Nerys stopped at the T-junction with Chester Road and twisted in her seat to look at Michael.

"I think you're projecting."

"I'm doing what now?" said Michael.

Nerys smiled at him. She, like Michael, had a range of smiles. Several of hers were devious and capricious things.

"*You* are happy," she said. "And you now want to pretend that everyone else is happy. You and your tiny gymnast boyfriend are all cosy in your little pink paradise and you want to ignore the troubles in the wider world."

"That is not fair, Nerys Thomas," said the archangel grumpily. "*One*, I am not ignoring the troubles of the wider world. I help out at the St Michael's mobile soup kitchen on alternate Tuesdays and act as bouncer for the monthly senior citizen whist drives. *Two*, he is not tiny. He's perfectly proportioned and, heightwise, falls well within a standard deviation on a bell curve. And *three*, I don't know if you're being homophobic or not, but our little paradise is not pink."

"Okay, touchy. Jeez."

Nerys set off again.

"The lounge is a charming shade of watermelon," said Michael quietly. "But it's not pink."

The woman from Sutton Coldfield Union of Mums was, ultimately, very helpful. She listened to Clovenhoof's queries and then, in no uncertain terms, told him where to go: the supermarket. Clovenhoof went there, baby in pram (getting down the stairs was much quicker and more fun than going up; both he and Beelzebelle could agree on that) and returned within the hour with several bulging carrier bags. The pram might have been a cumbersome contraption, but its capacity for carrying goods in its various nets, pockets, and folds was amazing. Clovenhoof thought it might be worth taking to the pub some nights, in case he needed someone to wheel him and a goodnight takeaway home.

Clovenhoof mixed up a couple of bottles of formula milk, one for the baby and one for himself, fitted the rubber teats into the screw lids (not until after he had pinged one behind the fridge during his learning curve) and then plonked himself and Beelzebelle on the sofa. He put the bottle in her grasping hands, but held it up for her when he saw that it was perhaps too heavy for her to manage.

He clinked bottles with her.

"When in Rome," he said, and took a deep suck.

He pursed his lips and contemplated the bottle.

"It tastes like..." He paused to think. "If cornflour was a drink. It's like rice pudding but, you know, without the rice, or the sugar or cream. Or any flavour at all." He looked at Beelzebelle. "It's like bottled boredom. You really go for this stuff?"

Beelzebelle munched gummily on the teat, losing a good proportion of it down her chin, but Clovenhoof knew happiness when he saw it.

"You know what would liven this up," he said, leapt up and was back again in moments with a pair of glass bottles. "Lambrini or vodka? Lambrini? Good choice."

They sat side by side in quiet companionship for a while, each enjoying their bottle. Clovenhoof was impressed how the Lambrini had caused the baby milk to curdle and form huge sloppy clumps in the bottle. It was like a lava lamp and a drink at the same time! Groovy!

Gradually, a rich aroma reached Clovenhoof's nose. It had a gusty farmyard quality, meaty and mysterious, with some little sweet and acrid notes in the mix.

"Is someone cooking dinner?" he said and then looked at Beelzebelle.

She looked extraordinarily pleased with herself.

"Oh," said Clovenhoof. "Someone *is* 'cooking dinner'."

He poked at her midriff and felt the squishiness of a nappy beneath her pink baby-gro.

"I invented a man-nappy once," said Clovenhoof. "It was brilliant. But it didn't go down well. Apparently, if a baby craps itself in public it's fine, but if a grown man does it..." He rolled his eyes. "That kind of poo-prejudice. It's racist. That's all I'm saying."

"Victory!"

Clovenhoof stepped back and admired his handiwork.

The nappy battle had not been an easy one. Velcro, poo, and baby lotion were not a natural mix. Baby poop and baby lotion had blended to a fascinating consistency, like fresh bird droppings. The resultant substance had spread itself around the bed, Clovenhoof's face, Clovenhoof's eye and, because he had a pragmatic and unfussy approach to cleaning, the curtains. Baby lotion had also rendered the velcro useless, so Clovenhoof had to resort to other methods to fasten the nappy.

Thus it was that Beelzebelle now lay on Clovenhoof's bed, in a nappy held on with duct tape, the whole thing secured further with a knotted towel, and all held in place with a carrier bag in which Clovenhoof had cut two leg holes. It was a Marks and Spencer carrier bag because Clovenhoof demanded nothing but the best for his little house guest.

"Now it is sleepy-time," he said, not sure if he was talking about the baby or himself.

He arranged his grey and slightly crusty duvet around Beelzebelle so she couldn't roll off the bed.

"Right, some bedtime music." He turned on the stereo. "What do you fancy? Some Judas Priest? Megadeth? Slayer? Ah, no. You'll like this." He popped a cassette tape in. "Bootleg recording from the days when I had my own Heavy Metal band. That's right, my own band, Devil Preacher. Uncle Clovenhoof is one cool mofo."

As the caustic baseline of *Swallow My Fruit, Bitch* filled the room, Beelzebelle jerked her legs excitedly.

"I know, kickin'," grinned Clovenhoof. "Right. That website said you babies would be entertained by a mobile, so I picked this up." He put the phone he had bought in Beelzebelle's hand, and she immediately stuck it in her mouth and munched the corner. "It's only pay as you go, but I downloaded Candy Crush and Angry Birds, so that should be fun. And the website said you should have a cuddly toy. Toy..."

Clovenhoof looked around the bedroom but there were no cuddly toys. He had some specialist 'toys' hidden away at the top of his wardrobe, but he suspected they weren't quite cuddly.

He clicked his fingers.

"Ben has a whole bunch of furry things in his flat. You wait there. I'll get you something." He paused in the doorway. "Call me if you need anything, okay?"

It was a hop, skip, and a trot across the mouldy landing to Ben's flat. He did a rat-a-tat-tat on the door and scuffed it violently with his hoof for good measure. The high-pitched industrial whine within the flat stopped and, moments later, Ben had the door open. He was wearing a linen apron and goggles.

"Doing experimental cooking again?" said Clovenhoof.

Ben held up a length of metal tubing.

"Just forming the framework for Alexander the Bunny," said Ben. "Come in."

Ben, despite theoretically having a wife somewhere, lived the life of an unfussy, unfashionable, and unambitious bachelor. He had temporarily converted his front room into a taxidermist's workshop. The tabletop wargaming miniatures, the painting table, and the boxes of terrain building materials had all been put aside to make room for a skinning station, tubs of preservative chemicals, racks of blades and a lovely little jar full of glass eyes of all shapes and sizes. By the open window, a workbench was set up. Wire frames sat beside the partially stuffed rabbit skin and, at the end, a mounted rotary grinder spun. From mantelpiece, shelf, and window sill, Ben's creations stared at Clovenhoof. Here were arranged the mammals, reptiles, and birds that had not been considered good enough to go in Ben's shop window or to be given as 'gifts' to others. Surrounded on all sides, Clovenhoof felt like he had stumbled into a group session of Ugly Animals Anonymous, or a build-a-bear store from some weird parallel universe.

Ben waggled his tubing.

"I think a solid frame is key," he said, in the manner of one who was growing desperate in his attempts to improve on past failures. "I'm getting some custom polyurethane foam for the stuffing too."

"Tapioca not quite working out for you?" said Clovenhoof, prodding the nose of a rabid-looking chinchilla.

"Have you come to mock?" said Ben.

"Not at all, my geeky friend. In fact, I would like one of your... your... creations for my flat."

"Oh?"

"Something really furry and cuddly."

"These aren't toys, Jeremy."

Clovenhoof eyed a plastic tray containing a trio of jawbones. Lots of nice square teeth. "Of course not," he said. "What about that one?" And he swiped the bones and stuffed them in his jacket pocket while Ben was diverted.

"The pine marten?" said Ben.

"Yes, he's a spritely fellow. Would look great in my living room."

Ben gave him a sceptical look.

"You've done nothing but laugh at my efforts until now. Why the change of heart?"

"Oh, many reasons," said Clovenhoof.

"Such as?"

"The realisation, good buddy, that taxidermy is a means by which we can get to see nature, understand nature, close up. People see it as morbid, but actually it's the preservation of life, a celebration of the natural world."

"You just read that from that copy of Taxidermy Today," said Ben.

"No, I didn't," said Clovenhoof, sweeping the evidence off the table.

Ben shook his head.

"Listen, Jeremy, I ..." Ben stopped and then tilted his head. "Wait. Listen."

"You said."

"No," he scowled and raised a finger pointedly. "Listen. Is that... is that the sound of crying?"

The man was right. Beelzebelle was indeed crying.

"That's impossible," said Ben. "None of us have babies. There's no one living on the ground floor at the moment. Maybe it's an abandoned baby. We'd better call the police..."

Clovenhoof didn't particularly approve of the police. Actually, that wasn't true. He loved the tit-shaped helmets, the pepper spray, the tasers, and the riot shields. He just didn't particularly appreciate having them applied to him. The police, in his experience, were the ultimate party poopers.

"I can't hear any crying," he said loudly.

"Of course you can," said Ben. "It's getting louder."

"It's the belt on your sander thingy," said Clovenhoof.

"Grinder," said Ben. "And no, it isn't."

"Sure it is," said Clovenhoof, stepped over to the workbench, and turned up the speed on the machine. "Oh, yes. Listen. Wah-a-wah-a-wah. Definitely the grinder."

Nerys locked her car.

"Just come inside and speak to him," she said.

"It won't do any good," said Michael, but she heard the resignation in his voice.

"Thank you, Michael," she said.

She looked up at the subdivided house. A window was open on the first floor and the sound of machinery and raised voices appeared to be coming from within.

"I do fear Jeremy is a bad influence on Ben."

"You are a bad influence on Ben," said the archangel. "You're all bad influences on each other."

"Yes, but he's the only one who doesn't know he's got the devil for a next-door neighbour. Come on. Afterwards I will buy you a thank you tipple in the Boldmere Oak."

"Turn that off!" said Ben. "I told you I heard crying."

"It's probably just Nerys's TV," shouted Clovenhoof.

Ben made for the door.

"Yes, well let's go find out."

"Why bother?" said Clovenhoof.

"Are you hiding something, Jeremy?"

"Of course not."

Ben sighed and went to the door.

Panicked, Clovenhoof grabbed the partially stuffed white rabbit and threw it onto the grinder wheel.

"Oh, goodness," he declared. "How did that happen?"

"No!" shouted Ben.

The rabbit, snagged on the disc, was a white blur, a candy-floss whirl of fluffiness.

"What did you do?" yelled Ben. "Turn it off! Turn it off!"

Something – a paw, an ear – caught against the edge of the wheel, and the pelt jammed against the spinning mechanism. At once there was smoke and the smell of burning fur.

"I'm not much of a drinker," said Michael.

"Fine," she said. "Well, I have sorrows to drown and I need someone to hold my hair while I throw up, but if you're not willing to console a friend in a time of crisis..."

"Alcohol is no consoler. And what sorrows?"

"Oh, some jerk of a man who I think isn't taking me on holiday anymore, even though I..." She paused and looked at the expression on Michael's face. "Yeah. One problem at a time, eh?"

"Quite," said Michael. "In fact, these 'Clovenhoof' concerns. You're perhaps projecting issues in your own life onto an external figure."

"Can it, Freud. I'm not projecting anything."

"Really? Because I think Jeremy has calmed down a lot in recent months."

No sooner were the words out of his mouth than a flaming rabbit skin plopped down on his face and wrapped its fiery limbs around his head. Michael screamed. Nerys screamed. Twinkle barked and ran in little circles. Michael clawed the thing off but the flames had spread to the flammable product in his hair. Nerys stamped on the burning animal. Twinkle growled at it and snapped ferociously.

Michael wrenched his shirt over his head and smothered the flames with it, just as Ben came staggering out the front door.

"What the fucking Hell is going on?!" shouted Nerys.

Ben scooped up the smouldering remains of the once beautiful rabbit skin.

"Oh, no."

"Did you do this?" winced Michael.

Ben looked up.

"Jeremy, he..."

"I bloody knew it!" said Nerys. "That man..."

Clovenhoof leaned out the upstairs window.

"Are my ears burning?" he asked, grinning.

"*Your* ears?" hissed Michael. "You set my head on fire!"

Ben was moaning softly to himself, inspecting the ruined pelt.

"It's useless now. The hair's all burned."

"I thought it was a rabbit," said Clovenhoof.

"That's not funny," yelled Ben.

"Jeremy's calmed down, has he?" said Nerys to Michael. "Come on, let's go inspect the damage."

They took a booth in the corner of the Boldmere Oak and, while Ben got the drinks from the bar, Nerys and Michael read Clovenhoof the riot act.

"Someone could have been seriously hurt," said Nerys.

"Someone was," said Michael. Smears of lotion glistened on the edges of his bright pink ears.

"I didn't do it on purpose," said Clovenhoof.

"You never bloody do," said Nerys, and then added, "Except when you do do it on purpose. But it's always you. You're a sodding menace."

"I may not be officially assigned to monitor your behaviour anymore," said Michael, "but you need to just ..." He made a lowering motion with his hands. "... bring it down a notch or two."

"And what if I don't?" said Clovenhoof.

"I'll rip your balls off," said Nerys.

"You're not the boss of me," sniffed Clovenhoof.

She gave him a grim stare.

"I am now."

"Now?"

"Since I discovered you're the damned devil."

"Yeah, that doesn't make you Jesus."

"Get thee behind me, Satan."

"I don't know what you expect of me. You want me to just sit in my little flat, live a quiet little life until the Guy Upstairs grants me a quiet little death?"

"Sounds good to me," said Nerys.

"Find some purpose in life," said Michael. "Something that isn't going to get you into trouble or get people killed. You've got a job. Take pride in that. Add a little to your local community. Participate. But, yes, quietly."

"I don't do quiet," said Clovenhoof.

"We know," said Nerys.

"I do grand and bold. I attempted to overthrow the Almighty, for Hell's sake. If I'm going to do something with this puny mortal life I've been given, then it's something that must say 'Here was a man of vision! Here was a man of epic ambition! Here was the most bold, heroic, and downright manliest man you ever did see!'"

"Lambrini for you," said Ben, putting the glass in front of Clovenhoof.

"Thank you."

"Chardonnay for Nerys, G and T for Michael, and that leaves a cider and black for me. What are we talking about?" he asked, sitting down next to Clovenhoof.

"My world-conquering ambitions," said Clovenhoof.

"You?" said Ben, amused. "Conquer the world?"

"I invaded Spain last year," Clovenhoof retorted.

"You went on holiday," said Michael.

"My cover story. Covert warfare. That's just my style."

"I don't recall you declaring war on Spain while we were there," said Nerys.

"Although, what he did to the hotel plumbing could seriously be described as an act of terrorism," said Ben.

"Yeah," said Clovenhoof, nodding. "Paella bomb. Seriously dirty warfare. Anyway, I might yet conquer the world with my business empire."

"Dodgy pet cremations!" snorted Nerys. "Just another joke."

"Only ever inspired by you," said Clovenhoof. "I see you in your swish office, making deals, making money."

"Having to kowtow to sodding Tina ever since she was made office manager, you mean! You know nothing about business,

Jeremy. Pet cremations, indeed!" Nerys shook her head bitterly and, in doing so, caught sight of someone across the bar. "Ah, speaking of animals that deserve to be burned..."

Nerys stood, grabbed her wine and downed it in a single motion, and stalked over to the bar.

"Ed! Ed! I want a word with you!"

The miserable looking man at the bar looked up from his smartphone and swore.

"Not now, Nerys," he pleaded.

"Not now, when..." Nerys looked at her watch. "When we should be waiting to board our plane for – and I quote – the holiday of my dreams?"

"Shush. She's picking up."

Ed thrust the phone to his ear.

"Toyah! The taxi hasn't arrived yet, but I can still collect my ticket at the gate if ..." He kicked his stool back onto the floor as he stood bolt upright. "*You* cancelled it? That's... that's... well, two can play at that game, Toyah. I bought those tickets, I can cancel them. I'll call the ..." The words choked in his throat. He stared wide-eyed. Nerys attempted to insert herself in his field of vision, increasingly unhappy at being ignored. "Listen, Toyah, this holiday was just meant to be a holiday. Yes, I was planning to meet Mr Kimkemboi but any trade we make would be totally above board ... Toyah. Toyah! Do not go through that gate! You can't. What about your kids? Who's looking after them?"

Ben, who, along with much of the pub, had watched the man's telephonic meltdown, nodded.

"Children. As far as ambitions and legacies go," said Ben, "children are all most of us desire."

"Really?" said Clovenhoof, slurping his drink. "But when I came into your shop with a bargain offer..."

"I don't want children *now*," said Ben, "and I certainly don't want your stolen baby clobber but, one day, the chance to pass my wisdom, my very self onto ..."

Michael put his hand on Ben's.

"You're not suggesting Jeremy has children?" he said, alarmed.

"God, no!" said Ben, almost gagging. "Lord in Heaven, no! I wasn't suggesting that at all. I was just talking generally. Jeremy have children!" He grinned in disbelief. "Can you imagine the evil and twisted little psychos he would raise? Little Baby Clovenhoofs? Ugh! The horror!"

"Well, I'm glad we're of an accord in that matter," said Michael, failing to spot the fresh glimmer in Clovenhoof's eyes. "I think you've already done enough to shock and upset me today, Ben."

"Oh, you've reminded me," said Ben, opening the carrier bag beside him. "I wanted to make it up to you for this afternoon's 'accident'. I saw you'd got a bit of, er, cosmetic damage around your ears, and I managed to salvage some bits of the rabbit skin and I thought to myself, well... I've made these."

He produced his creation from the carrier. Ben had taken the very front portions of the dead rabbit and the hind legs and tail and artfully attached them to an alice band.

"What is it?" said Michael, taking them reluctantly.

"Earmuffs," said Ben. "Try them on."

"Put 'em on," said Clovenhoof. "Don't be ungrateful."

Michael slipped them over his head and carefully adjusted them.

"They are very fluffy," he admitted. "Although, I do wonder if I look at bit of a ..."

"Cock!" shouted Nerys, flinging the Animal Ed's drink into his face, their conversation clearly having ended poorly.

She stormed over to the table, but the fury on her face melted instantly when she saw Michael.

"I have been drinking," she conceded, "but surely I'm not the only one who can see that a rabbit has crawled into Michael's ear and got stuck halfway."

Clovenhoof checked in on the baby when he got home. She lay in his bed, quite awake, one arm wrapped possessively around the stuffed pine marten Clovenhoof had acquired for her.

"Any calls while I was out?" said Clovenhoof.

Beelzebelle kicked her legs excitedly.

"A funny thing happened this evening," said Clovenhoof, "Ben kind of suggested I should have kids. I mean, those weren't his exact words, admittedly, but that was the meaning I took away from it." He looked at little Beelzebelle. "I was going to sell you but, well, I don't want to seem too forward, but maybe we could try out this whole father-daughter thing. I am an excellent role model. You couldn't ask for a better parent. I'd impart all my worldly knowledge to you, mould you into a perfect mini-me, and you'd get to inherit Hell from me when I die. It's a pretty sweet deal."

Beelzebelle made a noise which Clovenhoof couldn't say was either agreement or disagreement.

"And I've made you some cool dentures to try out tomorrow," he said, holding out the sets of teeth he had fashioned from blu tack and the smashed remains of the jawbones he'd stolen from Ben.

"Let's have one last bedtime story, and we'll make a start on it properly in the morning," said Clovenhoof.

He said down on the edge of the bed and picked up one of the card picture books he'd picked up from the supermarket. He flicked through it and tutted.

"I'll do my own variation, I think." He opened the book so Beelzebelle could see the pages. "Right. This one's called Goldilocks Goes Burgling And Gets Herself A Nice Bearskin Rug. Ready? Once upon a time..."

Chapter 2 – In which Clovenhoof gets a monkey, pimps his pram, and Twinkle feels a little flat

Clovenhoof and Beelzebelle were out walking. More accurately, Beelzebelle lay asleep in her buggy, and Clovenhoof rode proudly on the Segway that he had attached to its handlebar. In principle, they were out for a walk. They had covered quite a distance already, and Clovenhoof was ready for a little light refreshment. He bent down to the straw to take in a decent slurp of Lambrini, but there was an empty, gurgling sound from the cup in the drink-holder.

"Quick pitstop, Beelzebelle. We'll be on our way in a moment."

He hopped off the Segway and rummaged in the basket below the pram for a fresh bottle. He popped it into the makeshift holder, a flower pot that he'd duct-taped onto the Segway's main post. He inserted the straw, humming a selection of Beelzebelle's favourite songs. She liked it when he did the hits of Abba in the style of a Satanic chant. He was just getting to a good bit when a car horn sounded loudly.

Clovenhoof looked up from the task in hand to see a most unusual vehicle. He'd seen stretch limousines before, even stretch Humvees. This, however, was a white stretch transit van, the tradesman's workhorse of choice, modified and lengthened limo-style. It was unnecessary, showy, and vulgar – things that Clovenhoof approved of very much. He also approved of the angry-looking man who was leaning out of the window and shaking his fist. His day was becoming more interesting.

"What do you think you're doing?" shouted the man.

"Just a little maintenance," said Clovenhoof.

"Get a move on!"

"This is a pedestrian crossing you know."

"Yeah, but it's a not a pedestrian stop-and-have-a-picnic. I've got an important meeting to get to, mate. Gonna need you to get out of the way."

"What's in the back of the van?" asked Clovenhoof, in no particular hurry.

"What?"

"What have you got in there? Loads of space in the back of there, what do you use it for?"

"You'd better concentrate on what you're doing with that bottle before ..." The man bit down on a swear word. "Before you drop it."

"It's fine, I'd finished that one," said Clovenhoof.

"What? You got broken glass all over the road!" The man opened the van door a crack to get out and then restrained himself. "Glass and tyres don't mix, pal."

"Is it, like, a crack den in there, or a low-key brothel?" asked Clovenhoof.

"What?"

Clovenhoof waggled a finger at the elongated van as he straightened his straw and – finally! – took a long satisfying drink of Lambrini.

"That's a filthy slur! I'm an important businessman. Fingers in lots of pies."

"No, I think mobile brothels are the thing of the future," Clovenhoof reassured him.

"Say sorry right now!" spluttered the man, literally frothing at the mouth, his bushy eyebrows descending in fury.

Clovenhoof walked on his way, worried that the man's shouting might upset Beelzebelle. He heard some more impassioned bellowing about broken glass, but he knew that the Segway's top speed would soon outpace any but the most athletic pursuers.

Nerys drifted along as Twinkle scampered at the end of the lead, sniffing out the intriguing, multi-layered doggy secrets of Boldmere.

It's going to be one of those days, Twinkle, she thought.

Tina, the branch manager of the Helping Hand Job Agency, had arranged a *coaching session*. Ever since she went on that management course, Tina had been dead keen on *coaching*. As far as Nerys could tell, coaching meant kicking your arse while pretending it's for your own good. Nerys gritted her teeth at the prospect. And Jeremy, never the quietest of neighbours, was getting noisier and noisier of late.

"Did you hear that wailing from his place today, Twinkle?" she said. "I blame Ben for getting him that Aztec death whistle for Christmas."

Twinkle yipped and tried to chase a fragrant chip paper into the gutter. Nerys didn't have the heart to pull him away.

"At least one of us needs to follow our dreams, Twinkle," she said, "and it's probably best all round if I don't act out those fantasies with Tina and the steam roller – oh!"

A huge elongated van hurtled round the bend, wheels riding up momentarily over the kerb. Nerys leapt back and wondered what kind of inadequacies a vehicle like that might be trying to address. The van braked sharply just beside her. A man leaned out of the driver's window, looked at Nerys and then, critically, at his tyres.

"Sent the tracking right out too, I bet!" he grumbled.

He had a face that was darkened with stubble and a pudgy, dangerous look about him. Not ideal man material.

The man revved his engine. It was only at that moment Nerys realised that the lead in her hand was dragging limp and empty. She looked down. The tyres span in the loose grit and disgorged the lifeless form of Twinkle, flinging him like a dirty rag at her feet.

Nerys screamed, a primal and terrible thing. Part of her brain told her that there were rational and useful things that she ought to do, like get a look at the registration number, but the primal and terrible part was in charge. She wanted to hurt the man who had done this. At the very least, she needed to throw something. As usual, there were no half housebricks or anvils around when needed. She took the only thing to hand and hefted it into the air with all of her might as she let out another blood-curdling scream. The recently filled bag of dog mess sailed through the air with uncanny accuracy and in through the open window of the departing van.

Clovenhoof was unable to get the combined bulk of the Segway and the buggy over the threshold of the Boldmere Oak, so he parted their duct tape coupling and dragged them in separately.

"Lennox, pop a Lambrini onto my tab, would you?" he called out as he approached the bar.

"You can't have a tab. I'm going to need payment in cash," said Lennox the barman pleasantly.

"Not you as well! You know I've been blacklisted by the payday loan companies too."

"They've got your picture up behind the counter in Lend-U-Like and a sign saying 'Do not give money to this man'."

"Have they never heard of rewarding loyalty? Even loan sharks won't come near me."

"You shot the last two loan sharks who came to your flat," Lennox pointed out.

"The police shot the Coddington brothers," Clovenhoof corrected him. "It wasn't my fault the police thought that we were all bank robbers."

"You're the very devil himself," said Lennox, "Everything's your fault."

"Hmph, I've had a lot of expenses lately. The baby bouncer was a costly item. There was the cost of buying it, and then there was the cost of rebuilding the doorway after I personally stress tested it."

"You got in it?"

"Better safe than sorry. Beelzebelle will thank me one day. You can see why I need a drink, can't you? I'm run off my feet. I had no idea it was so much work to look after a baby."

Lennox continued to wipe down the bar, smiling at Clovenhoof.

"Well, luckily, I came prepared for this eventuality. Ben's penny jar it is then," sighed Clovenhoof, upending a huge pile of coppers onto the bar. "I read once that your average penny is contaminated with traces of urine and faeces from dozens of people."

"You can't believe everything you read."

"I wasn't sure if it was a general statement or a legal requirement, so I pissed in the jar before I came here."

50

Lennox paused only momentarily in sorting through the coins. The barman of the Boldmere Oak had a sanguine and easy-going manner, a valuable quality in a publican, particularly one who had Satan as a regular.

"While you're counting it out," said Clovenhoof, "get one for this poor chap too."

Animal Ed Lawrence, staring forlornly into his pint just along the bar, looked up.

"Oh, cheers. Wait," he said, as he recognised Clovenhoof. "Did Nerys send you to break my arms or something?"

"Nerys hasn't sent me, just extending my generosity – well, Ben Kitchen's generosity – to my fellow man."

"Need all the help I can get right now, and that's the truth. Up the creek without a paddle, as they say."

Clovenhoof nodded in understanding.

"To be honest, I've never let that bother me. If God had meant us to wipe our arses, he should have given us non-stick butt cheeks."

"No, that's not what the phrase means..."

"Having said that, I've now been lured in by the hedonistic pleasures of the baby wipe warmer. You tried them?" he asked. "I've got one in every room now, so I don't get caught short."

Animal Ed's confused gaze flicked between Beelzebelle's buggy and Clovenhoof's dreamy expression, but the question never quite made it out of his mouth.

"Er, no. I've managed to get myself into a difficult position."

"Ah, working your way through the Kama Sutra, eh?"

"No. I'm supposed to get a load of exotic animal samples for a research lab, and, as you know, my trip to Kenya's fallen through. I'm in trouble. Debt trouble and unfulfilled order trouble."

"There must be something you can do," said Clovenhoof.

"Nothing."

"There's always something. I find running away from problems often works."

"I can't leave all my animals. I've got responsibilities."

"Or pretending that all my problems have run away. That also works, and it's better because you don't actually have to go anywhere."

"I might have to let my monkey go," admitted Ed.

"Well, don't let me stop you," said Clovenhoof, glancing around, "although Lennox might prefer it if you found somewhere a bit more private."

Ed stared at Clovenhoof.

"It isn't a euphemism," he said.

"It doesn't matter what size it is."

"No. It's a real monkey."

"Right," said Clovenhoof with a leer. "And I bet it needs spanking sometimes as well?"

"It would be cruel to spank it. I really do have a monkey. A capuchin."

"That's a coffee, not a monkey. I'm not stupid."

"He's highly trained," said Ed.

Clovenhoof leaned forward in interest. "Trained? Like Olympic level poop-flinging accuracy?"

"No, trained to help people. They can take the lids off jars and switch on lights, things like that. They train them up in the US to help disabled people."

"So why have you got this one? You've got full use of all your bits and pieces, according to Nerys," said Clovenhoof with a salacious wink.

Ed gave him a sideways look.

"Gorky was placed with a wheelchair user obsessed with Feng Shui and smoking excessive amounts of cannabis. It didn't end well. The programme had to let him go, he can't be returned to the wild, so I've had him as an attraction in the shop for a few months now. He's worth a couple of hundred as a pet, if I can find a buyer."

"I'll give you fifty, if he really can open bottles and do, you know, useful things."

"You want my monkey?"

"This parenting lark is hard work. I could do with an extra pair of hands."

Ed looked hard at Clovenhoof.

"I can't go lower than eighty."

"I'll tell you what," said Clovenhoof, reaching into the basket of the buggy, "let's see what's in Ben's fifty pence jar. I'm sure we can come to some sort of arrangement."

Nerys walked hurriedly down the path leading to St Michael's church, her phone to her ear.

"Listen, I can't come in today, Tina. There's... there's been a bereavement. Yes, a death in the family. Yes, thank you. I should be in tomorrow, yes."

She ended the call and blew her nose with her free hand. She held a shoe box under her arm, but that didn't feel right. She held it out in front of her, cradling the box in both of her hands, as she entered the church.

Michael, alone in the church, sat in prayer halfway down the aisle.

"Where's the font?" Nerys called.

Michael blinked and looked round.

"Sorry?" he said.

"Holy water. Don't you need that?"

"Need it for what?"

She held out the shoe box towards him.

"To bring him back. What else have you got here? Any saintly relics?"

"I don't understand..."

"We need everything this church has got. It's an emergency!"

Michael was on his feet. Nerys held out the box. Michael peered inside.

"Oh," he said. "Oh, Twinkle."

"Bastard van driver didn't even see him."

"Oh dear. I'm sorry, Nerys."

He looked at her.

"I can't," he said. "I'm really sorry."

"You're sorry? *Really* sorry?" She held him in a challenging stare. "If you were sorry, you'd fix him."

"He's dead, Nerys. I can't change that." Michael fixed her with sorrowful eyes and gave her shoulder a gentle squeeze.

"Rubbish!" spat Nerys, pushing his arm away. "You're still an archangel. You said so yourself. You might not have special powers, but you've got... *connections*, you know you have. Help me fix Twinkle. He's up in Heaven and he's missing me."

"I'm sorry to say that animals don't go to Heaven, Nerys, they ..."

"Don't you dare say that!" hissed Nerys. "I've been there. I've seen them myself."

Michael smiled gently, and Nerys could see that his genuine concern, an unguarded moment of compassion, was now slipping behind one of his masks.

"Ah, dear me, Nerys, this is a complex subject," he said. "Suffice it to say that there is, of course, an *idea* of animals in Heaven, so that those amongst the blessed dead who relish the natural world can surround themselves with familiar sights."

"Bullshit!" spat Nerys, conscious of where she was, but not caring, as hot tears ran down her cheeks. "You're making this stuff up. It's so stupid! I just want you to help me!"

"I will help you as a friend, Nerys. I *want* to help you get through this difficult time, but I can't help you bring back the dead."

"I don't want to get through! I want it sorted!"

Nerys swivelled and stormed out of the church, anger suffusing her entire being. At that moment, she wasn't sure which was worse, the ignorant idiot who had killed her beloved dog, or the self-righteous idiot who was withholding the only possible avenue of practical help.

"If God can't do something good for us when we need it most, then what bloody good is He?" she shouted. "No wonder Jeremy thinks He's an almighty tosser!"

A fat-bellied figure at the back of the church pushed a broom and unconvincingly pretended he hadn't noticed there was a mad woman in the church.

"Darren!" called Nerys.

Darren Pottersmore, the church's zealous helper, and wearer of his mother's experiments in creative knitwear, looked up.

"Oh. Nerys, isn't it? Didn't see you there," he lied.

Today's sweater was in the style of a stained glass window, although the Heavenly cherubs were distorted around Darren's considerable girth. Nerys approached, thinking Michael wasn't the only avenue for practical help.

"You used to go by the name of Pitspawn," she said.

"What?"

"Pitspawn."

Darren looked at her, and his eye twitched slightly.

"I think I knew someone called that, a long time ago."

"No, it was you. Back in the days when you were a practising Satanist. You had all sorts of books, as I recall."

The incident in question, a couple of years back, had involved summoning rituals, demonic powers channelled through the dubious conduit of crystal animals and, critically, Nerys being dead for far longer than was considered healthy. Either the powers of Heaven or simple Post-Traumatic Stress had wiped the incident from Darren's mind (and put the fear of God into the boy).

"You knew rituals," she said. "Summoning the devil, raising the dead, that sort of thing."

Darren whimpered slightly and shook his head.

"No. Not since Stephen and I were kids... I've been good... I've been good."

"Snap out of it, church boy," said Nerys. "I get that you don't go in for that stuff anymore, but I really need to know how to raise the dead. It's an emergency."

"We shouldn't meddle with dark forces."

"Do you want me to tell your mother that, on the cub camp, you let the boys use one of your jumpers as an emergency bivouac and then told your mum it had been stolen by badgers?"

"You wouldn't!"

"Right now, I'm one of those dark forces you shouldn't meddle with," said Nerys.

Darren groaned.

"Look, if I get you the book and stuff, will you leave me alone?"

"To live a blameless and holy life? You betcha," said Nerys.

Clovenhoof had a monkey.

Clovenhoof had a capuchin monkey.

Jeremy Clovenhoof had a capuchin monkey.

He owned – paws, tail, fur, and teeth – a real-life capuchin monkey.

The monkey had small questing fingers, wide child-like eyes, and was generally brown but for a cowl of blonde hair over his head and shoulders. The monkey was called Gorky.

Clovenhoof had a monkey and, if he had known how instantly happy it was going to make him, he would have got one years ago.

Like the battery-powered spaghetti fork, the Lambrini hat, the electric hoof-buffer, and personalised toilet paper (printed with the faces of whoever you wanted), the monkey was one of those items Clovenhoof didn't realise he needed until he got it and then found it almost instantly indispensable.

Clovenhoof arrived back at the house with his new capuchin monkey riding on the back of the baby buggy. He wheeled into the hall and considered the prospect of hauling everything up the stairs again.

"What can you do then, Gorky? You gonna help me get this stuff up there or what?"

Gorky sprang off the buggy and snatched Beelzebelle out of the buggy. Despite the baby girl being much heavier than him, Gorky carried her easily up the stairs and stood at the top, looking expectantly at Clovenhoof. Beelzebelle burbled and poked Gorky's ear.

"Oh, fine. Leave the heavy lifting to me," said Clovenhoof. He carried the buggy up. It was a bit easier with no baby in it, but, on reflection, he could have got Gorky to make another trip with the Lambrini stash.

"Good work, Gorky. I think you'll make a commendable addition to our little family," he said as he opened the door to his flat with a flourish. "Welcome to my domain."

Gorky scampered across the threshold and carried out an inspection of the rooms that Clovenhoof called home. The kitchen seemed to hold great interest, and Clovenhoof followed him in there after a few minutes to see what he was doing. The monkey was evaluating the contents of the fridge and seemed to feel that there was something lacking. He was making this evident by the way that he was transferring the contents directly to the bin.

"What do you think you're doing?" said Clovenhoof. "Findus Crispy Pancakes are an unparalleled delicacy!"

Gorky ignored this and continued through the contents of the fridge, until he eventually came across a mouldy orange, squashed against the back wall. He peeled it away, cradling it carefully in his hands. He held it up for Clovenhoof to see, a look of deep sorrow on his face.

"All right, I get it," said Clovenhoof. "You like oranges, and you prefer them a little bit fresher than that. Fine, if I promise to get some oranges, can we move on?"

Gorky stepped away from the fridge, apparently satisfied with this.

"I think we need to set out a few ground rules," said Clovenhoof, beckoning Gorky back into the living room. "Let's talk."

He sat Beelzebelle on the settee and indicated that Gorky should sit next to her.

"Right, listen up, the two of you. You might want to take notes. We each have our roles to play in this family. My role is to impart my considerable wisdom. I've been around for quite some time, so there really aren't many things I'm not an expert on. Pay close attention at all times, especially you, Beelzebelle. After all, you're my daughter now, my protégé, and you've got a lot to learn if you're going to grow up in my image. Gorky, your role is a supporting one. I will expect you to do all of those things that I don't fancy doing myself. You'll get as many oranges as you like if you play your cards right."

Beelzebelle patted Gorky's face with interest. Gorky carefully took her hand, making her giggle.

"I hope you're paying attention, young lady, because the first lesson is about to begin."

Clovenhoof puffed out his chest and looked upwards, seeking inspiration. His gaze travelled over a large cobweb.

"Housework. Yes, right. When you've got important stuff to be doing, which you definitely will when you're grown up and as skilled as I am, you won't want to be wasting your time on menial tasks. There is always a way to get someone else to do it. Always. If you can't convince somebody to tidy the place up for you because you deserve it, then plan 'b' – a small fire every once in a while –

takes care of things." He thought for a moment. "A big fire will work, too."

Gorky looked up to where Clovenhoof was staring and, in the blink of an eye, scrambled up the curtains, leaned across, and swiped the cobweb from the ceiling. He then looked at his hand and nibbled delicately at the cobwebby mess.

"See what I mean?" said Clovenhoof proudly. "Circle of life, Beelzebelle, and we're at the, er, top, you and me."

He frowned slightly. Beelzebelle's attention seemed to be focussed on Gorky, as he hung from the picture rail, eating more cobwebs. He was about to point out the ground rule about paying attention to him at all times when he became aware of a subtle popping in his ears. He tasted the air with his tongue and detected the prickling sensation that indicated some sort of interference in the dullness of earthly normality.

"Interesting."

He followed his nose out of his flat's front door and up the stairs to the top floor, and flat 3. He knocked on the door and pushed his way inside.

"Nerys? What are you doing?" he called.

"A little privacy, if you don't mind!" yelled Nerys, standing in the middle of the floor, all the furniture pushed back. "I was just starting to get the hang of this chanting thing."

"Is that 'Satanism for Dummies'?" asked Clovenhoof, looking at the book that she held, "and I recognise that crystal dolphin. Darren's mom gets really angry when he takes her ornaments, you know."

"She'll get them all back," said Nerys hotly. "Darren said the crystal helps to focus the force of the pentagram or something. Now go away and let me get on with the ritual."

"What's in the box?" Clovenhoof stepped forward. As he entered the pentagram, there was an implosive *glump* sound, and the magic seeped out of the room.

He peered at the lifeless and quite *flat* form on the floor.

"Someone's let the air out of your dog."

The punch Nerys threw connected powerfully with Clovenhoof's chin and made his teeth snap.

"Don't you dare make a joke out of this," she wept.

Clovenhoof rubbed his jaw.

"Your dog's dead. I get it," he said and then, surprising himself, added, "Sorry."

Nerys glared at him.

"You've broken the spell."

"Hasn't hanging around with me taught you anything about messing with Satanic forces?"

"Christ, you sound like Michael. I have to try. Heaven's no help, maybe Hell can sort this out."

"Not sure I'd do that if I were you," said Clovenhoof, as he turned to leave. "You have no idea what it might cost you."

Nerys stamped a foot in frustration, fists balled at her sides.

"What? I thought you'd be all for it! No wonder you got sacked as Lord of Hell. You're a rotten salesman!"

Jeremy paused at the doorway.

"You know what?" he said thoughtfully. "I've never actually seen someone stamp their feet in anger before. I thought it was just something people did on TV."

"And you're a lousy friend too!" she shouted, as he closed the door behind him.

As he descended the stairs, Clovenhoof heard something that sounded like a crystal animal hitting a wall.

Ben was arranging a jolly taxidermy mouse choir on a shelf between piles of self-help books. Each tiny mouse corpse held a tinier hymn book and had its mouth open in mid-song. He thought it might cheer up people who were looking for books about depression. The door to the shop opened.

"Nerys."

She gave him a weak smile.

"I heard what happened to Twinkle," he said. "You'll be needing a cup of tea."

Nerys sat down while Ben tried to find a cleanish mug in the kitchenette behind the counter.

"The maniac that ran him over only stopped because he thought he'd damaged his stupid van!" growled Nerys.

"Would you know him if you saw him again?" asked Ben, rubbing a cup with the hem of his t-shirt.

"Oh yes. Him and his stupid van. If I saw that van again, I'd smash the windscreen into tiny pieces."

"Hmmm, yes," said Ben, setting the tea down. He'd realised that this required breaking out a packet of rich tea biscuits. He put them down next to Nerys's mug. "Whatever makes you feel better. Although, breaking safety glass probably won't be as satisfying as you're imagining."

"What?"

"It will just crumble rather than smash and, besides, he'll get a new one in no time. You might want to dent some of the body panels, preferably a wing. It will be much more expensive to fix those."

Nerys gave him a smile, and reached across to squeeze his hand.

"Thank you, Ben," she said. "It's great to get some practical advice. Michael and Jeremy have been useless."

"You asked them how to smash up a van?" said Ben, incredulous.

"No, no. Just about Twinkle. About what to do with him."

"What *are* you going to do with him?" asked Ben, eyeing her sideways. "Because I might be able to help."

Nerys took a rich tea biscuit, but simply looked at it.

"If you're thinking of turning him into another hair accessory for Michael ..."

"No, nothing like that. I can make sure he looks just as you always remember him though."

"I don't know. Stuffing animals. It's a bit... tacky."

Ben spread some photos across the counter.

"I've collected a load of pictures together to use as a reference."

He glanced at Nerys. Her eyes misted over as she sifted through the pictures.

"Who knew there were so many pictures with Twinkle in them?" she mused. "It's a bit of a shame that Jeremy's in so many of them being, well, Jeremy." She put the biscuit down, uneaten. "Lovely to see these though."

Nerys walked over to look at the mouse choir and gingerly touched its head. She narrowed her eyes and looked more closely.

She pulled on its ear and it came away. She held it in her hand, small, delicate, and pink, with a curious bright stripe along the hidden edge.

"Ben, these mouse ears are made from false fingernails! This one's even got nail varnish on it! It's almost as if you got it out of my bin or something."

Ben looked uncomfortable.

"Waste not, want not," he mumbled. "I've got much better since I did that one, Nerys."

"These aren't... appalling," she said.

"I promise I'll do a good job with Twinkle. You'll be able to see him every day, and he'll look just like you always remember him. Just think about it, yeah?"

Clovenhoof tapped the counter in the Helping Hand Job Agency. Ordinarily, he'd call out for Nerys, but she was summoning the dead rather than coming into work today.

"Hello! I can't see any astronaut vacancies in the window," he called.

Her lips were set into an exaggerated pout, and glistened with such an extraordinary amount of lipstick that Clovenhoof was reminded of a freshly painted post box. Clovenhoof read her name badge.

"Tina."

"That's right, sir," she said and ran a talon-like fingernail across the slogan under her name. "Happy to help. We've met before, haven't we?"

"I was in the market for a job a while back. You helped."

She smiled.

"And how did that position work out for you?"

Clovenhoof thought. He remembered the screams, the tears, the vast quantities of fake blood. It was one hell of a school assembly.

"Rather well," he said.

Tina indicated a low table with some comfy chairs in a corner by the window. "Perhaps we can have a chat and work out what your next step on the career ladder might be."

She tottered over in her high heels to one of the chairs. She crossed her legs after sitting down, and gave a loving glance down at her shiny, metallic shoe, dangling her foot so that it bobbed between them.

"Nice shoes," said Clovenhoof, feeling that nothing would be done until he had admired them.

"Thank you," said Tina. "Not everyone can walk in five inch heels, but as a professional working woman, I know that I need to look my very best."

Clovenhoof was hit with a strong sense of déjà vu. That sounded like something Nerys would say. He imagined that Tina and Nerys must be the very best of friends. He was sure she had mentioned a Tina recently...

"Tell me about yourself," said Tina, settling a clipboard onto her knees.

"Well, I have a small daughter, great kid, you'd love her, but expensive all that gear she needs. So now, I've got Gorky, my au pair."

"East European?"

"South American, I think. Anyway, I'd like to take on a bit of part time work to bring in some extra cash." Tina jotted notes in a meticulous, loopy hand. "I can see me doing something in the evenings, when she's sleepy. Gigolo would work, if you've got anything in that general area?"

Tina looked up sharply.

"Sorry, I thought you said... I wonder if you meant something else, like serving coffee or ice cream...?"

"Whatever the ladies require."

"I tell you what, shall we start with your name and address, for the form?"

Tina smiled brightly, pen poised.

Clovenhoof reeled off his details. Tina paused.

"You live at the same address as Nerys, a colleague of mine. Do you know her?"

"Yes, everyone knows Nerys," said Clovenhoof with a saucy wink. "Although she'll maybe calming down her *socialising* for a few days. Her dog died, you know."

"Oh goodness me, has her dog died as well?" Tina gave a sad little pout at Clovenhoof.

"As well?"

"Yes. Didn't you know? There's been a death in the family."

Clovenhoof shook his head. Apart from one sister in Cheshire and another on the other side of the world, all of Nerys's family lived in North Wales and he was certain that, if one of them had popped their clogs, she would be on the road to Wales rather than performing demonic rituals.

"Nah," he said. "Don't think so. Carefree and single, our Nerys. She's got no one, certainly no dependents like me. Costs me a fortune on nappies and oranges."

"But she said..."

"Nerys just worries when she has to pay full price at *Kinky and Frilly*."

Tina's face hardened. "Are you telling me that Nerys has taken the day off for the death of a pet? A pet!"

"No, Twinkle's not just a pet, he's more like a..." Clovenhoof reached for the right words. *Nemesis* wasn't right, neither was *annoying ball of fluff*. Then he realised that they described his own relationship with Twinkle, and that Nerys's was probably different. That might go some way towards explaining her determination to resurrect him from his present state (which Clovenhoof actually thought was an improvement in terms of his behaviour). "Actually, yes. Pet. You'd call him a pet," said Clovenhoof.

Nerys held the phone to her ear and listened with growing dismay.

"Yes, I am aware of the company policy, but can't I just take a day? One day?"

She raised her eyes to Ben, but he was mollifying a woman whose child had started to cry after seeing dead mice on the bookshelf. The mouse choir hadn't quite engaged customers in the way he had hoped.

"No, of course I didn't send him in to be annoying and offensive to you," said Nerys. "He's annoying and offensive to *everyone* ..."

Nerys gritted her teeth.

"Within the hour? Yes. Yes, of course. See you soon, Tina."

The call ended, she stared at her phone for a long moment.

"Jeremy Clovenhoof, you are a selfish, ridiculous bastard and I'm going to show you what I think of you!" she yelled.

The mouse-spooked child started crying again.

"Any idea where he's gone?" she called to Ben.

"Jeremy? He said something about going to the park and *'letting his little one run wild in the bushes'* this afternoon," said Ben, pulling a face. "He has got some filthy habits."

"He'd better hope I don't find him before he gets himself arrested," said Nerys, and made for the door.

Clovenhoof brought the Segway-buggy combo to a halt under a spreading oak tree on the plush grass of Sutton Park. Gorky rode on top of the buggy, chattering at Beelzebelle as he peeled an orange with a dizzying speed.

"Right, gang, let's decide what we'll do to start with," said Clovenhoof, holding up a book to show them. It was entitled *50 Things To Do Before You're 11 3/4*. "I am taking my duties seriously, as you can see. We need to start work on these nice and early, Beelzebelle. I've seen several other titles in Ben's shop. *Boutique Hotels to Stay in Before You Die* might have to take a back seat – a bit pricey. I did some calculations, and if we attempt to do all of them before you go to school, we need to get through at least twenty five every day. If we apply ourselves, we can get through this book this afternoon, what do you say?"

He flicked through the pages.

"We'll come back to kayaking. I need to figure out where to get a kayak. It's a kind of moose, isn't it?"

Gorky squeaked at him.

"Let's start with tree climbing, shall we? There's one right here."

Clovenhoof walked over and slapped his hand on the enormous trunk. It looked like a good one. He picked up the book to see what it said about climbing trees, but it was very light on detail. The branches that looked climbable started well above his head. He tried to grip the bark and dig in his feet, but he just slipped straight off.

He turned to the others.

"I think this might be an unsuitable activity for those of us with hooves," he said. "Your upper body strength isn't what it should be, Beelzebelle, so I can imagine you might struggle with this, too. I wonder if I put the Segway against the trunk, whether I can give you a leg up onto the first branch?"

Gorky leapt off the top of the buggy and rummaged in the basket below until he found the baby sling. He carefully put Beelzebelle into the sling and twisted himself into the straps, so that she was suspended in front of him, suspended with her knees and feet dragging on the floor. She laughed and patted his face as they were pressed close together.

"Well done, Gorky. It's useful to know that you can do that," said Clovenhoof. "Not sure how it's helping with our current predicament though. Oh."

Gorky scrambled speedily up the trunk of the oak tree with Beelzebelle in the sling. Clovenhoof examined the bark, wondering if he might follow, but he had no idea what Gorky had used as hand holds. Maybe he had suckers? He'd check later. He stepped back to watch as Gorky climbed higher and higher, with Beelzebelle emitting squeals of delight.

"Well, that's one we can tick off the list," called Clovenhoof. "You can come down now. Mugging squirrels is *not* on the list, Gorky! Oh, all right, have it your way. I guess we all like nuts."

Moments later they were all reunited on the ground. Clovenhoof took Beelzebelle and carried her on his hip as he read aloud from the book, munching the nut that Gorky had passed to him.

"Right, we have to find and handle squishy bugs. That should be pretty easy. Let's head down there towards the pool. There should be some properly squishy bugs in the muddy part. Tell you what, after we're done with the bugs, we'll come up here to this hill. Rolling down a hill is on the list, and that's definitely something we can all do."

The three of them sat at the edge of Keeper's Pool, grappling through the mud, looking for bugs, or eating it in Beelzebelle's case.

"You know, Gorky, that was a really good idea, taking the nut off that squirrel," said Clovenhoof. "We should do more foraging for food, you know, living off the land. I picked up a book in Ben's shop about making homebrew. Lots of wild plants are suitable for brewing." He picked up a nearby leaf and rubbed it between his fingers, giving it a sniff. "This has some of the subtle fragrance that belongs to Lambrini, Gorky. I bet I have what they call a 'nose'. If I make Lambrini out of everything that smells good, it stands to reason it would be awesome, right?"

He handed the leaf to Gorky, who sniffed it, screeched, and threw it vigorously away. Clovenhoof grabbed armfuls of vegetation and stuffed it into a spare carrier bag.

"That was rude," said Clovenhoof, straightening, "although I can see that you find anything other than oranges a bit of a challenge. You should be more open-minded, like Beelzebelle. What *is* that she's eating?"

He wandered over. "A slug! Well done Beelzebelle, you can tick another one off your list. Foraging too, I'm going to call that an extra point for ingenuity. Right, it's time to roll down that hill."

"Oi, Jeremy! I want a word with you!"

Clovenhoof looked round.

"Nerys!" said Clovenhoof in surprise. Nerys strode towards him with her fists clenched and a scowl on her face.

"Why on earth did you have to go and talk to Tina? She gives me enough trouble without you giving her any more ammunition!"

"Really?" Clovenhoof was genuinely surprised. "You've got such a lot in common with her. I sort of assumed you'd be best buddies."

Nerys stood for a moment and absorbed this comment, and then her eyes bulged, she stepped forward, and used her handbag like a sap, whacking Clovenhoof repeatedly as she screamed at him.

"That is the most horrible thing you could possibly say to me! Do you ever think a sentence through before it comes out of your mouth? *Ever?*"

Clovenhoof thought for a moment, and shook his head with a small shrug.

"I've told you about Tina. I moan about her all the time. Don't you listen?"

"No, but in my defence, I read an article somewhere that said women's voices are too high-pitched and whiny for most men to hear."

"God damn it, Jeremy! I know *you're* not normal, but can't you at least try? You're still wheeling that baby buggy around. What's that all about? Everything that you do is creepy and weird!"

Clovenhoof beamed.

"That wasn't a compliment, you twat!" she snapped.

Clovenhoof's face fell. Nerys was being a little harsh, but that was perhaps understandable, given the loss of Twinkle. What was a more immediate cause for concern was the absence of Gorky and Beelzebelle. Where had they gone? He and Nerys stood alone on the bank of the pool, the buggy nearby. A small electric whine made them both look behind them.

"There you are!" Clovenhoof said as Gorky barrelled towards them on the Segway with Beelzebub hanging from his chest in the sling. Clovenhoof could see an immediate problem with this arrangement. To hold onto the handlebars, a diminutive capuchin monkey had to extend his arms as high as he could, so steering was somewhat compromised. "When I said *roll down the hill*, I'm not sure that this is quite what the authors intended."

Clovenhoof wondered whether Gorky had a plan for stopping. He suspected not, from the look of panic in his eyes as he approached. He wasn't sure that Nerys had yet processed the reality of what was approaching them, so he stepped in front of her.

"Sorry Nerys, we need to – oof!"

The Segway hit him in the midriff, and he leaned over the handlebars, winded. Somehow or other, the Segway kept going, and shifted direction, although Clovenhoof clearly heard the sound of Nerys splashing into the pool accompanied by a string of Welsh invective.

"Did we have a plan here?" grunted Clovenhoof, dangling over the handlebars of the Segway as it carried him backwards at high speed. Gorky's screeching told him everything that he needed to know. There were sounds from behind, as pedestrians and cyclists threw themselves out of the way. The trees got thinner, and the noise of traffic came to Clovenhoof's ears as they approached the entrance to the park, and the road that ran alongside it.

Clovenhoof was aware of two things at the same time. One was a look of intense fear in Gorky's eyes, and the other was the honking of a car's horn. Gorky reacted by stepping expertly off the Segway, taking Beelzebelle with him. Clovenhoof saw him give a final sad little wave as he stood at the kerb.

There was the sound of brakes screeching. Clovenhoof twisted to see what lay in his path and was surprised to see the same stretch transit van he'd encountered earlier in the day.

As he somersaulted through the air, horns gouging the paintwork and shattering the sunroof, he was dimly aware of the Segway landing heavily on the vehicle's rear end. His very last thought before blacking out, suspended upside down inside the van's interior, was that the space in the back of the van was not at all what he'd imagined.

Chapter 3 – In which Twinkle gets stuffed, Michael gets a new church, and Clovenhoof goes off-road

Nerys put a hand to her mouth, speechless.

"It's... it's..."

"Horrible?" suggested Ben. "Wonky? An affront to all human decency?"

She blinked rapidly and there were tears on her cheeks.

"You," she whispered hoarsely. "You..."

"Failed? Betrayed me on a level previously thought impossible?"

"And I'm..."

"Leaving? Going to kill you?"

Nerys stepped forward shakily and reached out for the stuffed and mounted Twinkle that Ben had placed on her kitchen counter.

"It's terrific," she said.

Her tone sounded positive, but Ben had been caught out by feminine conversational nuances before.

Nerys ran her fingers through his fur.

"Incredible," she breathed.

She plucked the little dog up and wrapped her arms around it. She pressed her face against the stuffed Yorkie's and spun in a little circle on tiptoes.

"You like it?" said Ben,

Nerys grabbed Ben and placed a fat kiss on his cheek.

"He's gorgeous, Ben. I've never loved you more."

"I didn't know you loved me."

"I don't, but I've never loved you *more* than I do now. For once, you've not screwed up."

"Thank you," said Ben, and then, after consideration, added, "I think."

He was relieved that Nerys liked the mounted Twinkle. It was, he thought, his best work yet. He had arranged the dog stood on all fours, although with a bend in the back legs as though the little beast was about to jump up (he had worried it was going to look like it was about to take a crap, but he had somehow avoided that). He had arranged Twinkle with his mouth slightly open, tongue just visible. In so far as it was possible to put a smile on a dog's face, Ben had achieved it.

"I had my doubts," said Nerys, tickling Twinkle under the collar. "I thought it might look tacky or stupid, but no."

"No?"

"You've given him back to me," said Nerys.

Ben blushed.

Nerys placed Twinkle on the floor by the dog bowl.

"And mummy's so glad," she said.

She reached for a box of dog biscuits on the counter and poured a liberal quantity into the bowl.

"And I should think you're hungry after all your adventures," she said.

The words "It is dead," closely followed by "Stuffed animals don't eat, you know?" attempted to escape out of Ben's mouth but, with uncommon foresight, he quashed them.

"I must offer you something," Nerys said to Ben. "This means the world to me."

"I'll take a cup of tea before I head to the shop."

"Tea it is," she said, and filled the kettle at the sink.

When she turned the tap off and the sound of running water ceased, there was a biscuity crunching sound. Both looked down. The stuffed Twinkle sat by his bowl, perfectly still.

Of course he'd be perfectly still, Ben chided himself.

"Do you know," said Nerys with a foolish grin, "for a moment there, I thought ..."

She stopped. There was the crunching sound again.

Their gazes snapped downward. Ben even leapt a little, pressing himself back against the fridge. Twinkle was quite still. The noise had stopped.

"Ben," said Nerys quietly.

"Yes?"

"When you... restored Twinkle, you didn't...?"

"What?"

"No, I'm being silly now."

"Please, go on."

"You didn't turn him into a cyborg?"

Ben kept his eyes fixed on the dog.

71

"Robo-Pooch? I wouldn't know where to start."

The crunching sound came again. Twinkle sat motionless.

Maybe Nerys had a rat infestation, thought Ben.

Nerys slapped Ben on the arm.

"Ben, quick question," she whispered.

"Uh-huh?"

"When you came in with Twinkle, did you also bring a stuffed monkey with you?"

"A what?"

On the counter by the door sat a brown and gold capuchin monkey. It was in a pose not unlike that of Hamlet contemplating a skull except, in this case, it was not a skull, but a handful of dog biscuits.

"No," said Ben, quiet and insistent and more than a little weirded out. "Is it stuffed?"

Perhaps realising the game was up, the monkey gave them a toothy grin and stuffed the remaining dog biscuits in its mouth.

"Lambrini me, Lennox," said Clovenhoof.

The Boldmere Oak barman took a bottle from the chiller cabinet behind the bar. Clovenhoof was pleased that, in the years since his arrival, the pub's stock of Lambrini had gone from one lonely bottle to a whole fridge of the stuff. Clovenhoof didn't know if it was reflection of his own personal alcohol consumption or if he had sparked a renewed fashion for the drink. He was happy with either.

"This one's on me," said Ed Lawrence, coming up to the bar.

"I never refuse the offer of a free drink," said Clovenhoof.

"Well, I owe you one and, maybe – just maybe – I can see the light at the end of the tunnel."

"I had a neighbour who had that. I think it was cataracts."

"I meant financially."

"Or possibly excessive wanking."

Ed shook his head and paid Lennox.

"The research company have given me an additional cash advance."

"Drinks on the house then."

"The cash is to procure those samples of exotic animal DNA. Cheers."

Clovenhoof clinked glasses with Ed and downed the glass of fizzy perry.

"So, you're off to Africa?" he said.

"It's not *that* much money. I've got to be a bit more creative."

"Well, I'm an exotic animal. I could sell you some of my DNA," said Clovenhoof, and waggled his glass at Lennox for a refill.

Ed laughed and pulled a folded sheet from his pocket.

"It's a very specific shopping list and you're not on it."

"The cheek," grinned Clovenhoof.

"Anyway," said Ed, "how are you and Gorky getting on?"

"Like a house on fire," said Clovenhoof. "He's at home, looking after Beelzebelle right now. At least, I assume he is."

Ed pulled a screen device from his canvas shoulder bag and switched it on.

"Yup," he said. "He's at your place, although I can't guarantee he's actually doing any childcare. I made no promises about his abilities as a babysitter."

"What's this thing?" said Clovenhoof.

Ed tilted the screen for him to see. Clovenhoof could see dots on a local map, lines trailing out behind them like snail slime.

"GPS tracker," said Ed. "Did you not notice the collar around his neck?"

The collar was quite unobtrusive, and consisted of a fat bead on a plastic collar which sat beneath Gorky's neck fur.

"I thought it was a fashion thing," said Clovenhoof.

"They're quite similar to the ones naturalists use to track animal populations. I actually got mine off a website for parents who want to track their children. I've just got into the habit of putting them my more expensive and important animals. And girlfriends."

"Girlfriends?" said Clovenhoof, impressed.

"Charm bracelet. Necklace. Sewn into the lining of her purse."

He was dimly aware that putting tracking devices on loved ones, particularly without them noticing, was the kind of thing that Nerys would call "balls out creepy", a fact which made Clovenhoof all the more impressed.

73

"It has saved my skin on more than one occasion," said Ed.

"Didn't work that time your girlfriend caught you and Nerys re-enacting the face-hugger scene from Alien."

"I can't keep my eye on two things at once."

"Multi-tasking is hard," Clovenhoof agreed.

"Anyway, you just log onto track-my-child.com and it can show you everywhere your kid or monkey or girlfriend has been. If you make your profile public, other people can see too."

Multi-tasking was indeed not Clovenhoof's greatest strength. Most days, even single-tasking was too much effort. However, two distinct and separate ideas – mind-blowingly stunning ideas – had formed in his mind.

"Would you lend me that thing?" he said to Ed.

"The tracker? You can just log onto the website with your phone."

Clovenhoof put his phone on the bar with a heavy thunk.

"Okay, maybe not that phone," said Ed. "I'm sorry, Jeremy, but this is an expensive bit of kit."

"But maybe I could help you out in return."

"Help how?"

Clovenhoof unfolded Ed's piece of paper and looked at the list of animal names.

"Serval, bat-eared fox, bushbaby, oryx, spotted-necked otter," he read without recognising a single one. "I can get these for you," he lied.

"You can? How?"

"Contacts," said Jeremy, tapping his nose.

Ed looked at him shrewdly.

"I heard there was a guy with connections at Dudley Zoo."

"I couldn't possibly say," said Clovenhoof with an air of mystery. "Obviously, these things don't come cheap."

Ed thrust the GPS tracker device into Clovenhoof's hands.

"Get the samples and then we'll discuss a price."

It took Ben and Nerys and a broom to chase the monkey out of Nerys's flat. They stood on the top floor landing, uncertain where it had gone, but happy that it was out of the flat. Nerys protectively held Twinkle under her arm.

"Did I tell you that I saw a monkey in the park?" said Nerys.

"In the park?" said Ben.

"With Jeremy. At least I think it was a monkey. There was a baby too."

"A monkey baby?"

"A baby baby. It all happened so quickly."

They looked up down and around for the capuchin.

"You know," said Ben, "there's this documented psychological effect where people who are constantly subjected to traumatic events – war, natural disaster, Jeremy Clovenhoof – eventually stop registering them. The brain has a sort of limited capacity for awful shit."

Nerys nodded reflectively, stroking Twinkle all the while.

"I *think* I saw a monkey and a baby in the park."

"It does sound like the kind of thing Jeremy would be involved in."

"He's a madman," said Nerys. She looked at her stuffed dog. "Some people are just crazy, aren't they, Twinkle?" she said in a squeaky baby voice and pinched Twinkle's nose affectionately. "Yes, they are, aren't they?"

Michael sat in St Michael's church and prayed.

Michael sometimes wondered why he continued to pray. As an archangel, he was an extension of the will of the Almighty. Even if The Guy Upstairs knew everything imaginable and directed everything, he knew and directed his angelic host that bit more. On top of that, was praying in a church that bore his name the equivalent of praying to himself?

Whatever, Michael prayed. He prayed because he loved the Almighty with all his heart. He prayed because he hoped that the Almighty would listen and, perhaps one day, answer him. Most importantly, though, he prayed because praying was what good people did, and Michael was certain that he was 'good people'.

It was, however, difficult to pray with the sound of Netty Fairfax grinding away on the stone floor, moaning and gasping with every thrust.

Michael attempted to put the sound out of his mind, and tried to recall where he was up to. He had been thanking the Lord

75

for the gifts of love and of honest work, mentally phrasing it so that he clearly wasn't just bragging to the Lord about his boyfriend and his job. He resettled his thoughts and opened his mind to the Almighty. *Ah, yes, Dear Lord...*

"Oh, Netty, that is lovely," said Reverend Zack.

"It's all in the elbows," said Netty, breathlessly.

Michael tutted loudly and opened his eyes. Spiritual communion with the Divine was clearly going to be impossible today.

"I'm sorry," said Zack. "We weren't disturbing you, were we?"

Michael looked at the Reverend Zack Purdey, an individual who, whilst occupying the body of a youngish church rector, had the earnest and prosaic manner of a middle-aged chartered accountant. He looked like he should have had a moustache and pipe, despite having never owned either.

"You're not disturbing me," lied Michael. He could be a particularly bad liar when he chose.

"I just had to admire Mrs Fairfax's efforts," said Zack.

Netty knelt on the flagstones, soapy to the elbows. A stiff-bristled brush was in her hand, and the sin of pride was all over her face.

"I don't think I've ever seen the floor so clean," said Zack.

"Just doing my bit, rev," said Netty.

"I think you've done a wonderful job. She's an absolute angel, isn't she, Michael?"

Michael blinked.

"I'm sorry."

"Netty. Her work. Absolute angel."

"I don't think angels would be seen scrubbing floors on their hands and knees, Reverend."

"It's just a turn of phrase," said Netty.

"But an inaccurate one," Michael informed her. "It wouldn't be right to associate the angelic host with something as... as... earthy as this."

"I understand the point you make," said Zack diplomatically.

"You believe in angels then?" said Netty.

"What? Yes," said Michael. "Of course, I do."

"My mam believed in ghosts."

"Well, that's not exactly the same..."

"She said there was a little Victorian girl called Esme who lived up our chimney and that's why she wouldn't put the fire on, even in winter."

"Angels are an integral part of the faith."

"I think she was just tight-fisted and didn't want to pay for gas."

"I think there's room for a range of beliefs on the matter," said Zack.

"No, there's not," said Michael. "Angels are mentioned several times, and quite clearly, in the Bible."

"But the word 'angel' does not necessarily come with all the wings and halo baggage. It just means 'messenger'. It can even refer to the message itself."

Michael stood up and gestured wildly at the huge tapestry at the back of the church, the one of the Archangel Michael – him! – defeating the Great Dragon, Satan.

"I can't believe we're having this conversation in a church dedicated to *an angel*! One of the chief angels! Look at him. Michael. Of course I – *he* – is real. Who else threw down Lucifer?"

"Isn't it all just a metaphor for good's struggle with, but ultimate victory over, evil?"

"No, it's not," said Michael crossly.

"It's like a lot of the Bible, isn't it?" said Netty.

"What?"

"Thingy. Allegory. It's not really true."

"I will admit," said Michael, slowly, cautiously, and prepared to backtrack at any moment, "that there are a couple of historical facts – number of people who died in certain battles, the order of succession of certain kings – that need to be carefully evaluated and put into a, er, broader contextual truth but, no, Mrs Fairfax, it's all true."

"Adam and Eve in the garden?"

"It's true. It happened."

"Noah and the flood?"

"True."

"The virgin birth?"

"Without a doubt!"

Netty gave him a look of pity.

"You're what they call a little naïve. Some things are just too unbelievable."

"They are not!" said Michael in a loud and forceful voice that was not shouting, but only just. "It's called faith, Mrs Fairfax! Faith!"

In his rage, Michael fumbled the picking up of his coat, tripped over his own feet, and nearly slipped in the soap suds on the floor as he did his best to storm out dramatically.

Clovenhoof plonked Gorky in the pram beside Beelzebelle, and positioned the tracker screen next to them both. Beelzebelle giggled and stuck a sticky hand on the monkey's belly fur. Gorky made a throaty noise of enquiry at Clovenhoof.

Clovenhoof did a couple of practice lunges and grunted in his manliest manner.

"No Segway today, my friends. Never mind that I wrecked it pancaking onto Mr Chip Malarkey's stretch transit, today's baby-walking goes off-piste."

He tapped Gorky on the nose.

"You, my monkey pioneer, are going to record our journey. Sit proud and point the way."

As Gorky sat upright and peered like a sea captain on the prow of his ship, Clovenhoof pushed the pram down the Chester Road. Within seconds, he felt a child-like thrill of glee at seeing their progress mapped on the device screen. It was like having an etch-a-sketch as big as the world.

"There are no limits but our imagination," he declared theatrically, and broke into a jog.

Beelzebelle clapped as she was jiggled along.

Clovenhoof was not necessarily one for excessive exercise (from the flat to the bookies and then to the pub was a veritable marathon in his eyes), but he was one for the grand gesture and, in this instance, the grand gesture required some exertion.

Down the Chester Rd he went, to Green Lane and then left towards Sutton Coldfield town centre. Onto the Birmingham Road and past the Horse and Jockey pub, Clovenhoof began a long sweeping loop around the shopping centre. Clovenhoof had a very specific route in mind. Sadly, the town planners of Sutton Coldfield had not taken that into account, and Clovenhoof had to stray from the pavement on more than one occasion. With a careful eye on his GPS tracker, Clovenhoof swung round the Gracechuch shopping centre, cut through Halfords car park and then, eschewing the wheelchair access ramp for the more direct stairs, in through the front door of Friday's New York Grill and Burger Bar.

"Can I help you?" said a server in a stripy hat and a vest covered in tin badges.

"You can clear those tables out of the way," said Clovenhoof, and pressed on immediately.

"Tuck in, tubby!" he yelled at a diner. "Move it, grandma!"

The staff gave chase once he was past the bar and exiting through the kitchen.

A cook tried to block their way, arms waving, but Clovenhoof warded her off with a snatched ladle. They barrelled through the fire exit, tumbled down the concrete steps and through beeping traffic onto Lower Queen Street.

Beelzebelle squealed with delight. Gorky passed her a buttery corn on the cob he had liberated in the diner. Beelzebelle gummed it happily.

Clovenhoof rolled his eyes.

"Gonna have pebble-dashed nappies tonight, then," he said. "Now, here's where it gets interesting."

The course he had plotted along Sutton's streets involved going from Holland Road to Elms Road. Unfortunately, Holland Road was a cul-de-sac, and a row of gardens stood between him and Elms Road. Internet maps had only provided the sketchiest of details, but Clovenhoof had selected what looked to be the weakest point.

"Buckle up, Beelzebelle."

Gorky checked the baby's straps and resumed his position on top of the pram. Clovenhoof lowered his horns and accelerated. The driveway of number fourteen was clear, and the garden gate was a thin thing of creosoted panels.

With only a moment to consider the value of reinforcing the front of the pram, perhaps with some bull bars off some rich wanker's jeep-tank-range-rover-thing, Clovenhoof sprinted up the driveway and straight through the gate. Gorky leapt off at the last moment, not away but up and over, swinging along the house guttering and maintaining pace with Clovenhoof.

"Good Lord!" exclaimed a woman, kneeling by the flower beds.

"Lovely garden," called Clovenhoof, racing past.

Actually, Clovenhoof couldn't give a damn for gardens or gardening. He had been a resident in the world's first garden and, frankly, felt he had done those two naked kids a favour when he'd got them kicked out. Gardens were peculiar things, gardeners doubly so, and British gardeners triply so. If an Englishman's home was his castle, then his garden was the grounds to his estate, treating it as though the natural world was something that needed to be tamed or improved upon. If these lawn-loonies attended to their spiritual and moral lives with the same puritanical diligence as they did their gardens, Hell would have far fewer British residents.

"Mind the bougainvillea!" shouted a man.

In addition to frilly pansies, drooping magnolia, and some weird trellisy thing, these nutters had decided that their garden required a decorative rockery. It stood by the rear fence, several feet high, home to sprouting greenery and prickly cacti, and entirely in Clovenhoof's way.

Gorky ran down the trellis and shrieked at Clovenhoof.

"No retreat! No surrender!" said Clovenhoof through gritted teeth.

Clovenhoof ran at the rockery, hoisted the pram above his head, an act that required more strength than he actually possessed, took one, two steps up the craggy mound, and leapt over the fence before his arms and legs realised that what he was attempting was impossible. He cleared the fence and, initially, Clovenhoof came down on his hooves, which was a greater success than he deserved. The pram came down right way up which was, again, a matter of luck. Clovenhoof fell into a roll. The pram tottered on two side wheels. Gorky flung himself out to right the vehicle like an expert yachtsman. The pram jolted to a stop in a rut. Clovenhoof exited his roll and leapt up.

A dozen women, babies in hands, stared at Clovenhoof. They stood evenly spaced across this new garden, each in the same peculiar pose. Clovenhoof couldn't be sure if they were frozen in the middle of a battle with invisible ninjas, or if each of them was driving an invisible tractor.

"Ta dah!" declared Clovenhoof.

The women stared. The babies stared.

"Actually, it's called Tai Chi," said one of the women.

Zack found Michael deep in thought in the churchyard.

"Michael, Michael."

The archangel turned.

"I'm sorry, Reverend. I didn't mean to get annoyed at you and Netty but, sometimes, I can't cope with such faithless talk."

Zack offered a genial smile.

"It's not faithless, Michael. It's a different expression of the same faith. Not everyone can have your... zeal." Zack breathed deeply and took a moment to look at the exterior of his church. "There is more that binds us together than separates us, Michael. You, me, Netty, even Darren ..."

"I heard that," said Darren, who was weeding around a granite angel.

"... We're all united by our love, our good deeds, and the sharing of meaningful ritual."

"I know, I know. It's just..."

"Don't question the details," said Zack. "Our church and faith keep us going even when..." Zack closed his mouth and then looked around suspiciously. "Can I share a secret with you?"

"Yes, Reverend."

Zack leaned close and whispered.

"Some days, I don't even believe in God. It doesn't make me any less of a Christian."

Zack watched carefully for a reaction. There was a weird look of satisfaction on Michael's face. He looked like a child who had found a slimy, disgusting thing in the garden, horrified and smug all at the same time.

Michael turned and fled before Zack could say anything further.

"SCUM," said the woman.

"Most people are" said Clovenhoof.

The woman smiled. She was long-haired and rosy-cheeked, with a dress sense that seemed to be what would have happened if hippies had discovered tweed. She held a baby boy whose face was almost entirely spittle.

"No, you misunderstand. Us lot, we're all SCUM."

Clovenhoof nodded in agreement.

"Glad we've cleared that up."

"Sutton Coldfield Union of Mums."

Something clicked in Clovenhoof's brain.

"I went on your website," and immediately something else clicked. "And I spoke to you. You're Sandra DribblyBibbly-something."

"Millet-Walker."

"Dribbly-Bibbly-Millet-Walker. That's the one."

Sandra gave him a suddenly shrewd look.

"Were you the man with the – and I quote – 'five boob emergency'?"

There was a smattering of laughs from the others.

"Depends," said Clovenhoof.

"I've told all the women," said Sandra.

"We do like to laugh," said one of the others.

"At men, mostly," said another.

"Sorry," said Sandra.

Clovenhoof shrugged.

"Men. Women. I laughed at everyone."

"So this is ..." Sandra closed her eyes. "Belle, was it?"

"Beelzebelle."

"That's a lovely name. Is that Eastern European?"

"Philistine originally," said Clovenhoof.

"I do like the old names," said a woman.

Another woman wearing an outlandish headscarf approached with an expression of deep consternation.

"This is *my* garden, you know. You can't just leap in."

"I would have barged through," said Clovenhoof, removing a piece of garden gate that had got wedged on one horn, "but your neighbours left a pile of rubble in my way."

"Most people would have used the gate."

"No, it wouldn't work if we went round," said Clovenhoof, and then suddenly yelled, "Don't you move an inch, Gorky!"

Gorky froze in the act of returning a dummy to a smiling babe.

"Would he hurt us?" asked the mother.

"Dunno. Depends how hard you throw him. Gorky, we have to stay on the route. Let's not ruin it now by going goo-goo over a little pooper. Back on the pram."

"So, what is this?" said Sandra. "Some sort of parent and baby parkour?"

"Ye-es," said Clovenhoof slowly. "Yes, that's exactly what this is. We just like leaping off random street furniture. And we've still got some leaping to do. Gorky. Pram."

"How exciting," said Sandra. "Well, it was nice of you to *drop in*." She said it with the heavy emphasis and accompanying eyebrow waggling of someone who rarely told jokes and didn't expect people to pick up on the subtlety of her comedic efforts. Several of the women laughed, though not the somewhat miffed garden-owner.

"Perhaps you'd care to give us notice before you drop in again," she said.

"Ooh, perhaps he'd come to our swishing party tonight," said a mum.

"We do lack dads in our group," said another.

"But we're not called SCUD."

"Or SCUMAD."

"But we're all about acceptance, support and diversity," said Sandra to her colleagues, who were all white, Anglo-Saxon, and so middle-class it was probably stamped on their DNA.

Clovenhoof had only truly picked up on one word.

"Party?"

"If you're free," said Sandra, and presented Clovenhoof with a business card. "We start swishing at six."

"Count me in," said Clovenhoof, and consulted his GPS tracker. "Now, you'll have to excuse us. I need to do a testicle on Fourlands Avenue."

"Testicle?"

"I think it's a parkour manoeuvre," suggested a woman, as Clovenhoof aligned himself. "*Test a clé*. The, um, key test."

"Bollocks," said Clovenhoof.

Michael attempted to walk off his troubles.

He loved St Michael's Church – yes, partly because it was his church in more than one sense – but he couldn't get over the weird irreligious failings of both the congregation and the man who was meant to be shepherd of the flock. And it wasn't just Netty's lack of belief in key Biblical events or, more galling, Reverend Zack's utter lapses in faith. St Michael's seemed to favour a certain Christianity-lite in which the choice of coffee morning biscuits was more important than contemplation of the communion host, where the Christmas nativity took precedence over the church's apostolic mission.

Michael could have taken his concerns home and shared them with Andy, but Andy didn't share Michael's faith. Andy was prepared to pay lip service to Michael's beliefs, attending church at the most important times of the year, but he was gleefully unbothered by the finer nuances of religion.

A walk was a fine way to clear the mind and gain some perspective. Michael's mind-clearing was somewhat interrupted by the sight of Jeremy Clovenhoof running up and down the driveways all along Fourlands Avenue. The odd sight was made all the odder by the pram that Clovenhoof pushed in front of him, and the capuchin perched on the top of the pram.

"What are you doing?" called out Michael, as Clovenhoof came out of one driveway and into another.

"Pubes!" Clovenhoof shouted and was gone.

Michael's befuddlement at that carried him a considerable distance. It was only when he heard someone reciting from the Book of Matthew that he looked up and considered his surroundings. Ahead of him, on a wide sweep of pavement by the traffic lights, was a white transit van – not just a transit van, but a *stretch* transit van.

Clovenhoof had mentioned this vehicle, as had Nerys. Ah, yes, there were the signs of a repair in the roof, presumably where Clovenhoof had crashed through. And, Michael could see, Jeremy had not lied about the vehicle's interior. There was the plush red carpet. There was the altar rail and the altar of polished pine. And there was chalice, patten and a priest in a cassock administering communion to the short queue of people by the van's open side door. Meanwhile, on the pavement, a young woman read through a megaphone from an open Bible. A pair of men supervised the distribution of sandwiches and tea from the picnic table at the rear of the van.

Michael's feet carried him over.

"Hungry, sir?" said a stocky man, offering Michael a cellophane-wrapped sandwich.

"No, thank you," said Michael. "This is all fascinating."

"Just doing our bit," the man said. "Feeding those that need it."

"Are there many homeless people in Sutton?"

The man jiggled his head toward the tea-server beside him.

"Quentin here used to sleep rough behind the train station."

"S'true," said Quentin. "A horrible life of Scrumpy Thunder and petty theft. Cuppa?"

Michael accepted the Styrofoam cup.

"Our streetside missions offer sustenance to any who want it. But, of course, man shall not live on bread alone."

"But on every word that comes from the mouth of God," said Michael, finishing the quote.

A broad grin split the sandwich-bearer's stubbly face.

"A man of the faith!" he declared. "You belong to a local congregation?"

"Ah, well..." said Michael, feeling his spiritual unease resurface.

"We've recently opened a church on Beechmount Drive."

"Consecr8?" said Michael, surprised in having to reconcile this earnest grassroots work with the imposingly modern church building he had previously disparaged.

"That's the one, mate. The very Reverend Mario Felipe Gonzalez in the van there is our preacher-man, but I'm very pleased to admit I had a hand in its founding. I'm a builder by trade and, if there's one thing a church needs, it's a building."

The man stuck out his hand. Michael shook it.

"Chip. Chip Malarkey," said the man. "Maybe you'd like to come see our church sometime."

"Yes," said Michael. "I would like that."

Clovenhoof pushed the pram up Penns Lane at a speed that was less of a jog and more of a stagger. He had bruises across his back, rips in his finest green smoking jacket and his hair was so stuffed with twigs and foliage, from all the hedges he'd run through, that he looked as if he was auditioning for the role of Puck in regional theatre. All in all, it had been an exhausting outing. The scramble over fences into Pilkington Avenue had been followed by a slog across Walmley Golf Course, which had involved churning his way through several sandy bunkers and a running the gauntlet of half a dozen elderly golfers who had not been afraid to use their clubs to defend their right to a quiet game.

Clovenhoof's phone rang as he reached the end of the road and turned up towards home. He didn't answer it. To stop now would be to admit defeat.

"Almost... there..." he panted.

Once back onto the Chester Road, he felt a renewed energy. The end was in sight and his glorious little project would be complete. Gorky held on tight in that final dash, although did lean out to snatch a poster that had been tied to a nearby lamppost as they ran past.

In the closing moments, Clovenhoof braced his arms on the handlebar and lifted his feet off the ground, coasted along and then brought his hooves down hard. There were even sparks.

Gasping, he looked at the tracker screen which Beelzebelle was helpfully holding up for him.

"Work... of... art..."

Gorky put the screen to one side and gave Beelzebelle a bottle of formula milk. The little girl burbled and farted. Clovenhoof gave a fart of his own in reply, accompanied by a fist pump.

"Job well done, eh? What's this?"

Gorky had thrust a sheet into his hand, the poster from the lamppost.

In the centre was the headshot of a baby in a pink baby-gro.

"Missing," read Clovenhoof. "Beatrice Wilson. Abducted from her family in the Boldmere area earlier this month."

Gorky pointed at the picture and at Beelzebelle.

"What?" said Clovenhoof. "Oh, yeah. I know." He screwed the sheet up into a ball. "But all babies look alike. It's just a coincidence."

Chip walked Michael down to the Consecr8 Church. It was only a stone's throw from the ARC Company portakabin compound where Michael worked and took up the bulk of the reclaimed wasteland between the Sutton Road and the new housing estate that was going up by Wilmot Drive.

The great curving wooden edifice of the Consecr8 building was a modern – or was that even post-modern? – rose among the brambles and weeds of Sutton's architectural skyline. Automatic doors opened as they approached. Chip produced a plastic card and swiped in through a reader at an inner door.

"Security?" said Michael.

"Not at all," said Chip. "All are welcome day or night. This just records how often I come to church."

Michael understood instantly.

"That's clever. Not that attendance to church necessarily equates to personal piety."

"Of course not," said Chip, leading him through. "We have an app to measure that."

The interior curved like the exterior, making a giant compartmentalised bowl of the central space. Seating, vibrant hangings, and the musical and electronic trappings of a place of celebration ranged up the sloping walls.

Michael blinked at the majesty of it all. It wasn't opulent as such. The stylings were relatively modest, but the scale and presentation of it all was something else entirely.

"I beg your pardon?" said Michael, his brain catching up. "There's an app?"

"There certainly is, mate."

Lugging the pram upstairs took considerable additional effort and, once they were all inside flat 2a, Clovenhoof declared himself thoroughly knackered.

"Gorky! Findus Crispy Pancakes all round!" gasped the Fallen One. "And a glass of Lambrini for me."

Gorky chattered and bounded into the kitchen.

"Actually, make that a pint," Clovenhoof said. "I'm parched."

He unstrapped Beelzebelle and lifted her out. She smelled wonderful. That biscuity baby smell, baby poop guffiness, plus the faintly chemical buzz of a damp nappy. Shattered though he was, Clovenhoof laid her out on the sofa and, with the skill of a man who'd learned on the job in recent weeks, changed her. He tossed the wipes at the bin by the fire, merrily missing every time. He arranged it carefully and fetched his polaroid instant camera.

"Mmm, textured," he said as he took a nappy snap. "Beelzebelle, ma gal, if I ever get to do a father of the bride speech, there *will* be a slide show."

Gorky returned with a laden tray: Lambrini, milk, and an orange for himself. As Gorky began to play peek-a-boo with Beelzebelle, Clovenhoof savoured a drink well-deserved. He caught sight of himself in the mirror above the mantelpiece and saw the various twigs and leaves stuck in his hair.

"Decorative," he said, and then had a sudden thought. He pulled the bits of plant from his hair and horns and took them to the airing cupboard. There, on a wooden shelf above the heating tank, sat a glass demijohn of what Clovenhoof entirely expected to become beautiful sparkling Lambrini, but which currently resembled the water left behind after a rugby team's communal bath. He wasn't sure when the transformation would occur, but he was sure it would be soon.

"A few bits of local flora to sweeten the brew," said Clovenhoof, popping the stopper and stuffing the leaves and twigs in.

He returned to the lounge and, as he drank his glass of monkey-poured Lambrini, saw he had a voicemail on his phone. He played it.

"What did you do with Bea?" hissed Spartacus. "Mum's back from her holiday and we've only just discovered that she's not at my nan's. You were meant to hand her over! If you've cremated her, I will burn your house down! Call me!"

Clovenhoof stared at the phone.

"Well, that was rude," he said.

88

Gorky was blowing raspberries on Beelzebelle's tummy. The baby laughed and squealed. The two of them had bonded so well in their short time together.

"Break time's over," said Clovenhoof.

Gorky looked at him. Clovenhoof dug in a pocket and pulled out a set of keys, copies of the keys to the other flats.

"Brilliant plan number two," he said. "We're going to make ourselves a wad of cash. I need some plastic bags, a pair of scissors, and a little light burglary."

Chip went to a bank of tablets on the wall, swiped his card to release one from its docking station, and opened an app.

"I won't lie to you, mate," he said. "We adapted this from some software used by a vile and manipulative American cult. I won't mention it by name, but let's just say I'm betting Tom Cruise has got something very much like this on his iPhone."

"Really?" said Michael.

Chip waved his concerns away.

"We could have just as easily adapted something from Weight Watchers or the Open University. You see, in a narrow sense, faith is about goals. There are smaller goals to fulfil along the way, but there's one ultimate goal."

Chip looked to Michael for an answer.

"To return to Heaven," said Michael.

"Return? I don't think either of us have been there yet, Michael."

"Sorry. I meant to go to Heaven."

"Right. And what is Heaven?" said Chip. He provided his own answer before Michael could. "It is God. It is love. Our goal is to worship God and to be with him. As our Muslim chums would put it, to submit utterly to his will. And how do we do that? We follow his instructions. After all, he tells us what to do!" Chip said this last with the passion of someone who couldn't see how anyone could fail to understand this simple fact.

Chip tapped at the tablet screen and brought up a menu.

"The Jews had the right idea – I won't hear you say a bad word about them, Michael – they codified the laws of their religion. Do you know how many commandments there are in the Old Testament, you know, the Jewish bits?"

"Six hundred and thirteen mitzvot," said Michael.

"Very good," said Chip, surprised. "All the dos and don'ts, laid out clearly for them. You know what SMART targets are?"

Michael nodded.

"Specific, measureable, attainable, realistic, and timely."

Chip grinned.

"Oh, you are a man after my own heart, Michael mate. I think you can see my vision already."

"I think I can," said Michael. "'Measure what can be measured and make measureable what cannot be measured.'"

Chip laughed, reached into an inner pocket, and pulled out a retractable metal tape measure. The quote from Galileo was inscribed on the side of it.

"Who says builders can't be philosophers?" Chip put a hand on Michael's shoulder. "We can't presume to know the mind of God, but I think you were destined to come here, mate. Out on the street, I saw you a troubled man, spiritually lost. Maybe you've found your spiritual home."

Michael was taken aback. Chip's church and approach to faith was fascinating, but was he looking for a new spiritual home? Surely, St Michael's church with all its idiosyncrasies and flaws was already his spiritual home. Did he really need to move on? Shouldn't he just attempt to mend and renew his relationship with his current church?

"Tell me a bit more about this app," he said to Chip.

Stuffed animals, including the recently mounted and surprisingly perky looking Twinkle stood in a row on Clovenhoof's coffee table. Gorky and he had successfully liberated the lot of them from Ben and Nerys's flats. Next to the animals were freezer bags decorated with white snowflakes and blue penguins. Several of them had already been filled with various materials – scrapings from Clovenhoof's horns, claws snipped off some of the stuffed mammals, a skin sample from the one stuffed lizard.

Clovenhoof paraded up and down in front of the stuffed creatures, inspecting the list Ed had given him.

"Next. Bat-eared fox. What do they look like?"

Gorky turned the computer monitor on the corner desk so Clovenhoof could see it. Clovenhoof sniggered at the image on the screen.

"Seriously? Clearly one of the Big Guy's 'off' days. Stupid-looking thing." He sighed. "So, brownish-reddish-blackish fur. Let's see."

Clovenhoof yanked a few hairs from his own head and sprinkled them into a bag.

"Now we need something a little lighter."

Twinkle's tan-coloured fur was an ideal match. Clovenhoof snipped hairs from the little dog's belly and added them to the bag.

"It needs a little... ginger."

Beelzebelle, rolling on the floor, grabbed a ferret off the table and waved it about.

"That's white," tutted Clovenhoof. "Focus, girl."

He picked up a red squirrel.

"You'll do, Nutkin."

Clovenhoof cut off some wispy tail hair, added it to the bag and shook.

"What do you reckon?" he said.

Beelzebelle spat and wrestled with the ferret. Gorky squawked and did a backflip.

"Excellent," said Clovenhoof. "Let's get another couple of these done, and then we're off to our swishing party. No, I don't know what swishing is. I think it's what Nerys's parents did in the seventies. Now, what animal's next? Oryx. What the Hell's an oryx?"

Nerys parked up outside the flats after work.

"Thanks for the lift," said Ben, got out, and took the heavy bin bag off the rear seat. "I think I'd have struggled to carry this home."

"When you said you had supplies to bring home, I thought you meant shopping."

"Taxidermy supplies," said Ben.

Nerys locked the car and eyed the soft, shapeless bin bag suspiciously.

"But you don't mean needles and thread, do you?"

Ben attempted to give her an open and innocent look, but he failed almost instantly. Nerys was a scary lady – a friend, yes, but a scary lady nonetheless – and he found it near impossible to lie to her.

"I think the important thing to keep in mind," he said, "is that it died painlessly."

"Did it?"

"I should think so. The lorry was travelling at quite a lick."

Nerys almost dropped her keys.

"You put roadkill on my back seat?" she said.

"In a bin bag," Ben pointed out. "There was no actual goat-to-seat contact."

"Goat," said Nerys, to herself more than anything. "This hobby is getting out of hand."

"You were singing my praises this morning."

"And you did a wonderful job," said Nerys. "But it feels like you're just doing one after the next after the next. You've got them lined up for a personal stuffing."

Nerys opened the flat door.

There was a line of stuffed animals going up the stairs. They formed an orderly queue, the larger animals resting across two steps as though climbing up.

Nerys took a second or two to consider this.

"What the fuck, Ben?"

"This isn't my doing," said Ben, aghast.

"No, it's bloody Jeremy, isn't it? Twinkle!"

Nerys ran upstairs and snatched up her dead terrier from its position near the top of the first flight. She hugged the dog to her breast.

"What did the nasty man do to you?"

"It's just one of his little jokes," said Ben reasonably.

Nerys glared at him.

"Don't you find this weirdness, this invasion of our personal space and private lives intensely annoying, Ben?"

Ben thought about it.

"Yes, I do. But this is still sort of background noise level as far as Jeremy is concerned. Compared to other times, he's been quiet of late."

"Yeah, and that's even more suspicious. You must have noticed it. The weird smells coming from his flat. The cries in the middle of the night. The sound of him watching the Teletubbies at full volume. And that pram. Does he push his monkey round in it?"

"Lennox told me that he bought the monkey off Ed."

"Animal Ed?"

"Well, you'd be the one who'd know if the man was animal," said Ben.

Nerys kicked a stuffed hedgehog down the stairs at him. Ben caught it and then wished he hadn't.

"Ow."

"I'm going to talk to Ed and see if he knows what Jeremy is up to."

Ben picked up a scrunched up ball of paper that he had spotted on the hall carpet. He unfolded it and stared at it.

"No," he said softly, not willing to believe.

"What?" said Nerys.

"I might know what Jeremy's been up to."

"And?"

"I think we need to speak to Ed, right now."

Sandra's home was Victorian villa a short walk from the Chester Road. Clovenhoof, Gorky, and Beelzebelle stood on her doorstep shortly after six. Clovenhoof reached into his trousers and adjusted the spandex thong he'd put on for the occasion and knocked. Sandra answered the door, a cup of coffee in hand.

"Jeremy!" She looked back over her shoulder and shouted, "Well somebody's lost a bet!"

There were titters from a distant room.

"A number of them reckoned you would be too frightened to spend the evening with a gaggle of women," said Sandra.

"Why?" said Clovenhoof. "I like women."

"Yes, but en masse, some men find us intimidating."

"Can't say I've ever been intimidated by a woman," said Clovenhoof, wheeling the pram in, "but I'm willing to give it a go."

Sandra directed him through. Clovenhoof carried Beelzebelle on one shoulder. Gorky perched on the other. In a back room, a dozen women sat on low chairs, chatting and drinking while their babies bounced on their knees or rolled about on the floor. There were several bags piled high on the one table in the room.

"Does everyone remember Jeremy?" asked Sandra.

"How could we forget?" said a woman, and another laughed.

"I do have a memorable profile," Clovenhoof agreed.

Sandra introduced all the women present, and their children, and offered a potted biography of most. Here was Regina with her daughter, Clytemnestra, who had both recently returned from India. Here was baby Astra with mum, Jocasta, whose husband was the director of the Victoria Theatre. And this was Savannah and little Lyric, with the unfortunate eczema, who had a narrow escape when someone had smashed into their Octavia at the traffic lights.

Clovenhoof made an effort to remember.

Was it Octavia with baby Regina who had recently returned from the savannah? Maybe India and baby Eczema whose daddy worked at the Lyric Theatre? This was Jocasta and little Victoria with the unfortunate case of clytemnestra who had recently been involved in an accident with an Astra?

By the end of the introductions, all Clovenhoof was certain of was that there was a woman called Sandra and lots of other women who were definitely not Sandra.

"So," said Sandra, "tea, coffee, or can I tempt you to an alcoholic tipple?"

"Tempt away," said Clovenhoof. "I'm not driving, but I did bring my car keys."

Sandra frowned at him.

"You know," said Clovenhoof. "That bit where everyone puts their keys in a bowl and..."

Sandra thumped him in the shoulder playfully.

"Swishing, Jeremy! Not..." She laughed. "Oh, you are awful."

"Are we swishing then?" said one of the not-Sandras.

Clovenhoof was nonplussed.

"So what does swishing involve?" he said.

"We swap clothes," said the not-Sandra.

"Kinky," said Clovenhoof with an approving nod and began to strip.

A not-Sandra pulled open one of the bags on the table to reveal neatly folded blouses and jeans within.

"Swap clothes," she said.

"Oh."

"Like a jumble sale," said a not-Sandra. "But without the smell, the elbowing, and the money."

"Maybe we'll all find something nice and new to wear, without having to get all consumerist and splash out the dough," said another.

"Not sure if we have any men's clothes," said Sandra apologetically.

"I'm nothing if not adaptable," said Clovenhoof, not bothering to do up his shirt again. "Let's take a look, eh? Maybe I'll find that mankini I've been dreaming of."

While Beelzebelle floundered on the floor with several other babies and Gorky (who was in monkey au pair heaven) cheerfully supervised and played with the lot of them, Clovenhoof joined the ladies of SCUM in search of that ideal outfit.

Ed was not at the pet supplies shop, or in his flat above, but was to be found in a booth at the Boldmere Oak. He looked quite content and pleased with himself, until the moment he saw Nerys striding purposefully across the bar floor toward him with a slightly less purposeful looking Ben Kitchen in her wake and, oddly, he thought, a stuffed Yorkshire Terrier under her arm.

Ed coughed, spilt the foam on top of his fresh pint, and hurriedly sat upright.

"Nerys." He clutched a beer mat like a tiny, soggy, and entirely useless shield. "You're not still, you know, mad at me, are you?"

Nerys glared.

"Of course not, Ed. Past's in the past. Who wants to go to Kenya anyway? I've moved on. In fact, I'm seeing an absolute cutie at the moment. A, er, fireman. I tell you, one look at him, and I just fell into his arms."

"Really?" said Ben. "I didn't know that you were seeing anyone at the – ow! – The only date you've been on lately is with a tub of Ben and Jerry's and a box set of Poirot – ow! – Why do you keep jabbing me in the ribs with your – ow!"

Nerys smiled sweetly at Ed.

"We need to ask you some questions, Ed."

"Questions?" said Ed. "What questions?"

"Like why you gave a monkey to Jeremy?"

"I didn't give it to him. I sold it to him."

"Why on earth would he want a monkey?" said Ben.

"To help look after the baby, of course," said Ed.

"Baby?" said Nerys.

"Yeah, baby."

"Told you," said Ben.

"Baby!" squeaked Nerys.

"Yes. Baby," said Ed irritably. "You do know he has a little baby girl? You do live with him, don't you?"

"I think I'm going to faint," said Nerys.

"Really?" said Ben, rubbing his bruised chest. "If only there was a cute fireman whose arms you could fall into."

Despite the lack of drunkenness or sexual promiscuity or presence of a mankini, Clovenhoof realised he was actually enjoying the swishing party. He had found a skirt that he declared would be a passable kilt he'd wear to the next wedding he attended (or any church service, he decided). He insisted on modelling for the mums, and they gave him approving applause.

"A welcome addition to SCUM," said a not-Sandra.

"We do have a full programme of events," said Sandra. "We've just moved our play mornings to a new venue on Beechmount Drive. You'd be very welcome."

Clovenhoof looked at Beelzebelle. She and another spittle-faced baby were pushing plastic blocks back and forth. Elsewhere, Gorky wiped chins and picked up dropped bottles. When Clovenhoof had first taken Beelzebelle in, it had been a possessive thing, as though this little life was a vessel he could fill with his own personality and dreams. Now...

"Yes," he found himself saying. "That sounds nice. Bit of socialising for the girl."

One of the mums was breastfeeding her baby. She had unfastened her blouse and unleashed a large rounded breast that soon filled the hungry baby's face. The baby had a significant chunk of flesh in its greedy mouth, like a tiny cannibal. He wondered if the not-Sandra might get her other breast out if he asked her to, so that he could try to estimate how much boob a baby could get in its mouth. Michael would be proud of his scientific methodology.

"And you'll have to introduce us to parent and baby parkour," said Sandra.

"What? Yes? Well, that wasn't quite what I was doing. You see, there's this mapping website. Do you have a phone or tablet-thingy?"

Nerys stared, slack-jawed, as Ed explained all he knew of the baby situation.

"But didn't you think to alert the authorities?" said Ben.

"Alert them to what?" said Ed. "He's a man and he's got a child. That's not abnormal. Men *do* have children."

"Men, yes," said Ben, "but not men like Jeremy."

"He had a real paternal aura about him."

"Sorry," said Nerys, "are we talking about the same individual? Jeremy Clovenhoof. About this tall. Passing resemblance to Satan. Likes Lambrini, ugly print clothes, and making lives Hell."

"Maybe fatherhood has brought out his caring, nurturing side," said Ben.

"He doesn't have one," exclaimed Nerys. "He's fifty percent goat, fifty percent git. We need to find him at once, before something terrible happens. He's not at home."

"Have you got a phone on you?" said Ed.

"Why?"

"Go to track-my-child.com. I put a tracker on Gorky – that's the monkey – and it's probably in the same place as Jeremy. That's it. Account name is Ed underscore Lawrence."

Nerys fiddled with her phone.

"Which of the trackers is Gorky's? And what are all these other ones?"

"Um, animals I'm tracking," said Ed, quite unconvincingly. "Wild animals."

"Really? One of them appears to be in Harvey Nicks in Birmingham."

"Urban fox?" He cleared his throat. "Gorky's tracker is ..."

"Found it," said Nerys in a cold, flat voice.

"How did you know it's that one?" said Ed.

Nerys showed him the screen and then Ben.

"Yeah, that'll be him," said Ben.

"I'm mailing this to Michael."

"Why?"

"I think we're going to need an intervention."

She said the word as though intervention had taken on a whole new meaning, one involving baseball bats, dark alleys, and shallow graves.

Michael had spent a very informative evening with Chip Malarkey. He would not have thought it possible, but Chip had demonstrated that measureable religiousness was a possibility, a not-quite-perfected science.

Michael had downloaded the Consecr8 app to his phone, and signed up to the accompanying social media plug-in.

"Now, I'm not one for the Facebooking or Twitting," said Chip, "but if you give the app permission, it will scan your feed – is 'feed' the right word? – and evaluate your posts for accreditation in the Goodness Archive."

"And that will earn me Piety Points?" said Michael.

"That's right, mate," said Chip. "However, the Goodness Archive uses an algorithm to compare your Faith Score and Works Score and then calculate your overall Piety Points. You can't be saved through faith alone, nor through good deeds. Doesn't matter what you do if you don't have faith. 'None shall come to the Father except through me.' That's what Christ said."

"And the weekly introspection questionnaires monitor my spiritual devotion."

Chip held out his arms wide. "Do good." He brought them in to his chest. "Be good."

He opened a folder and removed a white and gold swipe card.

"We'll register this to you and your account. You can use this to access all our events and redeem your points in the celebration zone."

"Celebration zone?"

"It's over here."

Michael's phone vibrated.

"Oh, I've just received a message."

"It could be your registration with the website."

Michael opened the message. Before he could whisk it out of sight, Chip had seen it too.

"What is that, Michael?"

"Um. It would appear to be a message from a former neighbour of mine."

"Is that a...?"

"Map," said Michael firmly. "Yes. It's a picture of a map."

"But this stuff on it," said Chip, beginning to trace his finger over the lines on the map and then recoiling as though catching himself doing something obscene. "Is that...?"

"It would appear to be genitalia, Chip," said Michael, as casually as possible. "Someone has used GPS tracking software to draw an enormous penis and testicles on the streets of Sutton Coldfield. Oh, look, and they've shared it on the internet."

Chip grabbed Michael's hand to pull the phone closer.

"But that's my road! My driveway! What were they doing on my driveway?"

"Pubes," said Michael.

"Here!" said Ben, looking at his phone and pointing to a house on the left.

Nerys braked sharply and pulled up.

"Here?"

Ben showed her the tracker app on his phone.

Nerys looked up at the property.

"These are nice houses, Ben. What would Jeremy be doing here?"

"If we're in time, maybe nothing."

They got out, just as another car pulled up behind them.

"Well, that was embarrassing," said Michael as he got out. "I was in the middle of something spiritually important."

"But you're here now," said Nerys, "and you don't know the half of it. Babies."

"Babies?"

"Babies."

The three of them walked up the path. Nerys knocked on the door.

"Sounds like there's a bit of a party going on in there."

A woman opened the door.

"Oh, more newbies?" she said. "And, er, a stuffed dog."

"Yes, this is Twinkle. We were wondering if there was a man with a monkey here?" said Nerys, perfectly aware of how stupid it sounded.

"Friends of Jeremy's," said the woman. "Come in. We're busy planning an outing."

"Outing?"

The woman led them down the hallway to a back room where ten or more women were shouting and laughing as another woman took a marker pen to a large map that had been hastily pinned to a wall. The floor was a mass of clothing, through which various babies and toddlers crawled and flailed. Clovenhoof, stripped to the waist and wearing what looked to be a gingham skirt, stood on the table in the centre of the room in a pose that, to Ben's eyes, looked like someone pretending to carry a heavy rock at waist height, but was probably nothing so innocent. He struggled to maintain the pose because of the brown capuchin monkey bouncing on his head.

As the women hollered, the pen bearer tried to draw a representation of Jeremy on the map.

"Make it longer!" shouted one woman.

"Take it down towards Castle Bromwich!" shouted another.

"No! Now it looks like he's treading grapes!"

Drinks were pressed into the hands of the three gobsmacked visitors.

"This is obscene," whispered Michael.

A woman sidled up to him.

"Puts me in mind of the Rude Man of Cerne," she said. "We're all going to walk it out next weekend. Mums and babies."

Ben nodded.

"Well, ancient man did love his, er, phallic earthworks. It's no different really."

"But look where he's putting it!" said Michael.

"What?"

"The, er, tip. It's going right into Beechmount Drive!"

100

Ben peered.

"Oh, that new Consecr8 place." He chuckled. "That's quite funny. At least he's not sticking it in the front doors of *your* church, eh, Michael?"

Chapter 4 – In which social services intervene, Nerys finds little solace in religion, and alcohol proves to be the answer to everything

Clovenhoof hummed to himself as he bustled around the kitchen. It was Wiggly Fingers Baby Signing class at the Consecr8 church that afternoon, and he had a lot to do. Gorky sat on top of the cooker, peeling an orange. Clovenhoof felt the soggy pieces hit the back of his head as Gorky screeched at him to get a move on.

"I know, I know," he said. "But she'll be awake a lot sooner if you keep making that racket. Now, help me out and get some things together for when we go out."

Gorky shrugged and leapt down from the cooker. He grabbed a carrier bag, put ten oranges into it, and added some nappies and baby wipes on top. He cocked his head to one side in contemplation, and then added another three oranges as an afterthought.

Clovenhoof nodded in appreciation.

"Sorted. Nice work!"

There was a knock at the flat door. Gorky yelled, back-flipped onto the counter, and grabbed a whisk and colander as a makeshift sword and shield.

"It's not going to be the postman again," said Clovenhoof. "But you stay in here and keep out of harm's way."

Clovenhoof opened the door to find on his landing the moustachioed Police Constable Pearson and a woman in a dress with flowers so bright that they hurt Clovenhoof's eyes. A hearty wail pierced the air.

"Look what you've done," he said with a roll of his eyes. "PC Pearson. My favourite party-pooper."

"Not seen you in a while, Mr Clovenhoof," said the constable. "Have you been keeping out of trouble?"

"Not really," Clovenhoof replied honestly. "You know, every time I get arrested by someone else, I feel like I'm cheating on you."

"This is Diana Dickinson from our family liaison unit. We've come to take charge of the infant you have on the premises."

"Infant?" said Clovenhoof.

"Baby Beatrice," said PC Pearson.

"Never heard of him," said Clovenhoof.

"I wonder if we might come inside?" said Diana with a wide smile. Clovenhoof saw movement behind her as she stepped forward, and he realised that Nerys was standing on the stairs. She looked away and then turned and left as Clovenhoof closed the door.

"Right, I think we can soon clear this up," said Clovenhoof, as they entered the lounge. "There's no baby here."

"I can hear a baby crying," said Diana.

"It's a recording," said Clovenhoof, eyeing the progress that Gorky was making as he swung across the picture rail behind the heads of his two visitors. "From the BBC sound effects CD. Do you want me to turn it off?"

He picked up the remote control for his television as Gorky left the room, counted to five and pointed it meaningfully at the waste paper bin. The crying stopped, as he knew it would when Gorky picked up Beelzebelle.

"Neat, huh?" he said, indicating the waste paper basket. "State of the art media centre, that."

"Jeremy," said Diana. "May I call you Jeremy?"

"You can call me Dr Wonder-Nuts if you like."

"Why?"

"Always fancied being a doctor."

"Jeremy, we know you have the baby here. Concerned neighbours have given us all of the details."

"You mean Nerys."

"Concerned neighbours. Please can we see Beatrice now? We all just have the child's best interests at heart."

Clovenhoof pouted and stomped out to the kitchen.

"One moment, I'll be right back."

He glanced around for inspiration. He moved quickly and returned to the lounge, holding a bundle to his shoulder.

"There, there, Beelzebelle," he crooned. "You're going to be fine. We'll tell them all the things you like. Make sure they let you keep your cool new name."

He handed over the bundle with exaggerated care to Diana. She gave him a look as she weighed the bundle in her arms and pulled back the cloth.

"Jeremy, this is a bag of oranges wrapped in a tea towel. Please bring us the real baby."

Clovenhoof nodded, stalling for more time.

"Shall we share an orange in the meantime? They're navels. My, er, friend says they're the best. I can get you a Lambrini to go with it, if you like?"

"Perhaps I'd better take a look around," said PC Pearson.

"No, no, you stay there," said Clovenhoof, leaping. "I'll go and sort her out now."

He hurried through to the bedroom to see how Gorky was getting on. Beelzebelle was dressed and changed, and Gorky was fastening her into the baby sling as she gurgled happily.

"Over here," hissed Clovenhoof, opening the sash window. "You'll need to go down the drainpipe with her."

Gorky chattered with excitement and headed over to the window, threading his lanky arm through the sling as he went.

"I don't think so," said PC Pearson, striding across the room and sliding the sash down onto four sets of fingers. Gorky and Clovenhoof gave a yowl of pain. PC Pearson unfastened the sling and carefully lifted the baby into his arms. Beelzebelle giggled.

Clovenhoof scowled as he eased the sash off his fingers, and the capuchin screeched in fury. Diana stepped through the doorway and deftly removed the baby from PC Pearson, just as the angry Gorky leapt onto his shoulders and began to pull on his moustache.

Clovenhoof watched in interest, wondering what the policeman would look like with a bald upper lip, but noticed that his hand was reaching round for something in his belt.

"Ah, Gorky, you might want to watch out for – oh!"

The taser shot out and Gorky fell to the floor, twitching.

"Never make things easy, do you, Mr Clovenhoof?" said PC Pearson.

The next few minutes were a blur. Clovenhoof was vaguely aware of the muted conversation between the two police officers about the correct protocol regarding animal accomplices and their arrest. Diana scooped Gorky up and laid him out on a pillow. PC Pearson got out his handcuffs.

"Are those necessary?" said Clovenhoof.

"Yes," said PC Pearson.

"Probably so," said Clovenhoof. "I was still considering grabbing the baby and making a dash for the Mexican border."

"Well, that might be tricky, given that Mexico is on the other side of the Atlantic."

"Is it?" said Clovenhoof frowning. "What's that one with all the pasties and in-bred fisherman?"

"Cornwall?" said Diana.

"Ah," said Clovenhoof. "Explains a lot." He held out his hands to PC Pearson. "Cuff me, big boy. Cuff me good."

"Yes, do come in," Ben said, glancing up as Nerys stomped into his flat. She went straight to the window that overlooked the front.

"Look, they're taking him away. He's got handcuffs on."

Ben could see the reflection of the blue flashing light on the ceiling.

"It's not the first time, Nerys," said Ben. "They've probably got a cell with his name on it. He'll be fine."

"We did the right thing, didn't we?" she asked. "I mean, we couldn't just leave the baby there with him. What are you doing?"

Ben removed the jeweller's magnifying glass from his eye and rubbed the bridge of his nose.

"Knitting miniature chain mail," he said. "It's very delicate work. This is forty-four gauge wire, almost as thin as a human hair. I have to knit it using cocktail sticks."

Nerys peered at his notes, and the scattered diagrams on the table.

"You're making a chain mail tabard for a rabbit?" she asked.

"You'll barely see it underneath his armour, but you know I'm all about the detail."

"Oh, like this?" asked Nerys, indicating a squirrel dressed in full armour and thrusting a lance aggressively forwards.

"Yes, a bit like that," said Ben, "but I think a rabbit would want heavier weaponry than a squirrel. I'm thinking maybe a halberd, a maul, or a mace."

"Yes, yes, of course," said Nerys with a shake of her head. "Does it make you happy, all of this?"

Ben turned in surprise.

"I suppose it does, yes."

"You're lucky."

Ben was not one for reading emotional and social subtext; he was a man, and one of many men for whom social interactions and emotions, especially of those pertaining to women, were utterly beneath his radar. However, by pure fluke, his subconscious mind latched onto some critical nuance.

"You're still missing Twinkle?" he said.

"So much," said Nerys, plonking herself into the chair across the table from him.

Ben searched for something to say. His repertoire of consoling noises was limited in scope and mostly consisted of agreeing that no, the film wasn't as good as the book. Luckily for Ben, Nerys continued to speak as if he weren't really there.

"I'm even going to that new church of Michael's tonight."

"That's that 'Prayers 4U' place?"

"Consecr8."

"That's the one."

"Michael tells me it's given him so much more energy and focus. Maybe it can work for me as well."

"You're hardly of a religious bent, Nerys."

"I just need something meaningful to fill the void."

Ben's gaze travelled across the table in front of him, and inspiration suddenly struck.

"I've got it," he said. "How about I teach you how to knit?"

Ben contemplated Nerys's reaction for some time afterwards, as he cleared up the cocktail stick splinters from his carpet. It wasn't so much the swearing that bothered him (most of it had been in Welsh), nor was it the violence (he had plenty more cocktail sticks), but he had the sense, not for the first time, that he understood Clovenhoof more readily than he did Nerys.

The foyer of the Lichfield Road police station was harshly lit and furnished with hard plastic chairs in an unappealing shade of orange, so Michael had arrived prepared with a cushion and a sleep mask. He settled himself down for the inevitable wait, and concentrated only on the voices that could be heard from down the corridor. He knew that the two female voices belonged to the baby's mother and grandmother, after their loud entrance, moments earlier. The male voice belonged to the pleasantly unflappable PC Pearson.

"Where's my Bea? You can't keep her from me. I'm her mother. Her *mother*!"

"And, believe it or not, I'm the grandmother. I know, right? We get taken for sisters all the time."

"Shut up, mum."

"Ladies, can I please straighten a few facts out so that we can get through the paperwork? Now, Ms Wilson, I gather that you left the baby in the care of Mr Clovenhoof before you left the country for your holiday. Is that correct?"

"No! I sent her round to my mum's with my Spartacus."

"He's your son."

"Yes."

"That would be the Spartacus Wilson who put an actual man on the top of Sutton Coldfield Lions' bonfire last year?"

"That was a case of mistaken identity."

"He had the wrong guy, officer."

"Very good, droll even. So, the baby was left with Mr Clovenhoof, and you, Mrs Wilson ..."

"Call me Stella."

"... Mrs Stella Wilson, you later spoke with Mr Clovenhoof yourself and assured him that you were happy to leave Beatrice with him. Correct?"

"I didn't even know he had my granddaughter."

"And yet your grandson told you by phone, and, indeed, instructed you specifically to go to Buford's to collect her."

"I thought he was trying to sell me a funeral plan!"

107

"Mum! How could you be so stupid?"

"It wasn't my fault! He kept talking about my fish dying!"

"You've got him bang to rights though, yes? He's a kidnapper! He took her from me, and that's against the law!"

"I'm afraid to tell you, Miss Wilson, that the events you've described to me would appear to corroborate his story entirely. If there is a criminal case to be answered, it could very well be one of parental neglect."

Michael covered up his ears at the cacophony of distressed bellowing that followed PC Pearson's remark. It sounded like a flock of seagulls trapped in a phone booth.

A short while later, he could still hear shouting, but footsteps approached.

"Why you wearing that? You look like a twat."

"Hello, Spartacus," said Michael, lifting his sleep mask. "How's your family getting on in there?"

"My gran's faking a migraine and my mum wants her arrested. It's cool."

Michael didn't know what to say to that, so he nodded cautiously.

"Why aren't you Akela at cubs anymore?" Spartacus asked. "Darren gets out of puff just walking up the steps. He'll never be able to control us."

"Darren will do a marvellous job, I'm sure," said Michael, although, privately, he agreed with Spartacus on this point. "I have found that my faith has taken me somewhere different. I'm attending a new church now, so I'm passing on my duties at St Michael's."

"A *new church*? New one, old one, they all talk the same molten cack."

"You might be surprised." Michael pulled out his membership booklet. "Look. There's an RFID tag in the cover, so I get loyalty points added to my account every time I attend and swipe on the touch point."

"What? Like Nectar Points?"

"Take a look at the stamps I've collected for extra services."

Spartacus flicked through the pages.

"One of my mum's boyfriends had all these stamps in his passport. He was a drug mule or something. It was sort of neat, though, like this."

"You think that's neat?" said Michael. "What about this?"

He pulled out his copy of Bible Action Stories, a glossy creation full of cartoon strips in eye-popping colours. An excited member of the Consecr8 congregation had told Michael that it featured an artist who had worked on DC comics. Some of the pictures of women bordered on inappropriate in Michael's eyes – he knew, for one, that the real Esther had never been so... *pneumatic*, and Eve's fig leaves could probably have been a little more substantial.

Spartacus was mesmerised.

"I can keep this, yeah?" he said, as the voices of his family grew nearer.

"Of course. You can get the rest of the set if you get the right badges."

"I've got to go to church to get these badges?"

"Yes."

"To church?"

"Yes."

"To earn badges?"

"That's right."

The boy gave it some thought.

"S'pose I could do that," he shrugged.

"There's a renewal service this afternoon," said Michael. "Make sure that you tell them I recruited you. If you do go, I get points for that."

"Come here, Sparts. It's your sister!"

Spartacus and Michael both looked up to see Spartacus's mother pushing the baby buggy. His grandmother held a damp towel to her head, and leaned theatrically on PC Pearson's arm.

"Look at her little face, she's so excited to see us all. My precious angel! You want to push for me so I can take this call? Yeah, I'm going to cancel the Daily Mail interview. It's not appropriate for someone in my situation, apparently. Terrible pity when I've still got this lovely tan."

Spartacus shrugged, and took the buggy by the handle. Michael peered inside and saw that the baby was fast asleep.

It was another ninety minutes before Clovenhoof emerged into the lobby and announced to the world that he was free to go.

"Suppose you've come to have a good old laugh?" he asked Michael, as he followed him out. He rearranged his jumper as he walked, causing a small cascade of pens, paper clips, and rubbers to fall out from beneath. "You might not have any sympathy for me, but those police brutalised my monkey and took my baby! They'll be sorry though. Want a pen?"

"I would never laugh at you. I've come as part of my Christian duty, to support you as a friend," said Michael, a little too loudly.

"Why are you shouting? And what are you doing with your phone? Are you recording this?" Clovenhoof grabbed Michael's phone and stared at the screen. "What's this? 'Uploading to the Goodness Archive'. What on earth are you doing, you arse?"

"Now, Jeremy, I'm just taking my duties seriously, like all true professionals."

"Michael, you're a sodding archangel! What are you trying to prove?" Clovenhoof wheeled his arms around to indicate the huge absurdity of the situation. "Seriously, who *on earth* could you possibly be trying to impress?"

"It's a harmless bit of gamification," said Michael huffily.

"Gay what?"

"I think it's quite clever, especially if it encourages best practice. Anyway, your monkey is in the car."

"You let him in your car? Oh dear. Has he been in there long?" asked Clovenhoof. He could see him now, as they approached, hanging from the sun visor and jigging anxiously.

"Yes, why?"

"No reason," said Clovenhoof, giving a tentative sniff as he opened the door.

Gorky launched himself forward and grasped a handful of Clovenhoof's hair in a gesture that ensured he was paying attention. He urgently mimed the cradle manoeuvre, peering into Clovenhoof's face to underline the query.

"Aw Gorky, she's gone," said Clovenhoof, kicking the side of Michael's car.

Gorky squeaked.

"I don't know what we're going to do," said Clovenhoof.

Clovenhoof's shoulders tried to slump, but they didn't get very far. His head was snapped up as Gorky yanked at his hair.

"We had to give her back, mate," said Clovenhoof.

"I need to get back to the office. Can I drop you off on the way?" asked Michael, shouting to be heard above the keening sound that Gorky was now making.

Clovenhoof wanted to jump and screech like Gorky, but, somehow, he just didn't have the energy.

"Yeah, I suppose so," he said and climbed into the back of the car with his suddenly unemployed au pair monkey on his lap. "Nothing else on. We were gonna have such a fun time this evening. I got fireworks and sausages so we could go to the park."

"Jeremy, what were you even doing with a baby? Can you just imagine what people would think if they knew who you really were?"

"As with most things, Michael, it was a situation that was thrust upon me. One moment I'm footloose and fancy free, the next I'm father to a baby. I didn't ask for it, but I tried to make the best of it. Surely you can appreciate that? In fact," he growled, "why don't you upload it to your Goodness Archive, and swivel on it?"

"Surely you can do those fun things anyway?" said Michael, pulling away from the kerb. "You're footloose and fancy free again."

"It just won't be the same without Beelzebelle," said Clovenhoof. "Our day was structured around her. She'll be wanting her nappy changed about now, won't she, Gorky? I'm going to miss that smell of bubbling sulphur."

Michael pulled a face.

"Beelzebelle? I take it that wasn't her given name? Well, perhaps it's time for you to find solace in good honest labour again. Or maybe for the first time, I don't know. I can drop you off at Bufords now if you like."

"I work with dead people! What's the point in dead people? They're going nowhere. Beelzebelle was doing something new and different every single day. Only yesterday she said 'gah' to me, clear as a bell. 'Gah!' You heard her, didn't you, Gorky?"

Gorky increased the volume of keening in response, and rattled the door handle in agitation.

"Well, if you don't want to go to work, shall I just take you home?"

"No. No, stop here," said Clovenhoof.

Michael pulled the car over and looked out. The only building of note within sight was the Consecr8 church.

"Here?" he said.

"Here," said Clovenhoof and took Gorky's hand.

"Can you smell something?" said Michael, as Clovenhoof opened the door.

"I think it's your air freshener," said Clovenhoof quickly, with a sideways glance at Gorky, and then slammed the door.

"You're welcome," said Michael.

Michael passed the Consecr8 church and pulled up outside the ARC offices that occupied the scrubby wasteland between the Consecr8 church and the not-yet-finished Rainbow housing estate. It was a messy hinterland that was the subject of heated opinions in the letters page of the local paper, but, to Michael, it was the centre for much fascinating research.

His mood brightened at the prospect of a couple of hours of careful cataloguing. Oh, he knew that it would seem mind-numbingly dull to most people, but nothing was more pleasing than bringing order to chaos, and, in the pristine environment of the lab, he could impose a sense of calm. The lab was like his own private universe and he (he thought with a thrill of mild blasphemy) was like the Almighty creator. The difference between Michael's universe and the Almighty's was that Michael was wise enough to keep all the little lifeforms under tight control. There would be no serpent in this particular Eden. The DNA samples in the tubes and dishes here would not be escaping and smearing their filthy ways across all creation, as humans had done in the wider world. Michael's little universe was perfect and pristine, and he was a kind and just God with a ready supply of disinfectant.

In the laboratory, he removed the latest batch of samples from the deep freeze. They had arrived in little freezer bags, decorated with penguins and snowflakes. Michael frowned at the frivolous packaging in his immaculate, scientific workplace.

"Little A," he said aloud.

"Yes, Michael."

"Make a diary entry for me. I want to suggest to supplier number 255 that he should reconsider his packaging choices. Prepare a catalogue cross-reference of lab suppliers' specimen holders for me to attach."

"Yes, Michael."

Michael put on a fresh lab coat and added disposable sleeves and gloves before he headed into the sterile room of the lab. It was essential that the samples he prepared were untainted. He worked slowly and methodically, according to his exacting protocol. It was soothing to prepare and label test tubes, working on a single sample at a time. He had already prepared a stock of the reagent solution, so he added this to his ground-up samples with a pipette, and then used the vortex machine to mix it all up. He prepared all of his samples, and then popped them into the freezer for analysis the next day.

"And he looked upon His work and saw that it was good," said Michael.

"Sorry, could you repeat that?" said Little A.

"Nothing," said Michael.

Clovenhoof and Gorky arrived at the Wiggly Fingers Baby Signing class ten minutes late, and there was already a raucous din coming from the Consecr8 church hall. For something that was billed as a lesson in unspoken communication, there was a surprising amount of bellowing and braying.

Nobody was making more noise than Sandra, who spotted Clovenhoof as he entered.

"Jeremy, welcome!"

Clovenhoof, who had been dealing with a lot of unwanted and novel emotions in the last few hours, surprised himself as well as Sandra by throwing his arms around her and burying his face in the cradle of her neck.

"Oh," said Sandra. "This is intimate, isn't it? Is everything all right, Jeremy?"

Clovenhoof disengaged, teary-eyed and shaking his head.

"Is everything all right with...?" Sandra looked around. "Where's Baby Belle?"

Clovenhoof threw himself backward into an empty chair and gazed around at the tiny forms sitting in a warzone of plastic toys. He inhaled deeply and took in the unique nasal assault that comprised biscuity dribble, untended nappies, and wet wipes.

"I'm going to miss this," he sobbed.

Gorky gave a sympathetic moan, and started to root through the toy boxes, presumably checking whether Beelzebelle was hidden in any of them. He sagged in a morose monkey heap when he found nothing, and sat down on the carpet. He started to build a pile of bricks for a delighted pair of twin babies to knock over.

"What's happened to Belle?" said Sandra.

"She's been taken into care," said Clovenhoof.

There was a collective sigh-cum-gasp-cum-mutter of outrage from the Not-Sandras.

"Ridiculous!"

"How does this happen?"

"Nanny state gone mad!"

"There's nothing I can do," said Clovenhoof.

"That's appalling," said Sandra with quiet passion. "We've all seen you with Belle. You're such a great dad."

"I am, I am," agreed Clovenhoof earnestly.

"They can't just do that to punish you for having an alternative lifestyle."

"It wouldn't be the first time," said one of the Not-Sandras. "Fathers get a really poor deal."

"We do, we do," nodded Clovenhoof.

A lot of thought and design had gone into the Consecr8 church. The exterior was a cool blend of modern curves and hipster sensibilities, a spaceship built out of polished pine. But it was the interior that grabbed Nerys's senses. The layout and style were oddly familiar, and it only took her a moment to work out why; Consecr8 might have been a church, but it had the heart and spirit of a nightclub. There were no funky lights, disco balls, or bars – of course there weren't – but the décor, stylings, and mood of the place sent out the very clear message that this was the place where cool people came and, simply by coming here, one was instantly made cool. This was still a house of God but, boy, this was the one where God threw house parties.

And just like a nightclub, there were the bouncers: young men in identical charcoal-grey suits and with identically perfect teeth, like Mormon missionaries who had taken up free weights and a career sidestep into personal security. Michael swiped himself in at the door, but Nerys had to register with one of the bouncers/ushers. A young man took her details on a tablet computer and handed her a hymn book and a membership card. She tucked both into her bag, only half-listening to the murmurs behind her. Michael was checking that points had been allocated to his account for recruiting a new member.

Nerys gestured to the outward-sloping walls.

"Why's it shaped like that?" she whispered to Michael as they walked towards the pews.

"I believe it's to show that the church is embracing the Heavens," said Michael. "Bit of a dust trap, if you ask me."

"Tell me, Michael, why does God want us to go to church?"

"Sorry? Are you asking me why the Almighty wants us to believe in him?" asked Michael, his brow furrowed.

"No, no, not that. What I want to know is why it's not enough to believe in him quietly, while we're going about our lives? Why do we have to go to a special place and sing his praises?"

"Faith in the Almighty is not just about a relationship with God. Implicit in our faith is a fellowship with one another. If we are to love as the Almighty loves, then we must reach out to our fellow pilgrims."

"And join together for a big ol' love-in, eh?"

"Exactly. In this space, before God, we're all equal and as one. Every man, woman, and child stands side by – no, we can't sit there."

Michael steered Nerys away from the plush pews at the front.

"That's the celebration zone," he explained. "People can only sit there if they have shown exceptional service."

"Well, who's that woman sitting there? Jesus's mum?"

"That's Tessa Bloom. Very active woman in the local community and an example to us all."

115

Looks like she's got a broom shoved up her arse. There's no room anywhere else for us to sit."

"We can squeeze in here."

Nerys tutted.

"It's a bit elitist, isn't it? Better seats for teacher's pet?"

"Oh, you shouldn't worry," said Michael. "It's not elitist. I'm sure the people in the zone feel very humble and, of course, we're happy for them, aren't we?"

Nerys sidled into a cramped pew.

"I'd be a lot happier if I got me one of them luxury seats," she muttered.

A high-energy dance beat filled the church. Nerys saw a white-jacketed man standing off to the side, pushing sliders and buttons on a synthesiser. He punched the air in time to the beat, and used his other arm to make a beckoning motion to the audience. He turned his attention to each section of the crowd, making eye contact and urging them on to follow his lead.

"God, it *is* like a nightclub," said Nerys.

She was determined that she wasn't going to join in, but, moments later, she realised that she was the only person in the church without her hands in the air. She'd come along looking for some sort of meaning to her life. If she'd wanted to dance badly to synthpop music, she could do that any night of the week. In fact, come chucking-out time at the Boldmere Oak, it was exactly what she *was* doing most nights of the week.

"When do they break out the alcohol?" she said snidely but, after a few minutes, she had to admit that this felt a bit different. This place, this crowd, this scene. It was energising, being part of a gathering all enjoying the same moment. It actually felt... good.

Maybe, she wondered, it had something to do with being sober.

Down in the Consecr8 church hall, the bassy reverberations from the church service barely cut through the final Wiggly Fingers song. Clovenhoof and a dozen mothers frantically signed various animals and a flurry of E-I-E-Os while their offspring joined in, ran around, screamed, and generally did what they damn well pleased.

While the mums gave a self-congratulatory round of applause, Clovenhoof saw Gorky was forming baby signs to twin babies. Clovenhoof regarded them thoughtfully. If this particular Not-Sandra had two babies already, she wouldn't miss one of them, surely? He could take one of them back with him, maybe tuck it up his jumper, like he had the stuff from the police station. He absent-mindedly pulled a pair of handcuffs out of his waistband and jangled them over a nearby buggy, making the occupant giggle and reach out. He wondered if Gorky was also selecting a baby to steal, when Gorky rolled away from the pair and looked at Clovenhoof sorrowfully.

Clovenhoof understood that look clearer than words.

"Nah, it wouldn't be the same, would it?" he said.

These babies weren't quite right. They weren't the right shape. They weren't really *squishy* enough. He gave one of them an experimental prod. The infant squealed with delight, but Clovenhoof sighed. No, it just wouldn't be the same if it wasn't Beelzebelle.

His train of thought was interrupted when Gorky leapt onto the chair next to him and thrust his hand down Sandra's top, grasping fervently her breast.

"What in the blue blazes ...?"

She stopped when she realised that Gorky's other hand was pointing urgently to her baby, Jack or James or Jizbert or whatever it was called. Jack or James or Jizbert was signing the udder-squeezing hand signal that indicated she wanted milk.

"Well I never!" she exclaimed, firmly removing Gorky's tiny hairy hand from her top. "You've got him well-trained, Jeremy. He's really looking out for the little ones."

Clovenhoof gave Gorky the thumbs-up as Sandra undid her bra and unleashed her fleshy milk-boob.

"Nice work, monkey," said Clovenhoof.

"How could they take a child away from such a switched-on dad?" said one of the Not-Sandras.

"You've got visitation arranged though, yeah?" asked another of the Not-Sandras.

"No, nothing," said Clovenhoof. "I just can't see her anymore."

"Seriously? That's outrageous. You should see your MP!"

"Should I?" said Clovenhoof, not entirely sure why his massive penis was a factor in this discussion.

Nonetheless, Clovenhoof was impressed by the depth of feeling for his predicament. He realised that it was based on the entirely false premise that he was Belle's father, but it was touching nevertheless.

"What do you think you're doing?"

A man stood, frozen, in the doorway to the hall.

"It's the Wiggly Fingers Baby Signing class," said one of the Not-Sandras.

"Is there a problem, Mr Malarkey?" said Sandra. "I've have to say that we really like this space. Lots of natural light and the kitchen's much better than the one ..."

"You sit there flaunting your... your bosoms and ask if there's a problem?" said the man.

Clovenhoof abruptly recognised the red face, the wet lips, and the furious brows that seemed to wrap around his bulging eyes. Clovenhoof had seen it all before, staring from the driver's seat of a stretch transit van. It was the very important businessman, Chip Malarkey.

Sandra looked down. "Er, I'm just feeding the baby."

"Why would you do that in a public place? Have you no shame?"

"Shame of what?"

"This lewd and sexual display," said Chip.

"To be fair," said Clovenhoof, "she's only got one of her chesticles out and, if I'm honest, the other one is far more lewd and sexual." He looked at Sandra. "Seriously, it's a classic." He then worried that the other mothers might think he was being biased. "I mean you've all got top notch norks, ladies. Ten out of ten for effort."

Chip Malarkey's head shook and spasmed as though he was trying to get a bad taste out of his mouth.

"This behaviour is unacceptable. Couldn't you at least cover yourself with something, or go sit in a corner? Don't you know how uncomfortable this makes people feel?"

"What people, Mr Malarkey?" asked Sandra, her cheeks now flaring an angry red.

118

"Normal people!" he snapped. "This building is devoted to the worship of God. I took your booking in good faith, assuming it would be wholesome and appropriate, but I can see that my trust was misplaced."

"Mr Malarkey, this group is *very* wholesome, and I think that your views on breastfeeding are a little outdated."

"Does not Paul say that 'women should adorn themselves in respectable apparel with modesty and self-control'?" demanded Chip.

"I've no idea," said Sandra.

"And does not the Bible say, 'And you shall not go up by steps to my altar, that your nakedness be not exposed on it'?" demanded Chip.

"Does it?" said Sandra.

"Yeah," said Clovenhoof, "but it also says cripples, dwarfs, and blind folk can't worship at the altar either. The Good Book's kinda goofy like that."

Chip Malarkey growled. He actually growled, deep in his throat, like a cornered dog.

"My church, my rules!" he shouted. "I will not tolerate this licentious behaviour. If you want to cavort naked like witches, then you will do it elsewhere. I insist that you leave immediately."

As Sandra glanced around at the rest of the group in dismay. Clovenhoof approached the stocky, red-faced man. He knew he could talk him round.

"Listen, Chipster, we're talking about tits, yeah? Bazookas, puppies, melons, whatever. Why would you want to cover them up? They have all these neat little tricks. Have you ever noticed how nipples stick upwards, whatever position they're in? Mind you, I haven't yet found a woman who'll stand on her head so I can test that properly. These ladies here can even make milk come out of them! Bags of fun to be had with boobs, my friend. I bet Sandra would let you ..."

"Stop this utter filth! Let me hear no more of it. This man is proof that the degrading spectacle of naked women leads only to corruption. Get out, now!"

Some of the Not-Sandras were already gathering toys into boxes and strapping babies into buggies, eyes downcast.

Sandra touched Clovenhoof's sleeve. "Come on, Jeremy. I know you mean well, but I think we need to go."

Clovenhoof's eyes moved up to the ceiling where Gorky swung from a light fitting, eyes blazing with malevolence. It would be enormously satisfying to see him launch a surprise attack on the pompous stranger, but Sandra was ushering everyone out of the hall.

"Come on, Gorky," he sighed. "Save it for later."

In church, the white jacketed DJ had done an expert job of warming up the congregation and, as a square-shouldered fellow in a button-down collar approached the perspex lectern that stood in for a church pulpit, the DJ turned down the music to a low, pulsing bass.

"Welcome, everyone!" he said into the microphone. "Welcome!" There was a whoop from the crowd. "You all know me. You know Chip. I'm no preacher. Don't worry – I'll be handing over to the very, very Reverend Mario Felipe Gonzalez in a moment. I'm no preacher. I'm a listener and a follower. When God told me to build this church on this site, I listened and I followed." There were further whoops and hollers. "When God told me to reach out to the good people of Sutton Coldfield, I listened and I followed. I'm no preacher, but that doesn't mean I can't testify."

"Testify!" shouted a voice from the congregation.

"I shall," said the man, Chip. "I must testify to a shocking experience that I have just had. In this *very building!*"

As the man's passion rose, Nerys thought there was something very familiar in his bearing, in the set to his red face.

"Wanton cavorting!" he said fiercely. "Wanton naked cavorting!"

There were gasps in the congregation.

"That's right!" said Chip. "Shameless nudity. It is as was foretold. 'The Lord saw how great the wickedness of the human race had become on the earth and that every inclination of the thoughts of the human heart was only evil all the time.'"

"Wait. I know where I've seen him before," hissed Nerys.

"We must be ever-vigilant," said Chip, "as evil stalks the streets of Sutton and attempts to corrupt this precious house of

God. When the day comes – and you know the day I'm talking about – only those who are blameless will be saved and those who ..."

"Hey!" shouted Nerys, suddenly on her feet. "Aren't you the tosser that ran over my dog?"

Chip fell silent. He blinked rapidly.

"Dog?"

"What a fucking twat!" Nerys yelled. "Yeah! *My* dog? What gives you the right to stand up there all smug and righteous? You animal murdering shithead!"

"Nerys..." Michael started, but Nerys pushed past him and headed for the exit. The last thing that she heard was the odious tit in the pulpit talking about *further signs of pervasive wickedness.*

Ben poured himself a cider. He deserved a cider.

The chain mail vest, painstakingly knitted, was complete. It hung on a wooden stand in the lounge, ready to be fitted, and, every time he looked at it, tears pricked the corners of his eyes. It was so bloody beautiful. Ben definitely deserved a cider.

He shook the last drops from the can and raised the glass to his lips. There was a thunderous hammering at his door. Ben, startled, sloshed cider on his socks and got none of it in his mouth.

He opened the door.

A very unhappy monkey sat on Clovenhoof's shoulder.

"I'm going to get absolutely fucking wankered on homebrew Lambrini," said Clovenhoof earnestly. "And I don't drink alone, so you're coming too."

"You drink alone all the time," said Ben.

"Yeah, well, misery loves company, and I'm bloody miserable."

"What have you got to be miserable about? The police let you go, didn't they?"

Clovenhoof gripped Ben's shoulder hard, spilling more cider.

"They took my baby, Ben. They took *our* baby."

Gorky the monkey squawked ardently in agreement.

"So grab your fizzy apple puke and get over to my flat."

Ben sighed.

"I need to change my socks first."

Clovenhoof looked down.

"That's why I don't wear socks. That way, the piss slides straight off."

Nonetheless, Ben did change his socks, and grabbed half a dozen cans of cider. As he crossed the landing, he found Nerys sitting on the stairs leading up to her second-floor flat. She had stuffed Twinkle on her lap and stroked him with every morose sniffle.

"You all right, Nerys?" said Ben.

"What do you think?" she snapped.

"Do you perhaps want to join Jeremy and me for some drinks?"

"God, yes!" she said, grabbed a can from him, opened it, and downed it.

Ben led the way into flat 2a. Clovenhoof had a fat demijohn in his hand.

"It's Ben," he declared. "And he's brought booze, broads, and a dead dog."

"Don't talk to me," Nerys snarled around another mouthful of cider. "I'm in the foulest of moods."

Ben pulled a face to Clovenhoof, a sort of man-to-man "Women, eh? Who knows?"

Clovenhoof pulled one back, a sort of Satan-to-human "People, eh? You're all stupid arses."

"Well, is no one going to ask what's wrong?" demanded Nerys.

"You said we shouldn't talk to you..." said Ben.

"And I doubt your mood is fouler than mine," said Clovenhoof.

"Oh, really?" said Nerys.

"I've lost my baby," said Clovenhoof, "but then I think you know that."

"Ah. Um. Yes. Yes, of course."

Michael entered the flat, slightly out of breath.

"Nerys. I came as soon as I could," he said.

"Really? Oh, Michael, it was nice of you to worry about how I'm feeling."

"Oh, well, yes, of course I'm worried about that, yes." He coughed lightly. "Actually, I need to get the hymn book back off you. If it doesn't go back to the church, I'll lose even more points."

Nerys stopped and sighed. Nerys made throttled noises under her breath for a few moments, and then pointed a finger directly into Michael's face.

"I just met the dickwad who killed Twinkle. Turns out he's the leader of your precious church."

Michael winced.

"And your response is to worry about your Jesus points or whatever they're called?" she said, and then sighed. "But I'm prepared to overlook the crassness of your behaviour, because I know you think you're doing the right thing."

"That's very charitable of you," said Michael. "Now, about that hymn book..."

"There is one condition to my forgiveness, though," she said. "You have to stay here and get shitfaced with us, because it's *that* kind of an evening. And, no, you're not having the hymn book. I will be having a ceremonial burning of it."

Michael's face fell, and Clovenhoof slapped him on the back.

"That's the spirit. Now, we've all got reason to drown our sorrows!"

"Actually, I feel quite chipper," said Ben. "Sorry."

Clovenhoof gave him a viciously clean punch in the side of the head, sending him to his knees.

"Ow!"

"Now we've *all* got reason to drown our sorrows," said Clovenhoof. "And I've got just the thing for that."

Clovenhoof held the demijohn up to the light and admired its murky heart. He opened it. The airlock gave a sinister burp, and the room was filled with a pungent aroma. It was somewhere between a stagnant pond and the forgotten gorgonzola in the back of the fridge. It pleased Clovenhoof immensely. The sediment in the bottom drifted up like ghostly fingers.

He put it in the centre of the living-room table.

"Looks fantastic, doesn't it?" he said to the others. The others regarded it with well-founded suspicion.

"I'm already on the cider," said Ben, raising his now entirely empty glass from which he'd not yet drunk a drop.

"And, um, I promised to mix up some dry martinis for Michael and me," said Nerys. "He got me the glasses and everything for Christmas, if you remember."

"I will go and get them," said Michael quickly, almost tripping in his haste to get away from Clovenhoof's concoction.

Within ten minutes, Nerys and Michael had reclined side by side on Clovenhoof's sofa.

"Look, we've even got olives on little sticks," said Michael.

Nerys lifted the glass to admire her handiwork.

"If something's worth doing, it's worth doing well."

Clovenhoof shrugged, grabbed a handful of olives from the jar and popped them into the top of the demijohn. Then he went to the kitchen, rootled for a moment through a drawer before returning with a straw. He put it into the top and took a long draw on his homebrew. It didn't taste very much like Lambrini, but then he expected it would have characteristics all of its own, like any artisan brew. It was undoubtedly alcoholic, he could tell that much from the caustic burning sensation. There were interesting botanical flavours competing with the yeasty effervescence. He belched loudly and took another huge slurp through the straw.

"Now that," he said, "is a work of genius."

He heard a clattering from the kitchen and turned to see what Gorky was doing. He had the bottles and milk formula out on the counter. He expertly filled the bottles to the correct level and added the milk powder. He then popped on the lids and started to shake the mixture. He came back into the room, shaking the bottle with an exaggerated swing.

Nerys had Twinkle at her side, and petted his inanimate head absently.

"Jeremy," said Nerys. "Is your monkey mixing cocktails?"

Sure enough, Gorky continued the shaking routine with nifty passes behind his back and flipped the bottle into the air, spinning before he caught it again. They all clapped, and watched as Gorky prepared four bottles of formula. He then shared them out and motioned with the udder-squeezing signal that they should drink up.

"That's hilarious," said Nerys, toasting Gorky with her martini, "but I'm not drinking it."

Gorky glowered and pressed the bottle into her hand. Nerys glanced around at the others, then sighed and put the teat in her mouth. Nerys gagged and spat out the milk.

Gorky whisked Twinkle away from the spray of formula milk, and gave Nerys a chittering earful of monkey scolding. It was only when all the humans had mimed appreciative sucking noises on their formula bottles that Gorky looked away and they were able to hide them.

Gorky slapped at the milky droplets on Twinkle's fur, wrapping his scrawny arm around the dog's neck to apparently hold him still while he tried to brush it off. Ben watched, and Clovenhoof could see a thought formulating in his mind. It was sure to be profound or thought-provoking.

"Makes you wonder..." said Ben.

"How human-like some animals are?" suggested Nerys.

"I'm not drunk enough for your blasphemies yet," said Michael.

"Whether we should open a dog-grooming parlour staffed only by monkeys?" suggested Clovenhoof.

"No," said Ben with the tipsy irritation of someone who might have their train of thought derailed at any moment. "I was wondering... if there was a fight between a Yorkshire terrier and a capuchin monkey, who do you think would win?"

Clovenhoof was intrigued.

"Good question. I mean the capuchin's definitely got the dexterity..."

"But the Yorkie's got a much lower centre of gravity," countered Ben.

"And sharper teeth and stronger jaws," added Michael.

"But the dog's a one-trick pony," said Clovenhoof. "Bite and shake, bite and shake. The monkey... he's a master of a myriad fighting styles. I've even taught him a little of my own Hoofjitsu."

"Hang on," said Ben, opening a fresh can of cider, "is this about *a* monkey versus *a* Yorkshire terrier, or Gorky versus Twinkle?"

"Mmmm," agreed Clovenhoof, waggling his half-empty demijohn at Ben. "Point. Cos Twinkle doesn't know his arse from its elbow. Didn't. Didn't know. That would be a seriously unfair fight."

"It would be a darn unscrupulous promoter who would even let Twinkle in the ring with Gorky," said Ben.

"True. I have seen that dog lose a fight with its own tail," said Michael.

"Hey, don't talk about Twinkle like that!" whined Nerys and, with an emotional sniff, she got up to prepare another round of martinis.

"You taught your monkey martial arts?" said Ben to Clovenhoof.

"Well, he already knew monkey-style kung fu. I've got my own moves." Clovenhoof threw some drunken karate chops in the air. "We workshopped some other stuff. S'clever monkey. Hear that?"

Ben and Michael listened.

"That splashing sound," said Clovenhoof. "He's bathing the baby. A more devoted nanny, you could never find."

"What baby?" said Michael.

Clovenhoof frowned in difficult concentration.

"No, wait. We haven't got a baby any more. Oh, I'd forgotten to be miserable for a few minutes. Oh, Beelzebelle. I do miss her."

He slumped back in his chair and stared forlornly at the carpet.

A howl went up and all heads turned to the doorway. Nerys walked in, carrying a sodden, deformed Twinkle.

"Your stupid monkey was bathing Twinkle! Look at him, he's ruined!"

Gorky swung in behind Nerys and dropped a towel on her head.

"Oh dear, Nerys. I'm sure it can't be as bad as it looks," said Michael, picking up the towel and dabbing the wretched animal, while Nerys batted ineffectually at Gorky. "We'll just get him dried off a bit, oh ..." Michael looked at the tail that he'd just pulled off and promptly hid it down the edge of the seat cushion. "Can I get you another drink, Nerys?"

Twinkle stood drying on Clovenhoof's lounge table. Clovenhoof had popped an olive in his slightly open jaw. Nerys had lined up the cocktail sticks from her successive martinis on the table edge as a little wooden tally. Unfortunately, she couldn't quite focus enough to count them.

"Do you think...?" she said and hiccupped.

"Rarely," said Clovenhoof, swishing his straw in the sludgy depths of his homebrew Lambrini.

She wafted her hand at him to shut him up.

"Do you think Twinkle's in Heaven and looking down on us?" she said.

"Yes," said Ben.

"I'm afraid you know that's quite impossible," said Michael.

"I don't care what *you* think, Michael," said Nerys.

"Animals don't go to Heaven," he insisted.

"That's what Heaven's there for!" said Nerys, turning sharply. "If you lead a good life, you can go there and live in God's house for evermore! You told me that!"

"Humans, yes, but not animals," said Michael. "No soul. No special relationship with God."

"How about a squirrel and a guinea pig?" said Ben.

"No, none of them go to Heaven."

"No," drawled Ben drunkenly. "Who'd win in a fight?"

"Can one of them have a knife?" asked Clovenhoof. "I'd back the one with a knife."

"That's ridiculous, Jeremy," said Michael. "You might as well arm them with helicopters and ballistic missiles."

"I would," said Clovenhoof emphatically. "I would arm the squirrels *and* the guinea pigs and reap the profits while they destroy each other in their petty rodent war."

"No, you're both wrong," said Ben, "because hardly any animals could operate things like that. Now, if we were talking about using tools and weapons, it's well known that crows and monkeys have been seen using tools in the wild."

"So, what weapons of war could a crow use then?" asked Michael. "They can use a stone to smash a snail's shell, but you couldn't give it a sword."

"Have you tried?" said Clovenhoof.

"Maybe you could adapt a crossbow so that a crow could pull the trigger," said Ben.

"But a crow could never load a crossbow."

"Maybe that woozle could help it," said Nerys, and then frowned. "Wazzle. Woozler. One of them things," she said, pointing.

Gorky had come into the room, carrying an armful of stuffed creatures.

"Hey, he's been in my flat!" said Ben. "That weasel's only just finished."

"Gorky's only trying to help," said Clovenhoof.

The monkey tossed a misshapen and patchy-furred thing into Nerys's lap.

"See, he thinks maybe a new friend will make you feel better, Nerys. He doesn't know how special Twinkle was to you."

Nerys peered blearily at the possibly-badger-possibly-wombat thing in her lap.

"Twinkle," she sniffed. "He was the best."

"He was," agreed Ben.

"And he could have defeated all of you!" she declared, throwing an accusing finger out at all the stuffed creatures.

"A true hero," burped Ben. "A knight among dogs."

"The King Arthur of the dog world," said Clovenhoof.

"Are we all talking about the same animal here?" said Michael, confused.

"... Tiny, tiny King Arthur," said Clovenhoof in a squeaky, drunken voice.

"We will not see his like again," said Nerys.

"No, we won't," said Clovenhoof. "But we can give him in death what he never had in life. You know what he needs?"

"A wash and a blow dry," suggested Michael.

"No. I have just the thing," said Clovenhoof.

He went off into the kitchen and came back with a pack of fireworks, a child's tricycle, and a ball of string.

"I got the tricycle from the charity shop," said Clovenhoof. "Beelzebelle would have loved it, but I'm thinking that Twinkle can make use of it."

"I'm not sure this is right, Jeremy," said Nerys.

"Trust me, I know something about creating a kickass image. We're going to remodel Twinkle into the sort of warrior that could take on a crow and weasel crossbow team."

He sat the sagging dog on top of the tricycle and tied him in place with string.

"I was going to use the string to keep Beelzebelle in place. She's a bit too small to ride it herself," he said. Then he pulled a rocket out from the fireworks and strapped it to the right paw of warrior-Twinkle. He pushed him back and forth when he was done. Then he arranged the other stuffed animals to face him, so that warrior-Twinkle was prepared to fight several rabbits, squirrels, and weasels with chain mail and swords.

"Look at that! He's ready to do battle against all of your guinea pigs with flickknives or your crows with tanks," warbled Clovenhoof triumphantly.

Ben stood up and looked at it.

"Y'know, that's not half bad. I think he might be onto something, Nerys. It captures Twinkle's playfulness."

"I don't really know about that," said Nerys. "It doesn't seem very respectful to me. I'm such a bad mother, Twinkle. I'm so sorry. I couldn't keep you alive, and now I'm not even sure I can, uh, keep you properly dead either."

"We're all getting a bit morose," said Ben. "I say we break out the snacks. What you got in, Jeremy?"

"Pop the oven on, we'll break out the Crispy Pancakes," said Clovenhoof.

Ben disappeared, but then came back moments later holding up several small plastic bags embellished with penguins and snowflakes. He jiggled the dusty contents.

"Jeremy, are these drugs?" he asked, with a frown of disapproval.

"I've seen those bags before," said Michael slowly. "Jeremy, what have you ..."

"No!" screamed Nerys.

There was a moment when they all turned to see Gorky strike the lighter in his hand and hold the flame to the fuse of the rocket strapped to Twinkle. There was another, much longer, moment, when the fuse burned down and several inebriated people scrambled to get to it, but succeeded only in falling over each other. The longest moment was the one when the rocket went off, propelling Twinkle forward, in a shower of sparks, through the ranks of the other stuffed animals and under the table, where the rocket exploded. Michael grabbed the demijohn of Clovenhoof's homebrew and upended it onto the flames and, when that was emptied, grabbed the bottle of vermouth and used that as well, eventually extinguishing the flames.

Clovenhoof stood, wavering slightly from the powerful effects of his homebrew. Nerys was screaming, Ben was muttering about drugs, and Michael was accusing him of faking animal samples. Only Gorky made sense at this particular moment. The capuchin monkey shared his pain and sorrow with the world. Gorky held the flame of the lighter above his head and swayed sadly from side to side in a solemn vigil of grief. Clovenhoof saluted him and then passed out on the carpet.

Chapter 5 – In which Clovenhoof goes blind and goes babysitting, and Nerys bares all

When Clovenhoof woke, it was still dark. Not grey-light-of-dawn-edging-through-the-windows-from-half-a-world-away dark. Not even dark-but-for-the-light-pollution-of-a-million-Birmingham-streetlamps dark. It was as black as the deepest pits of Hell.

Clovenhoof turned to look at his radio alarm clock. Its glowing numerals were not glowing, were not visible at all.

"Powercut?"

Clovenhoof staggered out of bed. His hangover rolled around inside his empty skull like a bowling ball. The homebrew Lambrini had left him with a mouth that tasted like a highland hedgerow.

Clovenhoof felt for the curtains and flung them open. Black. No streetlights, no houselights, nothing.

"Big powercut," he said, and then shouted for his monkey helper.

Clovenhoof heard the door, and the sound of Gorky leaping onto the bed.

"Fetch me my mobile phone," said Clovenhoof.

Gorky gave him an earful of monkey chatter.

"Yeah, well she's gone now," said Clovenhoof grumpily, "so you're no longer a nanny. You're my monkey butler until such time you find a new job."

Gorky made a rude noise and disappeared into the darkness. When he returned, he did not pass Clovenhoof his brick of a phone, but threw it quite expertly at his forehead.

"Ow!" Clovenhoof caught it, fumbled it, caught it again, and stabbed at the buttons. The screen did not light up. "Hmmm?"

Clovenhoof felt his way to the door to the living room.

"Powercut. No lights inside or out," he mused. "No lights at all. Even battery-powered items don't work. There can only be one explanation, Gorky."

Gorky made an inquisitive sound.

"Electro-magnetic pulse from a nuclear explosion," said Clovenhoof. "Cancel all my appointments for the day, my furry manservant," he said cheerfully. "Nuclear Armageddon is upon us! The end of the world is truly nigh."

The carpet squelched wetly under his hooves. Through the haze of alcohol-fogged memory, Clovenhoof vaguely recalled something involving stuffed animals, a small explosion, a subsequent fire, and Michael wasting the remainder of his homebrew on putting it out.

"Get something to mop this mess up, Gorky, and get me some clothes. I don't want to face Judgement Day naked." He thought on this. "Well, maybe later. But, for now, clothes."

Nerys surfaced from unpleasant dreams in which a hairy demon squatted on her chest, watching her sleep. She rolled over and groaned at the too bright daylight. She had consumed nothing but alcohol in the last twelve hours, and her dog was still dead. Her stomach hurt, her head hurt, and her soul hurt.

There was a bang, as of a door closing elsewhere in her flat.

"Huh?"

Within her open wardrobe, a coathanger swung back and forth in the breeze.

She sat upright. There was no breeze.

Against the protests of her aching and dehydrated body, Nerys climbed out of bed. She was still dressed in yesterday's clothes, still wearing yesterday's make up. She avoided the gaze of any mirrors as she shuffled into the lounge; she didn't want to see the bride of Frankenstein staring back at her.

Everything in the lounge was as it should have been. The front door was closed. There was no sign of anything having fallen over. Maybe the bang had been a figment of her imagination, the final dregs of a dream.

She went into the kitchen. Again, all was as it ought to have been. Nothing notably out of place. She shrugged. Well, she was up now.

"Coffee," she said.

She reached out for the kettle. It was hot to the touch.

She recoiled in surprise as though it had burned her which, she realised shortly afterwards, was exactly what it had done.

Ben heard the sound of something large bumping into his flat door, followed by earnest and earthy swearing and then someone kicking the door in retaliation in what sounded like steel-capped boots. He opened the door. Clovenhoof clutched his head in pain.

"That hurt," hissed Clovenhoof.

"Alcohol will do that to you," said Ben, looking Clovenhoof's *interesting* attire up and down.

"I accidentally headbutted the door and jarred myself on my horns." Clovenhoof gritted his teeth and rubbed his scalp. "And, of course, by horns I meant nothing whatsoever." He stared with an unfocused gaze at a point just above Ben's ear. "I bet you're wondering what's going on, but I worked it out. It's the end of the world. Nuclear explosions have fried every electrical circuit in the country."

Ben nodded in interest.

"And is that why you're wearing pink leggings and a crop top that says 'Porn star in Training'?"

Clovenhoof ran his hands over his outfit. Ben noted that Clovenhoof's man-boobs filled the crop top quite snugly, although the sight of his hairy belly poking out from under it was frankly disturbing.

"They do feel rather tight. There's a surprising restriction in certain areas" – Clovenhoof pinged the elasticated material over his crotch – "not entirely unpleasant but – hang on! How can you tell what I'm wearing?"

"Because I can see it," said Ben. "And I can see that Nerys is going to be furious when she realises you've stolen her clothes."

"I just told Gorky to get me – no, no, no. See me? How can you...? Did the fallout radiation give you night-vision or some sort of ESP superpower? I wonder if I'll get a superpower. I mean, apart from the one I have already, the general super-cool aura of awesomeness. And my massive schlong of course, which is a superpower all by itself. It's so super, I gave it a name."

Ben was waving his hand in front of Clovenhoof's face and feeling a rare moment of genuine and deep-rooted concern for his neighbour.

"Jeremy?" he said.

"No, I'm Jeremy. That'd just be confusing. And I'm not calling him Little Jeremy because, let me tell you, this trouser snake is anything but ..."

"Jeremy! Just shut up for a second!" snapped Ben.

He threw a few V-signs in Clovenhoof's face to confirm his fears.

"I think you've gone blind, mate," he said, his shocked voice reduced to little more than a whisper.

"What?" said Clovenhoof and then tilted his head in thought. "Yes. That would also explain it." He waved a hand in front of his own face. His eyes darted blindly to and fro. "And you're perfectly fine?" he asked.

"Apart from a fuzzy head and pee that smells of apples, yes. But I was only drinking cider, not some crazy homebrew concoction. Let's get you back to your flat, eh?"

Clovenhoof let him guide him back across to 2a.

"I mean, I've heard of people getting blind drunk, but I didn't think it was an actual thing," said Clovenhoof. "You know, like shitfaced. No one ever actually shits out of their face, do they?"

Ben steered him towards the sofa. On the floor under the window was a blast mark on the carpet, surrounded by scattered and charred taxidermy specimens. The area was sodden with the drinks that had been used to put the fire out. Gorky was busily mopping the worst up, using a pair of jeans and a women's blouse.

"Look what you did!" exclaimed Ben sadly, picking up a singed and now legless squirrel and cradling its ravaged form in his arms.

"I hope you're not looking at me," said Clovenhoof. "I only tied the firework to the dog. I can't be held responsible for the actual fire."

"It was *your* monkey that did it."

Gorky made a short, sharp noise at Ben and continued to clean up with what appeared to be items of Nerys's clothing.

Ben sighed.

"We're going to need to get you to a doctor," he said to Clovenhoof, as he salvaged various damaged creatures from the mess on the floor.

"Don't like doctors," said Clovenhoof. "Arrogant and self-important. Always telling me I'm doing stuff I shouldn't. They're worse than God."

"You've gone blind," Ben pointed out.

"It will wear off."

"Yeah? Who knows what diabolical ingredients you put in that drink?"

"All natural ingredients, I'll have you know," said Clovenhoof. "All harvested from local parks and green spaces."

Ben found the remains of Twinkle. The little dog was far from whole. The firework explosion had ripped it apart and into several distinct pieces. Ben groaned, partly because the mounting of Twinkle had perhaps been his best work, but mostly because this destruction would break Nerys's heart.

"Come on then," he said wearily. "If you won't go see a doctor, then let's at least find out what you've poisoned yourself with. Some perfectly innocent-looking plants are quite poisonous."

"Then they should have warning labels on!" Clovenhoof retorted.

"Since when has that stopped you? And let's get these clothes of Nerys's back upstairs before she notices you've taken them."

"Blame the monkey."

"Sure and..." Ben cast about. "I'll see if I can find the rest of Twinkle."

Nerys rinsed her burned hand in the bathroom sink until the stinging eased. It was when she set to removing her make-up that her mobile on top of the toilet cistern rang. She saw the caller ID and, with a sinking heart, answered.

"Tina!" she said with a false and unconvincing brightness. "No. I'm not in the office yet. It's only – what – seven thirty. What do you want?"

As her boss spoke, Nerys heard the sound of a door closing elsewhere in the flat. When she had heard it earlier, she had been on the cusp of waking and put it down to imagination but, this time, she heard it clearly. It was not her imagination.

Nerys crept out of the bathroom to investigate.

"Sorry, Tina," she said. "Got distracted a moment there. Were you phoning to ask what I'm going to wear to the office today?"

The bedroom was as Nerys had left it. No one there.

"You didn't like what I wore yesterday?" she said. "Because I... because I clashed with your ensemble?"

Nerys tiptoed to the living room.

"You know this is work we're talking about?" said Nerys. "It's not like we're bridesmaids at a wedding. We don't need to colour co-ordinate our clothing every day."

Nerys reached for the door handle.

"I don't think I own any fuchsia coloured clothes. I have a lilac trouser-suit. No, I'm not saying fuchsia and lilac are the same thing."

Nerys stepped into the living room.

"I do think sending the right image to our clients is important. I'm just saying..."

The words died in her throat. On the floor by the front door was a pile of clothing; jeans, leggings, and a couple of tops, inexpertly folded, but folded nonetheless. They had *not* been there before.

"I've got to go," said Nerys, and she hung up immediately.

Doors slamming. Swinging coat hangers. Kettles turning themselves on. Clothes mysteriously appearing on the floor.

"What the Hell is going on?"

Did she now have a poltergeist too? Wasn't it bad enough having Satan as a neighbour?

Nerys picked up the clothes and, to her disgust, realised that several of them were wet. She flung them over the dining chairs and rushed to the bathroom to wash her hands.

It was only when she was drying her hands and returning to the bedroom that she saw the small ball-like lump under the bed sheets.

"If you're a ghost," she told the lump, "I'm going to smash your sodding face in."

She flung back the sheets.

136

Twinkle's stuffed head, decidedly unattached to its body, gazed up at her. There was a playful sheen to his eyes. Nerys howled in horror.

Michael entered the ARC labs, gave Freddy on reception a wave of greeting, and went through to the laboratory area. There were two things that inescapably caught his attention the moment he entered the sterile laboratory.

The first thing was the destruction. The freezer unit in which he had stored the previous day's samples was on its side, the glass front smashed, and various test tubes, some broken, some whole, were scattered across the floor in a pool of liquid. On a side counter, jars of solution had been knocked from their brackets and had spilled their contents across the counter, over Michael's file wallet and the laboratory computer.

The second thing was a dog. A small dog. A Yorkshire Terrier to be precise. It sat in the centre of the room, just to the edge of the pool of liquid spill from the freezer. Michael found the human trait of applying human traits to non-human things quite baffling and somewhat sacrilegious. Nonetheless, he could not help but feel that the dog looked very pleased with itself.

It stuck out a tiny pink tongue to lick its tiny black nose and then yipped at Michael.

"Oh, God," he whispered, appalled. He took several quick breaths to calm himself and tried not to think about the damage done, tried not to think about the work that had been destroyed, tried not to think about the contamination and the clean-up that would be required.

Michael couldn't bear to think of such things, so instead focused on the one thing that might yield quicker results and a small level of bitter satisfaction: the allocation of blame.

The only entrance to this room was through the airlock to the preparation lab and the only entrance to that room was the airlock to the outer laboratory room. There were no windows in any of the rooms. The air circulation vents were set into the ceiling and were only two inches across.

Michael narrowed the Yorkie's options for getting into room to three possibilities: one, the dog had rubber bones and had inserted itself into the room by squeezing down a two inch ventilation pipe; two, the dog had the punch-codes for the airlock doors (and a step-ladder with which to reach the keypad); three, someone had let it in.

Michael tapped his earpiece with a shaking finger.

"Freddy."

"Mr Michaels," said the receptionist.

"Who was the last person to leave last night?" Michael heard the tap of a keyboard.

"Me, Mr Michaels. Twenty minutes after you."

"No one else came in?"

"Not until I arrived this morning."

"The security guard people...?"

"Only patrol the outer fence."

Michael swallowed the knot of emotions in his throat. "Um. Freddy?"

"Yes, Mr Michaels."

"Do you know anything about a dog?"

"A dog?"

"A little Yorkshire Terrier."

"You mean the one your friend brought in?"

Michael considered this. The creature was indeed the same breed as Twinkle. Miniscule, vaguely ratty, and looking like Jennifer Aniston on a bad hair day. However, this particular dog was hairier, perhaps a shade darker and – and this was critically important – not dead and mounted by an inexpert taxidermist.

"No," said Michael simply. "Not that one. Freddy, I need you to get onto the sample suppliers. We are going to need replacements for ..." Michael tried to look at the devastation with a dispassionate eye. "... units CY243 through to CZ004."

"Okay, Mr Michaels." Michael pulled the earpiece from his ear.

"Little A," he said.

"Yes, Michael," said the computer.

"Could you bring up the footage from the lab security cameras for last night?"

"Yes, Michael. Would you like milk with that?"

"I'm sorry?"

138

"That's all right," said Little A. "We're all human."

Michael frowned. "Little A?"

"Wassup, Michael?"

"I asked you to show me the security footage from the lab cameras."

"Uh-huh. And then what happened?"

"Could you show me the footage?"

"I could. I can do lots of things."

"Little A."

"I can bench press three hundred pounds and cook the world's best omelette."

"Little A."

"You love my omelettes."

"Run diagnostic checks on your own software. Check for viruses, spyware, and any indications that we've been hacked."

"Right-o, sexy. One diagnostic check coming up. Hey, can anyone else smell smo..."

There was a snap of electricity, sparks flew from the laboratory computer and the liquids spilt across it steamed lightly. A second later, the lights went out.

Michael put his head in his hands and wept.

"Okay," said Ben, very slowly and very loudly. "We are now in the park."

"I'm blind, not deaf," said Clovenhoof.

"I was trying to sound reassuring."

Clovenhoof disentangled his arm from Ben's grip. "You're treating me like an old codger. I don't need looking after."

"You're older than me, Jeremy ..."

"You have no idea."

"... and one day you will need to learn to accept help from others. Old age and infirmity gets us all in the end."

"Want to bet?"

"Well, no offence, but you've left it too late to live fast, die young, and leave a beautiful corpse."

"The last thing I'd want to do is leave a beautiful corpse. I can think of a thousand things I'd rather do with it."

"You're disgusting."

139

"I refuse to be measured by your standards." Clovenhoof adjusted his sunglasses snootily and sniffed deeply. "Pond weed, pine sap, the faint aroma of week-old cider and tramp piss. We must be down by Keeper's Pool."

Ben was impressed and had to admit he was right.

"I have the nose of a stoat," said Clovenhoof.

"Do stoats have a good sense of smell?"

"And the eyes of a stoat."

"I don't think you've got eyes at all at the moment."

"And the ears of a stoat."

"Yes?"

"Basically, I've got a stoat," said Clovenhoof, taking the small stuffed animal out of his pocket.

"Be serious for just one minute!"

"I've been waiting all week to do that joke," said Clovenhoof.

"You might be permanently blinded and any chance of restoring your sight might be dependent upon us finding whatever it was you put in that drink."

Clovenhoof shrugged, unfazed, and pointed towards the nearby trees.

"I did most of my foraging in there."

They had only take a few strides towards the woods when something caught Ben's eye. "There's a woman waving at you."

"Waving at me?" said Clovenhoof. "Like I'm-mad-at-you-for-stealing-the-engine-out-of-my-mobility-scooter waving or come-hither-big-boy-I-need-you waving?"

"Neither," said Ben. "Just waving. Looks like she knows you."

"Not mad with me *and* doesn't fancy me? That really narrows it down," said Clovenhoof.

The woman, whose clothing was a mish-mash of the garish, the ethnic, and the cheap, and whose smile was bordering on trippy, hurried towards them, a young toddler perched on her waist and a child's buggy before her in which a misshapen teddy bear was mostly buried underneath collected pine cones, twigs and leaves.

"Jeremy," she said. "I thought it was you."

"Oh, Sandra," said Clovenhoof in realisation, "who indeed neither hates nor fancies me. How are you?"

140

"Very well. We've come down to the park to hug the trees and feed the birds. Jack-Jack loves the birds."

"Well, he's a man of the world, isn't he?"

Clovenhoof bent down and tickled the teddy bear on the tummy.

"Er, Jeremy," said Ben and nudged him in the ribs.

"You are funny," said Sandra.

"Oh, he's that," said Ben.

"Jeremy kept us ladies at SCUM smiling," she said to Ben.

"Scum?"

"Sutton Coldfield Union of Mums. You're a friend of Jeremy's?"

"More like a carer sometimes," said Ben.

"I hope you were shocked as we were when they took his little girl from him," said Sandra fervently.

"Oh, I had barely got over the shock of him having a baby girl in the first place," said Ben honestly.

"It's a sad business for certain, doubly so when it happens to a loving and responsible father."

"Responsible," said Ben thoughtfully.

"Responsible," agreed the blind Clovenhoof.

"Listen, Jeremy," said Sandra. "You can say no, perhaps recent events are still a bit too raw, but I wonder if you'd be willing to babysit Jack-Jack tonight? I'm meeting with some of the other mums to discuss our response to Mr Malarkey's barbarian behaviour yesterday. Paul's away at a conference in Newquay, and I've got no one else to ask."

"Unfortunately, Jeremy's been a bit ill recently," said Ben.

"Be delighted to," said Clovenhoof. "I do love children."

He crouched down and addressed the bear.

"You and me will have a kick-ass evening, eh, Jimbo?"

"Funny, funny man," said Sandra, genuinely amused. "I'll text you later with the details."

"Brilliant." Clovenhoof took a Mars Bar out of his pocket and waggled it by his ear. "I'll wait for your call. Now, you'll have to excuse us. Ben and I have some urgent business in the bushes."

Sandra gave Ben a mildly saucy, mildly embarrassed look.

"I will leave you two boys to it," she said, and steered the buggy away.

"You're a tit," said Ben.

"What?"

"Not only did you make her think we're a pair of old-timey gays out for a day's cottaging, but you agreed to babysit for her when – and I cannot re-emphasise this enough – when you are clearly blind."

"I think we can all see that I can compensate for the loss of one sense with my superb mastery of all the others," said Clovenhoof. He turned decisively and marched into Keeper's Pool.

"Mr Michaels."

Michael stopped his mopping and tapped his earpiece.

"Yes, Freddy."

"I've got the cat carrier you asked for."

Michael looked at the Yorkshire Terrier who was currently sniffing around the base of a stool.

"Good."

"And I also picked up a couple of cartons of BowWow."

"Bow-what?"

"It's dog food, Mr Michaels. The finest meats for that special dog in your life. I'm reading that off the label, but my friend, Chad, swears it's true."

"Fine," said Michael.

"And there's been a phone call for you," said Freddy. "The boss wants to see you this evening."

"Mrs Feckler?"

"No, *the* boss. The managing director."

Michael had no idea who that even was. He had been hired through an agency and had only met with the overall project manager, Josie Feckler.

"I think he wants to talk about the doggy incident," said Freddy.

"Well, who told him?" said Michael.

"Not me. I only mentioned it to Saqib when I asked for the replacement samples."

Michael sighed wearily. He shook the towels in his hand at the dog.

"If I get fired for this, I'm going to put you in a sack and throw you in the Birmingham and Fazeley Canal."

"But I have so much to live for," said Freddy.

"Ah-ha!" declared Ben loudly.

Clovenhoof leapt to his feet.

"What is it?"

"I think I have your culprit. Oh my."

Clovenhoof walked over to the dining table, tripping over a ruck in the rug but turning it into a pirouette to make it look like he had intended to do it all along. Gorky smoothed out the ruffled carpet behind him.

"Hit me with it, Kitchen. Which plant poisoned me?"

Ben's hands ran over the plant samples that he had laid out neatly and methodically on the table.

"Frankly, there's plenty of things here that aren't great for you. You were pretty much drinking fermented grass. However, this one is of particular interest..."

Clovenhoof shrugged.

"I assume you're pointing at something," he said. "But, you know, still blind."

Ben picked up a sprig of tightly clustered variegated leaves and consulted his smartphone.

"*Euphorbia helioscopia.*"

"A foreigner, eh?" said Clovenhoof. "One of them Latin types."

"Sun spurge," said Ben. "Its sap can cause skin irritation, inflammation and the seed oils are a powerful purgative. This website says that one, er, individual ate some and indeed went blind."

"But he recovered?"

Ben read and then nodded.

"After a course of anti-inflammatory drugs from the vet, sight was eventually restored."

"Vet?"

"Um," said Ben. "I'm reading this off a horse care website."

"Stupid horse," said Clovenhoof. "What was it doing eating poisonous plants?"

"Because that's so much worse than making an alcoholic drink from it," said Ben sarcastically.

Clovenhoof dusted his hands together.

"Well, that's one mystery solved. Now, babysitting."

"What? I've just told you you've ingested something that would blind a shire horse and you think you're still okay to look after other people's children!"

"What's the issue? It's not like little Jazbo is going to run out on me. Even blinded, I'm faster than a two-year-old."

"And how are you going to get there? And, before you ask, I'm not taking you."

"Gorky will take me."

Gorky, who was tidying up around the sofa and eating the occasional food crumb he discovered, made a questioning noise.

"You've got to walk to Penns Lane," said Ben. "And – I don't believe I'm having to point this out – monkeys can't read house numbers."

Clovenhoof huffed.

"Don't you go telling me what my monkey can and can't do. If we set off now, we'll be there in less than twenty minutes."

An hour and a half later, Clovenhoof knocked on another door. He smoothed his hands over the door.

"Well, at least this one isn't a shed or portaloo," he said, giving a stern glare at where he assumed Gorky to be. "Or an old door propped up next to a skip. You had me waiting at least ten minutes for someone to answer that."

The door opened.

"Jeremy. I thought we said six o'clock."

"Running a little late, Sandra. That's all."

Jeremy couldn't see that rare expression on Sandra's face, the expression of an incurably nice person who knows they should be really angry but just doesn't know how.

"You could have phoned," she said.

Jeremy held up the Mars Bar.

"It seems to be out of charge."

144

"Well, you're here," she said, "and I am incredibly late. Good news is Jack-Jack is already in bed and fast asleep. Help yourself to anything you like in the house. I'll be back by eight, nine at the latest."

Sandra squeezed past him.

"Call me if there's any problem!"

Clovenhoof waved her off. He actually waved at a hedge, but the hedge didn't bother to correct him.

"Right, Gorky," he said, feeling his way into the house. "You heard the lady. We can help ourselves to anything in the house. Loose change, jewellery, portable valuables. Let's get to it."

Michael attempted calming breathing exercises all the way from his flat to the address in Wylde Green, Sutton Coldfield's suburban neighbour. He wasn't sure they were working. Over a dinner that Michael was too stressed to eat, Andy had given him a little pep talk. Andy worked as a personal trainer and his pep talks were invariably of a "you can do it if you try hard enough and you work that butt" nature. Michael would have preferred something more philosophical and consoling, but he appreciated the gesture nonetheless.

The address he'd been given was for one of the grandly proportioned houses on Penns Lane. Clearly, the ARC Research Company paid its top people well. Michael couldn't imagine that he'd be joining their ranks any time soon.

Unable to put off the inevitable, he walked up the brick-paved driveway and rang the doorbell. As he waited for it to be answered, he mentally lined up his excuses. Sadly, most of them involved pinning the whole dog incident on Freddy, and this without any evidence whatsoever.

The door opened. Michael stared.

"Mr Malarkey?"

"Michael," said the church leader, taking his hand and pumping it furiously. "And it's Chip. Everyone knows Chip."

Chip Malarkey was dressed in his suit trousers and shirt, but his sleeves were rolled up, the top three buttons on his shirt were undone, and his hands (and now Michael's too, he realised) were covered in dark engine grease. Chip laughed at Michael.

145

"The look on your face," he grinned. "Chip Malarkey? Construction magnate, church founder, and tech-industry boss? Do I amaze you, Michael?"

Michael mouthed silently for a moment.

"You do, Chip. You do," he said honestly.

"Fingers in pies. That's me. Fingers in pies," said Chip. "Well, come in. I'll make a cuppa. I'm afraid we're drinking out of paper cups until I get a new dishwasher."

"Oh, dear," said Michael, stepping into the house and a hallway covered in dirty footprints. "What happened to your old one?"

"Left me, didn't she?" said Chip.

"Oh. I see. I'm sorry."

For a moment, Chip sagged, as though the weight of the entire world rested on him.

"It's a fallen world, Michael, my friend." And then again, almost inaudibly. "A fallen world."

Clovenhoof sat in a deep armchair in what he took to be the living room, Jack-Jack's baby monitor on a table beside him. There was, he discovered after a thorough tactile exploration of the room, no television for him to watch (or at least listen to) and, despite sending the monkey back three times to check, no valuables for them to steal.

"That's what I hate about the bloody middle classes," said Clovenhoof. "They're all doctors and solicitors and high-paid academics, but they insist on living like the Amish. Give me a working class home any day, with a TV in every room, and more expensive gadgets and doodads than you could fit in your swag bag."

Gorky screeched.

"No, he's asleep," said Clovenhoof. "It would be nice, I know, but if having Beelzebelle taught me anything it would be that, well, if it taught me *anything* it would be that the faces babies pull while pooping are just hilarious. But if it's taught me two things, the other would be that if a baby's asleep, you let it sleep."

Gorky made a disappointed noise.

"We'll just have to entertain ourselves. We could play a game of Which Orifice Did That Come From? Or maybe Book-Slam Finger Roulette?"

Gorky spat at him.

"You could groom me for nits."

Gorky humphed in his squeaky capuchin way.

"Or I could groom you."

With no real enthusiasm, Gorky climbed up onto Clovenhoof's knee and presented him with his back.

Michael followed Chip past a dining room, where the components of a stripped down car engine were laid out across the now ripped and oil-smudged tablecloth, and into a kitchen cluttered with piles of dirty crockery. Chip pulled out a kettle from among the pots and pans, and filled it at the sink.

"Let me ask you a question," said Chip.

"Ask away," said Michael.

"What is a man?"

"A man?"

Chip put the kettle on.

"You and me. Men. What are we?"

Michael wasn't willing to chance a guess.

"I don't know."

"We're builders, Michael." He held out his stubby but powerful-looking hands. "We make things. We dream. We construct. We add things to this world."

Michael didn't really consider himself a builder, except in the abstract sense. He devised systems and constructed computer programs, but actual manual work...? The one time he had tried to assemble a flat-pack coffee table, it had resulted in a nasty little Allen key injury and a late night trip to Accident and Emergency.

"Women don't build," said Chip.

"They don't?"

"No, mate. They have wombs. They grow things. Children mainly."

"I suppose," said Michael politely.

"I built this house."

Michael made a show of looking round at it.

147

"It's a beautiful house."

"Thank you. There are great men in the world. Builders like you and me. We build. We bring order. And we follow the rules. If I build a house without deep enough foundations, it will fall. So I don't. I follow the rules. If a man builds a car, he doesn't build it so you have to remove the head to get to the reservoir o-rings."

"He'd be a fool," agreed Michael, who had no idea what Chip was on about.

"He follows the rules," said Chip. "And if someone's made something complex and important, he will also provide a manual."

"Absolutely," said Michael, back on more confident ground again.

The kettle clicked off. Chip picked up a copy of the Bible that sat on the window sill between two dead, brown plants.

"Life needs a manual," he said. "This world needs a manual. And God gave one to us."

"You're preaching to the converted, Chip," said Michael.

"Ah, but the question is, mate, what to do when the masses don't follow the manual? When the wicked and sinful start tearing down not just the things *we* have built, our great institutions, our great nation, our great civilisation, but also the world that God has built? What do we do?"

Chip poured two cups of tea.

"I tell you what, Michael. There's no point in the righteous following the manual if no one else is. Doesn't matter if I put diesel in the car if my bloody wife keeps accidentally filling it with petrol."

He slammed the kettle down.

"The car grinds to a halt. That's what happens. We have to send it to the garage so it can be fixed again, made like new, and then – and this is the important bit, mate, so listen up – when it comes back, *someone* isn't allowed to drive it again. It's taken away from her because she can't be trusted to *follow the rules*."

"It's a powerful analogy," said Michael.

"Isn't it just? Thing is, I've had my eyes opened in recent times, opened by the wickedness and selfishness of others, and I've set myself a mission, a mission to fix and renew and to build afresh. There are those who would tear our world down with their wanton and salacious ways."

"You're talking about your church."

"And more besides," said Chip. "Fingers in pies, mate. My mission is a clear one, and everyone involved needs to follow the rules. We're building something, together. But when things go wrong, I have to question whether the person responsible is a builder or a wrecker. One spoon or two?"

"Sorry?"

Chip held up a bag of sugar.

"Oh, none for me," said Michael.

Chip gave him a dubious look and then shovelled four spoonfuls into his own paper cup.

"Now, we'll have our brew," he said, "and then you'll tell me all about this business with the dog."

The monkey grooming was ultimately short-lived and unsatisfying. Gorky was as fastidious about his own hygiene as he was about childcare and housekeeping, and there were slim pickings amongst his fur. The fingertip discovery of a crawly critter and what turned out to be a crumb of Cheesy Wotsit was the pinnacle of that brief diversion. Meanwhile, Jack-Jack remained resolutely asleep. Even Clovenhoof, blind and insensitive as he was, could tell that Gorky was disappointed. Someone else's baby might be a poor substitute to caring for Beelzebelle, but it was a substitute of a sort.

"Cheer up, chimp," said Clovenhoof. "If we don't cock this up tonight, we'll get invited back another time. Play the long game."

Gorky muttered to himself.

"Well, life is tough. And short. And it's always unfair. Now, go and get me something to eat and drink."

Gorky hopped off.

Clovenhoof was left alone with his thoughts and the darkness. He was, in a certain sense, enjoying being blind. It gave him licence to demand the help of others, it was an excuse for a multitude of sins, and it evoked a genuine nostalgia for the lightless depths of Hell. People often used the word 'stygian' to describe the dark, but they had no idea. There was only one stygian darkness, that of the Styx itself. Beneath the black waters of that infernal river, there was no light, no sound, no sensation; the ultimate sensory deprivation tank. Back in the Old Days, they had used it for those Hellish residents who, in life, had often wanted 'to get away from it all'. A couple of centuries at the bottom of the Styx made them remarkably sociable and garrulous...

Clovenhoof sniffed.

"Is something burning?" he called.

Gorky squawked from the kitchen.

"Are you sure?"

Gorky entered and placed a tray on Clovenhoof's lap.

"What's this?" said Clovenhoof.

Gorky guided his hands to a spoon and a hot bowl.

"But everything's okay in the kitchen?" said Clovenhoof. "Because I thought I could smell something."

Gorky lacked the vocal control to tut, but gave Clovenhoof a simian equivalent.

"Well, I can smell soup *now*. I meant something else."

There came the piercing high-pitched whistle of a smoke detector upstairs.

"Like that!" snapped Clovenhoof.

He stood up quickly, the tray nonetheless held carefully in his hands.

"You left the cooker on!"

Gorky screeched angrily at him.

"If a monkey is clever enough to cook soup, he can remember to turn the bloody gas off!"

From the baby monitor came the murmurs and sniffs of a baby tossing unhappily in its sleep. Clovenhoof turned to the door.

"You find the smoke detector and take the batteries out, Gorky. *I* will deal with the kitchen."

Clovenhoof took one step and kicked something hard, round and plastic. It flew through the air, bounced off the wall, and then landed, playing a tinny nursery rhyme at high volume.

"Bloody toys!" snapped Clovenhoof, stepped forward, trod on the same object again, and slipped over onto his back. The soup hit him a moment later, but it seemed a very long moment, probably because he knew it was coming.

Steaming tomato soup splashed across his chest, its gooey heat seeping through his shirt almost instantly. Clovenhoof leapt up, screaming, and ripped his scalding shirt from his torso.

The first hints of a cry warbled from the baby monitor.

"Gorky! Smoke alarm!" Clovenhoof yelled.

He hurried to the kitchen, guiding himself along the walls with soup-smeared hands. He felt the hard tackiness of lino beneath his hooves and knew he was in the right place.

"Cooker," he said, and felt his way along the surface.

His hands found the hob controls before straying onto the hot rings. Smoke filling his nostrils, Clovenhoof felt out the four controlling knobs, worked out which was the odd one out and, feeling very pleased with his logical deductions, twisted it to match the off position of the others. The faint sound of gas died.

The smoke detector was still going.

"Damn it, Gorky," he said and turned.

At that point, his midriff nudged something, and Clovenhoof tipped the pan of burning soup off the hob and over his crotch. Clovenhoof screamed again. Louder, naturally.

"Hot cock!" he yelled and, pained, stripped off his trousers and boxers to cool his tender parts. "You've melted my manhood, you maniac!" he cried. "Did no one ever tell you to always keep the pan handles turned in? You're a health and safety nightmare!"

The alarm still persisted. Clovenhoof could hear Jack-Jack crying.

Naked and lightly coated with slowly cooling soup, Clovenhoof scrambled blindly for the stairs. He ignored the bumps and scrapes he received on the way, bounced his way up, all the while heading towards the siren wail. At the top of the stairs, he could hear the alarm almost directly above him. He reached up, found the fast plastic disk of the alarm and ripped it from the wall. It continued to whistle in his hand, so he pounded it until it shut up. It took a bit of effort, and Clovenhoof felt plaster dust raining down all over the place before he succeeded.

He threw the defeated alarm down.

"Gorky!"

Clovenhoof heard a gurgle and laugh from along the landing. He approached, smearing soup as he went. Coughing on the plaster dust, Clovenhoof entered the room. He could see nothing, of course, but he could hear Jack-Jack in his cot. He could, he was certain, also hear the sound of a naughty little capuchin.

"I told you to sort out the alarm," said Clovenhoof.

Gorky made a dismissive noise and then give a curious grunt.

Clovenhoof gestured at his own naked, sticky, and dusty body.

"This is your fault," he said. "All of this. And look what you did to my knob! I'm sure even you can see it's red-raw." He thought about that. "Redder than usual. I'm going to be dipping it in ice-cream for a week just to soothe my pain."

The thought of basting his genitals with ice-cream distracted Clovenhoof and his anger for a moment.

"Well, you're looking after young Giblet now. You keep him occupied while I find some fresh clothes."

He turned from the room and worked his way along the landing to another room. The plush carpet underfoot suggested a bedroom.

"Bathrobe," he said to himself, feeling around. "Trousers. Anything."

He found the door handles of a fitted wardrobe and opened it. He ran his grubby hands along the hanging clothes.

"Too frilly. Too thick. Corduroy? In the twenty-first century? Jesus! Ooh."

Clovenhoof pulled out something light and silky. It could have been a kimono or a dressing gown; he couldn't tell. He struggled with the fastenings, spun in circles while he struggled into it, and then, huffing, pulled it down.

"A little snug in the chest, but not bad," he said. "Right, Gorky, I'm coming to take over."

He became disorientated in his manoeuvring and edged towards the nearest wall. His fingers found a door handle.

He opened it, slipped through and, almost instantly, walked into something.

"What?"

Realisation dawned quickly. The iron railings to the front and side of him. The cool air wafting around his exposed legs. The bedroom had a balcony, one of those pathetically small British balconies that was barely deep enough for one person to stand on. It was ostentatious and Clovenhoof was jealous. To be able to step out of one's bedroom and greet the morning, to feel the breeze rise up your skirts and soothe one's scalded nether regions...

The door behind Clovenhoof clicked shut. Clovenhoof could tell from the chunky nature of the sound that this was the click of something locking firmly into place, of a door rendering itself unopenable. Clovenhoof found and waggled the door handle. He was correct. The door was locked.

"Hmmm," he mused out loud. "Locked out on an upstairs balcony, covered in soup, and wearing nothing but what I now suspect is a woman's dress." He patted his pockets. "With no phone to call for help."

He felt beyond the edges of the balcony and found nothing to grasp onto, no neighbouring balcony to leap to, no drainpipe to shin down. He shrugged.

"I've been in worse situations," he said. "Probably..."

"So, no one knows how the dog got in," said Chip. "What does the CCTV show?"

"We also suffered a... computer failure. I've set about recompiling and restoring the systems. If we're lucky, we should have the computer systems and the CCTV back up and running very soon. That might provide some answers."

Chip took a mouthful of tea and mulled this over, humming darkly to himself. Michael shifted uncomfortably, awaiting the man's judgement. Chip swallowed, smacked his lips, and raised his eyebrows at Michael.

"What can I say, Michael? You're doing important work, valuable work, and I know you're giving it your all."

"I am," said Michael.

"We move on and we put this one incident behind us," said Chip, a heavy emphasis on the word 'one'. "But time is short."

"Thank you," said Michael and then, "Is it? Time, I mean."

"Oh, yes," said Chip darkly. "Let me show you."

Taking his tea with him, Chip moved on from the kitchen and down a corridor at the rear of the house. As Michael followed, his phone buzzed in his pocket. Automatically, he took it out and looked at it. He did not recognise the number.

"Excuse me, one moment," he said to Chip ahead of him and answered. "Hello?"

"Listen, Michael," said Clovenhoof. "I need you to come quickly. Bring a ladder or a rope and grappling iron, or whatever balcony-rescuing equipment you prefer ..."

"Jeremy, I'm a bit busy now," said Michael and cut the call.

Chip had stopped at a closed door. Michael smiled apologetically at him.

"Sorry."

Chip opened the door before him like Willy Wonka at the gates of his factory.

At first, Michael saw the interior of a perfectly ordinary garage, albeit a perfect ordinary garage that was long enough to accommodate a stretch Transit van with room to spare. At second glance, he saw that the length of one entire wall was taken up with a pinboard covered in newspaper cuttings, graphs, print-outs, and scribbles.

"Impressive," said Michael automatically.

"Signs of the end times, mate," said Chip and gestured for Michael to take a closer look.

There was an abundance of line graphs, most with either a markedly upward or downward trend to them. Here, a graph on the increased number of televisions in the average household with an additional line showing the number of 'adult' television channels in the UK. Here a graph of the rising divorce rate coupled with the declining number of marriages. Michael had to look twice at one.

"The diminishing size of dining tables and the rise in sales of instant gravy?"

"Oh, yes," said Chip. "It's not just the family that prays together that stays together. Families are falling apart because they're not breaking bread together. They all just sit round on the sofa or in their rooms, stuffing their faces while watching their dirty movies. The cornerstone of the family, of our great nation, is the roast Sunday lunch, made from scratch, made with love. But no one does that anymore. Gravy, proper gravy, not the granulated stuff, is the cement that binds us."

"An interesting theory," said Michael, agreeing with Chip's sentiment, although doubting the scientific rigour of his data-gathering, and also the professionalism of his building, given the gravy / cement analogy.

"It's no theory," said Chip, and planted an oily finger right in the centre of the largest graph on the board.

The combined line and scatter graph showed changes in the Earth's overall temperature in the past century, plus incidence of extreme weather events in the same period.

"The flooding of the Somerset Levels, last winter's storms, Hurricane Katrina... The conclusion is inescapable."

Michael waited for Chip to explain, but the look on Chip's face was clear. Michael had to show he, too, saw the truth.

"Loose morals are bringing about the end of the world?" he suggested.

"Got it in one."

"So not greenhouse gases then?"

"It's just another symptom, Michael. We must look deeper, at the lust and desire that pervades our society, at the sexual perversion and shameless nakedness that surrounds us." He tapped a graph entitled 'nipples per hour on the BBC'. "This is a sick world, and God is displeased."

Clovenhoof humphed at himself while he tried once more to remember and tap in Ben's number. Gorky, screeching at him from the bedroom, was not helping. However, the monkey had at least been helpful enough to open a bedroom window and toss Clovenhoof one of the household phones. Why the monkey couldn't open the balcony door for him was a mystery, although Clovenhoof suspected it was merely a ruse to allow Gorky to spend more time with young Jack-Jack.

"Shut up!" shouted Clovenhoof. "It's ringing."

"Hello," said Ben.

"Good. It's you," exclaimed Clovenhoof.

"Who else would it be?" said Ben.

"Well, so far it's been three angry old women, a tyre fitter, a pizza delivery place, and a man called Roy."

There was a pause.

"By any chance," said Ben slowly, "have your attempts at blind babysitting gone horribly wrong?"

Clovenhoof made a noise of disgust.

"Some people have no faith. You want me to fail in life, don't you? Just because a friend phones you up when they're locked out on a balcony in ladies clothes, it doesn't mean things have gone 'horribly wrong'."

"What's happened?" said Ben.

"Well, that doesn't matter. Look. It's easily fixed. Just get over here. Make it quick too. Someone will need to pay for the pizza."

Nerys turned off the hairdryer and listened again.

She had been jumpy all day. The mysterious noises of the morning, the hot kettle, and the magically appearing clothes had spooked her. She had spent part of the day reading up on spiritual possession and hauntings, but that had not eased her mind, particularly when Tina caught her doing it and clamped a hand on her shoulder. Nerys had, in one terrified action, screamed, leapt up, and slapped Tina across the cheek. The disciplinary meeting was pencilled in for the following Tuesday.

After a day like that, Nerys's only plan had been to put on some washing, take a relaxing bath, and settle down with a glass of wine, an Ann Summers catalogue, and a TV box set of Hercules Poirot. She had achieved the first objective, but now froze, hair half dried, sure she had heard another noise.

There was another rap at her door, more urgent this time.

With a towel around her, and a brush in her hand to defend herself, she crept to the door and then flung it open, brush ready to strike.

"Ha!"

Ben cowered automatically.

"I'm sorry," he whimpered.

"Jesus, Ben! I thought it was a ghost."

"Do ghosts knock? I know they do in séances, but in real life..."

She lowered the brush.

"I'm sorry to bother you," he said, "but there's a problem with Jeremy."

"There's always a problem with Jeremy."

"This one we might need to intervene in. I need you to drive."

"I am not exactly dressed for going out," said Nerys.

Ben said nothing, but just looked at her. The geeky little man did carry off the kicked puppy look quite well.

Nerys huffed. Most of her tops and trousers were in the washing machine. She reached for the clothes she had thrown over the dining chairs that morning. At least they were dry now.

"One minute," she said, and pushed the door to.

"Hurry," said Ben through the door.

"One minute. God, Ben. I'm not going to go out undressed. I have standards."

She heard Ben mumble something to himself.

"What was that?" she snapped, blouse in hand.

"Nothing," said Ben.

"The work you do at ARC is vital," said Chip, a paternal hand on Michael's shoulder. "The world God made – the world God built – is being destroyed. You are at the forefront of the rescue operation."

"I understand," said Michael.

"By collecting the genetic material of all animals, God's blueprints for life, you are giving us a chance to restore what may be wiped out in next to no time."

"A project like this could take years, decades even," said Michael, "but it has my fullest commitment."

Chip smiled sadly.

"I only hope we have that long."

"Oh, I think the planet will struggle on longer than we imagine," said the former archangel.

"Really?" Chip looked at his pinboard. He swept a hand over the racy tabloid front pages and the tales of moral decay from online newspapers. He pointed at a steeply angled red line. "Eighty-four percent of the internet is pornography. Did you know that? Eighty-four! If my calculations are correct, within ten months, you won't be able to find anything else online. It'll be bazoomas and wang-doodles from wall to wall."

"I'm not sure that's wholly accurate..."

"And when it goes beyond a hundred percent, what then? It'll spill out into our everyday lives. God's wrath will be upon us then. Scripture makes it abundantly clear. When a nation acts contrary to the good book, it will be beset by storms and strife."

Michael, who had had a hand in some of the lesser sections of the Old Testament, struggled to recall exactly which bit of the Bible said that lewd acts caused bad weather. He decided to be diplomatic.

"It's a sobering thought."

"Oh, yes," said Chip. He flicked a wall switch and the garage door began to open. He reached into the wine rack below the pinboard and pulled out a bottle of champagne. "As long as you understand the seriousness of the situation we are in."

"That I do, Chip."

"Good on ya, mate," said Chip. "We have to be vigilant, before vile acts are performed on every street corner."

He placed the champagne bottle in Michael's hands. "A little Krug. Open it to celebrate when we're back on track, eh? Now, I'll let you get home and deal with that doggy business in the morning."

Nerys parked up hurriedly on Penns Lane, mounting a kerb and nearly striking a lamppost.

"I said we had to get here quickly," gasped Ben from the passenger seat, "but maybe not quite that quickly."

Nerys shuffled in her seat irritably and got out.

"I'm just really uncomfortable," she said. "I need to stop and ..." She grunted. "... and itch."

As she began to scratch at her sides, a voice cried out from above.

"Coo-ee!"

Clovenhoof waved at them from a narrow balcony.

"Why's he wearing a Laura Ashley dress?" said Nerys.

"In a strange way, it sort of suits him," said Ben.

"Oh, Jesus!" said Nerys. "Put some pants on, Jeremy! I can see right up ... oh God!"

"The door's locked!" shouted Clovenhoof.

Nerys groaned as she writhed in prickly tenderness.

158

"It's getting worse."

She thrust her hand under her blouse and violently scratched herself.

At an upstairs window, Ben could see Gorky and a toddler, the monkey holding the baby against the glass. Both watched Clovenhoof and looked to be enjoying themselves enormously.

"Ben? Nerys?"

Ben turned. Michael stood in the driveway next door, a middle-aged man beside him. Both looked at Clovenhoof with unconcealed disapproval.

"What the Hell is this?" Nerys pulled a tiny piece of plant material from the folds of her clothes.

Ben squinted at it and then made a rapid and worrying series of deductions.

"Aren't those the clothes Gorky used to mop up the homebrew?" he blurted.

"What?" said Nerys.

"It's full of euphorbia!"

"What?"

"It's poisonous, Nerys! Get them off! Get them off!"

"What?!"

"It only made me go blind," called Clovenhoof. "He's exaggerating."

"WHAT?!"

Nerys, who had begun tugging at her buttons at the mention of poison, now ripped at her clothing.

"Oh, God! Help me!"

Ben, robbed of all thought in his panic, grabbed at her jeans. Nerys slapped at his hands.

"No, they've got to come off!" said Ben. "All of them!"

The blouse was off. Nerys in her haste to dress had not put anything on underneath but, for once, her general disregard for how much of her flesh was on show was actually of some practical use. Ben couldn't get a grip on her fiddly trouser buttons, so she pushed him away and, popping seams, slid them straight down over her hips.

"And you tell me I should put on some pants," snorted Clovenhoof.

159

Naked, Nerys kicked the jeans away as though they were on fire. Ben could see pink blotchy rashes had sprung up across her body.

"It looks bad," he groaned. "What? What are you doing?"

Nerys was pulling at Ben's shirt.

"I'm naked!" she squealed. "Give me your fucking clothes!"

"Not yet," said Ben. "We've got to wash the residue off you."

"Urine!" shouted Clovenhoof. "Aren't you meant to piss on jellyfish stings?"

"I have not been stung by a jellyfish!" bellowed Nerys.

"It might work," said Clovenhoof, hoisted up his dress and let rip. Being entirely unsighted, he had no idea where to aim and sprinkled next door's driveway with his uncontrolled pee.

Both Michael and his companion leapt back in horror as piss splashed over their shoes.

"Euphorbia's an alkali poison!" exclaimed Ben and pulled away from Nerys.

Unfortunately, she still had hold of his shirt, and buttons flew off as she all but tore it from his torso. Ben ran to Michael and grabbed the bottle of fizzy wine from his stunned hands. He ripped the foil as he turned back.

"The alcohol's acidic!" he yelled at Nerys.

The naked woman, two hands failing to cover much of her indecency, gave him a wide-eyed stare of bewildered horror. Ben popped the cork with an unlikely show of strength and then, shaking the bottle like a Formula One champion, sprayed it at Nerys.

Nerys had moved beyond the capacity for words and simply squeaked in misery and fear.

"Turn!" Ben yelled. "I've got to get you covered! Move your arms! Lift your... your, you know... Yes, like that!"

Beneath the squeals and the hollers, Ben heard Michael's stunned companion fume.

"Vile acts in the street!"

"I can't even begin to explain..." Michael said.

Yes, Ben found himself reflecting as the last of the plonk spurted out. The sight of a bare-chested man dousing a naked woman with champagne while a man in a dress peed from above did indeed defy explanation.

He realised there was a man in a motorcycle crash helmet next to him. Ben looked at the young man.

"Which one of you ordered the pizza?" the delivery man asked.

Chapter 6 – In which Clovenhoof has monkey problems, Nerys breaks in, and Michael tries to earn some brownie points

Ben opened the door to his flat with a yawn.

"Come with me," said Nerys.

"What?"

"Something funny's going on." She tugged his arm.

"Can I get dressed first?" Ben asked, indicating his droopy pyjama bottoms and faded t-shirt.

"Just pop that blanket around yourself, you'll be fine," said Nerys, pointing.

Ben stared at the fluffy comforter neatly folded on the back of a chair, confused.

"What's the matter? Come *on*," said Nerys.

"I don't have a blanket like this," said Ben. He shook it out and they both saw that it was made of pink fleece, patterned with hearts.

"No, it's not really your style," admitted Nerys, "but it does look quite cosy."

Ben draped it across his shoulders with a small scowl, in the manner of someone slightly afraid that pink and fluffy might be contagious, and followed Nerys up to her flat.

"Look!" she said, as she led the way into her kitchen and made emphatic pointing gestures that gave Ben no real clue as to where he needed to look. He scanned carefully for signs of something amiss. The surfaces were tidy, the cooker looked shiny and clean, a bowl of oranges was the finishing touch on an immaculate kitchen. He wondered if the kettle needed descaling. He walked over to look inside, but Nerys stamped her foot with impatience.

"It's not at all how I left it!" she wailed. "There were some dirty plates on the side there, and that bowl there with oranges in it had some leftover prawn crackers from the Happy Gathering."

Ben nodded in understanding. "Ah. It's obvious what's going on."

"It is? What are you thinking? Burglar, demonic possession, obsessive compulsive poltergeist?"

"You've got a monosodium glutamate hangover, I'd say."

Nerys fixed him with a hard look.

"It's the flavour enhancer that they put in ..."

"I know what it is!"

"Well, it gives you a sort of hangover. I bet you got up and tidied the kitchen without even realising it, while you were still groggy."

"That is the most insane thing I ever heard! Let's just say for a moment that I was so utterly incapacitated that I turned into a domestic goddess - never happened before, by the way - but did I also go shopping? I didn't even have any oranges yesterday."

"Have you got a better explanation?"

Nerys had to concede that she didn't.

Ben left Nerys staring suspiciously at the mound of shining oranges and went back to his own flat to get dressed. As he walked through the door he hesitated. He had the faint but insistent impression that things here had moved around too. His eyes flicked across the room. The battered but comfy armchair was in the right place. The taxidermy magazine on the table was still open at the interesting article about polishing eyeballs to make them look real. He moved closer to the table, checking his latest work in progress. It was a small spaniel that belonged to a friend of Nerys's. After the dog's unfortunate demise, Ben had been asked to treat it with the same care and reverence that he'd shown to Twinkle. Ben was doing exactly that, although he would miss out the parts where the dog was strapped to a tricycle, doused with alcohol, and set on fire. Something looked different though; the dog had moved. Surely that wasn't possible? Ben knew it was irrational, but he leaned over and tried to locate the dog's pulse point with his finger and thumb, just to be sure, although the fact that the dog was filled entirely with styrofoam stuffing would surely indicate that a pulse was rather unlikely.

Michael filed into his pew for the Consecr8 earlybirds service. Attending first thing in the morning meant that he could nourish his spiritual needs before starting work. As a bonus, it also attracted double Piety Points. As the music faded and Chip took his place at the pulpit, Michael let his mind drift, tallying up the points that he'd recently collected. His attendance was now optimised to gain maximum points, and he had connected his credit card with the church's website, so that making purchases from the supermarket and petrol station would also top up his account.

There was a new system which encouraged the purchase of Bibles and prayer books as gifts for friends and family. The points to be gained from this were generous, but Michael ran through his circle of friends and wasn't sure that any of them would appreciate the thought. Previous attempts he'd made to encourage Nerys to read the Bible had been met with much resistance. Michael realised that he hadn't been paying proper attention to Chip's sermon and quietly admonished himself.

"When you're adrift on a sea of sin, you will want help. You will *need* help. You will *all* need help." Michael nodded in agreement. "We are all beset, every day, by the forces of darkness. Only yesterday, I witnessed heinous acts of violence and indecency here on the streets of this town. *Our town.* Those sinful influences approach from every side, and we must all be vigilant. We must all follow the path of strict righteousness, for only the most pious, the most devoted believers will be provided for when the day of reckoning arrives. You must prove yourselves worthy in every way possible. This church has worked hard to provide a framework to enable you to do this, and now it's time to see whether you measure up. You can now see whether you will be saved, or whether you will drown in this sea of sin."

Michael frowned, not sure what was coming. Chip pressed a button on the pulpit and there was an electric whirring sound. All heads turned to see curtains being drawn apart, high on the wall. They revealed an electronic board, showing a list of names. Michael gasped as he realised that it was a leader board. Where was he? Surely he must be close to the top? There were at least three hundred names on the board, but only the top hundred-odd were green, all of the others were red. Michael Michaels was at number eight. There were seven people ahead of him!

He became aware of a rising level of noise in the church. Chip was winding up his sermon, but people were not really listening.

They were focussed on the board and their position on it. Michael made sure that his hands weren't visible above the pew, and discreetly turned on his phone. He accessed the church's online shop and paused for a moment as he decided how many prayer books and Bibles to add to his basket. He decided that a hundred would do to start with, and clicked through to make the purchase.

Clovenhoof was awake, and decided it was time for his breakfast in bed. He rolled over and rang the bell on his bedside table, waiting to hear the scampering of Gorky's feet.

"I'll have Lambrini on Coco Pops today, I think," he called out. He waited a few minutes, staring at the cracks on the ceiling, pleased that he was once more able to do so. He had put most of them there himself with a little bedtime airpistol practice. There was silence in the flat. "Don't worry too much about the Coco Pops, if you can't find any."

More silence. Clovenhoof sighed and climbed out of bed. Having a helper monkey was much more fun when it did what you wanted.

He went through to Gorky's room.

"Time to earn your keep, minion!" he bellowed, as he tugged the covers off Gorky's nest. "Oh."

There was no sign of him. Clovenhoof frowned and toured the rest of the flat, attempting the noise that Nerys used to make when she called Twinkle. It sounded something between a leaking radiator valve and a badly tuned radio, but he persisted, until he heard a faint scratching noise coming from the airing cupboard. He flung open the door and found that the side wall had a new hole in it. The hole was too small for him to look properly through, but it seemed as though it led to a narrow cavity between the walls. A faint scampering sound indicated that Gorky was somewhere inside it. The inside of Clovenhoof's airing cupboard had been transformed by his recent homebrew experiments, and was not a model of tidiness, but even he was surprised at the strange contents and the appalling smell. Towels and blankets that had been pushed aside to make room for brewing equipment had been carefully arranged into a huge, plush nest. In the centre of the nest a pair of eyes stared blankly at him. Clovenhoof knew those eyes. They had belonged to Nerys's Aunt Molly who had died a few months after his arrival on earth. They had been torn from a photograph and attached to the front of a strange, lifeless form in his airing cupboard. Clovenhoof picked it up. It was the approximate size and shape of a human baby, but this thing was a grotesque anomaly, even to a fan of the grotesque and anomalous. The limbs were taxidermy spares from Ben's flat, he was fairly certain of that. They had, at some point, belonged to a fox, or maybe a large rabbit. The claws gave it a demonic, grasping appearance. He pulled back the knitted baby hat on the thing's head to see what it was made from. It appeared to be a Spanish onion, and was clearly the source of the unpleasant smell, as it was seeping putrid fluid. The pieces were held together with some spectacularly bad sewing. In fact, it seemed to Clovenhoof that the creator of this bizarre doll had given up with the coarse black thread and had used cocktail sticks to spear the pieces together.

"You're coming with me, onion baby," he said.

He carried it across the hall to Ben's flat, dribbling the stinking onion juice.

"What is that horrible smell?" Ben said, covering his nose and mouth with a hand as he opened the door. "Don't you dare bring it in here! It's even worse than that time when you brought back that sofa that you'd found in the canal."

"That was a genuine lay-z-boy!"

Ben propelled Clovenhoof back across the hall, shaking his head.

"What did you do? If you'd wanted to have a go at taxidermy, I'd have been happy to show you what's what."

"This is not my work," said Clovenhoof. "I think Gorky made it."

Ben scrutinised him carefully.

"Have you been drinking this early in the morning? Seriously, Jeremy, there's no way that a monkey did this. That music's very loud by the way. You know how much Nerys hates heavy metal."

Clovenhoof didn't have time to tell him that the music had also been put on by Gorky, as they both jumped at the sudden shriek from above them in Clovenhoof's living room. Gorky swung across the room on the lightshade and grabbed the taxidermy baby with his free arm. He perched on the curtain rail and glared at them with eyes full of malice, stroking the baby tenderly.

"You dressed him up in clothes?" whispered Ben.

"I did no such thing," said Clovenhoof. "Don't you think I'd have chosen something a bit cooler than a baby's dress? I think that's one of Belle's outfits."

They both turned back to watch Gorky as he lifted the side of the dress to expose a satsuma breast. He held the baby carefully in place and supported its head as he nuzzled it against him. Small noises of simian contentment came to Clovenhoof's ears.

"I think your monkey's got a problem," said Ben.

"I think you're right," said Clovenhoof.

Nerys was quite certain that something was amiss.

The photo of Aunt Molly had been the latest thing to disappear, and the odd noises and disturbances continued. She'd heard them previously, when Clovenhoof was locked up in the police station, so, for once, she couldn't blame him. The internet had been no help at all, suggesting that modern-day hauntings were nothing more than the projection of a person's own troubles. Was she seriously supposed to believe that these were manifestations of her own 'sinful' lifestyle? Even if they were, what she wasn't prepared to entertain was the notion that clean living was the way to put a stop to it. There must be an alternative.

She lingered over a website that had a helpful grid. It cross-referenced different types of possession and hauntings with the best strategies for tackling them. She pulled a notepad towards her and started to make a shopping list.

Ben anxiously watched Clovenhoof preparing to enter the bathroom with his makeshift lasso. Gorky had closed the door on them a few minutes earlier, and was, apparently, changing the baby's nappy.

"Watch this," whispered Clovenhoof. "I need to get him somewhere I can reason with him. "Stand by that chair and you can help me hold him down when I've caught him."

Clovenhoof opened the door and plunged forward. Ben heard the briefest sound of a scuffle, then a thump, and then the repeated flushing of a toilet. He could barely bring himself to look, but eventually peeked around the bathroom door.

"What happened?" he asked, looking around at the empty bathroom.

Clovenhoof flushed the toilet again, peering down.

"Oh, well, Gorky shot into the airing cupboard again. He's got some sort of escape route through the wall. I was just dealing with his... thing. Did you know that it's almost impossible to flush a Spanish onion down the toilet? Almost."

Ben peered into the bowl and saw a paw circling below the surface and get flushed away. He recoiled in horror.

"Do you think that Gorky might be a little bit upset by you doing that?" he ventured.

"Well, it was for his own good," said Clovenhoof. "Anyway, he's just a tiny little monkey. What's he gonna do to us?"

A well-aimed bar of soap flew out of the airing cupboard and hit Clovenhoof in the face.

"Ow! Fucking boll..."

A second bar struck him in exactly the same place.

"Oh, I don't know," said Ben. "Stuff like that, maybe."

A nailbrush whistled past Ben's head. Ben heard Gorky move past them inside the wall, more purposeful this time, as if he had somewhere important to be.

"Come on," said Clovenhoof. "We need to keep track of him. It's time to teach that hairy little sod who's the boss."

They moved through the flat, trying to discover which section of wall held the angry monkey. All was still. They stood back to back in the living room, circling slowly so they wouldn't miss the sound of him moving. The sound of heavy metal from elsewhere in the flat wasn't helping.

"Jeremy," whispered Ben. "Look at the light switch."

The plastic cover swung outwards, and a pair of eyes stared out at them, malevolent, cold, and calculating.

"Has your monkey gone over to the dark side?" said Ben, and shivered involuntarily.

A long brown finger hooked the plastic cover back into place, and they heard the faint sounds of Gorky moving away.

"We've got him," crowed Clovenhoof in triumph. "That section over there is a dead end. There's nothing in that recess apart from the electricity meter. We can get him now!"

"What's that?" Ben cocked his head to listen.

A brief thumping noise, followed by an electrical sizzling. All of the lights went out and the music stopped abruptly. As they stood there dumbstruck, the noise of a monkey running across the ceiling space above them barely registered.

Nerys opened her door to Reverend Zack with a smile of relief. She led him inside her flat.

"Thanks for coming. I really wasn't sure if the modern church would take this sort of request seriously."

Zack smiled and touched Nerys on the arm.

"I take any form of crisis seriously, Nerys," he said.

She nodded and went to make tea, pointing out the place where the photograph had gone missing just hours before.

"So how does this work?" she asked. "Do you need any special equipment to do an exorcism? I'm surprised you work alone, to be honest. I thought it would be like policemen patrolling in twos when they expect trouble. I've got a crucifix, if that helps."

She took out the diamante cross pendant she had taken to wearing since the ghostly shenanigans had started.

"I'm not sure if it's an 'official' crucifix. It's really just disco bling, and I didn't know if a proper crucifix has the Pope's seal of approval stamped on it or something."

Zack smiled politely.

"That's a cross, not a crucifix. There's no Jesus on it. And, um, I'm an Anglican priest. We don't have a Pope."

"You see? That's the kind of technical know-how I need right now."

"Nerys, I really want to see what I can do to help you," said Zack, "and I'm not sure yet what that will be, but it won't be an exorcism."

Nerys's smile faded.

"An exorcism can only be carried out with the authorisation of the diocesan bishop," said Zack. "And the church has priests who specialise in deliverance ministry."

"I told you on the phone. I was very specific. I said that I needed an exorcism."

"And guidelines state, quite rightly, that a mutli-disciplinary approach is required, involving doctors, psychiatrists, and any other healthcare professionals."

"I'm not mad, you dingbat. Why have you changed your mind? Did you at least bring the holy water that I asked you for?"

"Nerys, I can bless some water for you, but I'm really not sure ..."

"Here," said Nerys, thrusting a bottle of water at him. "Do this then. Do it now!"

He sighed and muttered a hasty blessing over the water.

"Let's start at the beginning, shall we? You lost your dog recently, I understand. Let's sit down with a nice cup of tea. I'd like to hear all about your dog. Why don't you tell me about him?"

One part of Nerys was infuriated by the insipid cliché of the soppy-eyed, tea-swilling vicar who just wanted a nice chat, but it was quashed by the other part of her that really, really wanted to talk about Twinkle. She sat down with a sigh.

"He was a miniature Yorkshire terrier. Lovely dog. You know the ones, about this big?"

Nerys indicated a Twinkle-sized space on her lap. She still had the stuffed one, but he was in such a terrible state now that she'd shut him away in a cupboard.

"Ah, yes, I do. I believe Michael mentioned that he'd got one in the lab where he works. Perhaps they could be from the same litter?"

"Err yes." Nerys's mind was racing. Why would Michael have a dog in his lab? Surely he wouldn't be performing experiments on animals? She had no real clue what he did for a living, but Michael didn't strike her as someone who would condone that sort of behaviour. Or would he? That supercilious attitude of his, the arrogance that she knew lay beneath his soft and caring exterior. But animal experimenter? Vivisectionist? Could Michael really be callous enough to toy with and destroy innocent lives? He was an angel; it was likely that nothing that served 'the greater good' was beneath him.

Nerys's mind came back to the conversation, and she realised that the Reverend Zack was suggesting that she might find some solace in a special thanksgiving service for pets that was coming up. She promised him that she'd come along in an effort to accelerate his departure. She needed some time to think.

"Right, we can't fail now," said Clovenhoof.

He and Ben had both strapped on head torches and were clustered around the green glow of the tablet that showed the whereabouts of Gorky's GPS collar. "We can see which part of the house he's in. Look, he's over by the kitchen now, so if we move quickly, we can get things all set up in here."

Clovenhoof had called Ed and told him that there was a fox in the garden that they needed to trap. Ed had given him the number of a local wildlife trust, and an earnest young man had spent a long time asking Ben difficult questions about how much distress the animal had been in while he set up the humane trap in the garden. It had given Clovenhoof plenty of time to break into the man's van and remove various traps and useful-looking cages. He and Ben were now trying to set them up at strategic points around the flat.

"Looking good," whispered Clovenhoof. "When he comes out of the airing cupboard, there's a trap covering each of his exits. I've put oranges in them. He loves oranges."

"He seems pretty smart to me," said Ben. "Won't he just run up the wall like he did before?"

"I'm there ahead of you!" said Clovenhoof, slapping Ben on the shoulder. "I have created an inspired backup plan for that exact purpose. You've heard of glue traps for rats?"

Ben shook his head.

"Fly papers then? Yes. Well, I got that tin of super strong adhesive that you use for your emergency taxidermy repairs so that we can turn the rest of the room into monkey-strength fly paper!"

"Jeremy, that glue is really expensive - wait, where have you put it?"

"On the walls, the door, the floor. Everywhere we haven't got a cage, basically."

There was a pause.

Clovenhoof focussed his head torch on Ben, who was struggling to move either of his feet. He winced at the light in his eyes, his head immobile, and Clovenhoof realised that his back and hair was also stuck to the bathroom door.

"Lucky I thought to bring scissors," said Clovenhoof, with a roll of his eyes.

Nerys entered the ARC laboratory building and saw the young man at a reception desk. His hair, his clothes, and his desk were as immaculate as ever. He smiled at her, flashing teeth so white that it made her blink.

"Good morning, madam. How can Freddy help you today?"

"I need to talk to Michael. Can you let me in?"

Freddy gave her a sorrowful look.

"It's a carefully controlled environment. Very limited access, I'm afraid. Let me call Michael for you. Nerys, isn't it?"

Nerys nodded, and Freddy dabbed a button on his console.

"Michael, Nerys is here to see you."

Freddy paused, listening, and then dabbed the button again to end the call.

"Michael tells me he's very deep in his current task. Apparently, he might pop round and see you later with a small gift. He's certain you'll understand."

Freddy flashed his megawatt smile again.

"Oh, right," said Nerys. "I'll look forward to seeing him later on. Love your calendar, by the way. Are you a fan of designer shoes?"

"A design classic is a design classic, whether it's a shoe or anything else," said Freddy, pushing the little perspex box towards Nerys so that she could look more closely. "But yes, Freddy does love his shoes. Check out these Manolos. They're my favourites."

Nerys made genuine noises of appreciation and leaned over to take a proper look. As Freddy pointed out some other pictures, she reached round and took an electronic entry pass from his desk.

Clovenhoof and Ben both jumped as they heard the first trap activate. Their eyes met and Clovenhoof punched the air. A small frown appeared on Ben's face as another trap clattered shut, and another.

"We win," said Clovenhoof. "Let's go and see what sorry state the young reprobate's in after his time inside the walls."

Clovenhoof jogged towards the bathroom.

"Err Jeremy," said Ben from behind. "Are we perhaps going about this the wrong way? Maybe we should be addressing the root cause of Gorky's behaviour."

"Come on. Don't you want to see the little git's expression?"

Clovenhoof opened the door and saw that none of the traps contained a monkey. They did all contain toothbrushes, combs, and other paraphernalia that had been used to trigger them.

"He's taken all of the oranges!" said Clovenhoof. "All of them! And look, he's used toilet roll to make pathways across the glue."

"That's what I've been trying to tell you," said Ben, holding up the tablet. "Look, he's on the move again."

"Well, where is our furry friend?"

"He must be just outside the door."

Ben and Clovenhoof looked at each other in puzzlement, edging towards the door which was slightly ajar. There was a sound from outside. Clovenhoof lunged for the door handle, but at that moment the door slammed shut. He wrestled with it, grunting and twisting. Eventually, he sighed.

"Kitchen, I have two things to report."

"Is one of them that we're now stuck in the bathroom?"

"Yes."

"And is the other that you've got this half of the door handle glued to your hand?"

"Yes."

Michael wheeled a stylish trolley case containing his Bibles along Boldmere High Street. He'd concluded that there were many people who were happy to take his Bibles as free gifts, but not so many who were interested in the contents. Technically, it wasn't a problem, as he would still get the points for buying them in the first place, but what he really needed were some new recruits.

He had discovered that the frontrunners on Consecr8's leader board had earned most of their points by bringing new people along. One was a hairdresser, and had reduced the price of a cut and blow dry for those customers who signed up under her name. Michael was quietly furious at someone gaining the upper hand in such a devious way, but was determined that his free Bible scheme would change all that. He just had to get them into the hands of people who might read them. There was currently one propping up a wonky table in the Boldmere Oak, and another that had been deployed to squash a fly. The problem was that everyone was distracted. Trying to insert a serious religious conversation into the lives of people who were busy discussing last night's television wasn't easy. Michael needed a captive audience. He toured the park, looking for likely candidates. A man snoozing on a bench caught his eye. The man had an unkempt beard and wore a jacket with holes where the wadding poked out. Michael slowed his pace. He might be able to kill two birds with one stone if he took it slowly.

"Hello, sir, how are you?"

The man mumbled groggily, stirring from his nap. Michael sat beside him on the bench.

"My name is Michael and I'd really like to know if I can help you out. Would you like a meal and a new jacket perhaps?"

The man eyed him suspiciously, but eventually gave a small nod.

"Perfect. We'll get going in a moment, but first of all I'd like to take a picture of the two of us. A little memento of the sorry state you're in now, so that I can show the difference once we've been shopping. And *smile...*"

"What we need to do is to get inside his head," said Clovenhoof to Ben. "We'll never catch him otherwise."

Ben stared at the orange in his hand.

"Fine, I can eat an orange, but I'm not at all sure how it's going to help."

"Oranges first, then grooming," said Clovenhoof. "Gorky loves a grooming session."

"Yes, but Gorky's not here," complained Ben, "and I don't know if you've forgotten, but there's a door handle stuck to your hand."

"To catch a monkey, we need to think like a monkey," said Clovenhoof, gesturing emphatically with the door handle. "Now, remember not to smile at me. I might take it as a sign of aggression."

"Oh, I don't think there's any danger of me smiling," said Ben, peeling his orange.

Nerys watched the ARC lab building all afternoon. Actually, it hadn't been quite all afternoon, because Nerys had popped to the shops to pick up a few items she suspected she might need. Actually, it wasn't really a building either, more of a set of extremely expensive interlinked portakabins. It looked like the kind of thing astronauts would live in if they ever got round to setting up a base on the moon. The lab was situated between the scrubby wasteland of a building site that added to the lunar feel and a block of boarded up flats that did not.

In fact, one of the flats was still occupied. A woman with lank grey hair peered out at her a couple of times, so Nerys held her eye and hitched up her skirt, flashing her thigh as suggestively as she was able. Nerys liked to think that if she was ever called upon to impersonate a prostitute that she could turn in a good performance, so she was gratified to see that the woman quickly retreated. Nerys was fearful that she might be calling the police, but it stayed quiet.

Shortly after five, Freddy had emerged. The building was now in darkness. She waited until Freddy had turned the corner before slipping into the building. The stolen pass worked on the entrance door. No alarms went off, which was fortunate as Nerys didn't imagine she could outrun the police in high heels.

Nerys had brought a small torch with her, but lights came on automatically as she entered. She tiptoed past Freddy's desk, then stopped and asked herself why she was tiptoeing.

"It's not as though anyone's listening," she told herself.

Nonetheless, it just seemed the right thing to do, and she continued to tiptoe into the back rooms, through two sets of sliding doors, and into a room that certainly looked like Nerys's idea of a lab.

It was white, had counters and cupboards, but very little else. A brief inspection of the cupboards showed that they were empty apart from masks and surgical clothing. She went through the next door, where a similar room lit up on her arrival. This one contained some complicated-looking equipment, but nothing that looked like animals. She was wondering whether she was wasting her time, but then remembered that there was another door off the first room, so she backtracked to check it out.

As soon as she opened the door, she detected a faint jungle smell reminiscent of Ed's flat. The light came on and she saw that no actual animals were in there, but lots of jars lined the counter. She looked at some of them. Oryx Gazella (Oryx), Otocyon megalotis (Bat-eared Fox). She recognised Michael's precise handwriting, but was mystified as to what they might contain. Some of them looked like balls of fur and...

"Toe nail clippings?" she frowned.

She shrugged. This was science, so Michael must surely know what he was doing. A tiny yip from below the counter startled her, and she realised that there was a cat carrier down there. She kneeled to look and gasped when she saw that there was a miniature Yorkshire terrier inside.

"Awww."

It looked up at her with soulful eyes that made her heart burst.

"Oh, look at you, all shut up in there!"

Nerys unlatched the carrier.

"You do look a lot like Twinkle," she said. "Maybe your fur is a little bit more red, but..." She lifted it out. "... you are simply the cutest little thing, aren't you?"

She couldn't possibly leave the tiny creature in here. What on earth was Michael thinking? A dog like this just needed a warm lap and some tender loving care. Nerys had bought a simple collar and lead in preparation. They were both bright pink. Hardly ideal for a covert operation, but they were stylish and that was more important.

"Well, aren't you going to look smart in this, eh?"

She crouched over the dog and fiddled with the buckle. Her heavy diamante pendant swung free and got in the way. The Yorkie yipped.

"Just a moment," she muttered. "There, I think I've got it on..."

There was an explosion, or at least that's what it felt like to Nerys. She certainly imagined she saw a flash of light and a wisp of smoke before she was sent staggering backwards. She landed on the floor on her backside with an 'oof' of surprise.

The Yorkshire terrier began to whine, but the noise rapidly transformed into something stranger, deeper, and quite unsettling. Nerys blinked the stars away from her vision. The little dog was upright on its back legs, twisting and writhing, as though it was being throttled and crushed by invisible hands. Nerys was about to rush forward to help it when it suddenly... *changed.*

Its body shifted and inflated. Where before there were tiny limbs of gingery coloured fur, there were now huge muscular ones, inky black. Steely claws as long as fingers slid from its paws and drove furrows into the linoleum. Its shoulders rose, contorting its hide. Its jaw dropped and lengthened. The little pink collar pinged off its expanding neck and ricocheted off the wall.

The beast – and it was a beast now – dropped to all fours and turned to look at Nerys. It was bigger than any dog now, even bigger than those Japanese ones she'd read about in the papers which could swallow a child without chewing.

The beast's face was a snarling black mask of malice. Drool dripped from its fangs.

"Oh, God. It's fucking Cujo," she whimpered.

It roared at her. It didn't bark at her like a dog; it roared, like a lion or a bear or a blast furnace. Nerys scuttled backwards across the floor.

"You didn't like the pink collar?" she suggested, terrified. "There are other colours..."

The beast pawed the floor, raking the linoleum into shreds, and then it crouched low and launched at her. She shrieked and ducked her head. There was a huge crash and, when she looked up again, surprised to be alive, there was a ragged hole in the side of the portakabin. The creature had taken out most of the wall. Hardboard and metal sheets lay twisting on the ground outside.

178

More frightened than she recalled ever being before, Nerys stared out, agog. There was the beast, already distant and receding fast, bounding across the road and away.

Michael stood to take another picture of his new friend, whose name was Spencer, apparently. He'd got pictures of Spencer tucking into a slap-up meal, pictures of Spencer sporting a new wardrobe, and, just to make sure he got maximum Piety Points, Michael wanted to get pictures of Spencer reading his new Bible.

"Just there, like that. Perfect."

Spencer mumbled something.

"They won't see that you're blind. Oh, they might if you hold it upside down. Here you go."

Michael stood back and took another, satisfied with his work. His head snapped up as he heard an unearthly howl coming from close by. He looked around and then his gaze was drawn upwards by the sound of loose tiles. There was a creature on the roof of a nearby house. It appeared to be vaguely dog-like, but the only dog it even vaguely resembled was Cerberus the hound of Hell. Huge slavering jaws chomped nastily and, although Michael hated to attribute human characteristics to animals, there was rage in those eyes. Michael thought he'd be angry too, if he looked that ugly.

The beast saw the two men in the street below and advanced slowly down the tiles.

"No!" shouted Michael, waving his arms at the beast. "Get away!"

"Is there a problem?" said Spencer.

"Go!" Michael yelled at the monster. "By all that is holy, I command you!"

The beast growled deep in its throat, seemed to think better of attacking them, turned back up the slope of the roof, and bounded off. Michael had the presence of mind to raise his phone and begin to take some snaps, but the beast was gone over the rooftops.

Michael realised his heart was thumping and he was breathing hard.

"Good God," he panted. "Did you see that?" He looked at the blind man. "Oh, sorry. Silly question. Deeply insensitive." He shook his head at himself.

"I thought we were getting inside the mind of a monkey," said Ben, as Clovenhoof laid out his arsenal on the kitchen table.

"You heard him laughing at us," said Clovenhoof. "He was actually *laughing* when I was trying to reach out to him and be sincere. That monkey is just a psycho, and we need to take him down."

"Was that laughing?" said Ben, unsure whether he could tell. "I wouldn't be surprised. You *were* rubbing wee into your chest hair."

"It's supposed to be attractive to monkeys," said Clovenhoof. "The internet said it's a mating ritual. Is the internet ever wrong?"

"Yes, lots."

Clovenhoof shrugged.

"Not laughing now, is he? We've escaped from the bathroom and we're COMING TO GET HIM!"

Ben turned and looked at the hole in the partition wall.

"I suppose that's fixable," he said, "and it did help to get the door handle off your hand."

"Yeah, I didn't like that wallpaper anyway."

"So, which of these things are we going to try first?" asked Ben, indicating the equipment arrayed on the table.

"All of it," said Clovenhoof. He picked up the sledgehammer and walked to the wall. "Each room will need a flush point like this." He swung the sledgehammer back and pounded a series of holes above the skirting board. "It's thirsty work. You take a turn while I get a Lambrini."

Ben grasped the end of the handle and tried to lift the sledgehammer. It plummeted onto his foot and he cursed in pain.

"If you need lighter work, you can be on hosepipe and firework detail," said Clovenhoof. "These two walls *here* will have fireworks, which we'll set off simultaneously, and that will make him come round *here*, where we will flush him out, literally, with the hose." Clovenhoof continued hammering around the room, making holes.

"This does look as though it could make a fair amount of mess. Surely there must be a less destructive method," said Ben. "Can't we gas him out?"

"Have you got any gas?" asked Clovenhoof.

"Well, no," said Ben, then clicked his fingers. "I have got something, though. Hang on a minute."

He ran out of the door and returned, moments later, with a stuffed ferret. Clovenhoof eyed him sceptically.

"I'm sorry to say this, Ben, but his hunting days are over. I don't think he'd be much of a match for Gorky anyway."

"Well, that's where you're wrong," said Ben, with a triumphant glint in his eye. "Check this out."

He pulled out a remote control and flicked a switch on the underside of the ferret. It trundled along on some sort of caterpillar tracking, climbing easily over the rubble left by Clovenhoof's sledgehammer work.

"Cool," said Clovenhoof, nodding with approval. "It's an improvement over your static work."

"That's not all," said Ben. "I did this as a proof of concept. If I can get hold of a lizard of some sort, I had the idea that I might make a dragon. Watch this."

He clicked another button on the remote control and a small ignition spark was heard, then a flame shot out of the ferret's mouth.

"Butane cylinder," said Ben proudly. "I can turn that flame right up, see?"

He turned a dial and the flame surged ahead of the ferret as it climbed up the rubble pile and disappeared into the wall cavity.

Clovenhoof was staring at him.

"What?" said Ben. "Yes, I know it's unconventional but... what?"

Clovenhoof grasped Ben's shoulders with fierce affection.

"You know, Ben, sometimes I wonder if I have an influence here, if my wisdom and example are teaching anything to the sorry people of this world. And then I see your remote-controlled fire-breathing ferret and I think to myself, 'Yes, Jeremy. Your wisdom *will* live on.'"

"Actually, if you approve, then I'm having second thoughts," said Ben.

"No, this is a great idea."

"Well, we certainly can send the flaming ferret right round the room," said Ben. "It's a lot more controlled than fireworks."

"Control," said Clovenhoof. "Not totally sure that's the word I'd use for setting fire to the skirting board, but I'm happy to see how it all pans out."

Ben looked in dismay at the curls of smoke and flame that were licking up the sides of the skirting board.

"Coming through with the hosepipe!" he yelled.

A noise came to him through the wall, and he realised that Clovenhoof was right, it was laughter.

Nerys shakily unlocked the front door of the flats. She felt utterly drained by her bizarre experience at Michael's lab, and she needed a big glass of wine to even begin to redress the imbalance in her soul.

"Several glasses of wine," she said. "No, gin. Several glasses of gin."

Nerys could hear noises as she shut the door behind her.

"Oh, please, no more dramas tonight," she muttered.

She walked up the stairs to see Clovenhoof using a sledgehammer to smash a hole in the stairs that went up to her flat.

"What the fuck? Stop that!" she yelled, but Ben appeared from Clovenhoof's flat. He looked as though he'd been set on fire, although that didn't explain the holes that had been cut in all of his clothes, or why his feet were bare. He also had a strange new haircut that looked messy even by Ben's low standards.

"Nerys, he's doing that so we can get the hosepipe through and flood the cavity wall," said Ben.

"What? Think of the damage!" shouted Nerys, advancing towards the stairs.

"The thing is, my fire-breathing ferret has been captured by Clovenhoof's monkey," said Ben. "He's inside the walls, setting fire to everything. The whole house is going to go up in flames."

A light switch popped off the wall by the side of them. As they turned to look, they heard a manic cackling sound and a huge flame shot out of the hole.

"Have you rung the fire brigade?" asked Nerys, whacking the hole with her handbag, a futile gesture, as she could hear the monkey climbing upwards.

"Yes, but they thought it was a hoax. Perhaps I should have kept quiet about the ferret and the monkey."

It was clearly an evening for madness, thought Nerys. Perhaps none of this was really happening. Maybe she was in a coma somewhere, or in a mental hospital. Nerys sighed and put down her handbag.

"Is there another hosepipe? Jeremy, we'll need a hole in my floorboards upstairs, so we can flush him out from up there."

She trotted up the stairs to her flat, pushing past Clovenhoof as he demolished the staircase. He looked extremely happy for someone whose home was being destroyed.

"Hey, I can see inside your cupboard, Ben," he said. "Did you tell Nerys about the tripwire?"

Nerys heard this a fraction of a second too late, as she fell forward onto the top landing.

Michael thought carefully about how he wanted to phrase things as he waited for Chip to answer the phone.

"Michael, it's rather late. Do we have a problem?" said Chip gravely.

"Nothing that can't be sorted in the morning," said Michael smoothly, "but I thought I should let you know. There's been a disturbance at the lab. Quite a few repairs needed."

"Has it impacted upon your work, Michael? You know how important that is to me."

"No, Chip. Everything's fine, only the building came under attack. I saw the creature that did it. It was...most unusual. A huge beast."

"Beast?"

"It was sort of..." Michael closed his eyes. "Demonic."

"Was it a monkey?" Chip asked. "Someone local's got a monkey. Seen it a couple of times."

"Definitely not a monkey," said Michael. "Much bigger. Besides, I know where the monkey lives."

"Is that right, Michael? Do tell me more."

Nerys stumbled down the stairs to answer the insistent thumping. It was much too early to hope that Ben or Clovenhoof might be up already.

"Coming, coming!" she yelled.

She remembered to avoid the tripwire and the hole in the stairs. God, they'd have their work cut out sorting out the flats today. They had all retired to bed after being sure that the flaming ferret was disarmed. When it ran out of butane, Gorky had flung it at Clovenhoof's head.

She opened the door to see a man with a tie and a clipboard. He had a moustache and a serious face, but not in a good Hercule Poirot-ish way. This was a moustache and a serious face that looked like trouble.

"Good morning. Are you one of the tenants in this building?" he asked.

"Err yes. Nerys Thomas."

The man jotted a note.

"I'm employed by the solicitor who represents the leaseholder, Ms Thomas. We need to do an inspection, as there's been a complaint issued."

"What sort of complaint?" asked Nerys.

"It has been alleged that this house has an infestation of vermin. I'm sure you'll understand that we need to act urgently when something of this nature occurs."

"Uh huh. So when do you want to do the inspection?" asked Nerys.

"Now, Ms Thomas. I am here to carry out the inspection with immediate effect."

Nerys's mind whirled. There were so many things that this inspector should not see, she wasn't sure where to start. She could pretend to faint, but she didn't think that would stop him. Her best bet was to stall for time and alert the others.

"Don't you need to give twenty-four hours' notice before entering rented property? I'm sure I read that somewhere."

"If there are grounds for believing there is an immediate danger to the occupants then no."

"Danger?"

"Danger."

"Oh. Come in then," she said. "You'll know that the downstairs flat is empty at the moment. Do you need to go back for a key?"

"I have all the keys right here," he said. "I'll get straight to work."

Nerys left him downstairs and ran up to wake Clovenhoof and Ben up. They all gathered in Clovenhoof's flat and stared around at the devastation from the previous evening.

"How can we hide those massive holes in the wall?" said Nerys.

"Newspaper and aerosol spray," said Ben promptly.

Nerys rolled her eyes as Ben fetched his modelling supplies but, as he taped pieces of newspaper over the holes and then sprayed them in a colour that matched the wall, she wondered if it might just work.

"He's coming!" hissed Clovenhoof, who had just jammed the bathroom door handle into place with a huge blob of toothpaste.

"Have you had a fire in this building at all?" said the inspector as he entered the flat, sniffing.

"Not for a while," said Clovenhoof, standing casually against the door frame to hide the worst of the charring. "I have just burnt some toast though. Do you want some?"

The inspector ignored him and walked around the room. Ben was behind the sofa, doing the last of the holes, and the faint hissing of his aerosol could be heard, so Nerys coughed loudly.

"Water stains up there," said the inspector, pointing at the ceiling. "They look fresh, too."

"Ah, that was the bath I left running," said Nerys. "Silly me."

"Hmm, well, we need to be very careful with water damage," said the inspector, scribbling notes faster now. "It can create lots of problems you know. Perhaps I'll pop upstairs now and take a look at that before I continue in here."

Nerys gave a sickly nod and followed him out.

"Oh, there's a squeaky stair up there," she said, "where that rug is to, er, mark it. You might want to step around that part."

The inspector stopped and picked up the rug to look underneath. There was a gaping hole right through the stairs. Nerys's heart sank.

"Yeah, I did have a go at fixing it, but DIY really isn't my strong suit. I'll get someone in to take a look at that, shall I?" She tried her most winning smile, but the inspector was moving on.

"You did disconnect the tripwire, didn't you?" came a whisper from behind.

"Oh, oh no," cried Nerys, a hand going to her mouth, "Mr Inspector, Mr Inspector, I think I just saw a mouse!" Her voice dropped to a whisper as something registered. "What do you mean *disconnected*? Isn't it just tied to the bannister?"

"No, it was supposed to empty that water tank," said Ben, pointing upwards.

As Nerys looked up, she heard the sound of the inspector falling over the wire with an *oof* sound and sighed at the inevitability of it all. She saw that the giant water tank that hinged above them teetered on its support and then, against all the odds, righted itself again. She dared to breathe, and prepared to try and explain away the trip wire, but then a furry hand came around from behind the water tank and gave it a push.

The water cascaded down upon all of them, washing Nerys, Ben, and Clovenhoof straight down the staircase in the deluge. The inspector wasn't so fortunate, as the huge tank then landed across his legs. Nerys looked up through the tangle of limbs at the bottom of the stairs and wondered what the ominous cracking sound might be. They were getting louder, clearly audible over the screams of the inspector, who really wasn't happy.

Water started to spray out from the floorboards where he flailed, still trapped by the tank.

"Err, guys, did anyone think to turn the hosepipe off last night?" Nerys asked.

She didn't need to wait for an answer as further sprays of water appeared, like tiny fountains. The cracking sound turned into a huge, structural groan, and the floorboards erupted upwards around the inspector, who disappeared downwards with the tank.

As the floor collapsed, a further torrent of water burst forth from the walls, covering them all with soggy chunks of plaster.

It was several minutes before things stopped collapsing and piling on top of them. Nerys struggled to disentangle herself from Ben and Clovenhoof. She could hear the inspector bellowing about the duty of care pertaining to a leaseholder.

"He's alive," she said, not sure if that was good news or bad.

She rubbed her eyes to try and dislodge the plaster and dirt that coated it. She caught a small movement off to the side. The monkey was sitting on Clovenhoof's chest, picking bits of plaster from his face. Clovenhoof shook himself like a dog and sat up. The monkey hopped across to Ben.

"Told you he loves a bit of grooming, didn't I?" said Clovenhoof.

Chapter 7 – In which Clovenhoof and Ben spend a night with furry friends, and Nerys spends a night with an old man

Chip Malarkey knelt on one knee and ran his fingers along the grooves that had been clawed into the laboratory floor. He measured the space between them with his extendable tape measure and made a noise to himself.

"Is there CCTV footage?"

Michael gave Freddy a terse look. Freddy clicked on the laptop that had been set up to replace the water-damaged lab computer.

"Here we are, Mr Malarkey," said Freddy.

"It's Chip," their boss told him. "Everyone calls me Chip, even when they're a gnat's todger away from being fired."

Michael and Chip watched the low-res image.

"I had to set up a temporary security camera," Michael explained. "On the night the dog appeared, the broken samples leaked into the original computer and..."

Chip regarded the massive hole in the wall, the starburst of cracks that spread through the remaining plastic and steel.

"You're saying a dog did this?"

"Sir, I..." Lost for words, Michael pointed at the image on the screen.

Nerys crouched in front of the Yorkshire Terrier, a collar in her hands. And then the image shook, shadows raced across the screen, and something dark and indistinct swelled into being.

"What is that?" said Chip.

"The beast," said Michael.

"It's not particularly clear," said Freddy.

The shape shifted, gathered itself, and then there was a final juddering of the camera and the image froze. Nerys was caught in terrified profile, staring at the hole ripped into the side of the building.

"So," said Chip. "What's the impact on your work, Michael?"

"In addition to the seventy-eight samples lost when the dog appeared, a further fifty-four samples. Just under half of those are duplicates but, in total, we have lost sixty-eight unique species samples."

Chip breathed out heavily through his nose, his chest heaving with suppressed anger.

"Which means?"

"We've been set back four months."

"Why is this happening, Lord?" said Chip to the heavens, and then looked at his two underlings. "What has happened here, guys? Theories."

"Animal activists," said Freddy.

Chip blinked at him.

"They unleashed a lion or a bear or something in here," said Freddy.

"Why on earth would they do that? We're trying to preserve DNA here. We're on their side."

"Confused animal activists? A lot of them are vegans and a low iron diet can cause light-headedness and tiredness..." Freddy tailed off under Chip's unimpressed stare.

"I *saw* a beast," said Michael.

Chip shook his head firmly.

"Little dogs transforming into monsters? Demonspawn stalking the streets of Sutton? No." He pointed at the claw marks on the floor. "Do you know what did that? A bobcat."

Michael smiled kindly.

"Chip, I honestly don't think any cat, not even a North American lynx, could ..."

"Not a bobcat, man! A bobcat! A mechanical digger. Someone rammed that wall ..."

"The wall's actually been pushed out," argued Michael weakly.

"... and tore chunks out of my rented portakabin. This was planned and deliberate." Chip stabbed a finger at the screen, "I know that woman."

"Yes," said Michael. "She's the one who stripped naked in your driveway while one man peed on her from above and another doused her in your champagne."

"Oh. I was thinking of the woman who shouted obscenities at me in church," said Chip.

"Same woman."

"Really?"

Chip peered at the screen closely, perhaps trying to picture her without her clothes on. He gave a quietly furious sigh.

"I hate that woman."

Nerys and Clovenhoof stood on the pavement and watched a succession of men in hard hats and hi-vis tabards bring out their furniture and belongings and dump them without ceremony in the tiny garden space at the front of the house. The suggestion that they could reclaim their own things without the clumsy aid of workmen was brusquely ignored by the still-seething, limping, and waterlogged building inspector who was now engaged in a conversation on his mobile. Ben sorted the sodden, plaster-speckled items into three piles as the workmen brought them out.

"A replica Seleucid shield – dented! – mine. Poirot series three box set, Nerys's. Some sort of fuzzy electric belt."

"Stomach toner," said Nerys.

"And your 'men' folders. Volume one: Targets. Volume two: Acquisitions."

"Please, please, tell me they're not damaged."

"They're fine enough. This yours too? A severed mannequin hand. A jewellery holder perhaps?"

"That's mine," said Clovenhoof.

Ben frowned at him.

"For picking my nose," Clovenhoof explained, as though it were obvious. "You know, for when I fancy doing it with a little class."

Ben looked at the fingertip warily.

"And for the occasional self-administered prostate examination," added Clovenhoof.

Ben dropped it instantly.

"A crate of alcohol," he said, looking inside a charred cardboard box.

"What kind?" said Clovenhoof.

"Ouzo, retsina, sangria in a bottle shaped like a flamenco dancer."

"Exotic."

"My collection of horrible holiday booze," said Nerys.

"And Viagra," said Ben, looking from a blue plastic case to Clovenhoof.

"I don't need that stuff."

"Well, I don't even get the opportunity to need it. Which I don't," Ben added hurriedly. "You are a man of a certain age, Jeremy. It's nothing to be ashamed of."

"It's mine, all right," said Nerys testily.

"Dude!" said Clovenhoof, approvingly. "I knew there was something mannish about you."

"We've seen Nerys naked," argued Ben.

"Yeah, but maybe she – I mean he – does that thing where she – he – tucks it under and ..."

"It's not *for* me," she snapped. "Jesus! Sometimes, a gentleman friend has had a bit too much to drink and maybe I can help him along ..."

"Vermin!" said a workman.

"Easy now," said Ben, quick to leap to Nerys's defence.

The man threw down a plastic container.

"You've got a rat problem."

"They're not rats!" wailed Ben, pulling out sorry-looking examples of taxidermy. "Well, that one is but generally, oh!" He regarded a damp and patchy badger and a rabbit wearing a look of terminal surprise on its face. "Captain Brockleton! And Sergeant McFuzzyshanks!"

"He's lost his marbles," Clovenhoof said to Nerys.

"They were going to lead my woodland commando team," explained Ben. "You know, in some tastefully arranged diorama. Guns of Navarone meets Watership Down."

"Tasteful, yeah," said Nerys.

"You haven't seen any live animals in there?" Clovenhoof asked the workman. "Specifically, a little turd of a monkey who's definitely one banana short of a bunch?"

"Oh, him. Attacked our Brian on the top floor. Think it's hiding in the attic now. So, who does the nudie calendar belong to?"

The three flatmates looked at each other questioningly.

"Men or women?" Clovenhoof asked the workman.

"Men," he said.

Nerys shrugged.

"Not mine, but I'll take it."

"Male or female, I think nakedness is both hilarious and culturally satisfying," said Clovenhoof, and held out his hand to take the calendar.

Ben snatched it from the workman.

"That's not a nudie calendar! That's Warriors of the Ancient World."

"They're not wearing many clothes," the workman argued.

"They're from Mediterranean civilisations, and fighting is hot and sweaty work."

"I'll bet," said the workman sceptically. "And what are those guys with shields doing in November?"

"Making a tortoise," said Ben.

"Disgusting," said the workman.

The inspector was winding up his conversation on the phone.

"Yes, sir. Absolutely, sir. Sorting it out right now."

He turned to face them.

"Mr Kitchen, Mr Clovenhoof, Ms Thomas," he said. "Once all items of ..." He looked at Ben's pathetic mammalian commandos. "... of value have been removed, I will need to make a full assessment of the damage *you* have caused."

"Will it take long?" asked Ben.

The inspector consulted his clipboard. Most of the pages were wet and fused together.

"Four weeks," he said.

"Got to be fucking kidding," said Nerys.

"Four weeks. Minimum."

"But that's my flat. I own it. You can't kick me out of a flat I own."

The inspector attempted to look like he wasn't enjoying his revenge and almost succeeded.

"You own the flat but not the ground it stands on. The law on this matter is clear. In fact, the landlord may choose to bring legal proceedings against you."

"But it was him!" she said, pointing at Clovenhoof. "And his fire-breathing stoat."

There was a crash from inside the house. It sounded like a wall falling down. It was followed by a simian screech and a lot of swearing.

"I'll be sure to pass that on," said the inspector.

"And it was Ben's anyway," Clovenhoof said to Nerys.

"And it was a ferret, not a stoat," added Ben helpfully.

"But what do we do?" said Nerys. "We can't be homeless!"

"I gather that tens of thousands of people are," said the inspector. "I'm sure you'll pick it up as you go along. Oh, and this ..." He waved the tip of his biro at the sad piles of belongings on the ground. "The skip is coming in half an hour. Anything left here will be assumed surplus to your current requirements."

Ben stared, gobsmacked. Nerys quivered with incandescent fury. Clovenhoof stepped forward and punched the inspector in the face. The inspector stumbled, tripped over a stuffed owl, and went down, his hand clutching his busted nose.

"Jeremy!" said Ben.

"Oh, come on," said Clovenhoof. "You were both thinking it."

Ben and Nerys did not ask where Clovenhoof got the trolleys from. The fact that each of the three was marked with the name of a different supermarket either indicated he had been very even-handed in his trolley-stealing, or that he knew a central source for stolen trolleys, some sort of backstreet cut-and-shut trolley den.

With belongings piled high, they pushed all their worldly goods down Boldmere High Street to Ben's bookshop. Nerys led the way.

"She's got a fair turn of speed, hasn't she?" said Ben.

"Enjoying the life of a bag lady," agreed Clovenhoof.

"I don't want anyone to see me!" she hissed at them. "Now get this door open. My phone's buzzing like crazy. It's probably Tina. The office will be falling into chaos without me."

Ben unlocked the shop door with one hand while trying to stop the trolley rolling into the road with the other, and then helped the others squeeze their trolleys through the narrow doorway. Nerys closed the door behind them and stared morosely at her lot. Three lives in three trolleys. And what did hers amount to? A pile of clothes, knick knacks and jewellery, boxes of papers detailing her meagre finances, and a bunch of files in which she had catalogued her successes and failures with men.

"I'm struggling to remember a crappier day than this," she said.

Her phone began to ring again.

"Look," said Ben. "I'll get this stuff stored in the back. I'll put the kettle on. We can even think of making a temporary bedsit thing in the basement."

"God, not bloody likely," said Nerys. "As soon as I've explained the situation to work, I'm splashing out on a four star hotel and washing this crappy day right out of my hair."

She looked at her phone. It was indeed Tina.

"Right," she said, taking a cleansing breath. "Let's turn this shitty day around." She hit the answer button. "Hi, Tina."

"I'm fired?"

Tina shook her head regretfully.

"Fired is a strong word," she said.

"But it's the right fucking word," said Nerys, her voice rising shrilly.

"Come, now. Let's discuss it in my office."

The rest of the staff in the front office of the Helping Hand Job Agency avoided Nerys's gaze as she followed Tina into the tiny back office.

"Now," said Tina, "although you have grasped the fundamental headlines here vis-à-vis your departure from this company, I think it is critically important that we discuss the 'whys' and the 'what nows'."

"Absolutely bloody right. I want to know why I'm being sacked."

Tina nodded sympathetically.

"As you know, Nerys, Helping Hand's ethos is the delivery of customer-centric and outcome-focused brand experiences. Our emphasis is on building on past successes, working through current challenges, and achieving key deliverables and targets."

"Yes," said Nerys tiredly. "We find people jobs."

"No," said Tina. "We provide sector-relevant expertise, skill-actioning, and workforce enhancement. We insert ourselves and our product into industrial positions at key locations and time-critical periods. Do you know what we are?"

"An employment agency, Tina."

"We're lubricant. You and I exist to lubricate the needs of the captains of industry."

"I don't recall that being on the job description."

"Our product ..."

"People, yeah. The HGV drivers, secretaries, and shelf-stackers."

"... enables local and global businesses to function efficiently and achieve their potential. Like the lubricant in the engine gears, the more effective we are, the less we are noticed. We are the silent partners behind the scenes who ease the bumps, quell the upsets, and ease the passage of ..."

"Hang on, are we a lubricant or a laxative? And what the fuck has this got to do with me?"

Tina's genial manner switched off like a light.

"You're grit, Nerys."

"What?"

"Grit in the gears. We have standards of behaviour to maintain."

"If this is about the table-dancing at Dave's leaving do, I told you that someone had slipped me a ..."

"It's not about that – not just about that. We have to retain a level of decorum, of social responsibility. *Particularly* when it comes to interactions with our clients."

"I am always nice to the clients," Nerys insisted, "even when they're idiots."

Tina laid a tablet flat on the desk and tapped the play icon. It took Nerys several seconds to realise what she was looking at. She recognised the dog first, then herself, then the setting. She watched it to its blurry shaky-cam ending.

"Firstly," she said, "I was not there on work business. It was a mission of mercy carried out in my own time."

"I thought you said your dog was dead."

"That's not my dog. Trust me, that's definitely not my dog. And, secondly, the ARC Research Company is not one of our clients."

"In the past year, Helping Hand has placed more than two hundred workers in Mr Malarkey's construction and property management companies."

"Chip Malarkey? That's his lab?"

Tina nodded.

"So you can probably see why your situation here has become untenable."

"He's trying to get back at me," said Nerys. "He's the one who killed my dog! That small-minded, self-important, shit-rinsing cockweasel! You can't fire me for this!"

"Oh?" said Tina. "Well, once it became clear that you could no longer continue with Helping Hand, I cleared out your desk drawers and locker. And I found this."

Tina placed a sack-cloth doll on the table. It had yellow wool hair, sinister button eyes and half a dozen round-headed pins sticking out of it.

"Now, you know I've been suffering from significant lower back pain of late," said Tina, her voice cracking with emotion. "I'd be devastated to learn that it was caused by ... dark forces."

"Tina," said Nerys, "who says that's a voodoo doll of you?"

Tina pulled a rolled up scrap of paper out of a slit in the doll's back.

"'My name is Tina ...'" she read.

"Okay, but I've never seen that before. There's no saying that *I* made that doll."

Tina read the note in full.

"'My name is Tina and I'm a small-minded, self-important, shit-rinsing cockweasel.'"

"Mmmm, yes. I admit there's a superficially familiar tone to that."

"It's your handwriting."

"Ye-es."

Tina put it aside.

"Clearly, I've offended you in some way. I'm sorry that you did not feel you could discuss your concerns and grievances with me." She sniffed back her fake tears. "However, this meeting can also serve as an exit interview. Perhaps you would like to offer your thoughts both on this job/no-job transition process and your time at Helping Hand in general."

Nerys blinked.

"You want to know what I think?"

Tina nodded supportively.

"I think it's an important part of the process."

"Okay," said Nerys and cleared her throat. "Strap in, Tina. Here it comes."

Clovenhoof trotted merrily through the frozen food aisle of the supermarket. Having had to leave their food supplies back at the flats, Ben had charged Clovenhoof with the task of getting something in for dinner. The bookshop had a kettle and a toaster and a tiny microwave, so the cooking options were limited. However, Clovenhoof was quite keen to discover what toasted Findus Crispy Pancake and what microwaved Findus Crispy Pancake tasted like. He was even contemplating popping one in the kettle. It would probably make an intriguing crispy pancake soup.

A brief, but recognisable, gurgle snapped him out of his culinary cogitations.

Beelzebelle, sat back in the baby-seat of an unattended trolley, held out her arms to him.

Clovenhoof looked around. There was no one else in the aisle. He trotted over.

"I'm not really meant to talk to you," he whispered. "PC Pearson said I could go to prison if I did."

Beelzebelle clenched and unclenched her hands excitedly.

"How have you been?" said Clovenhoof.

Beelzebelle rocked against her straps.

"Does your mum take you rollerblading like I used to? Maybe a parent-child trip to the bookies? No?"

Beelzebelle frowned furiously, her face reddening. For a moment, Clovenhoof thought she was brewing something in her nappy, but then her lip wobbled and he saw that she was about to cry.

"Don't be upset," he said. "It wasn't my choice. And I'm sure your mum is able to provide you with all the things I couldn't. Like ... like ... towels and cushions and ..." He looked in Beelzebelle's trolley for inspiration. "... Alphabites."

The relative merits of letter-shaped potato products did nothing to appease Beelzebelle. The little girl keened unhappily and took a deep breath to begin some serious wailing. Clovenhoof tutted, looked up and down the aisle, then unclipped her restraints and lifted her out. The transformation was instantaneous. The nascent bawling became a coo of happiness.

"You're a bloody blackmailer," said Clovenhoof, and then, hugging Beelzebelle close, said, "A chip off the old block, aren't you?"

Beelzebelle clapped her hands inexpertly and grabbed Clovenhoof's horns and pulled.

"I'm not a space-hopper, you know."

"Oi! You! Perv! Security! Security!"

The pregnant woman in the tight blonde ponytail, pointed an accusing finger at Clovenhoof and waddled up to him as fast as her baby bulge would allow her. Clovenhoof vaguely recognised her, from parent pick-ups at St Michael's cub scouts, from Boldmere Oak karaoke nights, and from the occasional girl-on-girl fights in pub car parks.

"Toyah!" said Clovenhoof to Beelzebelle's mum. "I can assure you that this is not what it looks like."

"What are you up to then, eh?"

"Um. Why don't you tell me what you think I'm up to, and then I can assure you that it's something completely different?"

Toyah pulled her daughter from his arms. Beelzebelle flailed her limbs and cried.

"You're a fucking baby-stealing monster. I bet you sell them mail-order to rich Americans."

"You can do that?" said Clovenhoof, totally unaware that such an exciting business opportunity even existed.

Beelzebelle wriggled and squirmed and bawled out her frustration.

"I should call the fucking police," said Toyah.

Clovenhoof shrugged.

"Well, here comes the supermarket's own brand."

He nodded down the aisle. A broad-shouldered security guard was walking unhurriedly, almost reluctantly, towards them.

"His name's Ahmed," said Clovenhoof. "It's surprising how often he ends up talking to me."

Toyah had suddenly become edgy and anxious.

"Right, well ... Come on, Bea, let's go."

Toyah's fingers shook as she tried to put her girl back in the seat.

Clovenhoof looked from Toyah to the security guard and then back to Toyah's bulging stomach.

"Hang on," he whispered. "How long have you been pregnant?"

"Er ..." said Toyah.

Clovenhoof grinned.

"Leave it to me."

He reached into a freezer compartment, took out a pack of fish fingers, ripped them open and scattered them across the floor.

"Swim free, my darlings!" he shouted. "I have released you from your icy prison!"

Ahmed yelled and broke into a jog.

"Step away from the fish fingers, sir."

Ben had little need to go down into the basement of Books 'n' Bobs. Or, if he was honest, very little desire. He had watched enough horror movies in his time to know that bad things happened in basements. The single naked bulb hanging from the ceiling did not cast enough light to illuminate all the corners. Who knew what demonic horrors or grisly remains lurked there? Nonetheless, with their homes rendered uninhabitable, Ben felt there was no option.

The basement still contained some of the stock from the previous occupant's fancy dress enterprise, and Ben had added to it with those books that were too damaged, old, or niche to even warrant shelf space in a second hand bookshop. Ben spent a good hour shifting boxes of tinsel wigs, vampire fangs, and body paint, and piles of books with titles like *How I Tamed the Savage Hindoos of Rajasthan* and *Rousing Stories for Bigger Boys*. He had twelve boxes filled with copies of the recalled 1975 Bunty Annual, featuring an obscene and unforgiveable misprint, which a friend had rescued from the pulping machine and passed to Ben in the vain hope that they would be priceless rarities one day.

Ben, never noted for his upper body strength, balked at moving all those boxes, and then decided that, if they were going to make a bedsit of sorts down there, the boxes could serve as a bed base. He arranged the books into a large rectangle, and then brought his asthmatic Henry hoover downstairs and began the lengthy process of removing decades of cobwebs and brick dust.

"And you say I can't maintain standards!" said Nerys, her rant having entered top gear and now cruising down the motorway of bitter parting shots. "Do you know why we didn't get that account with Dempsey Feinstein?"

"No," said Tina.

"Could it be that the managing director's wife made a pass at our James at the spring conference event and the MD found the pair of them playing tonsil hockey by the chocolate fountain?"

"Really?"

Tina made a note.

"Oh, and speaking of chocolate fountains. You remember that time we had a break-in and the burglars did a dirty protest in the stock cupboard?"

"Unfortunately, I do."

"Actually, Vivian brought her Lhasa Apso in when her dogsitter was on holiday, and the mutt got a dodgy belly from scoffing your secret stash of jelly babies."

"I thought Eduardo the cleaner stole those. We fired him."

"That's okay. If my sources are correct, he was doing unspeakable things to your coffee mug after hours anyway."

Tina gagged.

"Oh, come on," said Nerys. "The crappy free tea and coffee we get in this place, I should think a splash of Eduardo's special seasoning would enhance the flavour."

"We don't have free tea and coffee," said Tina.

"Yes, we do. In the kitchen."

"That's the tea and coffee club. You have to pay a fiver a month for that."

"Well, no one told me that."

"We asked you when you joined. *Eight years ago.*"

Nerys tried to work out what a fiver a month for eight years added up to.

"Oh."

Forty minutes after the supermarket tannoy had called for "fish finger clean-up on aisle three", Clovenhoof emerged from the supermarket in the strong and capable grip of Ahmed.

"Perhaps you could consider doing your shopping elsewhere in future," said Ahmed.

"Oh, I'm a big believer in customer loyalty." Clovenhoof grinned.

Clovenhoof trotted out and found Toyah Wilson sitting on a streetside bench, struggling to get her daughter to accept a milk bottle. Toyah eyed him doubtfully.

"You reckon this makes us even?" she said.

Clovenhoof couldn't tell if it was a threat, a warning, or a reconciliation.

"How was the African holiday?"

Toyah shrugged.

"Bit shit. Lions are lazy buggers, aren't they?"

Clovenhoof nodded.

"Giraffes are funny, though," he said. "The day the Guy Upstairs made them, I knew he'd lost his grip."

"Did you know, there's no Nando's in Kenya?" said Toyah. "I mean, not one. Chickens, yes. Nando's, no. Not impressed. Stop squirming, Bea!"

"Here," said Clovenhoof, holding out his hands for her.

"You kidding?" said Toyah but, an instant later, handed her daughter over.

Clovenhoof slung her in the crook of his arm and offered her the bottle. Beelzebelle grabbed it and drank.

"What? You're like some fucking baby whisperer?" said Toyah.

"We communicate on a deep level, mostly through the secret language of farting."

With his free hand, he reached into his shopping bag, ripped open a pack of frozen crispy pancakes, and began to munch on one.

"You're meant to cook them." said Toyah.

"I call them pancake lollies." He looked at Beelzebelle. "Wednesday. We'd normally be at Mum-Baby-Zumba right now."

"What the Hell...?"

"Belle and I used to shake our things with the other girls. Bit of arse-wiggling, a few giggles, and a cup of coffee with the SCUM ladies."

"SCUM?"

"Sutton Coldfield Union of Mums."

Toyah scoffed.

"I can imagine. A bunch of self-righteous, middle-class cows, eating baby placenta with that quinoa stuff, planning what grammar school to send their babies to, and bragging about how much their husbands earn while he's off shagging his secretary somewhere."

"Oh no, they're not like that," said Clovenhoof. "At least *half* of them are not like that."

"Can't quite see me and Bea cutting it with that kind of crowd."

Clovenhoof spun Beelzebelle around, and she burped loudly in his face.

"It's these special moments I miss." He smiled. He looked at Toyah. "You could come with me?"

"Where?"

"To a SCUM event."

Toyah snorted.

"Why not?" said Clovenhoof.

"I don't know. Look, those women, I know the type. They won't accept ... you know, me."

"I'll be there to hold your hand."

"Yeah. And that. Look, it's a sweet suggestion, but I'm not looking for another man right now, particularly one who's so ..."

"Handsome? Daring? Aromatic?"

"Old."

"I think you've got this wrong," said Clovenhoof.

"No, really. You are quite a lot older than me."

"No, I don't want *you*. I'm sure you're very attractive, but it's Beelzebelle I'm interested in." Clovenhoof, rarely conscious of innuendo or social taboos, caught himself. "Not like that. Obviously, not like that. I mean ..."

Toyah was smiling. Clovenhoof reckoned she wasn't the kind of person who smiled openly or often.

"Okay, weirdo. WhatsApp me some time with the details."

"WhatsApp?"

"You know, WhatsApp?"

"I have no idea what's up."

"But at least you Facebook," said Toyah.

"I'm assuming it's like doing a facepalm, only more violent."

"You can install it on your phone," she said, and clicked her fingers for his phone.

Clovenhoof pulled his mobile out of his pocket. Toyah stared at it.

"God, you are old," she said.

"You have no idea, lady."

Toyah hoiked up her top, reached inside her 'pregnant' tummy and pulled out part of her shoplifting haul from the supermarket. It was a mobile phone in a fat cardboard box.

"That's what you get for sleeping with a robot," said Clovenhoof.

Toyah ignored him, opened the box, and snapped the back off the sleek thing within.

"Just give me five minutes," she said.

Nerys slouched into the Boldmere Oak. It wasn't easy to slouch in heels, but Nerys's mood was so low, all things had become possible. Michael was waiting for her at the bar.

"Chardonnay," she said to Lennox, the barman.

Michael gestured to the glass of wine he'd already ordered her. Nerys took it and downed it in one.

"Chardonnay," she said to Lennox.

"Tough day at the office?" said Michael.

"There won't be any tougher ones," she said. "I've been fired."

"For what?"

"Nothing I didn't deserve, I guess," she said.

Lennox, who usually kept a stoic and emotional distance as befitted the best barmen, looked at her aghast as he passed her a drink.

"They broke you," he whispered.

"No home. No job," she said. "God clearly hates me. Why?"

"That's more his department," said Lennox, jerking a thumb at the Archangel Michael, and went off to collect empties.

Nerys drank deeply.

"Well?" she said.

"The Almighty doesn't hate you," said Michael. "He loves unconditionally."

"What he's given me today doesn't exactly feel like love. Feels like a steaming plate of shit with a side order of rubbing my nose in it."

"He never gives us more ... woes than we can handle. And I'd be grateful if you could moderate your language when discussing the Lord."

"Fannybumwang to you, God," said Nerys with cheery spite. "So, did God tell you I was homeless and jobless?"

"No. The Almighty does not speak to me, um, directly these days."

"Sent you to Coventry, huh? I just assumed that, when you asked to meet me you here, well ..."

"Well, what?" said Michael.

"Can I stay at your place?" she said.

Michael was taken aback.

"Please," said Nerys.

"Oh. Um. I see."

"You know, I'm in need of somewhere to stay, and that bitch Tina deducted nearly five hundred quid from my final pay packet –

for coffee, for fuck's sake! – and I can't afford a hotel, and there's no way I'm dossing in Ben's basement, and ..."

"I would love to say yes," said Michael.

"It's very Christian of you."

"Would love to, but Andy and I have got the decorators in."

Nerys was momentarily robbed of speech.

"Ah," she managed eventually. "Decorators."

"Yes. Doing the bedrooms. Walls and ceilings. We've gone for a beautiful Tuscan colour range."

"Right. But they're not decorating at night, are they?"

"No. No. But Andy has got himself quite worked up, worried that they're going to leave splash marks on the furniture and woodwork. Things are a little ..." Michael pulled a tense expression, teeth gritted.

"No, sure," said Nerys, deflated.

"I'm sorry."

"I understand."

"Decorators."

"That's right."

"Tuscan."

"It's beautiful. Sorry."

Nerys sighed heavily, and then inhaled the remainder of her wine.

"So," she said, "why did you want to talk to me?"

"The beast," said Michael.

Clovenhoof's new phone rang as he clip-clopped down Boldmere High Street. There were no buttons on the slim and shiny device, only shifting icons on the screen. Trust humans to take something as simple and reliable as a button and fuck it up.

It took him several attempts to work out what the little green telephone symbol required of him but, as he shouted at it and pushed it with his fingers, something seemed to happen.

"Hello," he said into the phone.

"Where are you, Jeremy?" said Ben. "It's gone seven."

"On my way back. How's the dungeon bedsit coming on?"

"I've tried," said Ben tiredly. "I moved stuff out. I hoovered. I think the hoover's died now, choked on dead spiders and cobwebs.

It's still not particularly clean, and there's this weird, toilet-y funk in the air. All told, it's a bit gross."

"Sounds wonderful," said Clovenhoof merrily, and pushed open the door to Books 'n' Bobs. "Ding dong, I'm home."

He dumped his bag of supplies on the shop counter, and clattered down the stairs. The basement was just as Ben had described it. The essential grottiness of the basement had been retained, but Ben had cleared space for their belongings and a large double bed. Ben, rosy-cheeked and smeared with grime, stood in the middle of it all.

"Looking good," said Clovenhoof. "Job's a good un, Kitchen."

"It's not exactly the Ritz," said Ben.

"Oh, no. You'd have to go a lot further to find a room with this kind of charm." Clovenhoof tested the bed. It was high, but surprisingly soft. He looked under the quilt. Lumps and bumps distorted the sheet below. "You found a mattress?"

"Not quite," said Ben. "I knew we'd need something to sleep on, and I had brought a lot of pieces of taxidermy and I thought ..."

Clovenhoof's eyes sparkled.

"We're sleeping on a bed made of lots and lots of dead animals?"

"I'm not sure we should think of it like that," said Ben.

"It's brilliant!"

"Oh, well, if you're happy with it."

Clovenhoof clapped him on the shoulder.

"I'm impressed. This kind of ingenuity deserves a slapup tea."

"Thanks. I am rather hungry," agreed Ben.

"Good. The food's on the counter. You get cooking. I've got to set up my Twitter account," said Clovenhoof, waving his phone in Ben's face.

Michael and Nerys went to a corner where they could talk in private.

"For a moment, I thought I had imagined it," said Nerys.

"No, I saw it too," said Michael. "Perched on a rooftop, staring at me. As large as a tiger."

"Larger. What the Hell have you been cooking up in that lab, Michael?"

"It's not that kind of laboratory. I've seen the CCTV footage from when you broke in."

"Look, I'm sorry about that. I just had to see that dog."

"It's not Twinkle, Nerys."

"I know. And I shouldn't have done it, but your cock of a boss didn't have to send the video to Tina."

Michael grimaced.

"I think you got off lightly. The amount of damage done by ..." He straightened up and took a sip of mineral water. "So, tell me. What happened in the lab last night?"

"You saw the video."

"Yes, but I can't believe it. I want to hear it from you."

"Okay." Nerys put her hands flat on the table. "It was a dog. Just a dog. A little Yorkshire terrier. Friendly, lovely little thing. I was rescuing it. I was going to take it home. I reached down to put the collar on it and – Bam!"

"Bam?"

"It changed, like a bad special effect. It grew. Muscles, hair, teeth. It was the cutest little thing but then suddenly ... It ... It's like, you know, when you wake up after a night on the pull and you discover that the Johnny Depp you went to bed with has magically transformed into Johnny Vegas?"

"Er, no, but I take your point," said Michael. "But what you describe is not natural, it's not scientifically possible."

"Said the Archangel Michael." A thought occurred to her. "Was it a demon?"

"You think a demon has come up from Hell to terrorise suburban Birmingham?"

"I share a flat with Satan."

"Jeremy is not a demon. Technically."

"Nitpicker," said Nerys. "The thing is, the one thing that happened before the dog changed is that it touched my crucifix pendant." She held out the diamante pendant to show him. "You say it wasn't a demon, but the feeling I got from just looking at that thing ... I was so..." She struggled to find the words to express the religious terror that it had inspired in her.

"Cross," said Michael.

"I was too bloody frightened to be cross," she said.

"No. It's a cross, not a crucifix," he said. "A crucifix would have a little ..."

"Oh, shut up, Michael," she snapped. "And get me another drink."

"This is nice," said Clovenhoof, patting the covers as Ben put his cup of hot chocolate down on the bedside cabinet. His bedside cabinet was made from a stack of *Roy of the Rovers* annuals. Ben's was made from copies of Obama's *The Audacity of Hope*. Ben wore a miner's lamp on his forehead. Clovenhoof sipped his chocolate by the light of his new phone.

"I'm surprised Nerys didn't want to join us," said Ben, taking off his dressing gown and climbing in beside Clovenhoof.

"I did text her," said Clovenhoof.

"Maybe she's had a better offer. Anyway, three in the bed would be a bit snug."

Clovenhoof chuckled.

"You ever wondered what a threesome would be like?"

"With you and Nerys?" said Ben. "That's ... that's the most horrible thing I could possibly imagine."

"All right. The threesome of your choice. Mine would be me, obviously, and I think perhaps another me – because I am super sexy – and then the third person would be ... I'm tempted to say me again but I think I'll have to go with Eunice Gandridge."

"Who?"

"At the library."

"Dare I ask?"

"She's got this really strict manner," said Clovenhoof, and shuddered with pleasure. "Sometimes, I take books back late just so she can give me one of her looks. Also, she plays tuba in the Sutton Coldfield brass band, and I think if she can get her lips round one of those ..."

"Enough," said Ben. "Frankly, I think having sex with one person is scary enough. I can't imagine why anyone would want to do it with two."

Clovenhoof had lost interest. He was busily engaged in setting up accounts for every form of social media he could find and was currently creating @SatanColdfield on Twitter. He wasn't sure what Twitter was, or what it was for, but felt certain he should have it nonetheless.

"Anyway, it's been a long, tiring, and emotionally draining day," said Ben. "I think I shall say goodnight."

He flicked off his miner's lamp and shuffled down into the bed.

"Can I have some of the covers?" he said.

"You've got some of the covers," said Clovenhoof.

"Half the covers."

"Half? That's nearly most of them." Clovenhoof grudgingly pushed some of the quilt over.

"Thank you."

Clovenhoof looked at the red error message on his phone.

"Twitter wants to know how old I am. Why?"

"To ensure you're old enough to use it."

"Of course I'm old enough. Haven't they seen this face?"

"Just put in your date of birth. Now, I'm going to sleep. Goodnight."

Ben pulled the covers up closely and settled down. Seconds later, his eyes were open again as Clovenhoof dialled on his phone, his phone beeping loudly with each button press.

"What are you doing now?" muttered Ben, in the half-voice of a man trying to delude himself that he was on the cusp of sleep.

"I need to find out what my date of birth is."

"You don't know?"

"I need to know what it's *meant* to be."

"Meant? Are you in witness protection programme or something?"

"Something like that. Michael!"

"What is it, Jeremy?" said Michael. "I'm very busy at the moment."

This was only a half-lie, unlike the out-and-out lie Michael had told Nerys in order to avoid having to put her up for the night. It wasn't as though Nerys would have been the worst houseguest imaginable (that accolade belonged to Jeremy, of course), but the flat he shared with Andy was *their* flat, a haven from all the irritations, annoyances, and stupidity of the wider world. As far as he was concerned, the front door was an airlock, and he wasn't going to let any potential contaminant inside. He was sure it had been better to lie than to hurt her feelings.

On the other hand, he had only half-lied to Clovenhoof, because he was indeed busy, having left Nerys in the Boldmere Oak in order to pull an all-nighter at the lab, rebuilding the laboratory computer and restoring Little A to life. However, that mostly involved watching various percentage bars on the computer screen as the hardware and software reinstalled, reconfigured, and repaired the vital systems.

"How old am I?" said Clovenhoof.

"You phone me at ten o'clock to ask me that? You and I are older than time itself, Fallen One. We were there at the moment of creation. Do you not remember?"

"I'm not senile yet."

"More's the shame. I'm looking forward to the day you forget who I am and what my phone number is."

"Twitter wants to know how old I am."

Michael's brain leapt like a frightened gazelle and bounded to several rapid conclusions.

"No. Social media is not for you."

"Why not?"

"You are meant to be keeping a low profile while here on Earth."

"So are you, but I've seen you on the computer doing ... stuff."

"Yes, but I'm the responsible one."

"Fine. I'll just have to go to the registry office tomorrow and ask them to find my birth certificate."

Michael had a sudden image of the chaos Clovenhoof would cause at the register office, in search of a document forged by Heaven in the creation of Satan's earthly alias.

"Please don't," said Michael and, reluctantly, reeled off the date. "Do not give me cause to regret this," he said, and hung up.

Michael saw that he'd had a missed call while on the phone to Clovenhoof. There was a voicemail message. It was Andy, and he didn't sound happy.

"Michael. Dearest. I've just taken the strangest call from your friend, Nerys. I think she was drunk. She said that she knew she

210

couldn't stay at ours because of our bedroom situation, but suggested that perhaps we should put plastic sheeting down in the bedroom before the men came over so that the splash marks wouldn't stain the furniture. She understands that it can be quite messy – some men she's had in like to splash it all over the place, don't you know – but that if we just take sensible precautions, then I'll feel a lot more relaxed about it. You need to call me now, Michael, and explain."

"Good God," Michael whispered to himself.

The progress bars on the screen crept upwards very, very slowly. It was going to be a long night.

Nerys tottered back to the bar for her fifth glass of wine. Or perhaps the sixth.

"Lennox," she called. "Top me up."

"You really want another? Maybe it's time to move on."

Nerys pulled a face.

"Got nowhere to move on to, as you know full well."

"Life is full of hardships," he agreed, and opened a fresh bottle of Chardonnay.

"Hey, Lennox ..." she slurred.

"No."

"No, what?"

"The answer is no."

"You don't know what the question is yet. It might be, 'Hey, Lennox, would you like a million pounds?'"

"Is it?"

"Is it what?"

"Is it the question?"

"Er. No."

"Would the question be something along the lines of, 'Hey, Lennox, will you put me up for the night?'"

"Might be," she admitted.

"And the answer would be no." He passed her the glass. "Nerys, not that I advocate such things, but many's the night when you come here and go to a bed other than your own, if you catch my drift."

Nerys tried her best to look shocked, but she was drunk, and drunkenness ripped away the veil of social pretence and mock decency.

She turned around and scanned the bar. There was not much of a crowd in the Boldmere Oak on a Wednesday. There was a smattering of couples, and a bunch of men and women in one corner. Mixed sex groups were tough to break into, and it was always hard to figure who was paired up with whom. What she really needed was a single bloke or, failing that, a bunch of men together whom she could target generally.

She eyed her only option.

"Oh, well," she said. "Needs must when the devil knocks holes in your walls, floods your house, and gets you kicked out on the street."

She straightened her skirt, adjusted her cleavage, and strode over to the three men.

"So," she said, channelling her inner sex kitten, "which one of you stud muffins gets to take me home tonight?"

"Eh?" said one of them.

"I think she's saying your taxi's arrived, Arthur," said a second.

"I didn't order a taxi."

"Sorry, babe, I think Jim, Arthur, and I will just stick with our dominos, if it's all the same with you," said the third old man, and supped his pint of mild.

"Oh, come on," said Nerys. "When was the last time you felt the touch of a young woman?"

"It was during the three day week," said Jim. "I accidentally tripped and fell on my Jean during a power cut."

"What are the chances of that?" said the mild drinker.

"Quite low, Les," said Jim. "Had to do it three times before I got her."

"I think dominos is excitement enough for us," Les said to Nerys.

"You'd rather play children's games than ..."

She stopped as Jim held up a warning hand.

"Not a word more," he said. "The simplicity of the Game," he said with such emphasis, Nerys could hear the capital letter, "belies the complexity of the playing. A lifetime to master, dominos."

"Really?" she said.

"Really," said Les.

"Fine!" she declared loudly. "Then I'll make a bet with you. I'll play your piddling game and, if I win, one of you will give me a bed for the night."

"And if you lose?" said Jim.

"I'll ... I'll take off an item of clothing. Strip dominos."

"Does she have to?" said Les, distastefully. "I'd rather stick to my drink."

"Right. If I lose, I'll buy you beer."

"*And* strip off," said Arthur.

Nerys sighed.

"Have it your way." She sat down on a stool and nearly missed. "Deal me in, boys."

"You're stealing the quilt again," grumbled Ben, his eyes screwed shut, refusing to admit to himself that he was still awake.

"I've not moved at all," said Clovenhoof. "If you want it all, have it. I sleep above the covers most the time anyway."

"It gets cold. You'll have sciatica in the morning."

"No, I won't. I'll have Rice Krispies, like I usually do."

"Don't blame me if you get a chill."

"I'll find a way to keep myself warm," said Clovenhoof, and farted loudly.

"Oh, God!" choked Ben.

"Better out than in," said Clovenhoof.

"No. No, it's bloody not. It's never better out than in. In is infinitely preferable to out. Agh! What have you been eating?"

"Nothing. The usual. Crispy pancakes. A Lambrini night cap. That hot chocolate was nice, by the way."

"Thank you."

"I liked the chocolate chip sprinkles."

"I didn't put in any chocolate sprinkles."

"Who's Taylor Swift?"

"What?"

"He, or possibly she, has lots of Twitter followers. Should I follow him?"

"She's an American ..." Ben ummed.

"An American what?"

Ben exhaled, and thought for a moment. "Nope. That's all I've got."

"Do you think she'll follow me back?"

"No."

"Oh. Screw her, then. Ooh, God's got a Twitter account."

"Great. Now shut up and go to sleep."

"And the pope."

"Good for him. Go to sleep."

"And, look. A whole load of local shops and stuff. Follow, follow, follow."

Ben huffed mightily.

"Damn it, Jeremy! Are you tweeting, or just trying to annoy me?"

"I can do both."

Ben tried to roll himself more securely into his sheets, as though he could physically force himself down into sleep.

"Just quit it," he seethed. "And, while you're at it, whatever you're scratching, just stop. Consider it fully scratched."

"I'm not scratching anything," said Clovenhoof.

"I can hear you."

"Mate, I'm an expert at one-handed web surfing, but it takes both hands to tweet."

"Whatever. It's late now. Be quiet."

"Fine," whispered Clovenhoof.

Ben exhaled. The bed of mounted animals was very soft and, apart from the occasional paw or snout, very comfortable indeed. It would only a moment or two before he dropped off ...

"Findus Crispy Pancakes. Follow. SCUM. Follow. Lambrini. Follow. National Rifle Association. Follow."

Ben contemplated pulling a couple of smaller mammals out of the bed and stuffing them in his ears.

"Ooh, WeirdBrum has tweeted that a strange and unpleasant creature has been spotted roaming the streets of Sutton."

"Is that so?" fumed Ben. "That's odd, because I could swear blind that the strange and unpleasant creature is currently in this basement and irritating the living shit out of me!"

"Really? I can't see it anywh... Oh, you mean me."

"Yes, I fucking mean you! Frankly, any weird or dangerous creature would make a better bedmate than you!"

"I don't know. This artist's impression makes it look like a Hellhound on steroids."

"Christ, Jeremy. Can't you hear the exasperation in my voice? Why won't you let me get some sleep?"

"Free the nipple."

"What?!"

"It's this campaign on Twitter. Some of the SCUM mothers are following it. It's about getting your tits out to show gender equality, I think. I'm all for that. Follow."

"That's it!" shrieked Ben, sitting upright in the darkness. "I've had it!"

"Have you?"

"We can't share a bed!"

"Quite clearly, since you've got all the covers and won't stop shouting."

"Shouting? I'm only shouting because the dozy twat next to me won't turn his phone off, won't stop scratching, won't stop talking to me, and – for God's sake, Jeremy! – stop rubbing your feet against me! Are you wearing slippers or something?"

"That's a big fat no. Me and footwear tend not to get on. Er, Ben? You know taxidermy?"

"What the ...?"

"Do you always check that the animals are, like, dead before you stuff them?"

"Shut up, you moron! Shut up, shut up, shut up! Shut your idiotic pie hole and stop asking stupid questions!"

"It's just that there are two fellers sat on the bed, looking at me."

Ben formed the opening sounds of a stern and expletive-laden rebuke when his brain interrupted him.

The furry form rubbing against his feet. The scratching.

"Chocolate chip sprinkles?" he said.

He flicked on his miner's lamp and instantly wished he hadn't.

Thank God for stockings, thought Nerys. If she had chosen to wear one-piece tights that morning, she would have been forced to remove them *and* something even more intimate. Sitting in knickers and blouse (her bra having been artfully removed from beneath, in a move that nearly gave Jim a heart attack), Nerys felt confident she retained a level of dignity.

Jim had had to go off home for a bit of a lie-down. Les had his head on the table amid various empty glasses, and was now snoring. Arthur blinked rapidly and tried to focus on his dominos.

"S'your go," he said.

"Is it?" said Nerys, and pushed a tile onto the table. "Think that's right."

Arthur peered, shrugged, and then slammed down his last piece.

"Out!" he declared, and drained his pint. "I've won."

"Oh," said Nerys.

"Wha's me prize?" he said.

Nerys frowned.

"I think you get to take me home for the night."

"Whoopee. Come on then, luv."

Nerys helped Arthur on with his jacket, and then gathered her clothes up off the floor. She tried to put her skirt on, but gave up after three failed attempts to get one foot inside it.

"Balls to it," she said, and, half supporting him, half leaning on him, guided Arthur towards the door.

Ben and Clovenhoof beat a fighting retreat up the basement stairs. Ben had turned on the Henry hoover and waved the nozzle aggressively at the tide of curious cellar rats.

"I think one's gone up my tube!" he yelled.

Clovenhoof, who in a past existence had spent many a joyful hour in Hell's Pit of Carnivorous Rodents, smiled wryly.

"The Marquis de Sade said the same thing to me once."

"What?"

"Nothing," said Clovenhoof, and cheerfully batted a rat off a step with a copy of James Herriot's *All Creatures Great and Small*.

"There's one on my shoulder!" yelled Ben.

"Hang on," said Clovenhoof, raised his phone, and took a picture.

"Don't just stand there!" Ben screeched.

Clovenhoof typed a comment on his phone.

"There's a rat on ma Kitchen, what am I gonna do? Hashtag, best night ever."

"Jeremy!"

Clovenhoof casually picked up the brown rat, tossed it down the basement stairs, and closed the door. Ben frantically spun in a circle, checking himself for any further hangers on.

"That was fun," said Clovenhoof.

"Fun?" said Ben, on the verge of tears. "I've been traumatised and violated."

"Fun," agreed Clovenhoof. "Now what? Another cup of cocoa and down again for round two?"

"Christ, no. We've got to find somewhere else to spend the night. I bet Nerys has found some cosy hotel for herself."

"Maybe she'll let us kip on her floor," said Clovenhoof, and opened the track-my-child app he had installed on his phone. "It's a good job I slipped one of Animal Ed's GPS trackers in her purse."

"You put a tracking device on Nerys?" said Ben, surprised.

"Don't judge me."

"Actually, I think it's a pretty smart idea."

Michael threw the last of the ruined samples into the yellow biohazard bin. Waiting for the laboratory computer to rebuild itself had given him time to put the lab space in some sort of order. The rampaging beast had indeed set them back by months but, with the salvaged samples and data set neatly aside, at least the road ahead was clear.

As he tidied, Michael's eyes kept returning to the large square of chipboard that had been placed over the hole in the wall. Maybe it was because it was nighttime, but Michael couldn't stop thinking of how flimsy chipboard was, and the strength with which the beast had torn its way out of that very wall.

"Maybe I should ask Chip to park one of his vans in front of the hole," Michael mused.

"Shall I put that as a reminder in your calendar?" said Little A.

Michael looked around in delight.

"Little A!"

"Yes, Michael?"

All the progress bars on the screen had reached one hundred percent. Green ticks ran down the list of diagnostic routines.

"You're back."

"I think I might have been ... unwell," said Little A.

"Just a little too much to drink," said Michael. "Little A, show me your most recent activity log."

Dates, times, and events raced up the screen.

"What was happening in the lab before you went off-line?" said Michael.

"I offered to make you an omelette, and then you told me to run a diagnostic check, and then I said, 'can anyone smell sm...' and then I went off-line."

"No, before that. What happened when the dog appeared?"

A video screen popped up. In the centre was the sequencing cabinet. Low resolution prevented Michael clearly seeing what was going on, but a shape appeared to form inside the cabinet.

"What's that?"

"Sample CZ005."

"What do you mean?"

On the screen, the cabinet shuddered and then tipped over. Glass smashed, and a furry bundle rolled out and off screen.

"The dog was in the cabinet?" said Michael.

"Yes. Sample CZ005," said Little A.

"No, that's nonsense. Sequenced samples do not spontaneously turn into little dogs," he said, and then mentally added, and little dogs do not spontaneously turn into monstrous beasts. But this one did.

"Tell me about sample CZ005."

"It came from supplier 255. You have an open reminder to speaker to supplier 255 about his packaging choices."

"But what is it a sample of?"

"It was labelled as a bat-eared fox."

218

"That's no fox."

"However, I do have a full genetic analysis of the sample."

"Yes?"

"Canis lupis familiaris 43%."

"So, it is dog."

"Sciurus vulgaris 27%."

"Squirrel?"

"Martes martes, 19%."

"What's that? Pine marten?"

"Yes. And 11% unknown."

"Unknown?"

"Possibly capra nubiana."

"What's that?"

"Wild goat."

"Wild goat?" said Michael, confused. "How the Hell did that get in there? The only wild goat I know is Jeremy," he chuckled humourlessly.

The chuckle died almost instantly in his throat.

Arthur flopped back on the bed. Nerys pulled off his shoes, and dropped them on the floor. The old man focussed blearily again on Nerys.

"Why're you here, again? You're not the home help, are ya?"

"No, I'm Nerys," said Nerys. "You agreed to put me up."

"Ah," said Arthur. "Were we going to have sex?"

"I hadn't necessarily planned ..."

"Because I don't think I'm up to it, luv."

"Oh, well, if you're certain."

"I think I'd rather just have a cuppa. Could you do that for me?"

"With pleasure," said Nerys, giving the drunk old geezer a warm smile.

"Besides, you're not really my type."

"Oh. Right."

"I like more of your ... your wosname ... Beyonce type. With the ..." Arthur mimed a curvaceous backside.

"You get a lot of them round here, Arthur?"

"Man can dream," he said, and closed his eyes.

"How do you have your tea?" she asked at the door.

"Hot and sweet," he murmured.

"Course you do."

"Lots of sweet, sweet sugar," he said and, perhaps drifting off into improbable dreams of Beyonce Knowles, performed a mime that Nerys was sure elderly gentlemen had no rights to know.

Nerys was on a plateau of drunkenness. She knew she wasn't going to get any drunker, recognised that, technically speaking, she was utterly smashed but, in recognising it, was able to function in a very limited capacity. Moving cautiously, as though the floor was made of slick ice, she stepped out of Arthur's bedroom, past the empty bedroom she had ear-marked for herself, and went into the kitchen to make a cup of tea for the now snoring Arthur. It was the least she could do in thanks.

She found the kettle, momentarily fought to get it off its stand, and then filled it at the sink. At that point, she saw the horned figure leering at her through the kitchen window. She screamed, dropped the kettle, and sprayed much of the kitchen with tap water.

"Bloody Hell, Jeremy!" she yelled.

She then saw Ben, seemingly wearing nothing but pyjamas, stood beside Clovenhoof in the alleyway.

She went to the back door, unlocked it, and opened it.

"What the bloody Hell?" she said.

"We need somewhere to stay," said Ben.

"What about the bookshop?"

Ben's face paled.

"It didn't end well," said Clovenhoof.

"Well, you can't stay here," she hissed. "How did you find me, anyway?"

"Tracker app," said Clovenhoof, and held up his phone. "Hang on. Stay there."

The phone's camera flash momentarily blinded Nerys.

"Hashtag, don't fancy yours much," said Clovenhoof.

"You two need to piss off," she said. "And now."

"But we've got nowhere to go," said Ben.

"You've no idea what I had to go through to get a bed tonight," she said.

"Depraved and sordid acts," said Clovenhoof, nodding.

"Dominos," she said.

"The pizza?" said Ben.

"The game."

"I don't understand."

"I think it's a sex act. I think you have to crouch behind them and stick your tongue up their ..."

"The bloody game!" squeaked Nerys. "Tiles. Dots."

"What am I thinking of then?" said Jeremy.

"There's an old man in bed back there who will not be pleased to find I've let two strangers into his house."

"We'll be quiet," said Ben.

"Like perverts loitering in bushes," said Jeremy.

"Or church mice, perhaps," suggested Ben.

Nerys looked at the pathetically hopeful expressions on their faces and relented.

"You both sleep on the sofa. You get up at six ..."

"But it's gone two a.m. already," complained Ben.

"... *At six*, and you are out of here."

"Fine," said Ben tiredly.

They stepped inside. Clovenhoof looked at the half-filled kettle.

"And if you're making a cup of tea, that'd be great."

"I'm not making you a cup of tea, Jeremy."

Clovenhoof tutted.

"Ben made me a lovely cup of hot chocolate with sprinkles."

"Those weren't sprinkles," said Ben. "They were rat droppings."

Clovenhoof sucked at something between his teeth.

"Bold choice, Kitchen."

"Just get in here and let me get some sleep," said Nerys. "I've had the worst forty-eight hours of my life. I've not only lost my house, but I've also lost my job because Michael's been conducting freaky Frankenstein experiments in his lab and turned a little dog into some ravenous monster that's now prowling the streets of Sutton Coldfield."

"What?" said Ben. "A monster? Are you drunk?"

"Of course, I'm drunk," said Nerys. "But it's true."

"But how is that even possible?"

Clovenhoof suddenly clicked his fingers.

"A thought?" said Ben.

"Rusty trombone," said Clovenhoof. "That's what I was thinking of."

The first rays of dawn crept through the gaps in the chipboard of the laboratory wall.

Michael had been deep in thought for several hours. An archangel who had watched over the Almighty's creation for aeons, he was capable of sitting in thought almost indefinitely. He had reams of genetic data on the computer. He had the laboratory CCTV footage and the video on his own phone. In his left hand, he held a plastic freezer bag decorated with penguins and snowflakes. In his right hand, he held a pink dog collar that had been torn apart.

"It's Jeremy," he said.

"Sorry, Michael?" said Little A.

"Talking to myself," said Michael. "Actually, could you put a call through to Jeremy Clovenhoof?"

"Are you sure, Michael? It is only seven a.m."

Michael grunted appreciatively. Programming AI with manners and a sense of decency was tricky, but much underrated.

"To Hell with him," said Michael.

Clovenhoof was dragged from sleep by the peculiar sensation of his chest vibrating. For a frightening moment, he wondered if this was what a heart attack felt like. Then he remembered that he couldn't die, and relaxed.

He had been lying in a fat armchair, head lolling over one arm, hoofy legs dangling over the other. Ben lay curled up on the sofa. Additionally, an angry woman was banging on the window and swearing.

Clovenhoof gave her a cheery thumbs up, and answered the phone.

"Hello, Happy Endings Massage Parlour. No job too small. How can I help you?"

"Jeremy, it's Michael."

"Good. I'm glad we got that cleared up," he said, and killed the call.

Clovenhoof went to the window. He was surprised to recognise the woman. She had a furious look on her face. He opened the front door.

"It's Stella, isn't it? Belle's grandma?" he said. "Come to arrange the funeral plans for little Nemo?"

"What the Hell are you doing here?" she spat.

"I often ask myself the same thing. It's life's great conundrum."

"Where's our Arthur?"

"Arthur?"

"*Our* Arthur?" croaked Ben, waking up.

"Did he say you could crash here?"

"No, Nerys did," said Clovenhoof.

"Nerys?"

Clovenhoof's phone started to vibrate again.

"And you would be Arthur's, um ... better half?" said Ben.

Stella stabbed Clovenhoof in the chest with a gaudily painted nail.

"I blame you for the attitude I get from Spartacus. He used to be such a good boy, my grandson. Then you take Bea, my granddaughter. Try to make me look stupid while you're doing it! I hear you've been propositioning my Toyah. And now Toyah's dad! Sure, we've not been together for years but ..." She shook with anger. "Are you trying to muscle in on my whole family? And who the Hell are *you*?"

This last was directed to Nerys, standing in the doorway, in a blouse and knickers, and holding her head delicately. Her hair was all over the place, as though each individual strand was doing its damnedest to flee the hangover.

"What's going on?" she mumbled.

"Whore!" shouted Stella.

"Easy now," said Ben, disapprovingly.

Stella, moving with surprising speed for an older woman, leapt at Nerys, nails out like talons. Nerys squealed and hid behind the door.

Clovenhoof answered the phone.

"What is it, Michael?"

"I need to ask you a simple question," said Michael and then, "What's going on in the background?"

Clovenhoof assessed the scene thoughtfully.

"An old lady who wants me to cremate her fish is trying to claw Nerys's eyes out because she thinks Nerys slept with her ex, even though Nerys did nothing of the sort, but only played dominos with him, which is not a sex act but a game with tiles. Was that the question you phoned up to ask me?"

"No."

"Then shoot."

"Did you offer to sell Ed Lawrence a genetic sample for a bat-eared fox but actually give him cuttings of your own hair mixed in with that of Twinkle and various stuffed animals from Ben's taxidermy collection?"

"That's an oddly specific question, wouldn't you say?"

"Did you," said Michael with the slow, quiet tone of the deeply annoyed, "stop to think what would happen if the DNA of the Fallen One, the Prince of Hell, formerly one of the most powerful spiritual beings in all Creation, was fed into a DNA sequencing machine, if that mystical coding was unlocked by the tools of modern science?"

"No," said Clovenhoof, feeling an excitement grow in his belly. "Something terrible I should think. Or amazing. Was it amazing?"

Michael began to shout. And then he began to swear. It grew in volume until it eventually matched the profanities Stella was hurling at Nerys through the closed door. Clovenhoof listened for a minute and then, bored, put the phone down and went into the kitchen to make himself that cup of tea Nerys had rudely failed to make for him the previous night.

Chapter 8 – In which Nerys searches for a job, Ben searches for a beast, and everyone has to learn to live together

Nerys followed Clovenhoof as he unlocked the door of the garage and ushered Ben ahead of him. He flipped a switch to illuminate the large space. Nerys blinked at the brightness of the fluorescent strips, which contrasted sharply with the deepening shadows of outside. They stepped around the shining hearses and went through a discreet door at the back.

"Right, the stairs or the lift?" said Clovenhoof.

"Oh, lift please, my feet are killing me," said Nerys.

Clovenhoof opened a cage and indicated the space beyond with a wave of his hand. It was low and wide. Nerys peered down to stare at the dusty interior.

"You're an arsehole, Jeremy Clovenhoof," she said. "That's for coffins!"

"It can be, if it wants to be. Not everything has to have a label. It's that kind of judgemental thinking that cost you your job."

Nerys considered slapping him, but she was too tired.

"Well, it can take my bags at least."

She tossed a backpack and a large holdall into the lift. They trudged up two flights of stairs, through a door, and emerged into a large storage space.

"This place is a dump," said Ben.

"This is a funeral directors," said Clovenhoof. "Show a little more reverence and respect."

Nerys stared at the chaotic mess and wondered how they ever found anything.

"A funeral directors should be tidier than this," she said.

"You know, that's what Gordon Buford keeps telling me."

There were folding signs to indicate that a funeral was in progress; there had to be enough here to close the Aston Expressway. There were badly folded piles of sombre velvet throws. There were various stands, for coffins, for wreaths, and for other unclear purposes. But the main feature of the storage area, the thing one simply couldn't ignore, was coffins. They were piled up on every side, cheap pine coffins, fancy mahogany coffins, and something that looked like a chrysalis for an alien life form.

"Is that coffin cardboard?"

"That's the eco pod, we put dead hippies in those," said Clovenhoof. "Closest thing you can get to being thrown on the compost heap. You can have one of those if you like. I've got something comfier lined up for my sleeping quarters."

Clovenhoof pulled out a luxury coffin and tested the depth of the satin padding with a hand.

"Seriously?" asked Ben. "Then why did we get these sleeping bags from the scout hut?"

"You can put your sleeping bag on this concrete floor if you like, but I'll take a bit of padding and a draught-proof surround every time," said Clovenhoof.

Ben gave a small nod on acknowledgement and started to investigate the other coffins.

"So, this isn't exactly an official arrangement," said Nerys.

"Nope."

"How often do people come up here, Jeremy?"

"Hardly ever. I'm supposed to be doing a stock take at the moment, so I've told them all that if they want something from up here then they need to ask me. Genius, eh?"

Nerys rolled her eyes."

"No windows, that's handy," said Ben.

"Yup. So as long as we don't enter or leave during working hours, then we're fine."

Nerys realised that the lift hadn't yet arrived at the top. She went over to peer at it.

"Jeremy, the lift is stuck!"

He sauntered over, pressed the button, and sucked through his teeth when it made a distant groaning sound, like a wounded buffalo.

"Yeah, it does that sometimes."

"So, how can I get to my stuff?" Nerys asked, anxiety gnawing at her.

"We'll call the engineer in the morning. They normally get to us within a week or so."

"You're joking. You must be joking. Ha ha?" Nerys gave Clovenhoof a pleading look. "All the things that I brought here, which pretty much equals all the things I have in the world at this moment in time, are stuck in that lift?"

"Yup."

"And I can't get to them."

"Nope."

"Is that what you're saying?"

"I'm pretty sure it is."

Nerys stared at the lift entrance, trying to imagine how she was going to survive the coming days with no fresh clothes, no toiletries, and no gossip magazines in the company of a pair of buffoons.

"No," she whispered, "it's just not possible."

Ben and Clovenhoof looked on as she sank to her knees and tried to reach down to the lift cage, her hands clawing ineffectually at empty air.

Clovenhoof clapped his hands together.

"Right, let's get this show on the road. We've got everything we need in here. I'll get a meal on, shall I?"

Nerys turned around and slumped despondently against the wall.

Well, I'm sure some grub will make us all feel better," said Ben. "What's on the menu?"

"We're pretty much limited to Pot Noodles, as we've only got a kettle. Do you want beef and tomato or Chinese chicken? My treat for this evening, we can take it in turns to cook."

Nerys hugged her knees and tried not to scream.

"Beef and tomato, please."

There was a toilet, a kettle, and space for them all to sleep. Clovenhoof was pleased with himself. He'd got his friends out of a sticky situation there. He was dimly aware that he had been the one to cause the sticky situation, but he'd come good. It would mean that they all had to live closely together for a few weeks, until the flats were made habitable once more, but they were mates. They knew each other well enough to manage.

"What do you mean, it's the wrong way round?" snapped Ben.

"The new sheet hangs from the front, everyone knows that!" replied Nerys.

"No. Sorry," said Ben in what Clovenhoof recognised as his 'listen, madam, I'm not a sexist, but I'm a man, and you're going to have to trust me on this' tone. "That is utterly wrong. It looks wrong. I can't live with it like that."

Clovenhoof was surprised to hear his friends shouting at each other. Normally they would be shouting at him. He felt oddly left out. He wandered through to find them both outside the toilet cubicle, red in the face, staring each other down.

"Jeremy, which way round should the toilet paper hang? It's critical that Ben understands it should *not* hang down the back like that!"

"It's like you don't understand any of the basic ways that a bathroom works, Nerys!" said Ben. "I bet it's you who squeezes the toothpaste from the middle."

"What are you talking about now, Ben? What other way of squeezing it is there?"

"From the end, of course! You make sure that the flow is even and the weight of the tube is balanced."

Nerys rolled her eyes.

"You're talking about the olden days when toothpaste was in tubes made of lead or whatever it was. It was always difficult to get the last bits out of those, unless you were an OCD type who rolled it up from the end, but we've moved on now. The plastic ones sort themselves out. Oh! That's what you are, isn't it? You're so OCD that you're basically incapable of sharing a bathroom! If it wasn't the toothpaste, it would be that I moved your jar of bath salts."

"Those aren't bath salts. They're toenails."

"They're *what?* What kind of a person, grabbing the bare essentials for a shoestring existence in a funeral home, takes their toenail collection?"

"It's not weird or anything," said Ben.

"Yes, it is. Fuck Hell, it is. Back in the good old days, they'd lock you in the loony bin for that."

"The state of your nails is a good indicator of overall health. They indicate the levels of nutrients and impurities in the body. It's like ice cores or tree segments. It's a glimpse back into biological history."

"It's bloody crazy, you revolting man!"

Nerys's voice reached a high pitched scream, making Ben wince with its ferocity. Clovenhoof decided to give his ears a rest by retreating, but he'd captured the entire exchange on video using his phone, so he trotted off cheerfully to review his footage.

Ben was pleased with the space he'd created for himself in the storage room. He felt quite at home, surrounded as he was by the last remnants of his taxidermy supplies, a handful of salvaged wargaming soldiers, and the last remaining animals from his collection.

He had also been creating grand plans for his next piece of work. In pride of place on the wall was a large scale map of Boldmere and Sutton Coldfield. He had found a cupboard with some stationery supplies, and had spent a happy couple of hours using string, glue sticks, and pictures from the newspaper.

"What's this?" said Clovenhoof.

"Project Beast," said Ben, intoning the words in a low and ominous voice.

"Pardon?"

"Project Beast," said Ben, and then coughed as the cinema trailer voice proved too much for his vocal cords. "These are all sightings of the creature Nerys was talking about. She's far from being the only one who's seen it. I'm trying to spot patterns and clues in the seemingly random sightings that had been reported so far."

"Why?"

"Why what?"

"Why are you interested?"

"It's fascinating, isn't it?" said Ben, and then, "And, although I'm sure the authorities want to capture it alive, if they end up shooting it – and I must emphasise I'm not saying they should – then it would be nice if a local taxidermist was on hand to preserve this unique specimen."

Clovenhoof looked at one of the pictures.

"You do know that one's a tabby cat, don't you?" he said, pointing. "You can even see its collar."

"That's not a collar," said Ben. "The eye witness said it was bloody entrails, dragging behind it as it snarled at her from her garden path."

"Did the eye witness also say how big the beast of Boldmere was?" asked Clovenhoof.

"She says it stood four feet high at the shoulder," said Ben. "She managed to get her kids out of the way just in time."

"That's amazing," said Clovenhoof.

"Yes. Amazing to think that this thing walks amongst us," said Ben, his eyes bright. "It could be crouched around any corner, ready to spring out at an innocent member of the public."

"No, I mean it's amazing that she has a watering can that's four feet high. It's the same size as the beast. Must be back-breaking work to water her flowers with that thing."

Ben sighed, and squinted sideways at the photo.

"Maybe this one is a fake. It does seem to be a different colour in the other photos."

He pulled the suspect photo down from his wall, and picked up some fur samples, comparing them with the other grainy images.

"Would you say it's dark weasel, or is it closer to mole?" he asked.

"I'd say it's a dead ringer for Satan's pubes," said Clovenhoof.

"Has it got a webcam?" asked Nerys, as Ben set up the laptop on a handy coffin.

"Yes," said Ben, "this is my old laptop, but it's got everything you're going to want, I think. Only thing to watch is the keyboard. The *t* key doesn't work."

"I'll be able to manage, I'm sure. I won't need the keyboard to become a YouTube sensation."

"So, what is it you're doing, exactly?" asked Ben.

"Ooh, I'll practise my spiel on you," said Nerys, clapping her hands in excitement.

She shifted in her chair and assumed her presenter's face. Serious but sultry. Could she get away with an Angelina Jolie pout? She pushed her lips forward slightly. A bit more, maybe. Sultry.

Ben frowned.

"A bucket, Jeremy, quickly!"

"I'm busy!" Clovenhoof shouted.

"Nerys is going to puke!"

"No, I'm not, you idiot!" said Nerys, exasperated. "I was just, you know, trying on a face. That one's not working then?"

Ben shook his head.

Clovenhoof appeared, his phone raised.

"Where's the puking?"

"You're filming this?" said Nerys.

"False alarm," said Ben. "Nerys was just trying on a face. She's going to become a YouTube sensation, apparently."

"I was just about to explain what my videos are going to be all about." Nerys tried to compose her features into something less alarming. She smiled at them, and imagined her grateful viewers. "My name is Nerys Thomas, and I want to share with you the accumulated wisdom from my time in the dating game. It's a jungle out there, but I can help you find your way."

She gave a knowing smile.

"Which jungle animal are you, a cougar?" asked Clovenhoof.

"I'm far too young to be a cougar, Jeremy. I may not be love's young dream anymore, but I'm a long way off cougar. I see myself more as a MILF, only, you know, without any actual kids. Having said that, cougar dating advice has a nice ring to it. I might use that." She attempted a sexy feline yowl, but stopped when Ben advanced again with the bucket.

"Give us some advice then," said Clovenhoof, still wielding the camera phone.

"I think I'll start with clothes," mused Nerys. "Right, viewers, I'm assuming that you've done the necessary research on your dating partner. If not, we'll cover that in a separate video. I mean, that's dating 101 and, if you haven't done that kind of research, you really do need help. Anyway, you'll know if he's a boobs or bottom man by now, so you will select your outfit to showcase your assets accordingly. I recommend a push-up bra and some sort of laced-up top for boob men. They love to unleash the girls by undoing the top." Nerys thrust her chest forward and pointed, in case her audience was slow in catching on.

Ben shuffled uncomfortably.

"Do you think that people really want to see this sort of thing?"

Clovenhoof snorted. "From what I've seen, the internet was *made* for this sort of thing. Carry on, Nerys."

"Right, where were we? Oh, yes. If you've got a bottom man, then you'll be wanting the highest heels you can stand up in, so it makes your bum stick out. Don't worry about being able to walk in them. If you follow my advice, you won't be on your feet for too long." She winked at her audience, and then relaxed her features. "So, stuff like that. I'll be doing regular updates, guiding people through the delicate art of dating, step by step."

"The delicate art of getting laid you mean?" said Clovenhoof. "You'll be a hit, Nerys. The internet's going to love this."

He wandered off, tapping away on his phone.

Clovenhoof had already built up a substantial following on Twitter and Vine, and dozens of friends on Facebook, and they seemed hungry for more updates, so he uploaded the video of Nerys trying her weird faces and vocal styles, followed by her dating advice. He put some thought into the correct hashtag, settled on #shagmebigboy, and posted the video onto all of his social media channels. He then spent a few minutes arranging Ben's taxidermy animals into sex positions so he could take some pictures to upload later to Snapchat.

Clovenhoof was particularly enjoying the voyeuristic side of social media. He had found Sandra on Facebook without too much difficulty, and discovered that she had over a thousand friends. She only seemed to actively talk to about six of them, but it was like having tentacles that spread throughout the community. There was very little that occurred in a five mile radius that Sandra wasn't alerted to by one of her friends. He'd already set about systematically friending Sandra's many contacts, and their contacts too.

SCUM had its own Facebook group that shared parenting problems as diverse as which nappy brand was best (this was something akin to the war between Heaven and Hell, he discovered) to the delicate question of what time was considered too early to start drinking wine. Clovenhoof's own views on alcohol were straightforward (it was never too early), whereas the ladies of SCUM had built up a set of rules based on things like whether it was a school night and whether you were with friends or alone. He scrolled back through old discussions and discovered that very little was off limits to this group. He particularly enjoyed the lengthy debate about post coital clean-up rituals, and determined that his new aim would be to start a discussion as fruitful and entertaining as that one. He started them off with a "whose bum print is this?" photo competition. He hoped to find some entertaining responses, and maybe even some more pictures when he checked back later, rather than the slightly bland chatter about the next day's protest in the park.

The expulsion of the SCUM group from the Consecr8 church hall had stirred up some discontent among the mums, and so they were gathering for a picnic to stand up for mums' rights to breastfeed in public. Although the protest picnic sounded dull, he was all in favour of public breastfeeding. No, he corrected himself, it should be positively encouraged, if not mandatory. There was nothing like some al fresco chesticles on display to lift a man's spirit, and it was positively selfish of women to hide them away.

Clovenhoof went to clean himself up. The only thing he'd been able to find to make a bum print was a jar of raspberry jam in Ben's things. He was sure that, if he scraped carefully, he'd be able to get it all back in the jar before Ben noticed any was missing.

Nerys had lost her patience so many times that she decided it had left for good, in search of a better owner. She put on a brave face when Michael visited.

"Thank God! Someone who could pass for an adult," she said. "You have no idea how much I need a conversation that doesn't consist of mumbling or farting. How's the decorating going?"

"The what?"

"The decorating. You were having your bedroom done."

"That's right. Yes, it looks lovely now."

"So, it's finished?" said Nerys hopefully.

Michael caught the look in her eye.

"Er, yes, but we're now having a new en suite shower installed."

"In the bedroom?"

"In an ensuite, yes."

"After you've just painted?"

"I know. We should think before we do these things. And, obviously, that's going to take a long while, because we're not even sure of how to get the plumbing connected to that part of the house." He looked at her. "Sorry. I'm sure it's not that bad here."

Nerys scoffed.

"These two Neanderthals are driving me to distraction."

Michael smiled.

"Well, I can understand that being cooped up is frustrating. I brought you something that might cheer you up."

Nerys grinned.

"Ooh, presents! You are indeed looking at people whose worldly goods are in short supply. If you've brought me some underwear or make up, I might just die with gratitude. Oh."

Nerys's face fell as Michael pulled out a Bible and offered it to her.

"You're out of work, Nerys. You need the comfort that scripture can offer."

Nerys wilted. The look on Michael's face was so earnest, so – bloody – loving, and here he was giving her what felt like homework.

"The Bible? Really?"

"You can't tell me you don't have time to read it."

"But it's so long and so ..."

"Important?" said Michael.

The word 'boring' died in Nerys's throat.

"Fine," she huffed, and accepted the book.

It was heavy. It even felt boring.

"Just start at the beginning. It's powerful stuff."

"Sure. Well, as it happens, I've been very busy today," said Nerys, putting the Bible aside. "Not only have I taken the first steps in my new online venture, but I have also been working on my next job. I have, ahem, retained the login details for the Helping Hand software that matches a person's personality and skills to their ideal job. Apparently, I was in completely the wrong job! I should be a legal adviser."

"Goodness me," said Michael. "Well, it's nice to see you motivated, Nerys."

"Oh, I bounce back quickly."

"Don't you need a degree for that sort of job?" said Michael.

"Yeah," said Clovenhoof, rising dracula-style from a nearby coffin. "Do you have a university education, Nerys?" he asked with unconvincing innocence.

"I have had plenty of university-based education," she said carefully.

"And we don't mean learning how to score free drinks in the student union bar."

"Listen, the degree question is a grey area," said Nerys. "That part of the questionnaire was focused more around what level you're aiming for."

"I don't think it's a grey area," said Michael. "You either have a degree or you don't. It's not as if you're studying for one."

"Well, I could. I'm plenty smart enough. The key thing is that my skills and personality are a great match." She ticked them off on her fingers. "I'm an expert at making decisions that affect other people, giving advice, and organising others."

"Do they tell all bossy people that they should be legal advisors?" asked Clovenhoof. "It seems unlikely, given that they mostly seem to work in your old office."

"Take a look for yourself," said Nerys, turning the laptop screen to Clovenhoof. "Computers never lie."

Clovenhoof picked up the laptop and moved away with it.

"I have to put up with this sort of thing all day, Michael," said Nerys. "*That's* why I'm motivated to get a new job."

Michael moved over to the wall to look at the map that Ben had been working on.

"Well now, this is interesting," he said. "The famous Beast of Boldmere. Are you trying to track it down?"

"God, no," shuddered Nerys. "It's Ben's. I don't want to see that thing ever again. Jeremy's developed a bit of a fixation on the thing."

"Well, he would, wouldn't he?" said Michael, glaring at Clovenhoof.

"Why?"

"Oh, nothing. And this is Ben's obsession too, eh?"

"I think he wants to stuff it. I, for one, can't see why anyone want to seek it out, for God's sake."

"For God's sake indeed," said Michael, examining his fingernails. "Someone who wants to do good in this world for reward in the next might want to find it in order to protect others,"

"Seriously?" Nerys spat. "If you wanted to do good for others, you could've at least brought some alcohol with you."

"He's way ahead of you there," said Ben, entering with a tray of drinks. "Michael's brought us a couple of bottles of vino destructo."

"If it was good enough for our Lord ..." smiled Michael.

Upon second inspection, what Ben was actually carrying was a tiny promotional coffin lid with a set of urns on it.

"Are those for ashes?" Nerys asked, picking one up. She hesitated, but then downed the drink. "Whatever."

"I was just admiring your map, Ben," said Michael. "I have an interest in finding the beast as well."

"He wants to score brownie points with the Jesus freaks," explained Nerys.

"The sightings are all clustered within a similar distance from this area of Sutton Park," said Ben, pointing. "I'm convinced it's hiding out in the trees there."

"You may be right," said Michael, measuring the distances with his hand. "Are you planning to look for it?"

"Well, this is just a hypothetical investigation at the moment. This specimen, if it truly exists, is a dangerous predator."

"But I remember you sharing a wealth of knowledge with the cub scouts about traps and tracking last year."

"Well," admitted Ben, "I do have some ideas for some traps and snares, to capture it with minimal damage."

"Aren't there any options that cause *maximum* damage?" asked Nerys, knocking back a second urn of wine. "Those are the ones we want."

"Tomorrow," said Ben. "I'm going to the park tomorrow."

"I may join you," said Michael.

Clovenhoof was fascinated by the job search software. He was even more fascinated by the answers that Nerys had given to certain key questions.

Handling people tactfully and *listening skills* were apparently areas where Nerys had much skill and interest, whereas *using your hands in a skilful way* was apparently not something she was particularly good at.

"I think Animal Ed might disagree with that," murmured Clovenhoof, stabbing the keys on his phone. "And Twitter, apparently."

It seemed, as he flicked through her answers, that she had made a careful assessment of each question and answered it according to whether it might lead to a manual job – the sort of thing where she might chip a nail – or the sort of career that Nerys would like to imagine for herself.

Clovenhoof settled the laptop on his knee and went back through the questions, answering them in what seemed to be a more truthful manner. *Explaining ideas and information to people* got removed on the basis that Nerys had the patience of an ADHD child on Christmas morning. He also removed *solving problems*, as she rarely sorted out the ones that he created. He declared that she'd be happy to work weekends, evenings, and even night shifts in case she decided she wanted more than one job. Perfect. He ran the search, once he'd fine-tuned some other choices, and read the top matches.

He dismissed *Warehouse Operative* as being too dull. *Bar staff* sounded useful. Would you be allowed to give your friends free drinks? He bookmarked that one. Next was the grand title of *Entertainment Agency Worker*. Now this looked promising. He gave a cursory glance through the description. He knew he'd found the ideal job for Nerys. The emphasis was on being well presented, being in good physical shape, and being pleasant and charming to clients at all times. Clovenhoof mused on this for a moment. It read like code, he decided. One of those strange examples of human subtlety that he occasionally ran up against.

"So what it really means is *dress slutty, move like a stripper, and chat men up.* Oh, I see, it's a lap-dancing job."

Clovenhoof congratulated himself on seeing through the coy wording. He opened up an internet search engine and looked for local lap-dancing opportunities. Nearby, in Erdington, an establishment called *Discreet Liaisons* had an advert that looked like just the thing. Clovenhoof filled in the web form on Nerys's behalf and sat back, feeling smug after tweeting the details of his good deed to the followers he'd picked up with #shagmebigboy.

Nerys was last to bed. She wasn't very keen on the coffin-style beds, but she'd drained the last of the alcohol, and she really was very tired. She'd positioned herself as far as possible from Ben and Clovenhoof to avoid the inevitable disturbances that they would cause, but her coffin really didn't look inviting. She'd rinsed her underwear in the sink so that she could wear it again the next day, aware that her clothes were likely to be trapped for the foreseeable future. She was currently dressed in an oddly shapeless garment that Jeremy had found for her. She had a suspicion that it was some sort of shroud, but was beyond the point of caring. She slipped into the sleeping bag that was nestled inside the coffin, and had to admit that it was a cosy bed. Shaped to her body, there was an instant feeling of being isolated and protected that was almost womb-like. Her mind wandered to certain men she'd known who would have found this dangerous and stimulating, and she drifted off to sleep with the thought that she'd ask Jeremy about getting a discount coffin for her bedroom sometime in the future when she actually had a bedroom.

Next morning, Ben came into the room looking for Clovenhoof, a jar of jam in his hand.

"Jeremy, have you had some of my jam?" he asked.

"Yes, raspberry isn't it?"

Ben scowled.

"I don't mind sharing my things with you, but did you use a knife that you'd used on something else? I can see some smears in it."

"Yes and no ..." said Clovenhoof. "It was a spoon, actually, and, depending on your viewpoint, I suppose it did go ... elsewhere, yes."

"I knew it!" shouted Ben. "You've been double dipping!"

"What?"

"Licking the spoon and putting it back into the jam. You do know that's the worst thing you can do to a person's food, don't you?"

"No. I'm pretty sure that's not the worst thing."

"Yes! Yes it is!" yelled Ben.

"But, you know, we won't sweat the small stuff, will we? We're all just muddling along together, like the honest cheeky cockneys did in the Blitz, yeah?" said Clovenhoof.

"Well, we're not honest bloody cockneys, Jeremy, and this isn't the Blitz. Why do I have to put up with your bad habits just because you can't bring yourself to stick to the few rules of decency that make life possible?"

"There are people who enjoy the way I live my life. Hashtag skidmark got me loads of retweets. It's only you who has no sense of humour about that sort of thing. So, how bad is it, exactly, this double dipping?" said Clovenhoof. "Is it worse than using someone's towel, say?"

"Tell me you haven't been using my towel as well?"

"Well, I don't know where mine is. Yours was there," said Clovenhoof.

Ben put a hand to his brow and took a deep breath.

"Right, of course you did. Anyway, in answer to your question, I'd say that double dipping is worse than using a person's towel, on the basis that at least a towel is used after washing, so in theory – and I'm clinging to this theory – there are no bodily fluids involved."

"Oh," said Clovenhoof. "Bodily fluids. You might not like what I've been using your towel for then."

"What?"

"Hashtag skidmark. I heard you and Nerys fighting about the toilet roll thing. I was way too scared to even touch it after that ..."

Nerys positioned herself in front of the screen and hit record.

"Hello again, viewers! Welcome to the latest instalment of Nerys's dating advice. By now, you'll realise that there are many tools at your disposal in your hunt for the perfect date, so I'd like to talk about one of my favourites, horoscopes. You might think it's a lot of nonsense, but I've recorded my experiences over the years, and I see a consistent eighteen percent uplift in the conversion rate when I use horoscopes. I'm talking, of course, about the conversion rate from first contact to full intimacy. Eighteen per cent! So, what do you need to know?"

Nerys ticked off on her fingers.

"You find out his birthday first of all. Social media can help you with this or, if not, you need to drop a subtle question into conversation. Once you know which star sign you're dealing with, you can start to form a plan. Now, a Leo will want you to look good at all times, so don't let him see you in your lounging slacks. Libra is similar. They both like well turned out women. You'll be wanting a nice perfume to waft his way too. Who next? Scorpio. It's well known that Scorpios are all sex maniacs, so just turn up in high heels and a trench coat belted over your best underwear, and you'll be fine."

Nerys frowned and stopped the recording as the sound of shouting came from the other side of the room. Ben was red in the face, waving what looked like a jar of jam and looking extremely angry with Clovenhoof.

"... A new towel immediately! Burn the old one. Burn it! I don't ever want to see it again. You're worse than an idiot, you're a complete menace. I feel sick just thinking about that towel."

"Hey! Busy over here, keep it down, will you? I need to get this filmed this morning. I've got an interview for a job this afternoon."

They didn't seem to hear her. Ben looked as though his head might explode with anger, while Clovenhoof was prattling on about the towel just needing a good ninety degree wash.

"Oh, really, Nerys?" she said in a loud voice. "What interview is that? Oh, it's a position with a legal company in Erdington called *Discreet* something or other. Something about client confidentiality. Really, Nerys? Well done for getting an interview so quickly, and being so productive in the meantime. We'll just stop this nonsense and pay you the correct amount of attention, shall we?"

She huffed as she realised that they were still ignoring her. She'd been waiting for a chance to try out her latest idea for dealing with Clovenhoof. Back when she'd had a flat and a job, she'd taken the water Reverend Zack had blessed and decanted it into a tiny perfume atomiser. She wasn't thrilled that it was one of the few things to escape the destruction, as it was of no practical use, but maybe now it could prove its worth. She fished it out of her handbag and approached Clovenhoof while he continued to argue with Ben.

Which part of him to squirt, though? While she really wanted him to shut up and stop doing whatever had got Ben so riled, she wasn't ready to see him melt into a puddle or go up in smoke. She gave him a quick squirt on the tip of one of his horns. The nozzle stuck briefly and much more came out than she'd intended, going all over his hair. Quick as a flash, Nerys dived onto Clovenhoof, and tried to mop up the excess with her hands.

"What are you doing?" he yelled. "I know I'm hard to resist, but you need to control yourself, woman!"

"I'm trying to stop your brain melting, you stupid tit!" said Nerys, using the corner of her sleeping shroud to dab at Clovenhoof's hair.

He tried to swat her away with a hand.

"Jeremy's an unthinking, selfish twat," said Ben, staring at them both in puzzlement, "but I can't see how spraying perfume will address that in any way. He'll just be a slightly more *fragrant* twat."

"Need to stop it getting on his face!" grunted Nerys as she worked frantically. "I don't want to see his skull grinning at me through rotted flesh every time I talk to him."

"She's gone mad," said Ben.

"I would like you to get off me. Now," said Clovenhoof.

Nerys stopped and addressed Clovenhoof directly.

"Are you sure it's not hurting? Not at all?"

"Let me try and tell you how it feels," said Clovenhoof.

Nerys scooted backwards and studied him.

"Yes?"

242

"It feels like having a demented woman launch herself at you with perfume, being unable to fight her off. Tell you what it reminds me of – going through the ground floor of a department store."

"No pain?"

"No."

"No itching or swelling?"

"No. So what was it all in aid of? What did you spray me with?"

"Er, Lynx Africa."

Clovenhoof sniffed the air.

"They've changed the smell of it then. I always assumed it was called that because it would fell a charging rhino."

Nerys retreated and slipped the atomiser back into her handbag. Clearly holy water wasn't going to work to control Clovenhoof. Maybe she should get herself some Lynx Africa.

By a small copse of trees near Keeper's Pool in Sutton Park, Michael met up with Clovenhoof and Ben as planned. Clovenhoof had a wheelbarrow filled with spades, rope, and tools.

"Jeremy, I'm amazed at how well equipped you are!"

"You better believe it!" said Clovenhoof, as he grabbed his crotch with a hip thrust.

"I meant the tools you've brought," said Michael, indicating the wheelbarrow. "Haven't you lost a great many of your possessions?"

"Oh, these," said Clovenhoof. "I borrowed them."

"Well, as long as you put them back where you found them, I suppose I can overlook that," said Michael. He looked at Ben, who had his arms folded, his back to Clovenhoof, and was staring up at the sky. "Do I detect a slight frisson between the two of you this morning?"

Ben rolled his eyes.

"Jeremy is, quite simply, a massive prick who has no clue how to behave," he said.

Michael nodded in sympathy.

"That's hardly news. Well, let's see if we can work together to catch this beast. Do you have a plan?"

Ben instantly became more animated, his arms waving as he spoke.

"I've assumed that the beast will want to feed, so we've got a bag full of butcher's scraps as bait. I'm going to dig a pit over there, at the edge of the copse. We'll cover it over, lay down the bait, and wait."

"Sounds good," said Michael. He contemplated briefly whether he ought to offer his help with the digging, but he'd worn his cream chinos. "I need to, er, analyse the area for spoor and other signs of the beast. We can learn much if I can get a viable sample to the lab."

Ben shrugged and wandered off with his spade. After a few moments, he decided on the optimum place and broke the ground.

Michael turned to Clovenhoof.

"What's your role? You don't seem in a rush to do any digging."

"If I thought there was any danger of that, I'd have pinched a JCB rather than just a wheelbarrow," said Clovenhoof. "I might have a look round for some branches to cover over Ben's pit."

They walked off together.

"Here's one," said Clovenhoof, pointing. "Do you want to help me get it?"

Michael pulled a face and addressed Clovenhoof, hands on hips. His phone was ringing in his pocket, but he felt it more important to deal with Clovenhoof first.

"Jeremy, there are two things wrong with that branch. Firstly, it is so enormous that we wouldn't be able to carry it, even between the two of us, so it certainly won't break, as intended, under the weight of the beast. The second thing that's wrong with that branch is that it's still attached to a tree. Quite high up."

"Fine!" huffed Clovenhoof. "Hadn't realised you were afraid of heights." He slapped him on the shoulder. "I'll leave you to get the branches then. Nice low down ones. I'm off to have a chat with some friends I've just spotted."

Michael tutted. He looked at his phone. There was a voicemail message.

"Michael, dearest," said Andy, "I've taken yet another call from your friend, Nerys. She wasn't drunk this time. Once again, she had hoped to stay at ours, but realised that we had a lot going on in the bedroom. Apparently, she feels that cleanliness and hygiene are important and knows that *we* – I don't know if she meant you and I or, you know, the international federation of gays – do take pride in our appearance, but wonders if we should have thought ahead before mixing things up in the bedroom. She did suggest that, if we want to get it resolved quickly, I ought to get my plumbing looked at by a professional. Delightfully, she knows a man who can come sort things out with little fuss. Apparently, he's a wizard with the waterworks. You need to call me now, Michael, and explain."

Nerys had arrived a full hour early for her interview, and had some time to kill in Erdington. She'd phoned Andy to offer her own insights into the installation of an en suite shower (with the ulterior motive of reminding him that she was still looking for a place to stay, of course) and then, with dreams of moving into a proper home on her mind, stopped outside the window of an estate agent and gazed at the available properties. She sighed deeply. There were many flats in the local area. Nice flats with carpets, running water, and neighbours who wouldn't unleash insane monkeys into the walls and then demolish the building. All completely outside her current price range, though.

She went inside to examine some of the other boards. Since she couldn't afford to move anywhere, there was no point limiting her window shopping to the cheap end of the market. What would it be like to live somewhere quiet and stylish? Somewhere with private parking, or a doorman, or a rooftop pool ...

"We're interested in the house for sale on Warden Road," said a woman behind Nerys.

She turned. A young couple looked at her expectantly.

"Sorry?"

"Warden Road."

"Oh," said Nerys. "No, I'm not ... er ..."

Nerys looked at the one man in the office. He was on a phone call and looking the other way.

Nerys smiled at the young couple and reasoned to herself that, when she got her new job as a legal advisor, she'd have people coming to her for advice all the time, so she needed to practise.

"Let's see," she said. "Warden Road? Really, you want to move to that place with all those trees?"

"Leafy suburbs," said the man. "It's nice, isn't it?"

"Not really," said Nerys. "You'll never see any sunshine with those massive trees and the way it faces. Gloomy, if you ask me. And think of the tornados."

"Tornados?"

Nerys nodded earnestly.

"There are more tornados per square mile in the Birmingham area than the American Midwest. Do you know how many houses have trees fall on them? Stay clear, I say."

"Oh. I had no idea. You've also got a property on Church Road?"

"Yes, but the cracked pavements round there will destroy a decent pair of heels in no time. You do know that there was an accident on that road? Killed the vicar!"

"I'm sure there are accidents all over the place," said the woman.

"True, but, I tell you, if a woman of the cloth can't safely cross the road ... I'd look elsewhere if I were you." Nerys scanned the houses. "Now, this place here, on Maney Hill Road, is in another class. It's handy for the shops and all the decent pubs are up that end."

"We've not been looking up there," said the woman. "It's a bit out of our price range."

"This house really ought to be loads more money than they're asking," said Nerys, peering at the price. "I'm tempted myself."

Nerys realised that the estate agent had materialised beside her. She hadn't noticed him finishing his phone call. How long had been there?

"That's absolutely correct," he said. "We'd normally see properties on that road going for much more than this, but the owners are an elderly couple who really need to move into a care home. Tragic story. They keep telling the family that women with pushchairs have been breaking into their garden and climbing over

246

the rockery. Mummy and baby parkour, they say. Can you imagine?" He smiled. "Anyway, they're after a quick sale. Can I show you some details?"

The man shrugged. His partner nodded.

The estate agent gestured to some chairs. As the couple turned away, he leaned across to Nerys and passed her a business card.

"Nice work," he said.

Sylvester McIntyre – Estate Agent, the card read.

"I think you actually have them hooked," smiled Sylvester. He had a cute smile, and he smelled of hair product. Nerys thought there were worse things for a man to smell of.

"They thought I worked here," explained Nerys apologetically.

"Maybe you do, Nerys," said Sylvester and tapped the business card. "It is Nerys, isn't it?"

"Um. How did you know ...?"

"I've seen your YouTube video skits."

"Skits."

"Comedy dating advice. I'm a big fan. Funniest thing ever. Call me if you ever need a job."

Clovenhoof strolled over to where the Sutton Coldfield Union of Mothers had spread their blankets on the ground. Some of them had brought placards bearing slogans like *Only the breast for my baby* and *Feeding time is not a crime.* Sandra was distributing juice drinks from a cool box.

"Jeremy! How lovely to see you here. You didn't bring a placard."

"I do have a whole cupboard of pro-breastfeeding placards at home, but I just didn't know which one to bring."

"Would you like to write on one of the spares?"

Clovenhoof got busy with a marker pen, and then saw a familiar face approaching.

"Toyah!" he shouted. "Over here. Do you like my placard?"

He waved it above his head.

"*Get your tits out for breastfeeding*," read Toyah. "Stating the bleeding obvious, if you ask me. How you gonna do it otherwise?"

"No," said Clovenhoof. "It's a thing. I saw it on the internet. Women are supposed to get them out to show that boobs are not just for men to look at. I do think that maybe a man thought that up though. Genius."

Clovenhoof crouched and rubbed his nose against Beelzebelle's. She giggled, and playfully punched him in the eyebrow. Clovenhoof felt a warm glow within his chest. He wasn't sure if he liked that feeling or despised himself for feeling it.

"Love truly is the work of the devil," he said.

"Hello, hello! Is this a new recruit?" said Sandra, approaching Toyah. She bent down to the buggy and then popped up again, a surprised expression on her face. "Oh, goodness me, are you Belle's mom?"

Toyah looked Sandra up and down. Sandra was wearing a maxi dress and Birkenstocks, which contrasted sharply with Toyah's sequinned t-shirt with *Bitch Queen* embossed upon it.

"Yes," said Toyah, clearly biting down on a much sharper retort, "but her name's Bea, not Belle." She brought out a box of cakes. "I brought some cherry Bakewells for the picnic."

"Perfect!" beamed Clovenhoof. "A cake with a built in nipple. Pass one over."

Toyah was introduced to the other mothers and then she set Bea down on the blanket, where she could wriggle with the other babies. Sandra pulled Clovenhoof aside.

"None of my business at all, but I take it that the two of you aren't together?" she whispered.

Clovenhoof shook his head, a cherry Bakewell wedged between his lips.

"I understand. It must be so hard on you all." She dropped her voice to a conspiratorial whisper. "Although, I can't get used to Belle's new name."

One of the non-Sandra's looked at Sandra and tapped her watch.

"Oh," said Sandra. "It's time for the speakers. We've got a health visitor and a local councillor. Oh, and a performance poet."

Clovenhoof saw Toyah shoot him a look that clearly said that he was an asshole for dragging her along to this.

Sandra bent to another cool box and pulled out a pair of bottles.

"So, let's make sure that everyone's got a nice full glass of Prosecco, so we can enjoy the speeches."

Clovenhoof winked at Toyah, who hunkered down and reached for a glass.

Nerys entered the park and stormed across the grass at speed. The speed she was able to attain fell short of what she really wanted, but that was because of the clothing she was wearing.

"Ben! Michael! Where's Jeremy?"

She approached Ben and Michael, who were packing some tools into a wheelbarrow. They looked up at her in surprise. Ben's forehead was smeared with dirt.

"Nerys! How did the job interview go?" asked Ben.

"I was offered the job," growled Nerys, quivering with rage. "I was offered the damn job."

"Well done! said Michael. "When do you start?"

"I'm not bloody starting!" she yelled.

"You sure, Nerys? Sounds as if you're starting to me," said Clovenhoof, walking over.

Nerys was too furious to even ask why he was carrying a *Get your tits out for breastfeeding* placard.

"You! You unbelievable shithead!" she seethed. "You applied for a job in my name, without asking!"

"Yes, I did, and you're very welcome," said Clovenhoof. "I see you adhered closely to the dress code." He indicated her short leather skirt, low cut blouse, and impractical heels. "You obviously nailed the wiggle test and the pole trial?"

Nerys was momentarily torn between a perverse sense of pride and the anger that had been working its way to the surface and was refusing to leave.

"I scored in the upper quartile for the wiggle test, and my pole routine was so spectacular that apparently I can start at the advanced grade, where you get to choose the best shifts, but that's *not the point!* I don't want to work at a lap dancing club. I want to be a legal advisor. You not only sent me off to an audition to titillate pathetic businessmen, you've shared it all on social media!

249

Tina's been laughing her head off about this. Do you have any idea how that makes me feel?"

"Hashtag catfight?" said Clovenhoof.

Nerys roared in frustration and grabbed a spade from the wheelbarrow. She hefted it above her head and swung it at Clovenhoof. He parried, reducing his placard to *Get your tits out*. He was on the move before she could get him with a reverse swing, but he really didn't have to move very quickly to outpace her in the vertiginous heels she was wearing.

She tried to chase him anyway. Now she had the spade in her hand, she wanted to feel it connect with his skull. She knew that she couldn't kill him, which was actually quite a liberating thought. She could crack open his skull, and then maybe he might appreciate the depth of hatred she felt for him at this moment.

She could hear the others calling out, but ignored them. If there was something she was good at, it was focus, and, right now, she was focussed on pulverising Clovenhoof's head. Ben was more vocal that she would have imagined. A few short hours ago, he was baying for Clovenhoof's blood himself. He had just as many reasons to want to swing at their stupid neighbour as she did. Except that he didn't have the added humiliation of an ex boss's mockery over social media.

"Hnnnyaaaagh!" Nerys knew she wasn't going to catch Clovenhoof, so she hefted the spade at the back of his head and staggered to a stop. Except that she didn't stop. The ground gave way beneath her. Broken branches and leaves did little to break her fall into a large hole that she felt sure had something to do with her neighbours. She landed in a painful tangle with broken branches scratching and poking her exposed flesh.

"Nerys?"

Ben and Clovenhoof peered over the edge of the hole.

"Gah! I didn't even crush your stupid skull! When I get out of here, I'm going to make sure that the next thing I do is research how much pain you're physically able to feel, and then I'm going to make you feel it!"

"Ooh, nice. Hashtag fighting talk!" said Clovenhoof, holding up his phone to take a picture. "I think we'd better get going, Ben."

Nerys was speechless. The cowardly pair had retreated, rather than helping her out. She took a breath to shout for help, but then paused as she heard voices, and what sounded like applause.

"Those performance poets are brilliant!" said a woman. "Who knew they could inject such passion into such a short piece?"

"Yes, but I still don't understand what it had to do with breastfeeding," said another.

"The way I see it, the woman – representing the objectification and sexualisation of women – lashes out against the reasoned and liberal worldview that we represent."

"Oh, I see."

"But – and this is telling – we don't need to meet them with violence to defeat them. Those who would sexualise and diminish us will fall into a trap of their own foolishness – represented here by the physical trap in the ground."

"Powerful stuff. That woman is an astonishing actress."

"Well, you know who she is, don't you? It's the woman that does those parody dating advice videos. She's quite the local celebrity. Let's help her out of the hole. I want to see if she can do party nights."

Nerys looked up.

The first face to appear over the lip of the pit seemed somewhat familiar. It was whatsername Wilson – Toyah. Nerys had seen her in pubs and clubs here and there, previously hanging on the arm of ...

"Oh."

"You're the cow what stole Ed from me, aren't you?" said Toyah.

Nerys stumbled in her search for words.

"Stole is a bit strong. I didn't even do anything. I was just stood there and ... um, he has a thing for leopard print."

Toyah grinned at her.

"What? And now you're caught in an animal trap. That's iconic, innit, love?"

Nerys gave up.

"'Ironic', but yes. Yes, it is."

"And my mom tells me she caught you in bed with my dad."

251

"Now, that's not strictly true," argued Nerys. "He put me up for the night, but there was no, um, hanky-panky, and I understand your mum and your dad haven't been together for years."

Toyah was laughing.

"God, you're a pathetic bitch."

Nerys was about to fling an insult back, but Toyah had a hand held out to her. Nerys looked at it, then took it.

Clovenhoof and Ben had made an uneasy truce as they hurried back to Buford's.

"We need to come up with a good story. A really good story. Epic," said Clovenhoof, as they entered the temporary sanctuary of the storage room cum bedsit. "Shall we blame Michael?"

"That's hardly going to work when you stood there taking photos and sharing them on social media," said Ben.

"Yeah! Let's see how many likes and retweets I've got," said Clovenhoof, pulling his phone out. "Nerys is always a hit."

"Wait, have you put stuff on there about me too?" asked Ben.

"For some reason, the internet's less keen on you. Semi-clad women do a lot better. Oh, and cats. I've sent a lot of your stuffed animals to @craptaxidermy."

Ben's face suggested that an angry retort was on the way, but it was drowned out by the sound of the door bouncing open on its hinges and Nerys bellowing at Clovenhoof.

"You pair of shits! I know you're both capable of doing selfish ridiculous things – Lord knows that's why I find myself sleeping in a coffin and eating pot noodles for every meal – but at least we've always stuck together. Looked out for each other."

"Nerys, that's not true," said Ben, bristling with self-righteousness. "If you're looking out for a friend, you don't leave hairs on their soap."

"What?"

"Hairs. On their soap."

"What are you blathering about, you cretin? I'm talking about personal betrayal."

"Betrayal can occur on a number of levels. And, frankly, it's bad enough that we have to use the autopsy tables for showers, but my soap definitely had hairs on it, and I'm certain that they were yours, Nerys."

"You knob! Are you comparing that to digging a bear pit and leaving me in it? Seriously?"

"Yes! Yes, I am!" shouted Ben. "You both mock me for my habits, but I've always had my own set of standards, and now fate has dictated that I must live in close proximity with you. Well, I don't mind that. I'm very happy to share all I have with you, but you must act with some decency. It's like you're *trying* to make me angry when you wash the cups."

"You can't make someone angry by washing cups," said Clovenhoof.

"You both just swill them, and that's just not acceptable," said Ben.

"What's swilling?" asked Clovenhoof.

"It's when you just run something under the tap without actually washing it," said Ben, with visible distaste.

"Surely running something under the tap *is* washing it?" said Clovenhoof, puzzled.

Nerys rolled her eyes as if she knew what was coming.

"No!" squealed Ben. "No, it's not. You don't remove grease or kill germs that way. It's a filthy habit."

"Filthy habit? Using tap water?" said Clovenhoof. "Interesting. So, how bad would it be to use the water out of the loo, if you couldn't be bothered to walk all the way to the tap? You know, hypothetically?"

Nerys and Ben locked gazes with each other, and then they both looked at Clovenhoof. They each grabbed the closest thing to hand. In Nerys's case, it was a Prosecco bottle that she'd been passed by the SCUM ladies and, in Ben's case, it was a marble cherub from the selection of funereal statuary.

Both approached Clovenhoof with murderous intent, when there was a voice on the stairs.

"Hello? Is someone up there?"

"It's Mr Buford," said Clovenhoof. "This could be interesting. You two aren't supposed to be here."

"I thought he never came up here," whispered Nerys, alarmed.

"We could be arrested for trespassing," whispered Ben in reply.

"Get in your coffins," said Clovenhoof.

"From lap dancer to corpse. This day just gets better and better," said Nerys.

"Pull the lids over. I'll see what I can do," said Clovenhoof.

Nerys and Ben both reacted quickly, getting into their beds and gently lowering the lids into place.

The door opened, and Gordon Buford entered the room. The funeral director was a rotund fellow, with a cheery outlook on life and a taste in suits which aided the general impression that this was a man who had stepped straight out of polite 1950's British society. It was an impression that seemed to serve him well.

"Jeremy, I am surprised to see you here."

"People often say that to me."

"But what on earth are you doing?" he asked. "It's your day off."

"Oh, I'm a 'work the job' not 'work the hours' kind of man."

"We've had a call saying that there's some sort of fracas going on in here."

Clovenhoof nodded, and reached for the closest thing to hand.

"Yes, I wanted to come here when it was quiet to investigate the rodent problem," he said, holding up the taxidermy specimen.

"What sort of rodent problem?" asked Mr Buford. "That looks, for all the world, like a ferret."

"Yes, Sutton has an increasing ferret problem. Wild ones, gathering in quiet places like this. I was right, see?" said Clovenhoof.

"Why's it wearing a leather skirt?" asked Mr Buford.

"It's a humane trap I designed," said Clovenhoof.

"It's not that humane. It looks dead."

"Seems this one had a heart condition," said Clovenhoof. "The main thing is that I've saved Buford's from a serious ferret infestation. You can be sure that everything's under control."

Gordon Buford narrowed his eyes. He was man to whom negative emotions did not come easy, so even his most suspicious gaze looked more like short-sightedness.

"I'm really not sure what's going on here."

"Are any of us?"

"So I shall be getting back to my family barbecue now."

"You do that."

Mr Buford paused on his way to the door and regarded the stone cherub and the empty bottle of sparkling wine leant against it.

"Do not disappoint me, Jeremy," he said, and left.

Footsteps receded down the stairs and, shortly afterwards, there was the faint sound of a car starting and moving off. Clovenhoof looked around, savouring the peaceful atmosphere.

"Can we come out now?" whispered Ben.

"What's happening?" whispered Nerys.

Clovenhoof shushed them.

This was surely the quietest the room had been since they'd moved in. An hour or two more of this would be a wonderful idea. He could do with some quality Lambrini time. He quickly fetched a screwdriver and fastened the tops onto the coffins.

"It's all right," he said to them both. "I'm just having a drink on you."

Chapter 9 – In which beasts and beastly plans are uncovered

Nerys pulled up outside sixteen Station Road.

Two weeks into her new job, Nerys had come to a number of conclusions regarding the world of estate agents.

One conclusion was that working for an estate agent was not dissimilar to working for an employment agency. Both were about selling a product to a market: selling houses to homebuyers had replaced selling jobseekers to local employers. In both industries, the products were unique and came onto the market at irregular times. In both industries, the product frequently needed tidying up or renovating to make them remotely sellable and, sometimes, the product had to be heavily discounted if there was to be any hope of a sale. However, property sales had the distinct advantage that there was no fear of the product punching the buyer in the face and telling the buyer to shove the job where the sun doesn't shine.

Nerys climbed out of her car, and turned up her collar against the light rain.

A further conclusion she had come to was that there were a number of uncontrollable factors that made selling houses all the more difficult. One of these was the weather. A spot of sunshine made even the dingiest prefab in the arse-end of nowhere look inviting but, if grey skies rolled in, a house had better be fucking charming or there was no hope.

Another uncontrollable factor was the Beast of Boldmere. It had a name now. The few pictures that had appeared in the Sutton Coldfield Observer were blurry shapes at best, and the witness sightings were wildly contradictory, but once the damned thing had a name, it had gripped the imagination of the local populace and had impacted on house prices.

However, Nerys was working on a counterattack. She checked the papers in her work satchel and went up to the door.

As she did, she felt a thrill in her heart and a spring in her step. Yes, another conclusion she had come to was that she loved this job. She had often wondered what went on inside other people's homes, what weird little quirks, foibles, and decorating disasters could be found behind the front doors of England. Some might have said she was a people person and showed an *interest* in others. Others might have said that Nerys Thomas was just a nosy bitch.

The Sutton Coldfield Union of Mums gathered in the churchyard of St Michael's. They clustered close to the church wall to stay out of the approaching rain. As placards wavered in the breeze, Sandra addressed the women.

"I am so glad to see everyone who came to the protest picnic here again. And some new faces too."

She strode up and down the line, her skirts flapping.

"We took to the park to speak out against the sexism and discrimination breastfeeding mothers face. And what good did it do? Who noticed? No one. How many column inches did we get? None. What changed? Nothing," she declared loudly.

Clovenhoof couldn't help but think that she had the appearance of a latter day Wat Tyler, addressing the pitchfork-wielding members of his Peasants' Revolt. Clovenhoof had attended the Great Rising of 1381, mostly to point and laugh (the hunting and decapitation of Tyler was entertaining stuff, given that no reality television existed in those days). He had to admit that Wat Tyler had never worn a corduroy jacket, or carried a bemused baby in a papoose, but there was definitely something of the rebellious Kentish man about this woman.

"The media is not interested in polite people picnicking in the park, no matter how noble their cause. If we want people to sit up and pay attention, we have to go out and grab that attention."

"Yeah!" said Clovenhoof, trying to inject some peasanty spirit into proceedings.

"Our mission is increasingly vital. I've heard on the grapevine that the body fascists and chauvinists of this town want to oppress mothers further. A certain church, which banned breastfeeding mothers, has made a deal with a major formula milk manufacturer to distribute free formula to local residents. This isn't charity! This isn't kindness! This is covert oppression of a mother's right to feed her child how she chooses! And it will not stand!"

"Yeah!" yelled Clovenhoof, and was pleased to note that a certain Spartacus Wilson (who had come with his mum and sister) had joined in.

"We're going to march up the Boldmere High Street on to Sutton town centre and make sure that everyone – everyone! – hears our concerns."

A very middle class but nonetheless enthusiastic cheer went up from the SCUM.

"Onward!" said Sandra and waved the crowd toward the street.

Yep, very much like Wat Tyler. Clovenhoof wondered if this day, too, would end in a swordfight and a head on a stick. That would certainly grab headlines. He might suggest it to Sandra later.

Toyah and Spartacus fell into step beside Clovenhoof. Toyah pushed Beelzebelle in a pram. Spartacus looked up at Clovenhoof's placard.

"Get your tits out?"

Toyah gave him a clip round the ear.

"But you're always telling me to read more," he said.

"It did say more," said Clovenhoof of his placard, "but the bottom got chopped off by a madwoman with a spade."

He looked at Spartacus's placard.

"I heart boobs," said Clovenhoof looking at the stylised pictograms.

"He's very supportive of his old mum," smiled Toyah.

Clovenhoof frowned.

"But you don't breastfeed Beelzebelle anyway," he said. "I gave her formula when she was with me and you must have stopped – what do they call it? – spurting since then."

"Lactating."

"Really? Not spurting? Let's compromise and call it oozing."

"It's called lactating and she's called Beatrice."

"Potato, potahto."

"And it's not just about my rights to breastfeed. It's about my rights to do what I bloody well please with my body. I say, 'no one is the boss of me and no one is going to tell me where I can or can't show my naked flesh'."

Clovenhoof was tempted to agree and point out that he had heard a drunken Toyah exclaim those very words in the car park of the Boldmere Oak, when caught with a bloke in the bushes, but instead said, "Spartacus, I have to commend you on your boobs. Very lifelike."

"He spent all evening on the internet looking up pictures to copy them from," said Toyah proudly.

Clovenhoof passed Spartacus the plastic vuvuzela he had brought with him.

"What's this for?" said Spartacus suspiciously.

"Any decent protest calls for a vuvuzela," said Clovenhoof, "and the boy who drew those badonkadonks should be the one to blow it."

Clovenhoof took his phone out to take a picture of Belle.

"Come on, boy. Blow your horn. Tell the world the Nork Army are coming!"

The occupants of sixteen Station Road were Rory and Sarah Lilley. Rory worked in IT. Sarah worked in retail. Rory had an appalling taste in clothing. Sarah had an appalling taste in men. Both had an appalling taste in soft furnishings. Nerys commented on none of this when she went through the evaluation process.

Nerys put down the insipid cup of tea and took out her camera.

"I'm going to take photographs of all the rooms."

"We tidied up especially," said Rory, apparently impressed with himself.

"And your house looks lovely," she agreed. "I'd just like to move a couple of things first."

"Move?" said Sarah.

"To create a better sense of space," smiled Nerys. "Could we perhaps take a couple of those cushions off the sofa?"

"Cushions?"

"Just to create a better sense of space. Less clutter."

Rory did as instructed.

"Maybe a few more," said Nerys.

"Okay."

"And ... maybe a few more." Nerys nodded. "That's lovely. Well, that last cushion just looks lonely. Maybe we should ..."

"Put some back?" said Sarah.

"No," said Nerys. "Remove. That's it. Just stuff them all down the back. Good. Now, the curtains ..."

"Do you like them?"

"They are unique, aren't they? The woman with her face printed into the pattern ..."

"My mum," said Sarah.

"Wow," said Nerys. "I didn't know you could get that done."

"We had to search high and low to find a company that could do it for us."

"Really?" said Nerys. "I am surprised. Rory, could you draw them right back? Let's have some light in here. Yes, is there any way in which we can tie your mother-in-law back? We're selling the house after all, not your relatives." She forced a laugh.

"My dad's staying," said Sarah.

"Pardon?"

Sarah pointed at the wallpaper and Nerys realised that that diamond spot pattern on the wall wasn't composed of diamonds at all, but the infinitely repeated face of a quizzical bald man.

Nerys was wondering if there was a setting on the camera that would blur out the disconcerting crowd of baldies, when her thoughts were interrupted by a strident horn blart from outside.

"What was that?" she said. "Does the fox hunt come through here?"

"What fox hunt?" said Rory.

Sarah clung to her husband.

"You don't think it's the beast, do you?"

"I don't think the beast has a horn, Sarah," he said.

"Maybe they're hunting it," she said.

"There is no beast," lied Nerys.

The husband and wife exchanged a glance.

"Nerys, I think we have to be honest with you."

"Honesty is always the best policy," lied Nerys again, who had little time for honesty.

"The reason we want to move is because Mrs Benjamin at number twenty-two saw the beast in her garden."

"Really?"

"We've already put down a deposit on one of the houses in the new Rainbow housing development. There have been no sightings over there."

"True," said Nerys, lying for a third time in the full knowledge that the new Rainbow estate was a stone's throw from the ARC lab where the creature was born. "But I can assure you that every one of the so-called sightings has been debunked as either a hoax or mistaken identity. It's just public hysteria, like the Loch Ness Monster or the Biting Man of Sparkhill."

"But Mrs Benjamin saw it tip over her bins. She said it was like an enormous cat creature."

"Did she now?"

Nerys removed a sheaf of large photographic prints from her satchel. They were black and white. For some reason, even in this digital age, black and white added an air of authenticity and authority to images.

"Perhaps she saw this," said Nerys, and presented them with a picture of a horribly misshapen moggy lurking by a drainpipe.

"That's one ugly cat," said Rory. "What's wrong with it?"

Nerys shrugged.

"It's a large ginger tom, one apparently unhappy with the hand life has dealt it. People have made phone calls to the RSPCA about it."

"No," said Sarah. "Mrs Benjamin said it had a snout and a long muscular body."

"Like this?" suggested Nerys and showed them a picture of a contorted otter, skulking in grass.

"An otter?" said Rory.

"Spotted by the storm drain outlets," said Nerys.

"And is that a ... a little spear it's carrying in its hand?"

"Noted tool users, otters," said Nerys.

"But what about the other sightings? The bones buried in Sutton Park?"

"Dogs," said Nerys.

"The claw marks on the rooftops?"

"I think I have a picture of a rogue owl in here somewhere."

"It trashed the supermarket."

"Youngsters."

There was doubt in Sarah and Rory's eyes, and doubt was enough.

"You want to move house," said Nerys. "That's lovely. But you also want to sell this house."

"We do," the couple agreed.

"I think it would help the speedy sale of your home if you put your neighbours' fears to rest. Show them the pictures and help quash these terrible rumours."

Nerys held out the pictures. The doubt in their eyes revealed the inner conflict between the truth that they had accepted – and which, utterly incidentally, was the actual truth – and the need to make a quick sale.

"Of course," said Rory.

"Lovely," smiled Nerys. "Now, on with the photos."

The rain drummed on the window of Café Ole, the geographically confused pan-European café on Boldmere High Street. Michael was trying to consume a breakfast basket of churros and croissants, while simultaneously holding a phone conversation with Chip.

"Finished?" said Michael. "I'm not sure I understand."

"I should have thought it would be a fairly straightforward question, mate," said Chip. "When will the DNA library be complete?"

"Right. Yes, that's the question I have a problem with. Complete how?"

Chip sighed.

"Listen, Michael. When I started out in this game, building conservatories, the customer could say, 'Chip, when will the conservatory be finished?' and I would say, 'ten to twelve weeks' and they'd be happy. When the bank asks me, 'Chip, when will the Rainbow housing estate be completed?' I can say, 'two to three years' and the bank could include that in their calculations. So, I'm asking you, Michael, when will the animal DNA bank be completed?"

"Yes," said Michael.

"Yes?"

"Yes, I'm acknowledging the question. I just don't know the answer."

"Why not? It's simple really. How many DNA samples do you have?"

"Have, fifty-two thousand. Sampled and catalogued, approximately nineteen thousand."

"Good, and how many animal species are there?"

Michael grimaced.

"Just under nine million."

Michael could hear the tip-tip-tap of a calculator.

"So, in the time you've been given and with the wealth of resources I've put at your disposal, you've found less than one percent of all known species on earth."

"Oh, no," said Michael. "More like four percent."

"Are you doubting my maths?"

"Not at all. Best estimates put the number of species on earth at around nine million, but humans have only discovered a fraction of those. Most remain undiscovered. Nine million is our best guess."

"And how soon will the rest be discovered?"

"I think we – and I mean scientists generally – are discovering new species at an approximate rate of fifteen thousand a year."

"But how long will that take ...?" said Chip, and tapped at his calculator again.

"Don't forget," said Michael helpfully, "most of those will become extinct before we even find them."

"Oh, dear Lord," said Chip.

"Chip, if I may, I think it's important to regard the work at ARC Research Company as a process, not a finite act."

"But time is short!" said Chip passionately. "Can't you hear that?"

"Hear what?"

"The rain! The rain!"

Michael had no idea how to respond to that.

"We need to pick up the pace, Michael," said Chip.

"I'll try, Chip, but we are constrained by the amount of equipment we have. If we had larger premises and more machines then ..."

"Fine," said Chip. "You make the orders. I'll write the cheques."

"We're talking hundreds of thousands of pounds, Chip," said Michael.

"Let me worry about that."

A commotion on the pavement outside drew his attention. Several dozen people, mostly women, many with young children, were walking purposefully up the high street. Maybe there was a sale on maternity clothing somewhere ....

"Until the new portakabins arrive," said Chip, "you can take up some of the unused space in the Consecr8 building."

"That's very kind," said Michael. "I'll take a look later this morning."

From amongst the crowd of possibly bargain-hungry mums came an angry trumpet blast.

"What's that?" said Chip. "Are you driving?"

"No, I think someone's blowing a vuvuzela on the high street."

"Bloody menaces."

Michael stood up to peer into the crowd.

"I think you're probably right."

The SCUM march had begun in an orderly fashion, keeping to the pavement, moving in line, and generally being as rebellious as a primary school trip to the swimming pool. However, Clovenhoof found, with a little nudging and encouragement, the mothers and their toddlers could tap into their inner revolutionary and, by the time they had reached the parade of shops on the high street, they had spilled out into the road, blocked the traffic, and were singing at the top of their lungs. It was perhaps unlikely that many protests had been accompanied by *The Grand Old Duke of York* or *Incy Wincy Spider*, but there were children present and they needed entertaining.

Shoppers stopped in their tracks to watch them go by. Men in the bookies paused in their contemplation of the laws of probability and peered out. Ben Kitchen, looking exactly like a man who had not had proper access to washing facilities or a good night's sleep in nearly a month, stood on the doorstep of Books 'n' Bobs and watched with bemusement.

"Oh dear," said one of the not-Sandras, failing perhaps to grasp the purpose of their march. "I think we're causing a bit of scene."

"Damn right, we are!" shouted Clovenhoof.

"Those police officers don't look too happy though."

A police car was parked outside the supermarket. Two police community support officers were ambling casually towards the head of the march, hands raised for them to stop.

"They're not real police!" said Clovenhoof, emboldening his fellow marchers. "The hobby bobbies can't stop us! Mow 'em down!"

The PCSOs spread their arms as though to catch the thirty-odd-strong band of protesters. Clovenhoof was shocked to see this tactic appeared to be working. Those at the front slowed. Maybe they were sorcerers.

Then one of them uttered the magic incantation, "What's going on here, then?" and the protestors stopped, and Sandra started to explain.

"Don't reason with them!" hissed Clovenhoof. "Trample them!"

"Kick their shins in," suggested Spartacus.

"Yes. What he said."

There was scaffolding across the front of the supermarket, and a team of builders in hi-vis jackets had paused in their work on the frontage to watch the spectacle unfolding in the street. Clovenhoof saw PC Pearson and Ahmed the security guard, two of his favourite people, chatting in the supermarket doorway. Clovenhoof waved at them.

PC Pearson smiled and waved him over.

Since the march seemed to have ground to a temporary halt, Clovenhoof trotted over.

"It's amazing," said Ahmed, shaking his head at Clovenhoof.

"Speak of the devil," said PC Pearson.

"And he shall appear," said Clovenhoof proudly, and did a little tap dance and even threw in some jazz hands. Unfortunately, one of the jazzy hands was holding a placard and it nearly hit Ahmed.

"Get your tits out?" read PC Pearson.

"No," said Clovenhoof. "Special requests and happy endings cost extra."

PC Pearson turned to Ahmed.

"I never used to believe in that old nonsense about criminals returning to the scene of the crime."

"Who's doing what now?" said Clovenhoof.

PC Pearson smiled, not unkindly, and said, "Jeremy Clovenhoof, I am arresting you on suspicion of breaking and entering with the intent to carry out acts of theft and vandalism ..."

"Where?"

"Where?" said Ahmed. "Here! Where you broke in last night. Or were you too drunk to remember it?"

"What did I do?" asked Clovenhoof.

Ahmed glared and pointed to the smashed panelling and store sign that the builders were repairing.

"I attacked the sign?"

"As you made your escape."

"And I stole what exactly?"

PC Pearson twitched his moustache.

"Come. Let us peruse the scene of the crime."

He took hold of Jeremy's elbow and steered him into the closed shop.

The aisles were in shadow, only half-lit. On each aisle, boxes, jars, and bottle were strewn, as though a drunkard with outstretched arms had ricocheted through the place. A chisel-faced woman in a trouser suit moved through the mess, taking photographs.

"Is this him?" she asked.

"Later, Ms Donnelan," said PC Pearson.

"I will be putting together a full account of damages caused."

"Yes, Ms Donnelan."

"Oh," said Clovenhoof. "Did I do this?"

PC Pearson and Ahmed both gave him a look.

"What makes you think I did this?" said Clovenhoof.

Clovenhoof was prodded along to the freezer aisle. One of the cabinets had been smashed open. Food boxes had been flung out across the aisle and ripped apart. Clovenhoof's mood of general curiosity and amusement was turned to horror when he saw the red and white packages, the logo that was the universal symbol for tastiness.

"Crispy pancakes," he whispered in dismay.

"Now, do we know anyone who particularly likes Findus Crispy Pancakes?" said PC Pearson.

"Yes, but ..."

"Did we perhaps have the late night munchies, perhaps after a little ..." He mimed someone smoking a spliff between thumb and forefinger.

"Blowing tiny cocks?" said Clovenhoof.

"You were definitely in a hurry, man," said Ahmed and traced a line along the edge of the smashed cabinet. Dried blood glistened dully on the jagged edge.

"Now, it would be rather incriminating if you had a corresponding cut," said PC Pearson. "Perhaps on *this* arm."

PC Pearson pulled Clovenhoof's sleeve up. He looked at the devil-red flesh, hairy but injury-free.

"Nothing up my sleeves," said Clovenhoof, pulling up the other sleeve too.

PC Pearson humphed.

"Seems the only thing you've got on me is my perfectly reasonable and rational love of crispy pancakes," said Clovenhoof.

"Oh, no," said Ahmed. "Not just crispy pancakes."

PC Pearson, still flummoxed by the lack of cuts on Clovenhoof's arms, took a moment to collect himself.

"Indeed," he said. "Shall we take a walk round to the drinks aisle?"

Nerys backed into Ben's bookshop, her arms full of papers and folders, and momentarily let in the noise of the crowd.

"Is it still going on out there?" said Ben from behind the counter.

"What *is* going on?" said Nerys.

"Something to do with breasts. Jeremy's involved somehow."

268

"Course he is."

"If they stay there much longer, I think I might arrange a bosom-based display in the window."

Nerys blinked.

"And do you have many bosom-based books?"

Ben slapped a pile of books that he'd made on the counter.

"*Knit Your Own Breasts*?" said Nerys.

"Apparently, they're used in teaching mums about breast-feeding."

"*Boobs of Britain*? Is that for real?"

"It's actually a book of rude spelling mistakes, but it seemed to fit. And I thought I could throw in some art books, like this Rubens one. I've got a collection of photos by that Finnish artist, Heinz Takala, who does all the nude flashmobs."

"Not one of your worst ideas," said Nerys, "but, speaking of which ..."

She pointed at Ben's current efforts on the counter.

Half a dozen stuffed rats were posed in a circle on a wooden board. Some were squatting, others were poised on tiptoes, others held aloft cubes of cheese. It looked like a furry folk dance-off with a spring-loaded rat-trap in the centre.

"Now, I consider myself to be an ethical taxidermist," said Ben, "but I do also have a rat problem in the cellar."

"Yes?"

"What I've done here is mount the rats I have trapped and killed, and arranged them in a sort of, well, welcoming committee. A sort of 'come to the dance, oh ratty friends. There is nothing to fear here' and then – Snap!"

"That's fairly fucking creepy, Ben."

"It's a work in progress."

"Quite. Anyway, I would like to borrow some more of your taxidermy efforts for my photography project."

"You can't debunk the Beast of Boldmere with badly staged wildlife shots."

"It's worked so far. The couple on Station Road were convinced, and are going to share the evidence with their neighbours. Actually, maybe there's something else you can help me with."

Nerys dumped her papers on the counter. One of the gaily dancing rats fell over. Ben attempted to stand it upright again.

"This is some of the paperwork for the Lilleys. They're selling up and moving to the Rainbow housing estate."

"The new development."

"Right."

"So, we've already had some clients either selling up to move there or fixing their mortgage through us for properties on the estate."

Nerys unfolded a map of the large scale map of a section of Wylde Green. The map included the Rainbow development, the mostly abandoned tower blocks around the edge of the site, the ARC labs on Beechmount Drive, and the Consecr8 church nearby.

"What a weirdly shaped building," said Ben, tapping the oval outline of the Consecr8 building.

"Now, look here," said Nerys. "This is Dove Close and this is the property the Lilleys want to buy."

"Number nine."

"Well, yes, and no. You see it's marked on here as number nine, but they've put a deposit down on 9b."

Ben looked at faint line running through the property.

"It's been subdivided."

"That's what I assumed. It was built as a four-bedroom house, but is being sold as two two-bedroom houses."

"Okay."

"And so's this one. And this one. And all of these."

Ben nodded.

"So, the plans are out of date."

"Okay," said Nerys in agreement. "That's what I thought. So, I looked at the financial records and there's a mortgage on this house, on number nine. And all of these. Not 9a or 9b or anything else a, b, or c. There are existing mortgages on all these properties, for the property as it was originally built."

"So someone has borrowed against the four-bedroom house."

"While, simultaneously, the Lilleys and dozens of other homeowners are also borrowing against their own little homes. And it hasn't been flagged up because they are notionally different properties. 9, 9a, 9b, and so on."

"It's a mistake," said Ben.

"Or a scam."

Ben smiled.

"What?" said Nerys.

"Is Nerys Thomas sticking her nose into the nefarious doings of other people again?"

Nerys sniffed. "Got a problem with that?"

"No. I just think you've still missed your true calling. You should have been a private detective."

Nerys considered it.

"That would be fun. Well, Ben, this little detective is going to visit the local planning office and ask some questions."

"Really? Is that part of your job?"

"No," smiled Nerys.

Clovenhoof's knees nearly gave out at the terrible scene in the drinks aisle.

"It's like ... It's like a Lambrini graveyard," he whispered.

Shards of glass lay in a wide pool of spilled perry, sharp glittering islands in a sea of deliciousness. Clovenhoof was tempted to get down on all fours and start lapping it up.

"Lambrini and crispy pancakes," said PC Pearson.

"Don't pretend it wasn't you," said Ahmed.

Clovenhoof shook his head.

"Let me get this straight," he said. "You're saying I broke in, scoffed all the pancakes, drank all the Lambrini, and then escaped via the roof?"

"Through the office space upstairs and out the skylight."

"And you caught this on CCTV, no doubt."

"You know we didn't," said Ahmed, "because you trashed the computers along with the office furniture upstairs, before you went on your little rampage."

"And how did I get on the roof, in the first place, to break in? It'd have to be a twenty foot jump to the roof edge."

"No," said PC Pearson. "You used the roof to escape."

"Oh. So how did I break in?"

PC Pearson and Ahmed exchange a glance.

"The service door?" suggested PC Pearson.

"The air vent?" suggested Ahmed.

"Do I look like Bruce Willis?" said Clovenhoof.

A doubtful look crossed PC Pearson's face.

"Hang on," he said softly. "Jeremy destroyed the surveillance computer before he got down here."

"Yes," said Ahmed.

"So he must have been upstairs first before coming down to the shop floor."

"I suppose."

"So, he must have broken in through the roof."

"Except I couldn't have," said Clovenhoof.

"He must have had a ladder," said Ahmed brightly.

"Or," suggested Clovenhoof, "your perpetrator was someone – or some*thing* – that could leap up onto a twenty foot roof."

"Now, let's not entertain silly rumours," warned PC Pearson.

"And then, after raiding the store, the beast escaped by the same route," said Ahmed, warming to the idea.

Clovenhoof looked up to the windows of the offices set into the mezzanine level of the supermarket.

"Or it never left," he said, in his most sinister voice.

After Nerys left in search of answers to questions she had no right to ask, Ben saw that the protestors weren't moving anywhere, so did as promised, and put together a little breast-themed window display. He initially arranged some of his taxidermical woodland readers about the display, but the look on the badger's face seemed somewhat lecherous, and the sight of cute little stoats and harvest mice scampering among books on the female form looked a little sordid, so he moved them on elsewhere.

Happy with his efforts, he stepped outside into the rain to gauge public opinion. Some of the banner-waving ladies who saw it appeared sceptical, rather than delighted.

"I like it," said a voice.

It was Spartacus Wilson, juvenile delinquent of the parish.

"Thank you," said Ben.

"I like the woolly boobs. They'd make good hats."

Ben would have argued, but the knitted knockers did have a certain bobble hat quality to them.

"Who is this man?" asked Spartacus's mum.

"This is Ben," said Spartacus. "He used to be Baghera at the cub scouts."

"Oh, right," she said. "I'm Toyah."

"We've met," said Ben.

Toyah frowned.

"I didn't go to many of the cub things."

"No, I held your handbag for you last year, while you went twelve rounds with those two Essex girls in the Boldmere Oak car park."

"Oh, yeah," she said, and smiled in fond memory. "Hold this for me."

She thrust an open cloth bag into Ben's hand and rooted through it one-handed as she lifted Beelzebelle out of her pram.

"Hey, Belle," said Ben, and gave her a little wave.

She blew a bubble at him and squirmed in her mother's grip.

"Her name's Bea," said Toyah, finally retrieving a bottle of formula milk from the bag. "So, you one of Jeremy's friends?"

"Friend is a strong word. Victim comes closer." Ben looked round. "Where is he, anyway?"

"Oh, he went off to talk to the fuzz and got arrested," said Spartacus.

"Again?" said Ben unsurprised. "You know he leaves a permanent overnight bag at the police station, don't you?"

Belle (or was it Bea?) latched onto the bottle and sucked noisily on it. One of the other protesting women, a tall woman in dungarees, looked at her.

"A bottle on a day like today?" she said. "I know it can be easier sometimes but, if there was a time to show that public breastfeeding is not only acceptable, but the right thing to do, it's today."

"I'm fine, thanks," said Toyah, embarrassed.

"I express milk for my Tristram sometimes, but I ..." The woman paused. "That looks very creamy. It's not formula, is it?"

"Perhaps," mumbled Toyah, angling her body away.

The tall dungaree-wearer pulled a disgusted face.

"I don't mean to scoff, but that stuff's practically poison."

273

"I think it might mention something about that on the tin if it was," said Ben.

"Everyone knows breast is best," said the woman.

"Well, it rhymes anyway," agreed Ben.

"I was unable to breastfeed Bea for a few weeks," said Toyah, "and ..."

"Why?" snapped Dungarees.

"Um, I was on holiday."

Dungarees's look of disgust was replaced by one of even greater magnitude. It was so powerful that, if Toyah had then revealed she drowned kittens and ate old people's faces, Dungarees's face wouldn't really have had anywhere to go.

"Nothing is more important than your baby's well-being," said Dungarees. "Any loving mother knows that."

Ben saw an immediate change in Toyah's expression. Whatever shame or class-consciousness or guilt had allowed her to be browbeaten by the other woman vanished instantly. Ben had seen that expression on Toyah's face before, shortly before he had been given a handbag and two Essex women had regretted ever coming to the West Midlands.

"Are you suggesting I don't love my children?" said Toyah.

Dungarees's eyebrows shot up, and she glared pointedly at the formula bottle in Toyah's hand.

In the shabby-looking corner building that housed a down-at-heel shopping centre, the Moo Moo Club nightclub, the Sutton Coldfield town library, and the city council's regional office, Nerys looked through screeds of maps, plans, and documentation that she barely understood. The council worker, Surinder, hovered nearby and tried not to look uncomfortable as Nerys untidied the precious paperwork.

"Perhaps if you told me what you were looking for?" she said.

"I'm interested in the company that holds the freeholds and mortgages on these properties," she said.

"ARC Residential and Construction," said Surinder, tapping a document Nerys had already looked at.

"And what does ARC stand for?" said Nerys.

"Er, ARC Residential and Construction. A. R. C."

"The A in ARC stands for ARC."

"Apparently."

Nerys shook her head.

"But who are they? What are they?"

Surinder pulled out some fresh files, surreptitiously tidying up some of the existing ones as she did.

"Touch of the OCDs?" said Nerys.

"Nothing wrong with liking order," said Surinder happily. "Here." She passed Nerys a paper-clipped file. "It's the company's property portfolio within the city. Own a lot, don't they? Here's the planning permits. Oh, they own that new church on Beechmount Drive."

"What?" said Nerys, and snatched the papers from Surinder.

"Can't say I like it myself," sniffed Surinder. "Any self-respecting building should be rectilinear. Keeps things nice and neat. But the committee approved it. Signed by our own Councillor Bloom."

"I've heard of her."

"Oh, she's a very ... active woman. Councillor. Justice of the Peace. Wouldn't be surprised if she runs for parliament sometime. But, look at this, honestly."

She was holding the plans for the Consecr8 church.

"I mean, it's not bad enough that they can't build the thing square, but they got all these unnecessarily weird links to the water and electricity in the basement, and a dubious floating foundation. If this thing was in an earthquake zone, it would be rolling off down the street at the first tremor."

"And, are we in an earthquake zone?" asked Nerys, not really interested in plans, but utterly taken by the links between the church, the housing estate, and a possible financial scam.

"No, but that's not the point."

"It's Chip Malarkey."

"It's what?" said Surinder.

"He's behind it. He built the Rainbow development. He built that monstrous eyesore of a church. He owns the ARC lab and this ARC residential thingy. He's funded it all by taking out mortgages on properties that he's already sold to other people and ..."

Something caught Nerys's eyes: one line on the list of properties owned by ARC Residential and Construction.

"That evil clusterfucking cockthistle!" she exclaimed.

"We searched up here when we first realised there'd been a break-in," said Ahmed.

"Yes, we're not complete idiots, Jeremy," said PC Pearson.

Clovenhoof crept up the stairs to the upper floor. Hooves weren't ideal for creeping. He had previously considered inventing some hoof-slippers for covert ops, and now wished that he had followed through with that idea. He could have pitched it to Dragons' Den and everything. Hoof-slippers for horse-riding in noise reduction areas. Hoof-slippers for, er, goat ninjas ...

"Just have your taser ready, plod," he said.

"We don't carry tasers."

"Your big whacking stick then."

He opened the door onto the admin area. This level of the supermarket was built directly into the roof. A metal apex roof was above them, dotted with frosted glass skylights. One had been smashed in. Clovenhoof inspected the granules of glass on the floor.

"So, the beast broke in here."

"It's like seeing a master at work," said PC Pearson sarcastically.

In this room and the office beyond, boxes, desks, and computers had been tipped over and flung aside.

"It was angry," said Clovenhoof.

"Or *he* was very drunk," said PC Pearson.

Ahmed gave a start at a scrabbling sound above them.

"The beast!" he whispered.

"Builders," said PC Pearson, and sighed wearily. "Right, lads. Fun though this is, you know how they say the modern police force is hampered by too much paperwork? Well, I've got this lovely mountain of paperwork on my desk back at the nick and, astonishingly, I'd quite like to get on with it. Let's wrap this charade up and get you down to custody, Jeremy."

Clovenhoof ignored him utterly.

"If I'd broken into a supermarket," he mused, "eaten all the crispy pancakes and drunk all the Lambrini, where would I go next?"

"Yes," said PC Pearson. "Where did *you* go next?"

"I'd throw up," said Ahmed. "Not that I've ever drunk, obviously. It's haram."

"Funny that," said Clovenhoof. "The Guy Upstairs tells one bunch of the faithful to quaff wine every time they think of His son, like it's some kind of weird drinking game. And then He tells the next bunch that all alcohol is sinful. It's almost as if He makes it up as He goes along." He clicked his fingers. "The toilet!"

"What?" said PC Pearson.

"To throw up," said Ahmed.

"Or just have a kip," said Clovenhoof.

He led the way, through the devastated rooms, to the end corridor and the single staff toilet. The door was closed.

"I'd bet money it's in there," said Clovehoof.

"I'll give you fifty quid if there's a burglar in there," said PC Pearson.

"And if it's the Beast of Boldmere?"

"A thousand pounds."

"Done."

Clovenhoof approached cautiously. Ahmed, realising how close he was, scuttled round to stand behind PC Pearson.

"Really?" said PC Pearson.

"I'm on minimum wage," said Ahmed. "You're not."

"Ready?" said Clovenhoof.

He reached out slowly, turned the handle, and opened the door. A dark shape filled the small space, half-draped over the toilet bowl, half-hugging it. Two eyes, as big as pool balls, glared at them.

"Oh, crap," whimpered Ahmed.

PC Pearson's moustache quivered as he gargled and stammered.

"It ... it ... it's some – it's a wolf, a bear a – oh, crap."

"It's a thousand pounds, thank you very much," said Clovenhoof. "I think I'll be using it to kickstart my hoof-slipper business."

Ahmed was descending into a crouch, curling up into a ball, as though he could hide inside his own hi-vis security jacket. PC Pearson had reached for his police radio, still burbling.

"Control, this is Lima Zulu Papa Wolf Bear Tiger thing."

"Come again, Lima Zulu Papa."

"Lion, lion. Dog. Teeth. Big, big fudging animal."

Clovenhoof smiled at the beast. It was a magnificent monster, all muscle, sinew, fangs, and take-no-prisoners attitude, wrapped up in a sleek coat of midnight. There was no mistaking the lineage of this half-ton beauty.

"Hi," said Clovenhoof. "I think I'm your dad."

The beast bared its fangs and growled. A waft of the most deliciously foul breath surrounded Clovenhoof.

"Well, me and a Yorkshire terrier and some other dead things. It was sort of a group effort," said Clovenhoof.

"Come in, Lima Zulu Papa," crackled the radio. "Matthew, are you there?"

PC Pearson readjusted his grip on his truncheon.

"Get back, Jeremy," he said, his voice trembling.

"It's okay," said Clovenhoof.

"Get back!" PC Pearson hissed. "I do not want to die saving your life. That would be a truly shitty way to go. Worse than embarrassing."

Clovenhoof smiled. "It's fine. We're fine."

The beast roared.

"Lambrini hangover?" said Clovenhoof. "Tell me about it."

The beast pounced.

A full-scale slanging match had broken out between Toyah and the dungaree-wearing mother, and Ben wished he could be somewhere else entirely.

"What you saying?" said Toyah. "Just because I don't breastfeed my kid, I'm a bad mum?"

"As mums," said Dungarees, adopting a super-calm and condescending tone that would probably earn her a punch in the gob within seconds, "our role is to care for and nurture our children. We are responsible for raising the next generation."

"And – what – because I ain't done this one thing, I've failed? I didn't breastfeed Spartacus here. Did I fail to raise him properly, yeah?"

"Perhaps not the best example to use," Ben muttered quietly to himself, although not quietly enough to avoid getting a kick in the shins from the ten-year-old thug.

"Breast milk is superior to artificial substitutes and, moreover, it's free. You'd be a fool to not breastfeed your child."

"Free?" snapped Toyah. "How the fuck is it free? It's only bloody free if you've got the time to be there for them! If you've got to work a fucking zero hour contract, five hours here, two hours there, at a bloody shop that's a two hour bus ride from home, how the fuck am I going to be there to breastfeed her?"

"Does your mum have a job?" Ben whispered to Spartacus.

"Not the point," Spartacus replied smoothly.

"It's only fucking free if you've got a toffee-nosed twat of a husband who earns enough dosh so's you can stay home and play mum!" shouted Toyah.

"*I* don't play at being mum," retorted Dungarees. "Parenting is a full-time vocation and the most important job there can be. And, even if you're scrubbing the floors at Lidl ..."

"It's Aldi, bitch."

"I thought you said she didn't have a job," whispered Ben.

"She really gets into character," said Spartacus.

"... You should still have time to express milk for your baby," said Dungarees.

"Time?" shouted Toyah. "Time is a bloody luxury. I don't have the time to cook Alphabites and Turkey Twizzlers like Nigella fucking Lawson every night. Frankly, they're lucky if they get Pom Poms and a Capri Sun sometimes."

"Not really winning the argument there," said Ben.

"Well," said Dungarees, "if you're not able to provide the time or nourishment your children need, then maybe you shouldn't have had children."

Toyah stepped back, stunned.

"Take Bea," she said, and thrust the baby into Ben's arms.

Dungarees should have taken that as a signal to run. Run far and run fast. She either didn't notice it, or chose not to heed it. The builders mending the supermarket frontage were yards away, and they were able to spot it. They paused in their work to watch as Toyah squared up to Dungarees.

"You telling me you should decide who gets to breed and who don't?" said Toyah.

"With parenthood comes great responsibility," said Dungarees.

"Is she quoting Spiderman?" Spartacus whispered to Ben.

"I am responsible!" snarled Toyah.

"Responsible mothers do not jeopardise their children's health by feeding them nutritionally deficient milk!"

"I believe that there's no conclusive evidence to suggest that children raised on formula suffer significantly worse health or are more likely to suffer life-limiting illnesses than children who are breastfed," said someone, and then Ben realised it was he himself who had said it.

Toyah and Dungarees stared at him.

"Children who are breastfed are much less likely to suffer from conditions such as obesity, asthma, and ADHD, you idiot," said Dungarees.

"Um, yes," he said, wondering where the Hell his mouth was taking him. "However, that might be a reflection of the type of households those children were raised in. It's like children raised in houses with lots of books do better at school, but it's not the books that are responsible, but the parents who, incidentally, read themselves. I believe that sibling studies, where one child is breastfed and one isn't, show no real difference whatsoever ..."

Ben trailed off under the glare of more than one passionately pro-breast mother.

Dungarees shook her head in disgusted disbelief.

"I don't know what poppycock your husband is spouting ..."

"He ain't my husband," said Toyah.

"Boyfriend, whatever."

"I'm not her anything," said Ben. "I'm married, I think, but not to her."

"But if you're not in favour of breastfeeding, then what the Hell are you doing on this protest march?"

280

"Because," said Toyah softly, and only softly because she was going to build to an almighty crescendo, "I hate the idea of some jumped up little Hitler telling us that we can't breastfeed our babies in public because it somehow offends them. I love my children, and how I choose to raise them and feed them is up to me. If I want to parade up and down the high street, flashing my tits, I can."

And she did exactly that. Toyah whipped off her top and, seconds later, her bra.

"Mum," moaned Spartacus, mortified.

"These are my children and this is my body, and neither of them is anyone else's fucking business. It's not their business to tell me what I can and can't do, and it certainly isn't fucking yours either!"

Ben expected one of two things to happen then. One was Dungarees to launch into a loud retort. The other was for Toyah to launch a topless and unarmed assault on the woman. He wasn't expecting the mothers of SCUM to erupt in loud applause, but that's what they did.

"Well spoken," said a SCUM mum.

"The right to do as we wish," said another.

Toyah and Dungarees were equally wrong-footed by this turn of events.

"Er, thanks," said Toyah.

Dungarees bowed her head, cheeks aflame. "Maybe I misspoke," she mumbled.

Ben saw the builders on the scaffolding tut and roll their eyes. They'd been treated to a bit of unexpected nudity, but had been denied a full-on pavement brawl. And then something far more pressing caught Ben's attention. Above and behind the two builders, a powerful clawed creature was thrashing about on the roof by a skylight. It looked like a sharp-faced dog-creature, albeit one the size of a small horse. In fact, it looked like it could eat a small horse at a single sitting. And gripping tightly to its neck ...

"Jeremy?" said Ben.

The beast and the idiot riding it rolled across the rooftop. Ben couldn't tell if Clovenhoof was trying to subdue it or simply stay on its back and out of the reach of those claws.

Ben pointed high.

"Look. Look."

One of the builders turned. The beast flung Clovenhoof from its back and skidded on the tiles. The builder gave a cry of terror and pitched over the scaffolding rail. Clovenhoof rolled off the roof entirely and down past the builder, who clung one-handed to a lower rail. As the first gasps rose from the crowd, fingers pointing not at the beast, but at the fallen men, the beast slipped over the corner of the roof and out of sight.

Ben ran forward. The builder, despite his mate trying to reach him, lost his grip on the rain-slicked rail and fell the dozen remaining feet to the ground, landing awkwardly on the pavement and spilling over. The builder then proceeded to grasp his ankle and swear violently.

The ability to swear being a clear sign of rude health, Ben ran past him to Clovenhoof, who lay sprawled over a row of parked supermarket trolleys.

"Jeremy!"

Clovenhoof groaned, eyes closed.

"Don't move," said Ben.

Clovenhoof feebly patted the air with his fists as though they were trotting feet.

"... tiny goat ninjas ... I'll be a millionaire," he murmured, and passed out.

Chip kept an office at the Consecr8 church, a room at the rear of the building with a wide, gently curving window that commanded a view over the new Rainbow estate and, further to the south west, the currently damp-looking city of Birmingham. Michael thought it likely that being owner of various enterprises, Chip had any number of offices in various establishments, but he imagined that this was the most impressive.

It was the size of a small flat, would provide more than agreeable accommodation for one person, and, judging from the little corner of bedsheet poking out from a wall panel, possibly did just that. The walls were covered with an eclectic mixture of religious paintings, pre-Raphaelite prints, maps of both the UK and the globe, and a version of the immorality-causes-climate-change pinboard Michael had previously seen in Chip's garage.

Chip's desk was a vast oval map table, inset with a relief map of the world.

Michael had only been in the room a few times previously, but only now saw it for what it really was: a stateroom.

"Good afternoon, Chip," said Michael.

"I hope it is, Michael," said Chip, putting his coffee mug down on Greenland. "Talk to me about the DNA bank. Do we have the space we need in this building?"

"Oh, yes. Absolutely, Chip. The unused holds, I mean halls, would provide all the room we need. Obviously, there's the power supply, and even the emergency generator, which is just a boon and, er ... Chip?"

"Yes, mate?"

Michael found himself laughing at that. "Would that be *first* mate, Chip? Or should I say 'captain'?"

Chip gave Michael a look. "What's the matter, Michael?"

Michael unrolled a plan of the church building and put it on the map table.

"You're going to think me mad, but when I was looking at the plans to best place the additional laboratory space, I ..." Michael cleared his throat. "This building is one hundred and fifty nine meters long, twenty seven metres wide, and sixteen metres high."

"I know," said Chip. "I built it."

"Which, in itself, is not unusual, except if one converts it into cubits, then – you know what a cubit is?"

"I do."

"Well, it's three hundred cubits by fifty by thirty."

"Exactly."

"Just as God told Noah in Genesis."

"Correct."

"The building is made of wood."

Chip was now smiling.

"Well spotted."

"And the bottommost levels are curved under and water-proofed like a, like a ..."

"A boat?" suggested Chip.

Michael made a noise to himself. He knew what he had to ask. He knew Chip knew what he had to ask. Both of them already knew the answer. So why was it so hard to ask?

"Chip?"

"Yes, mate?"

"Is this an ark?"

"No," said Chip.

"Oh."

Chip stood.

"This isn't just an ark, Michael. This is *the* ark. I've looked. This is mankind's only current and credible attempt to preserve human life and, of course, the genetic data for God's creatures in the event of the inevitable deluge."

Michael let the confirmation of his suspicions wash over him. The church was a ship, an actual ship, sat in deep curved foundations, but not fixed to them. Over a hundred miles from the sea, Chip had built a ship, an ark to be precise. Questions queued up in Michael's mind.

"Who?" he said.

"You've seen the leader board in the church. You know how the Piety Points system works."

"When?"

Chip shrugged and smiled. "When? No man will know the day or the hour, but it's coming." He gestured to the window and the rain. "This downpour could be the beginning of it."

"Why?"

Chip blinked. "Why? Why would anyone want to save the faithful? Why would anyone want to do God's work?"

"No," said Michael. "Why ...?"

"Why me?" said Chip. "That is a perfectly reasonable question. Here."

He directed Michael's attention to one of the many pictures on the wall. It was not a religious painting. It portrayed a narrow stream between two plant-crowded banks and, in the stream a young woman, floating on her back, a string of flowers in her hand.

"This print, this very one, hung in my parents' bathroom when I was a child. Either they just thought it was pretty picture of a bathing woman – bathing in her dress, mind – or they had a

284

strange sense of humour. If you laid in the bathtub, you could not avoid looking at it. As a child, I thought it was sinister. I hated it. Do you know what it is?"

"Ophelia," said Michael, "by John Everett Millais."

"Very good!" said Chip. "Brownie points for you."

"Piety Points?" asked Michael hopefully.

"The Lord does not give salvation in exchange for general knowledge questions. If that were the case, Heaven would be full of pub quiz teams. I have a fear of drowning, mate, and I partly put it down to having that picture fixed in my vision throughout my childhood. And, yes, partly because of that time big Simon Jenkins pushed me in the Birmingham Fazeley Canal when I was twelve. I don't want to drown when the rains come."

"And you are so sure that the flood is coming?" said Michael.

Chip nodded.

"I am, even if others are not. Look at that picture. As we can see, Ophelia is not yet drowning. What is she doing?"

"She's singing, Chip," said Michael, who, as an extension of the omniscient will of the Almighty, was well-versed both in the works of the immortal Bard and the perfectly praiseworthy pre-Raphaelites.

"She's singing," agreed Chip. "I'm a plain-speaking man, Michael. I speak as I find, and I'm not usually one for metaphor but this ..." He wagged a finger at Ophelia. "... This is a metaphor for the blindness and the wickedness and the madness of our world. We're drowning in sin. We're drowning our world with pollution and greenhouse gases. And what are people doing? They're drinking and they're whoring and they're watching their YouTube and their rude tube and they're refusing to see that their skirts are filling with water and that their wickedness is going to drag them down." He looked Michael square in the face. "My eyes are open, mate. Wide open. I see perfectly clearly, even if the idiots in the street cannot."

The office door slammed open, and Nerys stormed in, with Michael's receptionist Freddy scuttling nervously in her wake.

"I tried to stop her," said Freddy weakly, "although there's only so much Freddy can do. And I was taking a message at the time."

Nerys strode up to the map table.

"You colossal cock!" she snarled at Chip. "You jumped-up petty excuse for a builder's mate! How fucking dare you!"

"I'm sorry," said Chip, a superior half-smile on his face. "Have we met?"

"You know full sodding well who I am!"

"Your face looks vaguely familiar."

"I know what you're up to," she said.

"Nerys," said Michael in reasonable tones, "whatever's upset you, maybe you should go home and have a nice ..."

"Shut it, pixie-wings!" she snapped. "I'm talking to the organ-grinder, not his flying monkey." Nerys threw down a handful of papers on the table, obliterating much of central Asia. "I know how you funded this church, Chip! Property fraud! You've borrowed against properties which you don't even own. Hundreds of thousands! Millions!"

"That's a slanderous accusation," said Chip, "and I mean that in the full legal watch-that-your-mouth-doesn't-land-you-in-court sense."

"I have all the evidence here."

"Oh, financial law and property conveyance are your areas of specialisation, are they?"

"Sir, if I may," Freddy tried to interject, "there's been an incident you should be aware of."

Chip ignored him completely.

"You see, Miss Thomas, I thought you worked at a recruitment agency. That is what you do, isn't it? Or *did* do."

"You lost me my job. You killed my dog. And you – you! – got me kicked out of my own home!"

"Nerys, please," said Michael. "You know full well that it was Jeremy's impromptu demolitions that led to your ... accommodation problems."

"Yeah, but *he's* the one who owns the bloody land our flats are built on. I saw the paperwork. It was *his* solicitor and *his* building inspector who had us evicted."

Chip was shaking his head sadly. "You think I did that? You think I personally oversee the actions of all my businesses and individual employees? Do you honestly think you're that important?"

"It's your bloody fault I have to live in the sodding storeroom above an undertakers and, yes, damn it, you are doing this on purpose! You've got your name written on half the land in this town and you think you own it. You're a horrible, ugly octopus sat in the middle of its web, with your tentacles in all the pies and ..."

"Do you mean a spider?" suggested Freddy.

"What?" snapped Nerys. "Yes! Fine! Spider in its web, and you think you can push us all around and I'm not going to stand for it."

"Oh, dear," said Chip, entirely unafraid.

"I'm going to expose what you're doing, you pathetic little man, and I'm going to bring you down! This ..." She performed a wild expressive movement that Michael judged was meant to be a cross between a world-encompassing gesture and some form of you-go-girl streetwise sass but simply looked weird. "... This is fucking war."

At that, she turned on her heel and stormed back out again.

Chip gripped the edge of the table and breathed heavily. Michael decided it was probably best to say nothing for now.

"You know," said Chip, eventually, "I might have previously mentioned that I don't like that woman."

"You might have," agreed Michael.

"You had a message for me," Chip said to Freddy.

"Oh, yes," said Freddy. "I quite forgot in all the hullabaloo. I thought you ought to know that there's been an accident. One of your construction workers has slipped off the scaffolding outside the supermarket."

"What happened?"

"As best as I understand it, there's been some sort of protest thingy going on in town. Mothers and babies angry about milk or something. Anyway, one of the women flashed her, you know, lady cushions, and your chappy took a tumble."

Chip closed his eyes. Something dark and furious rumbled in his chest.

"Is he hurt?" he said.

"He's been taken to Good Hope, but it's nothing critical," said Freddy.

Chip made a noise, an unexpected noise. It was a laugh.

"Not critical?" he said. "Some crazed woman goes around exposing herself, causing injury to an honest, hard-working man, and you say it's not critical?" He fixed both Michael and Freddy with a steely stare. "She's right."

"Who is?" said Michael.

"This is war," said Chip.

Chapter 10 – In which Clovenhoof has his day in court, and things get rather heated

Toyah Wilson's first appearance at the Lichfield Road magistrates' court on a public indecency charge had been a brief event, only enlivened by her colourful protestation of her innocence. Her second appearance, just under a month later, looked likely to be a longer and more intriguing affair and, subsequently, by the time Ben and Nerys sat down, the public gallery was almost full. There was barely a face they did not recognise.

"The SCUM are out in force," said Ben, regarding the various mums (for once without their sticky little offspring).

"And the real scum," said Nerys, nodding towards the surprisingly happy-looking figure of Chip Malarkey.

Chip caught her gaze and a look of oily smugness washed over his face. Nerys shuddered in disgust.

Toyah's mum, the fiery Stella Wilson, sat on the front row of public seats, flanked by a number of large men and scary women Nerys took to be the extended family. They kept giving cheery waves and thumbs up to Toyah, who sat, sullenly and silently defiant, in the dock beside the court security officer.

"Family outing," said Ben.

"Probably a rite of passage," Nerys replied. "I bet the magistrate has seen each and every one of them at some point."

"All rise," said the court usher.

The public stood, along with the advisors, solicitors and defendant, as the three magistrates – two women and a man – entered and sat beneath the royal crest.

"Tessa Bloom," Nerys whispered to Ben.

"Who?"

"The chief magistrate. An old friend of Chip Malarkey and a regular churchgoer."

"Ah," said Ben, eyeing the red-haired woman suspiciously. "Totally impartial then?"

As the public sat once more, Nerys looked round.

"I thought Jeremy was coming."

"Me too," said Ben. "I'm sure he said he had to pick up some things on his way down."

Nerys laughed grimly to herself.

"Probably best that he misses it," she said. "Knowing him, he'd do something stupid and get charged with contempt of ..."

She was interrupted by the courtroom door slamming open and a ridiculous figure in a black gown and grey barrister's wig swaggering in.

"Sorry, your honours," said Clovenhoof loudly, hefting a large bag with him. "Didn't have the outfits in my size. Had to make do with Sexy School Teacher." He gave a twirl of his cape as he approached the solicitors' desks.

"Who is this person?" said Mrs Bloom to the court at large.

"Defence solicitor, your worship," said Clovenhoof.

"But the court has appointed a defence solicitor."

"But Toyah, showing infinite taste and wisdom, plumped for me instead."

"And who are you?"

"Jeremy Clovenhoof, your judgeness."

"You were meant to be looking after Bea," Toyah hissed to him.

"She's with Spartacus," Clovenhoof hissed in reply.

"And are you qualified to practise criminal law?" asked Mrs Bloom.

"Practise is all I do."

"Where with Spartacus?" Toyah demanded.

"Laserquest."

"I find that it hard to believe that you are a solicitor," said Mrs Bloom.

"I like scepticism in my judges," said Clovenhoof.

"For one, you are wearing a wig. We do not wear wigs in this court."

"Wig, madam? This is all perfectly natural," he said, and stroked his grey locks.

The magistrate raised her hand to signal the court security, but Nerys saw her stop at a glance from Chip Malarkey. Something unspoken passed between them. Chip nodded in assent and Mrs Bloom turned the gesture into a dismissive wave.

"Well, if no one objects ..." she said.

"Oh, crap," said Nerys.

"Parcel for you," said Freddy, stepping through the sliding door into the ARC Research Company laboratory.

Michael, who had been working through samples of various South American vertebrates, clocked the company label on the box and grinned.

"Excellent."

Perhaps his grin was too obviously child-like, because Freddy lingered to watch him open it. Michael took a scalpel to the binding tape.

"Is it those cryo-tubes you've been waiting for?" said Freddy.

"No."

"That centrifuge that you said you were going to get?"

"Nope."

Michael sliced under the folding panels.

"This, Freddy, is a ticket to salvation."

"Oh," said Freddy, in the manner of someone who wished to appear excited but had no idea what was being discussed.

"Chip may not realise it yet, but I'm going to do a great service for the people of this parish."

Michael pulled out a close-fitting suit, seemingly composed of black leather and a inordinate number of straps.

"Is Salvation that bondage club off Broad Street?" asked Freddy.

"It's a camouflage suit," said Michael. He carefully removed a pair of complex and green-lensed goggles from the packing foam at the bottom of the box.

"My aunt and uncle used to go to these 'special parties'," said Freddy. "He sometimes wore a snorkel, which is odd because there's not much snorkelling to be had in Four Oaks."

"There's a beast," said Michael. "Hungry. Prowling. Dangerous. I'm going to hunt it."

"Okay," said Freddy, with a wink. "Well, as long as you and your 'beast' have fun – and take sensible precautions – that's all that matters."

Clovenhoof showed considerable restraint and managed to stay still and silent while the prosecuting solicitor set out his case. His first witness was the accused herself and, before asking her anything other than the most perfunctory of questions, had a loop of CCTV shown to the court on the large wall screen.

The footage was taken from a camera outside a nearby shop, looking past the supermarket towards the gathered protesters.

"Here we see the illegal protest march," said the solicitor. "The police were not informed of the intention to march through the town. Traffic was severely disrupted, and it was only due to the diligence of local officers that the march was stopped here. Now, Ms Wilson, would you agree that this person here in the picture is you?"

"Of course it is," said Toyah. "Ain't it obvious?"

"Yes, it is," agreed the solicitor. "You appear to be engaged in a discussion with this other woman in dungarees. And then, as we can all see, Ms Wilson, you remove your outer garments and expose your breasts. Now, exposure of breasts for the purpose of breastfeeding is protected under the Sex Discrimination Act, but you weren't breastfeeding, were you?"

"No," Toyah admitted.

"In fact, you did it to draw attention to your sensationalist cause and, indeed, caused such shock and distress that a construction worker fell from nearby scaffolding and was caused serious injury."

"Don't know nothing about that," said Toyah.

"No," said the solicitor. "I don't think you considered the consequences of your actions, but consequences there were. We will come to Mr Thrimble and his injuries shortly. By exposing your body with the intent to shock and offend, you not only committed a public order offence, but also engaged in sexual activities in the presence of children, contrary to the Sexual Offences Act."

"Sexual activities?" said Toyah.

"Objection!" shouted Clovenhoof. "Counsel is badgering the witness."

"I have no further questions," said the prosecuting solicitor.

"Damn right," said Clovenhoof.

There was silence in the court until Mrs Bloom coughed politely.

"Do you have any questions for the witness, Mr Clovenhoof?"

"Indeed I do, your holiness," said Clovenhoof and jumped to his feet. "I've googled a few things on the way over and I think I've got this all wrapped up. Miss Wilson, Toyah, has been accused of being topless and thereby breaking the law. It is indeed illegal for a woman to be topless in public," he paused for effect, "*unless* they work as a clerk in a tropical fish store."

Nerys and Ben exchanged glances.

"Senile dementia has hit early," suggested Ben.

"I will show beyond all reasonable doubt that my client was working in a tropical fish shop at the time of the incident," said Clovenhoof, and reached into his big bag.

"I'll stop you there," said Mrs Bloom. "I am aware of that peculiar little law. But it is not applicable here."

"Oh?"

"Firstly, it is reported to be a byelaw pertaining solely to the city of Liverpool."

"I thought we might overlook that in this instance."

"And secondly, it is made up. An urban myth. No such law exists."

"Ah," said Clovenhoof. He removed his hand from his bag, bringing with it a rather sad-looking goldfish in a plastic bag. "I won't be needing this then. Never mind!" he said brightly. "Onward! Miss Wilson, the prosecution asserts that you aired your nipples in order to cause shock and offence."

"But I didn't," said Toyah.

"Why did you do it then?"

"I was trying to make a point."

"With your nipples?"

"Er, yes."

"And what point were your nipples trying to make? What, indeed, were these most versatile and communicative of nipples pointing out?"

"They – I mean I was pointing out that women should be able to use their bodies – our bodies – as we want. We ain't harming no one. It's my body. Leave me alone."

"I'm impressed," said Clovenhoof. "Such expressive boobs you have. So, was there intention to shock or offend?"

"No way," said Toyah.

"In fact, it was a philosophical point they were making, an argument about personal freedom and women's rights?"

"I s'pose so."

"Then your fun bags weren't offensive or shocking, but actually informative and educational?"

"Er."

Clovenhoof turned to address the court, leaning on the wooden bar of the dock in a manner Nerys was sure he had deliberately borrowed from some TV courtroom drama.

"I ask the jury, can you condemn a woman for having educational fun bags?"

"Mr ... Clovenhoof, was it?" said Mrs Bloom. "There is no jury in this court and can you please refrain from your coarse language. Breasts, I think, would be the appropriate term."

"Breasts it is. I bow to your superior medical knowledge, your highness."

Despite Freddy's playful mockery, Michael was very pleased with the camouflage suit and night vision goggles. If he was going to track the Beast of Boldmere, the unholy progeny of Jeremy 'Satan' Clovenhoof, then he needed something to give him an edge.

He inspected himself in the full-length bedroom mirror at home. Even in combat gear, Michael cut a truly fine figure. The close-fitting black leather and thermal-dampening synthetic weave made a living shadow of him. He could already picture himself, perched on the rooftops of Sutton Coldfield like some dark guardian, a cloaked avenger ready to leap into action and protect the local citizenry from the forces of darkness. And, when the creature was safely dealt with and Michael's great deed was publicly

294

recognised, then a grateful Chip would have to promise Michael a seat on ...

"Is this something we need to talk about?"

Michael whirled round.

Andy stood in the doorway. Andy, the small but perfectly formed package, with a quizzical look on his face and a half-eaten crackerbread in his hand.

"Do you think we need to spice things up in the bedroom or something?" he said.

"What?" said Michael. "Why does everyone think this is something kinky?"

"That's a lot of leather. Is it some sort of midlife crisis thing?"

Michael tutted.

"If you must know, this is a ... it's a work thing."

Andy munched on the crackerbread and considered this.

"Yeah. That doesn't make it sound any better."

Adrian Thrimble, construction worker and ARC Residential and Construction employee, wore a medical support boot and a neck brace to show just how *horribly* injured he was. Nerys reckoned he must have also sprained his acting muscles, because his testimony was so stilted and obviously scripted that poor Adrian appeared to be in danger of collapsing under the strain.

"So, you were shocked?" asked the prosecuting solicitor.

"I was," said Adrian. "I was shocked and offended and ..."

"Alarmed?"

"Alarmed and distressed," said Adrian, and breathed a sigh of relief at having reached the end of the sentence.

"There is no doubt that Miss Wilson exposed herself – we have heard that admission of guilt – but the court wants to know how that immediately affected you."

Adrian nodded. "I was shocked and offended and alarmed and ..."

"No, not that bit. The next bit. What happened after you were exposed to Miss Wilson's nude body?"

Adrian licked his dry lips. "I was so shocked that I tripped and fell from the scaffolding."

"How long have you worked in the building trade, Mr Thrimble?"

"Eighteen years, sir."

"But, surely," said the solicitor, "a man of your experience wouldn't let something like this cause you to stumble and fall. Do you fall off scaffolding much, Mr Thrimble?"

"No," he said, with the sudden confidence of someone permitted to tell the truth for once. "Not had a single accident in all those years. And not a day off sick neither."

"So, are you telling the court that this act of indecent exposure, shocking and distressing as we know it to be, was the sole cause of your only work-related accident in eighteen years in the business?"

The nervousness was back. Nerys saw the man's eyes flick to Chip Malarkey, just for a moment.

"Yes."

"Thank you. I have no further questions," said the solicitor.

"Right. My turn," said Clovenhoof. He beamed at the witness in the box. "No need to worry. Just some routine questions, Mr Thrimble."

Adrian nodded and smiled awkwardly.

"Now, have you heard of Malebolge?"

"What?" said Adrian.

"Never been there?"

"No."

"Oh. Because it's where you're going."

"Is it in the south of Spain?" Ben whispered to Nerys.

"And there you'll be burned and scourged and forced to endure dropsy or leprosy or one of those hilarious diseases," said Clovenhoof.

"What?" said Adrian.

"It's the eighth circle of Hell," explained Clovenhoof, "reserved for liars and falsifiers."

"What?"

"Mr Clovenhoof!" said Mrs Bloom.

"Sorry, your chiefliness. To put it simply, Mr Thrimble: Liar, liar, pants on fire. You were not knocked from your perch by Miss Wilson's nipples, but were frightened by a monstrous beast."

"Well, I ..."

"A beast created in the laboratories of the ARC Research Company not more than a mile from where you had your accident."

"Slander!" shouted Chip.

"A beast cooked up from the DNA of a Yorkshire terrier named Twinkle, assorted dead mammals, and the most handsome devil there's ever been."

"Did he say Twinkle?" said Ben.

"I've been told ..." Adrian began to say.

"Mr Clovenhoof!" snapped Mrs Bloom. "You will not sully this court with ridiculous rumours of the so-called Beast of Boldmere. Mr Thrimble has given his version of events and the court accepts them at face value."

Clovenhoof tutted. "Fine. If you can't handle the truth," he muttered. "Let's proceed in this ludicrous fiction that you were knocked off the supermarket roof by Toyah's breasts."

"But ... but I was," said Adrian.

"I see. And so we need to fully establish that they caused you distress and alarm for, without distress and alarm, there can be no case of public indecency under the Sexual Offences Act." He whirled to the public gallery and waggled his eyebrows at his neighbours. "That's right. I read something."

Clovenhoof turned back to the witness. "Mr Thrimble, you say you were shocked and offended. Are you shocked and offended by the sight of breasts?"

Adrian frowned. "I suppose. Isn't everyone?"

"I wouldn't know, Mr Thrimble. I haven't conducted a survey. Have you?"

"I'm sorry?"

"I'm sure you are. So, this is a personal issue. Are you mastophobic?"

"Am I what?" said Adrian.

"Do you suffer from an irrational fear of breasts?"

"No."

"But you were offended and distressed by Toyah's?"

"Um, er, yes."

"So you don't like breasts generally?"

Adrian struggled. "No. I, er, I like breasts." He blushed at his own unexpected words. "I mean, I don't mind them. No, I mean ... I mean I'm a man, aren't I?"

"Are you?"

"Yes."

"Well, it's nice that you're certain of at least one thing."

"No, I mean men like breasts. Straight men, I mean and, er ... lesbians?"

"I'm sure we all like lesbians, Mr Thrimble. I am confused that you have expressed a personal liking of breasts but are nonetheless offended and distressed by them."

"I just think they shouldn't be out in public. That's not right."

"Oh," said Clovenhoof surprised. "Do you have issue with other body parts being publicly displayed? Elbows? Ears?"

"Er, no. But breasts, nipples, they're, er ... sexual, aren't they?"

"Mr Clovenhoof," said Mrs Bloom. "I do not see this questioning leading anywhere, apart from causing the witness acute embarrassment."

"It will, your grace. I'm just trying to ascertain the nature of the witness's shock and offence. So, Mr Thrimble, nipples are sexual, eh?"

"Yes."

"But they're not genitalia."

"No, but they're ..."

"Arousing?"

"If you say so," said Adrian, his tone making it clear that the word was Clovenhoof's not his.

"Very good," said Clovenhoof ,and removed several large mounted photographs from his bag. "So these are arousing, yes?" he asked, holding aloft a picture.

"Yes, I guess," said Adrian.

"Where did he get that from?" said Nerys.

"The internet?" suggested Ben. "I think he's just cropped it and blown it up."

"They do look inflated," she replied. "Those must give her chronic back ache unless they're full of helium."

"So, you are aroused by this image," said Clovenhoof.

"Someone might be," said Adrian.

298

Clovenhoof shuffled the picture to the back to reveal another set of breasts. "And these are arousing?"

"Yes," said Adrian.

"And these?"

"Yes."

"And these?"

"Yes!"

"So, someone whips these out and men get aroused and fall off scaffolding. Is that it?"

"Yes."

"If she whipped those out, I think someone would end up with concussion," said Nerys.

"I'd like to show the court a short video clip," said Clovenhoof, and skipped over to the screen with a DVD.

The screen fuzzed and then showed what appeared to be an Olympic diving event.

"What is this, Mr Clovenhoof?" said Mrs Bloom.

"London 2012," Clovenhoof replied.

"And why are you showing us this?"

"Because ..." He hit pause and pointed to an indistinct blob in the spectator stands. "Is that you, Mr Thrimble?"

"How can anyone see from that image?" argued the prosecuting solicitor.

"It is," said Mr Thrimble.

"This would be young British diving hopeful Tom Daley about to win the bronze medal," said Clovenhoof. "Did you enjoy the event, Mr Thrimble?"

"Um, yes. A great achievement. Proud to be there."

Clovenhoof nodded, pressed play, and made a show of watching the screen. "Were you shocked and offended?" he asked.

"What?"

"Young Tom's nipples are clearly on show, in a public place no less. Were you offended?"

"What? No."

"Whyever not?"

"Because he's a man. I don't ..."

"No, I understand," said Clovenhoof. "You've limited yourself to admiring only lady bits. Fair enough. But were the straight women, gay men, bisexuals, and the generally unfussy shocked and offended by Tom's nipples? Look at them. Must have been cold in the pool. Like hat pegs, they are."

"Of course not," said Adrian. "He's a man. Men's nipples are different."

"Non-functioning, you mean."

"No. They're just not the same!"

Clovenhoof stroked his chin thoughtfully. "Sounds like you're being a wee bit sexist there, Mr Thrimble."

"I'm going to have to stop you there," said Mrs Bloom.

"Getting too close to the truth, eh?" said Clovenhoof.

"No. You're wasting too much of our time. There are other cases to be heard today, and your prattling serves no purpose. Mr Thrimble expresses a reasonable disgust at women parading their breasts – their secondary sexual characteristics – in public, and I don't think there's any value to be gained from further dissection of the issue."

"But I had further evidence, and a list of surprise witnesses."

"I'm sure you did. However, this court has already come to a verdict, so sit down."

"Has it?" said Nerys to Ben.

Mrs Bloom tidied her notes and, with a nod of approval from her fellow magistrates and the court legal advisor, said, "This court finds Miss Toyah Wilson guilty of the offence of indecent exposure, contrary to the Public Order Act. Though the defence contends that Miss Wilson had not *intended* to offend Mr Thrimble or cause his injuries, UK law does not deal with *intentions* but with outcomes. Deliberately or as a result of unthinking negligence, Miss Wilson caused offence, not only to Mr Thrimble, but to our great town. She also caused a workplace injury that could have been avoided if she had been more modest and considerate in her actions."

"Considerate?" shouted the SCUM leader Sandra from the public gallery. "She was taking part in a peaceful protest!"

"You will be quiet, madam, or you will be arrested for contempt of court," warned Mrs Bloom. "And, peaceful or not, this court and this borough has little time for your juvenile cause. It is clear to anyone who has eyes to see that we do not want you to impose your breasts upon us."

"I don't mind that sort of imposition," said Clovenhoof.

"Silence! I, for one, am sick of these parenting Nazis telling us decent folk how we should raise our children. I come from a whole generation raised on formula milk, the three 'R's, firm discipline, and a sound respect for good and honest British values. Keep your New Age philosophies to yourself and, most importantly, keep your body covered!" Mrs Bloom took a moment to compose herself. "Miss Wilson, you will be fined two hundred pounds and will serve forty hours of community payback."

"Unfair!" yelled Sandra.

"Security, take that woman down," said Mrs Bloom.

As the court security officers pulled Sandra from her seat, there were boos and jeers from the public. Clovenhoof joined in with some armpit farts for no good reason. Toyah gave Sandra a small smile of thanks and solidarity as the SCUM leader was taken away.

"There will be silence in the court!" shouted Mrs Bloom.

The court subsided quickly, less out of fear and respect and more because they'd had their bit of fun and it was over.

"It is clear," said Mrs Bloom, "that there is alarming anti-social behaviour throughout the borough, and there needs to speedy action to deal with it. I will be making a recommendation to the borough council for a new byelaw forbidding all upper body nudity in public spaces and within businesses open to the public. Today it was a builder falling from his scaffolding. Who knows? Tomorrow, a waiter with a hot bowl of soup, or a bus driver carrying dozens of passengers? This menace must be stopped."

Toyah was taken down and the court was cleared. As they filed out, Nerys paused beside Chip Malarkey.

"Stop this now," she said.

"Stop what, Miss Thomas?" he said innocently.

"You've got your hand in this, and I've got a dossier on your dodgy dealings *this* thick. Sort this travesty out or God help you ..."

He smiled. "God help me indeed."

Reverend Zack Purdey, priest of St Michael's Church, was moderately surprised to see a large shadow creeping across the churchyard at dusk. As a spiritual man, working in a historical building surrounded by a graveyard, he had seen more than his fair share of ghostly apparitions. Most had turned out to be cats, windblown bags, wandering drunks, or, on one memorable night, Mr Jeremy Clovenhoof leading the St Michael's cub scouts on an impromptu zombie walk. Armed with his faith, Zack generally took these incidents in his stride, but recent rumours of a wild beast gave him cause for trepidation now.

However, when the shadow tripped and gave a hushed cry of "Oh, bother", Zack relaxed.

"Is that you, Michael?" he called.

The shadow dropped into a ninja crouch and then immediately decided it wasn't worth the effort.

"Hi, Reverend."

"Thought it was you. It's been a while, hasn't it?" He took in Michael's combat overalls cum gimp suit. "Planning on some undercover worship?"

"No, Reverend."

"Because you don't have to sneak back into this church. The door's always open."

"Thank you."

"We've missed you."

"That's nice."

"I could give you a quote about a lost sheep and a shepherd willing to sacrifice all else to rescue that one wandering soul, but I imagine you'd know it better than me."

"I imagine I would."

Michael was momentarily taken aback by the realisation that his current church demanded he fight tooth and nail to stay at its heart, and yet here was his old church telling him, even when he had abandoned it, that it would always hold him dear.

"So, why are you here, exactly, Michael?"

Michael grinned sheepishly. "I was going to ask permission. Well, I wasn't, but I hoped you wouldn't mind. I had planned to climb up the spire and sit on the roof."

Zack pulled a thoughtful face. "Would never have guessed that. Can I ask why?"

"Because of the unparalleled view it offers of the surrounding area."

"Right. So, no suicidal thoughts or anything?"

"Goodness me, no," said Michael. "I'm generally against that kind of thing and, in my case, it probably wouldn't work."

"Wouldn't work?"

"I hoped that I might better see the Beast of Boldmere from up there."

"You believe it's real?"

"I know it is. I've seen it. Stared into its demonic eyes."

"You're speaking figuratively, of course," said Zack uneasily.

Michael said nothing.

Zack looked up at the spire. "I doubt we're insured for this kind of thing."

"Any damages would be paid for."

"And if you slipped ..."

"I shall not slip," said Michael. "And if I did, it would be my own misadventure."

Zack struggled to find further argument.

"Mi casa, su casa," he said with a shrug.

There was an angrily passionate buzz in the Boldmere Oak that night. The women (and man) of SCUM had gatecrashed the weekly pub quiz and, between rounds, cursed the legal travesty they had witnessed that day and toasted the brave spirits of those who had fought the law and lost. Following Sandra's arrest, Clovenhoof had run up a dozen or so T-shirts emblazoned with 'Free The Boldmere One' and was more than put out when Sandra turned up, having been released on bail, pending a future court appearance.

As drinks were pressed in Toyah's and Sandra's hands, and women drank as only young mothers with a night of freedom can do, Nerys drew Clovenhoof into a corner.

"What were you playing at, Jeremy?" she asked.

"Silly buggers?" he suggested, not having a clue what she was on about.

"Your idiotic turn in court. Did you honestly think you could win?"

Clovenhoof gave her the most amazed of stares.

"Win?" he grinned. "Winning wasn't really the point. I didn't plan to win. You know who I am. I did it for the same reason I do everything."

She frowned.

"Because I thought it would be fun," he said, and laughed. "Win? Wow, you are funny."

The pub PA system popped as Lennox turned on the microphone.

"Speaking of fun ..." said Clovenhoof.

"Right," said Lennox. "We have a special bonus round in tonight's quiz, in honour of the women of SCUM."

The Union of Mums cheered loudly.

"The questions and the special 'booby' prize have been provided by Jeremy Clovenhoof. Any issues, take them up with him. I'm just reading the questions. Question one, what is the name of the largest city in Brittany's Finistere departement in Northern France?"

"Clever," said Ben, pressing a fresh glass of Lambrini into Clovenhoof's hand. "I see what you've done there."

"What?" said Nerys.

"It's Brest."

"Question two. The shape of champagne glasses is said to be modelled on which Frenchwoman's breasts?"

"Ten questions on the theme of tits?" said Nerys.

"It would have been twenty if Lennox had let me do a picture round."

Sandra appeared out of nowhere and wrapped an arm around Clovenhoof's shoulder. It was evident that this particular heroine of the hour had gone from nought to plastered in less than fifteen minutes.

"Soooo, Mr Defence Lawyer, what's our next step?"

"Vodka jelly shots," he said.

"I meant after that."

"Curry!"

"No, no," slurred Sandra. "What should our next move be on these horrible totali-ti-ti-tarian small town despots?"

"I wouldn't be asking Jeremy for that kind of advice," said Ben hurriedly, narrowly beating Nerys to it.

"Well," said Clovenhoof, ignoring them, "after the jelly shots and the curry, I would see if they try to implement their stupid cover-me-tits law and then ... and then we should all break it."

"An act of mass disobedience?" said Sandra.

"What?" said Toyah. "Everyone stripping off?"

Clovenhoof nodded, sincerely and drunkenly.

"A big massive Boob Out."

"Making a bold statement regarding our hu..." Sandra hesitated, looking like she was about to throw up but then reining it in. "... human rights?"

"If you like. I'm just saying we should hit them with both barrels, so to speak. A sea of nipples as far as the eye can see."

Clovenhoof's eyes glazed over as he was lost to his drunken vision.

"Question three," said Lennox, "Cameron van der Burgh holds the Olympic record in which discipline?"

"Breaststroke," said Nerys, "and DON'T even think about it, Jeremy."

Clovenhoof was frozen with his hand and his eyebrows raised in the manner of someone who had been cruelly prevented from demonstrating a hilarious visual pun.

Michael regarded himself as a being of considerable talents, and he climbed the spire with ease. He tucked himself into a crevice between two carvings (one a much eroded and sad-looking representation of himself) and looked down upon the surrounding urban landscape. Birmingham, despite its grim industrial history, was an exceptionally green city, and it was only the very tallest trees that impeded Michael's view of the local streets. He scoured the streets with his binoculars until the last of the daylight was entirely gone, and then slipped on his night-vision goggles.

Michael was a shameless technophile and had insisted that he buy himself the very best in surveillance gear. This particular pair of goggles had cost the price of a small car and were equipped with lenses for detecting ultraviolet light, infrared and – he shuddered with delight – thermal imaging. He switched to infrared, scanned the Chester Road, and tapped his ear-piece.

"Little A."

"Yes, Michael," said the computer.

"Continue to scan police radio frequencies."

"Scanning for keywords 'beast', 'creature', and 'animal'."

"Nothing yet?"

"Nothing, Michael."

"Very well."

Michael zoomed in on three figures emerging from the Karma Lounge Restaurant on the Boldmere High Street. Even at a quarter of a mile and in infrared, the hoofed feet were unmistakeable.

"A late night curry for the devil and his apprentices," noted Michael, and smiled.

He realised how much he enjoyed being on this lofty perch. Be it physically, morally, intellectually, or spiritually, he did just love looking down on people. And, thinking that, he had one of those rare and deep moments in which he missed his angelic wings.

"Little A," he said.

"Yes, Michael."

"Have the prices of jet-packs come down at all since we last looked?"

"No, Michael."

"Shame," he said.

He switched to thermal imaging for a clearer view of Clovenhoof, Ben, and Nerys. There seemed to be a miasma of warmth around Clovenhoof's trousers and, as Michael watched, a fresh cloud of hot air tooted from his rear end. The thermal image of Nerys – hot-headed, Michael noted wryly – put a hand to her nose and shoved Clovenhoof in the shoulder.

"Yes, I'm much happier up here," said Michael.

A moving heat source on a nearby roof caught Michael's eye. Closer inspection revealed it to be a domestic cat. When he refocused on the high street, the three people had gone, behind a transit van and into their temporary home.

As Ben shut the door to their coffin-filled bedsit behind him, Nerys gagged with horror.

"Jeremy! Please stop!"

Jeremy went to their mini-fridge and rooted around in the vain hope that there might be a previously forgotten bottle of Lambrini in there.

"What? It's a perfectly natural bodily function."

"Fine, but you've just spent the last ten minutes fogging up the high street with your toxic curry guffs. There's no bloody need to do it indoors too!"

"What can I say? I'm a man with a lot to give."

"Oh, quit it, the pair of you," said Ben. "I'm going to have a cuppa and get down to some taxidermy."

Nerys looked at the clock she'd propped up between the arms of a memorial cherub. "Are you sure? Isn't it late, and aren't you a little drunk to be playing around with needles and hot glue?"

"The alcohol steadies my hand," said Ben. "I do my best work drunk."

"I tried to tell Gordon Buford that," said Clovenhoof, "but apparently it's 'grossly inappropriate' to be drunk in a funeral directors."

Ben put the kettle on, changed into his pyjamas and dressing gown, sat down at his work bench, and inspected his latest project. For the past few weeks, after things had gone a bit quiet on the beast-hunting front, he had returned to the idea of combining his interests of taxidermy, ancient history, and wargaming and was currently building a recreation of the ancient battle of Ipsus. Antigonus's soldiers were represented by a band of grey squirrels, and the Seleucid forces by a small posse of red squirrels. Ben was very pleased with his Seleucid Argyrisapdes, which he had armed with spears formed from old tent pegs and silver shields made from the tin foil bases of mince pies. He had also bought the remains of a ninety-year-old leopard tortoise from a zoo in Wales that he hoped could be used as a Seleucid war elephant.

As he wondered when the mail order tortoise corpse might arrive, and daydreamed of how magnificent it would look in this powerful diorama, he worked on the Antigonid sandals he was currently sewing.

"Can I smell burning?" said Clovenhoof.

"I can't smell anything," said Nerys, slouched on some drapes that served as a beanbag. "You've totally destroyed my sense of smell."

Ben sniffed. There was a faint scent of wood smoke. He looked at the kettle, their small gas heater, and his soldering iron. Nothing was amiss.

"Maybe it's just dust."

Nerys rolled tiredly to her feet, sniffed the air, and then went to the door and looked downstairs.

"We're on fire," she said simply.

Ben leapt to his feet.

"What?"

Nerys pointed to the open door and the wisps of smoke that were now coming through. "We're on fire!"

Clovenhoof's phone began to ring.

"Michael. Hello," he said. "How's things?"

"Jesus!" snapped Nerys. "We're on fire!"

Ben was at the door beside her. Smoke filled the staircase, and down below there was nothing but an orange-yellow glow.

"Oh, Hell!"

"That's right," said Clovenhoof blithely on the phone. "We're still staying above Buford's. Uh-huh. Yeah, that's what we thought. Thanks for letting me know."

He hung up.

"What are we going to do?" said Ben.

"That was Michael," said Clovenhoof. "He says we're on fire. The ground floor is a furnace and the first floor is burning nicely too."

"How the Hell does he bloody know?" said Nerys. "Has he called the fire brigade?"

"Didn't ask," said Clovenhoof, busying on his phone. "I can tweet them though."

"Just call them!" said Ben.

Nerys slammed the door shut. "Right, we hole up in here and wait for the firemen to rescue us."

"This second floor room with no windows?" said Ben, and coughed meaningfully. "And not much air?"

"Then we run downstairs and out," said Clovenhoof.

"We'd be burned to a crisp," said Ben.

"Stupid flammable humans," said Clovenhoof.

A smoke haze was starting to drift up through the floorboards. Ben padded in his socked feet. The floor was getting warmer. Much warmer.

Nerys considered the old brick walls.

"Maybe we can break through. Create a hole for some air."

She went to the shelves of stacked coffins. Underneath the bottom one was a folding, wheeled gurney for pushing them around.

"A battering ram?" she suggested.

"There's a window immediately in front of the stairs on the floor below," said Clovenhoof.

"So?"

"And a long sloping roof just outside that window."

"So?"

"If we could get downstairs and through that window, we could climb onto the roof and get away into the rear yard."

"And again," said Ben, "we'd be burned to a crisp."

"I wouldn't," said Clovenhoof.

"What?"

"Now, we see your true colours," said Nerys, eyes narrowed. "Leave us to die, eh?"

Clovenhoof lifted up the gurney and shook it to unfold it. He then dragged a richly varnished hardwood casket off a shelf and onto the gurney.

"The crematorium ovens have to reach three hundred degrees to burn through one of these bad boys," he said.

"What?" said Nerys, but Ben was several pages ahead of her and could see where this idea was going.

"We'd suffocate," he said.

"Nah," said Clovenhoof. "A single person can last for up to sixteen hours in one of these."

"How could you possibly know that?" said Nerys.

"I've spent considerable time with some of the deeply disappointed individuals who've experienced it. Obviously, that disappointment was within the context of then meeting me."

"I've no idea what you mean," said Ben, "but it's a mad idea anyway. Ouch!"

The floor had transcended warm and was now hot.

"What idea?" said Nerys, coughing at the smoke.

Ben looked at Clovenhoof. "All of us in one coffin?"

"Just the two of you."

"You'll die."

"Care to bet?"

"Someone tell me what the bloody idea is!" growled Nerys.

Ben clambered onto the gurney and knelt in the coffin. He held out a hand to Nerys. "All aboard."

Michael listened as Little A relayed information to him, and then he called Clovenhoof.

"Wassup?" said Clovenhoof.

"The fire brigade is six minutes away."

"Right-o."

"How are Ben and Nerys?"

"I've just put them in a coffin. You know, in preparation."

"Dear God," said Michael. "They're not even dead yet. Are they?"

"Gotta go," said Clovenhoof. "We're going for a ride."

Clovenhoof ended the call.

Michael looked at Buford's Funeral Directors. There was no longer any need for the night vision goggles. The undertakers was entirely aflame, and cast its fiery glow along the length of the high street.

Clovenhoof slammed the lid of the coffin twice.

"Ready in there?"

"What do you think?" came Nerys's muffled reply. "Ben, what have you been eating?"

"Punjabi egg Masala and onion bhaji."

"And I thought the fire was hot!"

Clovenhoof took that as an all clear and, with the gurney-mounted coffin before him, charged at the door. The plan was simple: he would race the gurney down the stairs, open the window, flip the coffin lid, and follow his annoying-not-flameproof flatmates out onto the safety of the sloping roof. He saw it with such obvious clarity in his mind's eye, he was quite taken aback when it didn't work as anticipated.

They smashed through the door just fine and, while Nerys and Ben screamed, plunged onwards down through the billowing smoke and oven-like heat that filled the stairway. Clovenhoof could see nothing ahead of him as he juddered down the steps, and struck the first floor landing far harder than he had intended. The gurney bounced off the floor and Clovenhoof tripped. Ben shrieked. The gurney, wreathed in flames, slammed off the wall directly ahead and the coffin flew off, straight through the window. Clovenhoof, already running/falling at a speed, leapt the gurney and followed the coffin through the smashed pane, grasping at one of its handles as he did.

Nerys was swearing, but it was drawn out into a yell so long, Clovenhoof had no idea what the swear word actually was. The coffin, with Clovenhoof now dragged in its wake, came down on the tiled roof and slid onward towards the roof edge and the yard beyond.

"...uuuuuuuuuuuuuuuuuuuck!" screamed Nerys, clearing up one mystery in Clovenhoof's mind.

The coffin toboggan smashed the plastic guttering at the edge of the roof, flew off, and landed with a bone-jarring clang on the roof of the white stretch transit van parked in the rear yard.

"My head!" exclaimed Ben.

"Hey, guys," Clovenhoof whispered through the coffin lid.

"Are we out?" said Nerys.

"Yes."

"Out of the fire?"

"Guys," said Clovenhoof, "do we know more than one person who owns a stretch transit van?"

"What? No."

"Ah, then I think I might know what started that fire."

"Listen!" said Nerys severely. "Are we out and safe, Jeremy?"

A head momentarily appeared out of the driver's side window, and then the van engine started up.

"Out, yes," said Clovenhoof. "Safe? Um."

The van accelerated out of the back gates of the yard and swung onto Redacre Road.

"What's happening?" yelled Ben.

Clovenhoof lay spread-eagled across the coffin, braced in an effort to try and keep it and himself on the roof.

"It's a little bit hard to explain," Clovenhoof panted.

Michael knew that some individuals regarded him as essentially humourless. Likewise, he had never seen evidence of a sense of humour in the Almighty. However, he found a certain irony that, on the first night he had taken to the heights to search for the Beast of Boldmere, he was given a peerless view of a catastrophic building fire and the sight of a van trying to shake a coffin-riding demon from its roof. *And*, surely, if there was proof of the Lord's sense of whimsy, it was at this very moment, with these spectacles to distract him, that Michael saw the beast he was searching for.

The Beast of Boldmere, big as a polar bear, lithe as a puma, agile as a gibbon, bounded from rooftop to rooftop, throwing tiles and chimney pots aside as it cut across the town towards its obvious target.

"Really?" said Michael to himself.

He made to phone Clovenhoof to warn him, and then stopped, knowing the old devil was in no position to answer any calls.

Nerys had few things to be thankful for.

She had spent what felt like an age in the casket, pressed up against Ben, being flung back and forth and side to side, being slammed into a variety of very hard surfaces, all the while having to breathe in his currified breath. She had also, with the exception of the handbag she had instinctively grabbed, left her life's belongings behind in that burning building: all her clothes, all her personal documents, all the recordings for her Youtube channel, and, gallingly, every scrap of evidence she had on Chip Malarkey's fraudulent dealings.

Nerys had few things to be thankful for, but one of the few was that she had insisted on lying on top in the coffin. Ben was barely larger than her but, even in an inferno, she hadn't been willing to have him weighing down on her. More importantly right now, she was glad she was on top because, in all the violent commotion, she was convinced she was going to throw up.

"I'm sorry, Ben," she wailed.

"It's okay," he whimpered. "You've done nothing wrong."

"It's not what I've done ..." she began to say.

"Hang on!" yelled Clovenhoof.

There was a screech, a thump, and they were suddenly airborne once more. Nerys, arms pinned, clutched at Ben's shoulders. They struck the ground hard, and rolled. The lid cracked violently, and they tumbled out at speed onto tarmac. Nerys scraped along the road and came to a rest in the gutter. She bit her lip at a thousand minor pains, and rolled into a sitting position. Ben was crawling towards her, dazed and groaning, his dressing gown ripped along one side. Clovenhoof was even further down the road, in the messy ruins of the crashed coffin.

And nearby was the oddest sight. A white stretch transit van – Chip Malarkey's stretch transit van – was stopped askew in the road, and the Beast of Boldmere was tearing at its tyres, bumper, and grill with tooth and claw. Nerys knew some dogs chased cars, but she never imagined what they would do if they caught one. Here was a beast that had caught a van and was fully equipped to do something about it.

There was the rending sound of stressed metal, and the wheel arch panel came away in the beast's jaws.

"Jesus, that thing's big," gasped Ben, collapsing next to Nerys in the gutter.

"Still want to stuff it?" said Nerys.

"Shhh, it might hear us," he said.

The unseen driver stuck the van in reverse and powered back up the street. The beast held onto the radiator grill and smashed in the headlights with a free claw as they went.

"That thing doesn't like Chip Malarkey, does it?" said Clovenhoof, limping over while clutching his side.

"It's got good taste," said Ben.

The van swung backwards round a corner and out of sight, the beast still clinging to it.

"Or maybe it doesn't like that van," said Nerys. "It's the one that killed Twinkle."

Ben, battered and bruised, put a comforting hand on her shoulder.

Nerys smiled and then, without warning, vomited all over his shoes.

It started to rain.

Chapter 11 – In which beasts come home to roost, Clovenhoof goes underground, and it all goes a bit Scooby Doo

In the end, they went home.

Buford's funeral directors was a fiery ruin, Ben refused to consider spending another night at his rat-infested shop, and Nerys argued that three smoky and soot-stained individuals checking into a local hotel on the night of a huge fire might result in a swift transfer to the local cop shop. So, they went home.

"ARC Residential and Construction," growled Nerys as she read the banner hung from the scaffolding across the front of their house on Chester Road.

"I can't believe Chip Malarkey started that fire," said Ben.

"The man's a grade A nutjob," said Nerys.

"Worse," said Clovenhoof, unlocking the front door. "He's a believer."

Ben stepped first into the hallway. The carpets had been taken up, and the walls were partially replastered.

"I don't think that's fair," he said. "We know plenty of God-botherers, and they're quite nice people. Actually, they're the nicest people we know."

"What?" laughed Clovenhoof. "Even Michael?"

Ben's footsteps echoed hollowly as he made his way upstairs. "Even Michael. He's a bit of a zealot, but he's a sane and pleasant guy. Perfectly sane and normal."

Michael perched on the edge of the spire's parapet and spied on the town through his surveillance goggles.

Fire crews had arrived at Buford's fifteen minutes earlier and were fighting to put out the blaze. Several streets away, two police cars were parked beside the mysterious, shattered remains of a coffin. Michael had tried to keep a tab on each of the players in the evening's chaos, but all had disappeared. Clovenhoof and his unfortunate human companions had gone off somewhere towards the south. The beast had lost its grip on the van somewhere around Emmanuel Road, and the van had skidded off into Penns Lane.

Michael didn't want to believe the evidence of his own eyes, but that van looked awfully like Chip's. Surely, the man's misguided grudge against Nerys couldn't extend to attempted murder ...

Michael's phone rang. It was Chip.

"Morning, Chip," said Michael, glancing at the time readout in the corner of his goggle display. "You're up late. I was just, erm, thinking about you."

There was silence for a time but for the heavy, ragged breathing of a man who was either out of breath or scared, or both.

"That beast," said Chip.

"Yes?" said Michael.

"It's real."

"I'm afraid it is," said Michael.

"I ..."

"Did you ... encounter it?"

"What do you mean?" said Chip, sharply.

"I ... heard that it had attacked a builder's van a bit earlier."

"What? That thing is the work of the devil."

"Demonspawn," agreed Michael truthfully.

"It must be stopped."

"I did suggest that someone, a faithful member of the church, might be able to track it and capture it."

"Kill it," said Chip flatly.

Michael nodded in the dark.

"I assume that the individual who performed such a valiant and righteous act would earn quite a number of Piety Points."

"Their salvation would be guaranteed," said Chip.

Of the two first floor flats, Ben's was marginally more habitable. Walls had been stripped to the plaster, floor coverings and even some floorboards ripped out. There was not a stick of furniture left. But it was clean, warm, and out of the rain.

Nerys sat curled up in a corner. Ben rolled up some plastic sheeting to make a pillow and hugged his dressing gown about him. Clovenhoof simply laid out on the hard floor.

"It's been a funny old night, hasn't it?" he said.

Ben blinked and stared at the ceiling. "What happened to us?" he said.

"We got drunk, set on fire, rode a coffin round Boldmere, crashed, and then watched a mutant monster savage a transit van."

"No," said Ben. "What *happened* to us? I used to have such a simple life. I had a little flat and a little shop and a two-thousand strong scale replica of the Seleucid army and a burgeoning collection of mounted animals and ... and ... it's all gone. What happened?"

"I'd have thought that was obvious," said Nerys.

"No."

"Jeremy Clovenhoof, Ben. That's what happened to us. We were fine and happy. I had a job I enjoyed, a string of men waiting to wine and dine me, my little flat with my Aunt Molly and her little dog Twinkle. And then *he* came along."

"And that's when your lives truly began," grinned Clovenhoof.

"No," said Nerys. "That's when the crap began. The noise, the *smells*. The fires. I nearly lost my job twice because of you. You succeeded on the third attempt. You've crashed my car. You've upset my neighbours. You've stolen so many mobility scooters, I've lost count. The police come here so often, I'm thinking of giving them their own key. You bring dead things into the flats. Random drunks. Loaded weapons. A baby. A psychotic monkey. It's always you, Jeremy. You, you, you. And now ..." She sighed, exhausted. "No flat. No Aunt Molly. No dog. No man. No future. No life. God, there isn't even any alcohol to numb the pain."

"I don't think we can blame Jeremy for *everything*," said Ben. "It's all very sad and that, but we can't blame him for Twinkle. Or for your Aunt Molly."

"Can't we?" said Nerys. "Do you not see that everything he touches turns to shit?"

"That would be a cool superpower though," said Clovenhoof. "Shit-man!"

"It is a superpower, isn't it?" said Nerys with a cold malevolence. "It is what you do. I think it's time Ben knew the truth."

"Truth?" said Ben.

"Truth?" said Clovenhoof.

317

"Do you not think it odd that this ... individual appears in our lives without warning one day and, immediately thereafter, things just start going wrong? This ... character who behaves like no one else on earth, says things none of us would dream of saying, does things that no sane human would do. Yes, it's almost in-human, isn't it?"

"Inhuman is a strong word," said Clovenhoof.

"It's like he's some alien being or evil visitor from some diabolical realm," said Nerys. "I mean, look at him."

Ben rolled onto his side and looked at Clovenhoof.

"I mean, really look at him," said Nerys. "He doesn't even look normal when you really, really look at him."

"I know it's been a tough night ..." said Ben.

"No. Look!" insisted Nerys. "I think it's time you knew who Jeremy Clovenhoof really is."

"Is it?" said Jeremy, mildly panicked. "Does Ben really need to know?"

"Oh, he does," said Nerys between gritted teeth. "Because I can't manage this alone anymore, and Ben needs to see you for what you really are."

"What is he?" said Ben.

Nerys narrowed her eyes. "He's a git."

Clovenhoof's jaw dropped. He had been expecting something else and had his 'Me? The devil? How ridiculous!' counterarguments all lined up in his mind.

"A git?" he said.

"A bloody stupid git," said Nerys.

Clovenhoof considered this. "I would add," he said, "a bloody stupid git with over a thousand Twitter followers."

Ben nodded and rolled onto his back for sleep. "You're right. A bloody stupid git," he said, comforted by the thought.

"Yeah, but a bloody stupid git with over a thousand Twitter followers and the sweetest baby girl on the planet."

"She's not yours," said Nerys, as she struggled, and failed, to find a comfortable sleeping position.

"She was," he said. "And Toyah says I can look after her two days a week if I want."

"Because she knows free childcare when she sees it."

"And I should think I'll have more free time now that my workplace has been burned to the ground. Every cloud has a silver lining."

"You're an idiot," said Nerys.

Clovenhoof scrolled through the photos and videos on his phone. With the exception of some rudely shaped vegetables and photos of angry people he had met in his daily doings, they were all of Beelzebelle. He watched the videos and let his wonderful little girl lull him to sleep.

The rain didn't let up and, in the hours before dawn, the gutters became babbling brooks, orange and silver in the streetlights. Michael, atop St Michael's, had become a gargoyle, perfectly still and staring stoically at the town beneath him.

The Buford's fire was out, but there were still fire engines and police cars at the scene. Flicking between infrared and thermal imaging, his eyes roved the rooftops and alleys. For the last few hours, there had been few sightings of note. A few people walked (or, more frequently, staggered) through the night. A couple of cats and a one soggy-looking fox braved the rain.

It seemed that the excitement around midnight was going to be the high point of his vigil, but then something slunk into view down the Chester Road. It was prowling along the row of detached garages that ran behind the houses, sniffing this way and that, sensing its way cautiously along the backs of the houses.

"Are you hunting?" Michael mused. "Or going back to your lair?"

The beast padded down from the garage roof and towards the back of one of the houses.

Michael grunted to himself when he realised which house it was.

Nerys woke with a crick in her neck, a stabbing headache, and the mother of all bad tastes in her mouth. It was still dark beyond the curtainless windows. She staggered to her feet in search of paracetamol and water. She grabbed her handbag and popped some pills from the foil. The taps in the kitchen worked – thank God! – and she swilled her mouth under the tepid trickle.

She decided she would take another small nap and wait for the worst of her headache to subside, but then she heard a noise. It was hard to be certain above Ben's snoring and Clovenhoof's farting, but there was definitely a noise coming from above. A scraping, shifting sound.

"Ben! Jeremy!" she hissed. "I heard something!"

"Yeah," mumbled Clovenhoof, rolling over. "That was a wet one."

"No, not that. Someone's upstairs!"

"Not possible, Nerys," said Ben. "Those stairs aren't safe."

"Right, of course. Axe murderers are well known for carrying out risk assessments."

Ben sat up and fastened the cord on his dressing gown. "Maybe it's Gorky," he said.

"Oh, Hell," said Nerys miserably. "That monkey's a bloody psycho."

Clovenhoof was up, and clapped Ben on the shoulder.

"Come on then, let's go and see. Lead the way, Nerys."

Nerys grabbed her handbag as she went to the door, knowing what an ineffectual weapon it was. Perhaps she should put something heavy inside.

The three of them crept up the remains of the stairs, the sounds becoming more distinct as they went. Snuffling, chomping sounds.

"That doesn't sound particularly monkey-like," said Ben.

Clovenhoof's phoned beeped. The other two shushed him.

"It's Michael," he whispered. "He thinks he knows where the beast's lair is."

"One crazy creature at a time, please," said Nerys.

Clovenhoof's phone beeped again. He read the text.

"Ah."

"Ah?" said Ben.

"Yes. That one creature at a time thing. Probably not going to happen."

Nerys stared at him.

"You mean ...?" She pointed up towards the door of her flat.

Clovenhoof shrugged. "Michael. Pff. What does he know? Go on."

Nerys looked back at Ben, who urged her forward with hand gestures.

She edged along the landing to look inside the doorway of her old flat, and gasped with horror. The beast that she'd unleashed from the lab was indeed there, lying on a pile of cardboard, its long limbs stretched out, and its eyes half-closed. Gorky, that ridiculous monkey that caused a great many of their current problems, was sitting on its back, gently scratching between its ears and grooming its fur.

"That's nice," said Clovenhoof, peering round the door frame. "Gorky's found something else to look after. This has got internet meme written all over it. Let me take a picture."

Ben was the last to peek round the doorframe, and, as he did, his foot went through a broken floor board. He made a tiny sound of despair and horror. The beast snapped its head up and roared. Nerys screamed and backed up, tripping over Ben as she did so.

The beast sprang up, spilling Gorky of its back.

"Ooh, who's not an early morning person?" said Clovenhoof.

The beast leapt over them and ricocheted down the stairs. Gorky squawked in rage, frisbeeing the remains of crispy pancake boxes at the intruders.

"Why are there crispy pancake boxes everywhere?" warbled Ben, dazed and alarmed on the floor.

"It's simply what happens when you're top of the food chain," said Clovenhoof. "You eat the best of everything."

Gorky, having seen how ineffective a cardboard frisbee attack was, picked up the jagged remains of a Lambrini bottle and charged at the humans.

"Monkey!" yelled Ben, panicked. "Monkey! Monkey!"

The crazed capuchin coiled like a spring and launched itself at Clovenhoof's face.

"Hey, good bu..." Clovenhoof managed before Gorky enveloped his head like an alien face-hugger.

Clovenhoof flailed, giving out muffled screams.

"Help him!" shouted Ben.

"I think he's doing just fine," said Nerys callously, as she disentangled herself from Ben.

Clovenhoof punched at the air. A random stabbing thumb must have connected with his mobile, and Nerys heard the soundtrack of some video that Clovenhoof had taken of himself and Toyah Wilson's baby girl. Gorky's onslaught stopped, and the monkey looked at the phone screen.

Gorky made a querying sound.

"Mmm mmf ffle park," said Clovenhoof, still with a face full of monkey tummy fur.

Clovenhoof blindly swiped the phone and a fresh video started. He wriggled and huffed to free his face.

"And that's the day we went clay pigeon shooting," he explained.

Gorky cradled the phone in his hands and brought his face close to the image of the burbling baby girl. He cooed softly, and stroked the screen.

"Getting bigger every day," Clovenhoof replied. "Her mum lets me look after her sometimes."

Gorky looked at him.

"I'm sure she'd be delighted to see you again," he added.

"Touching," said Ben. "Now that you've made friends with one dangerous beast, could we perhaps get after the one that's just escaped?"

"Chase it?" said Nerys. "A moment ago we were all cowering in fear of it."

"A momentary lapse in courage," said Ben.

"You're wearing a dressing gown. You're not exactly well-prepared for monster chasing."

"The Arthur Dent look is in this year."

Nerys looked at the room, still startled but also thoughtful.

"The thing I don't get is, why would it make its den here?"

"It's attracted to penthouse living," suggested Clovenhoof.

"It's as though it knows this place. As though it remembers it." She pictured the room as it had been when it was furnished, imagining the little blanket-filled basket that had once stood where that cardboard nest was now. "It remembers having lived here before."

"Before?" said Ben.

"I know it's not scientifically possible, but it's like memories of its previous life have been carried in its DNA. It remembers what – who – it had once been."

"Yes, I'm sure," said Ben doubtfully. "Come on, let's get after it."

They piled down the stairs – two humans, Satan, and a monkey perched on Satan's shoulder – and out of the front door. The rain had worsened, if anything. The pre-dawn sky was slate grey and water had pooled across the front path.

"Where did it go?" Ben asked.

Nerys pointed as something bounded over a low brick wall that bordered the road a few hundred yards away.

"What's down there?" asked Ben, as they crossed over to take a look.

It looked like an overgrown ditch and rushed with rainwater.

"A drainage culvert," said Clovenhoof promptly. "It goes under the road and into a tunnel."

"How on earth would you know a thing like that?" asked Nerys.

"It's a highly desirable tunnel that sleeps three comfortably. Some mates of mine showed it to me," said Clovenhoof. "Dan and Quentin know a lot of interesting things about the area. Did you know, for example, that there's an office in the town, I forget which one, that's got these old radiator pipes where you can dry your socks if you ever need to?"

"That would be an estate agents' office," said Nerys, her eyes narrowed, "and it explains a lot about the funny smell that we sometimes get after it rains."

"So do we need to get down into that ditch to follow it in?" asked Ben, peering at the drop.

"No, there's a manhole cover we can use," said Michael, suddenly beside them.

"Jesus!" gasped Nerys, surprised at his stealthy appearance.

Michael considered this. "Close. Not quite."

Clovenhoof looked Michael's sleek black outfit up and down.

"Did the gimp convention finish earlier than expected?" he sneered, and high-fived his monkey.

"Are those NVGs?" said Ben, interested.

323

"Top of the line," said Michael, slipping the goggles off his brow and letting Ben have a look.

Nerys gave the archangel a sternly unimpressed look. "Gonna take a wild stab here, but is someone hoping to capture the beast in order to win favours with his loony messiah-complex church leader?"

"Chip does not have a messiah complex," argued Michael.

Clovenhoof snorted.

"What?" said Michael.

"There's a pit in the Old Place waiting for Mr Malarkey. He'll be able to play tennis doubles with Jim Jones, David Koresh, and Marshall Applewhite."

"Enough snide remarks," said Michael. "We have a duty to track this monster. Nerys, I'm sure you, of all people, understand the need to contain such a menace, now it's been released."

Michael walked over to a manhole cover and pulled it up.

"I really don't see that it's my duty at all, especially with a hangover," grumbled Nerys, but she followed Clovenhoof as he climbed down the ladder.

Nerys reached the bottom and was relieved to find that there was something solid to stand on. What was less pleasing was the sound of rushing water that seemed very close by. She could see nothing.

"Where are you?" she asked and, just for once, was relieved to hear Clovenhoof's voice.

"Right here. I'll take your hand if you like, just let me give Mr Big a quick shake now I'm all done."

"Are you having a wee?" asked Nerys, incredulous.

"I'm very suggestible," said Clovenhoof. "The noise of running water does it to me every time."

"Jeremy," said Michael, brushing Nerys's side as he stepped off the ladder. "I take it you came down here with a plan? Tell me you've at least got a torch."

"I've got one in the pocket of my dressing gown," said Ben, as he clattered down the steps. As he hit bottom he turned it on. "Better?"

Nerys decided that it was much better. They were stood on a metal grille walkway, six inches above the flowing water. Behind them, the culvert ran out into the open. Ahead, Ben's torch shone a light on the T-junction that split north and south along Chester Road.

"We need to split up and check both of these tunnels," said Michael.

Nerys rolled her eyes. "We only have one torch."

"I have night vision," said Michael, tapping his goggles.

"And I can see in the dark," said Clovenhoof.

"Since when?" said Ben.

"Well, you know how rabbits can see in the dark because they eat lots of carrots?"

"Allegedly."

"I thought I'd learn a lesson from the natural world."

"You don't eat carrots," Ben scoffed.

"No. I eat rabbits. Not sure when the night vision superpowers are due to kick in. Any second now, I reckon."

"Splitting up is such a rookie error," said Nerys. "We're here in the sewers with a fearsome beast. Everyone in the entire world knows that you don't split up or it will just pick us all off, one by one."

"Fine," sighed Michael. "This way then," he said, and led them on.

"They always split up on Scooby Doo," said Ben.

"This isn't Scooby Doo," said Nerys.

Water rushed beneath them, and strange plops and groans echoed along the tunnel.

"It's a bit like Scooby Doo," said Ben quietly. "Four young people ..." He looked at Clovenhoof. "... Young-*ish* people, chasing monsters and solving mysteries."

"They had a dog."

"We've got a monkey," said Clovenhoof, and Gorky squeaked in agreement.

"And we're chasing a dog – of sorts," said Ben.

More true than you know, thought Nerys. The beast was, by all accounts, part-Twinkle. And it couldn't be coincidence that it had made its bed in the same spot as the original Twinkle's bed. Was there more than just a trace of her old pet in that monstrous creature?

"This is like a Scooby Doo chase, and you're all relying on me, the only one with the sense to have a torch," said Ben. "That makes me Fred, by my reckoning. Or maybe Velma, the one with the brains."

Clovenhoof snorted loudly. "Fred? I don't think so. There's only one of us with the looks for that. You can be Velma."

"Neither of you can be Velma," said Nerys. "She's a girl, in case you hadn't noticed."

"Sexist," said Clovenhoof.

"It's clear that I'm the one here with Velma's brains. I just happen to have Daphne's looks as well."

"Michael can be Daphne," said Clovenhoof.

"And this is a female character?" asked Michael.

"Very concerned with outward appearances," said Ben.

"Always fashionably dressed and checking herself in the mirror," said Clovenhoof.

Michael silently reflected on this and offered no complaints.

They continued in silence for a little way.

"I'm not being Shaggy," said Ben sullenly. "Okay. I'm *not* Shaggy."

He slapped the side of his torch. The light was very faint and seemed to be getting fainter.

"When did your torch last have new batteries, Ben?" asked Nerys.

"Never. It came out of a cracker a couple of Christmases ago," said Ben. "Don't blame me, at least I had a torch. Which of you rang the police, by the way?"

There was a silence as nobody responded.

"No signal on my phone," said Michael.

"Me neither," said Clovenhoof, "but I've got wifi from somewhere. I'll tweet them instead."

"You're tweeting the police?" said Nerys. "Is that even a thing?"

"They're always tweeting about their dogs and their helicopter," said Clovenhoof. "I don't see why not. There."

"What have you said to them?"

"Well, remember we can't go over the character limit so I said @WMPolice, *we need your help. Give us a go with your helmet and I'll cum quietly.*"

There was silence.

"Why on earth did you say that to them?" asked Nerys, eventually.

"It's what I always say to them. My little police joke," said Clovenhoof.

"Well, all I can say it that it's a good job you didn't actually say where we are," said Michael.

At that moment, Ben's torch gave up the ghost and died.

"And now we're stuck in the dark."

"Here," said Clovenhoof, and cranked up the brightness on his phone. The bright screen lit up the tunnel ahead. Nerys felt momentarily better, and then she saw the glint of eyes ahead of them.

"Look!" she hissed.

They peered into the gloom. The eyes glittered and drew nearer, accompanied by a skittering sound.

"Rats!" gasped Nerys, as a small creature rushed past them through the tunnel. "I really hope that's a one-off. Foul creatures."

Even as she said it, there were more sets of eyes coming towards them.

"Are they running away from the beast or the water?" asked Ben. "Because I don't know if anyone else noticed, but the water level is rising. My slippers are sopping wet."

Clovenhoof shone the light from his phone towards the floor to see that water was now swirling across the walkway.

"Right," said Michael briskly. "We need to hurry up and find this beast, and dispatch it if we can."

"Dispatch it?" said Nerys. "Surely, we can be more humane than that."

"Subdue it at least," said Michael.

"What weapons have we even got between us?" asked Ben.

"I picked up a housebrick back there, and put it in my handbag to give it some clout," said Nerys, "and I imagine Ben's got a pocket knife on him somewhere."

"Be prepared," said Ben, flourishing a Swiss army knife. "Motto of the boy scouts."

"And paranoid survivalists everywhere," said Clovenhoof.

"Good, that's settled then. On we go," said Michael.

"It could be anywhere by now," said Nerys witheringly. "Or were we planning on just whistling and waiting for it to come?"

Clovenhoof clicked his fingers.

"We can tag it!" he said. He fished a half-eaten crispy pancake from his pocket and waved it under his nose. "Irresistible. Gorky, your collar."

Clovenhoof helped Gorky slip off the plastic collar about his neck.

"And Nerys, check inside your handbag," said Clovenhoof. "I think you might have a small makeup compact that isn't yours."

"Don't be ridiculous," said Nerys, rummaging. "I know exactly what's in h... Oh. That's strange. Wait, did you put that there?"

"Yup," said Clovenhoof. "It's the tracker that helped us to find you when you shagged Spartacus's granddad."

"For the last time, I did no such thing!"

"You do have a certain reputation," said Michael.

"Hey, don't judge a book by its cover," said Ben gallantly.

"No, I judge it by how many library stamps it's got in it," said Clovenhoof.

"What's the plan?" said Nerys loudly.

"Oh. We get the beast to swallow one of these, and we can track it wherever it goes," said Clovenhoof proudly.

"Those trackers won't work underground," said Ben.

Michael scrutinised the tracker in Nerys's compact. "They might work. It's using active RFID so it will transpond with any radio or wireless signal."

They tucked the devices into different chunks of crispy pancake. Clovenhoof tossed one down one tunnel and gave the other a brief, wistful lick before tossing it in the other direction. He pulled out his phone and activated the app.

"It's there, I can see it!" he said. "I can see where we are on here as well, we're right under your Consecr8 church, Michael. I'm on their wifi. See if the app will install on your phone, Michael. I'm not sure yours is up to the – oh, you've done it already."

Clovenhoof rolled his eyes. They walked on, peering into the shadows and feeling the water very definitely sloshing around their ankles.

"Should we go back?" asked Nerys. "This water could get to be a problem if it comes any higher."

"Scared?" said Clovenhoof.

"No," she said. "Although I'm not entirely sure what you think we're going to do once we've cornered it."

"We're going to fell the beast with a housebrick and a Swiss army knife," said Clovenhoof.

"It had better be a bloody fearsome Swiss army knife," she muttered.

"It's got a corkscrew and a pair of nail clippers," said Ben proudly.

"Great. We can offer it a manicure or ply it with wine," she said. "It's not much good really, is it? I wonder if we could poison it? Have you got any more of those pancakes Jeremy? I've got some paracetamol," said Nerys.

"How many?" asked Clovenhoof.

"About six."

"I don't think that would even take the edge off a minor headache for that bad boy," said Clovenhoof. "We need some other plan. Could we trap it inside that bit underneath the church, maybe?"

"I don't think that's a good idea," said Ben.

"Why not?" asked Michael.

"Because then we won't have its corpse to, er, prove it's really dead," said Ben.

"You mean you won't have its corpse to turn into another crazy-ass display to frighten your customers with," said Nerys. "I don't want to kill it."

"And maybe we don't need to," said Clovenhoof. "We just need to show it some understanding. I was so close to getting through to it when I found it in the supermarket."

"Was that before I saw it fling you from the rooftop?" said Ben. "I hope you've thought of something fresh to say to it by now."

"It was in a bad mood."

"Wait!" hissed Michael. "It's on the move! And it's eaten both the pieces of bait."

"Can't resist that pancake goodness," said Clovenhoof.

They all stared at the various phone screens.

Gorky chirruped.

"Yes, it's gone off towards the side," said Clovenhoof.

"How can that be?" said Ben. "I didn't see anywhere off to the side."

"We go back and find out," said Michael. "Quietly now."

There was silence, broken only by the sound of water rushing by and their feet sloshing through the flood. The sound of Clovenhoof loudly breaking wind brought a tut from Nerys and a shush from Michael.

"It was my monkey," he protested.

Gorky gave a little flatulent toot, though whether this was corroboration, disagreement, or sheer coincidence was unclear.

Clovenhoof stopped when he reached the point indicated by the tracker.

"Here," he whispered, indicating a recess in the wall, leading off to a smaller tunnel that they'd walked past. "This bit looks new."

"I've seen the plans for this," said Nerys. "We're under the new church, right? Well, the plans show a set of passageways and chambers where it connects up with the drains and sewers. The completely OCD woman from the council said that it was non-standard."

"Non-standard how?" asked Michael.

"Apparently, it's a bit like the arrangement that you get under portakabin toilet blocks, where you can isolate the mains from the building. She said that it might be that they want to install some eco toilet thing like a reed bed in the future."

"Something like that," said Michael.

"Surely we don't want to actually follow it in there?" said Nerys. "I'm not ready to put my faith in a half brick and Ben's multi-tool."

"And the Lord," added Michael. "We've come this far, haven't we?"

"Although we don't know it's the only exit," said Ben. "What does the tracker say. Jeremy?"

Clovenhoof started at his phone. "Oh. Look at that."

"What? What?" Nerys urged.

"My police tweet's had eleven retweets."

"Jeremy!"

"And @WMPolice have replied."

"Fantastic. Are they coming?

"No, they're just saying the same old, same old about #thinkbeforeyoucall. I can never seem to get them to play."

"And the tracker?" said Michael patiently.

"Hm. It looks as though the beast has gone in a sort of semicircle. See?"

Michael craned over and nodded.

"I think it's doubling back to another access point. We need to move quickly," he said. "Ben, you and I will go where it's heading, and try to get it fastened shut before the beast emerges. Jeremy, can I leave you and Nerys to do this one? I'm sure you'll find a cut-off just through there. Each group has got light and a weapon."

"Knife," said Ben.

"Half-brick," said Nerys unhappily.

"By the way," said Ben, angling a thumb at Michael as he addressed the others, "if we're splitting up and I'm going with Daphne, that means I must be Fred."

"Does not!" retorted Clovenhoof.

"Shaggy, Scoob, see you around," said Ben, and followed the archangel down the tunnel.

As Michael and Ben disappeared into the distance, Nerys turned to Clovenhoof, hands on hips.

"In you go then. I'll be right behind you."

"Hang on a minute." Clovenhoof stabbed at his phone, his face a mask of concentration. "I just tweeted that I was getting wet and wild with my neighbours, and there are some people who want to join in. What do you think?"

"I think the internet's full of weirdos. I'll tell you this for nothing though, none of those people want to come and wade through the sewers. Now get through that door. You've got a beast to chat up!"

Ben and Michael consulted their phones.

"Good. It's still in the same place, just through this entrance. Hopefully it's tired. Have you got the knife?"

"Yes," said Ben, feeling less brave now he was faced with the very real prospect of trying to take down a monstrous beast with a two-inch Swiss army blade. "Shall I go and look for something better, like a chainsaw or a rocket launcher?"

"Have some faith Ben," said Michael, edging into the smaller tunnel. "Everything's going to work out just – oh."

"What can you see?" hissed Ben.

"What appears to be a large puddle of vomit."

"Nasty."

"It looks like mostly crispy pancakes with a side order of GPS tracker," said Michael.

"Ah."

"Which leaves us with the question, where, actually, is the beast?"

Nerys was pleased to be able to stand up straight. They had come through a tunnel that was so low they had to crouch down, but now they were in some sort of room with a higher ceiling. Multiple pipes wove through the space, making it impossible to see right across the room by the light of their phones. Gorky jumped onto a pipe and chittered at the dark.

"How do we close the door then?" asked Nerys.

"I reckon it's this thing here," said Clovenhoof, grunting as he gripped a wheel-shaped handle and struggled to turn it.

"Are you sure?" asked Nerys. "That looks to me as if it's part of that pipe there. Actually, at the risk of being dull and obvious, there's an actual door we can ... "

Clovenhoof's efforts were rewarded when the wheel suddenly freed up, and the pipe that he was facing disgorged a forceful jet of liquid, sending him reeling backwards. Nerys was struck with three simultaneous thoughts. One was that she'd been right about the pipe and, if people would only listen to her more often, then they might do better. Two was that, although they were in a storm culvert, built for the management of excess rainwater, Clovenhoof had undoubtedly opened a sewage pipe. The eye-watering stench was already threatening to overwhelm her. Three ...

"Crap," she squeaked, terrified.

"I know," tutted Clovenhoof. "I do have a sense of smell."

She pointed. They were not alone in the chamber. The beast was approaching the prone form of Clovenhoof. Muscles rippled across its back as it edged forward, tensed to spring.

Nerys looked all around for a weapon. Was there any value in trying to get it to swallow the paracetamol? By the looks of things, she would just need to balance them on Jeremy's face, and the hungry beast would swallow them in a flash.

"Well, hello again! Who's a beauty, hm? Come here and give us a hug!"

Clovenhoof was grinning widely and talking to the beast in a cutesy voice that would have made Nerys hoot with laughter at any other time, but now she worried that he'd got concussion. She hunted around in her handbag for those paracetamol.

"You're just boisterous, aren't you, big fella? I know you just want to play. Come on, wrestling match!"

Clovenhoof clapped, gave a little whistle, and slapped his chest. The beast leapt through the air and landed on top of him, growling and slobbering. It clamped its teeth firmly around Clovenhoof's throat, shaking its enormous head. Nerys screamed and pulled her hand from her handbag. She had a perfume atomiser. Great. She held it up and sprayed it anyway.

There was a momentary sucking and popping noise, which Nerys felt rather than heard, over the sound of sewage rushing from the pipe, and the beast seemed somewhat ... diminished.

It was still there, still a beast, but now it looked like a large and shaggy wolf, not some beast born out of a nightmare.

"Holy water!" she yelled in realisation.

The creature was part-demon after all! But hadn't the touch of her diamante cross, a holy icon, brought the beast out of the little Yorkshire terrier in the first place? Why would holy water have the power now to turn it back?

She pumped the atomiser again. The beast shrank further, but continued to savage Clovenhoof's neck like a rabid hyena.

Maybe it was like electricity, she thought wildly. A small shock was enough to startle and provoke an angry response from it, but a powerful jolt was enough to send it scurrying back, to knock it out completely ...

Nerys continued to spray, but the little bottle was spent.

Clovenhoof gargled as though he was choking on his own blood.

"Gghhh-ad boy! Downnggghhh!"

Gorky did agitated back-flips on the pipe above. In amongst it all, Nerys heard the splash of running feet and warning shout.

Ben and Michael sprinted in. Ben's dressing gown cord wrapped around his leg and he pitched forward noisily into the water, disappearing from sight. Michael stared at the sight of Clovenhoof and the now smaller beast thrashing about in the shallows.

"What the ...?"

"We need holy water!" Nerys yelled.

Michael frowned and then understood.

"Jeremy, old boy, I'm afraid this might sting a bit," he said without a hint of remorse, and plunged his hand into the filthy waters that filled the chamber.

He then said something. To Nerys's ears it sounded a bit like Latin. Actually, it sounded more Latin-y than real Latin, a sort of super-Latin, a language that was to Latin what Latin was to normal modern tongues. Whatever it was, Nerys thought it sounded very impressive.

There was the briefest flash of light and something rippled out through the water from where Michael's hand touched it.

"Holy shit!" yelped Clovenhoof, which was, Nerys supposed, an accurate assessment of the situation.

The beast resting on Clovenhoof's chest now occupied much less space than it had previously. In fact, it occupied the exact space needed for a miniature Yorkshire terrier.

Ben came up from under the water, gasping.

"This isn't rainwater!" he moaned most unhappily.

The dog looked at Nerys and gave a small yip of a bark. She picked it up and tucked it under her arm, as she had done with Twinkle a hundred times.

Clovenhoof hissed in pain as he got to his feet. His already devil-red skin had taken on a deeper, burned tone.

"That stung," he grunted.

"You look like you've got sunburn," said Nerys.

"No one ever got sunburned testicles before," Clovenhoof groaned.

"What's going on?" said Ben. "Where's the beast?"

"Here," said Nerys, jiggling the little dog.

"No. It can't be," said Ben. "The beast is huge and that's ... that's ... Twinkle."

"You know that's not really Twinkle, don't you?" said Clovenhoof. "It's a laboratory experiment. Frankentwinkle. Twinklestein."

"Twinklestein," said Nerys with a smile. "I like the sound of that."

"It's an unholy beast," said Michael.

The beast squirmed in Nerys's grip, and one of its paws expanded and raked the air with huge black talons.

"He's not an unholy beast, he's just a very naughty boy!" said Nerys, rapping it sharply on the nose. "If it does that again, then little Twinklestein won't get any nice treats when we get home."

The claws retracted. The little dog gave a small whine and licked Nerys's nose.

"Better," she said. "Now, let's get out of here."

Gorky swung down from the pipes and landed on Nerys's shoulder. Twinklestein barked at him, and Gorky tickled him behind the ears.

"Do you want to sort that pipe out, Jeremy?" suggested Michael.

"God, yes," said Ben, confused and miserable. "That smell. What on earth is that *smell*?"

Clovenhoof gave a tentative sniff and nodded. "The sewage for this area displays an extraordinary variety. Beef tindaloo, doner kebab and Special Brew are the high notes," he said thoughtfully, "with a dash of soya and halloumi struggling to keep up. Not a bad party game, this. We should play it more often. It's just a shame it wouldn't work on Twitter. Hashtag 'guess what I ate today' would be a lot of fun."

"I think I'm going to throw up," said Ben.

"Come on," said Michael, and helped the poor man out of the chamber.

Clovenhoof turned the sewage pipe handle to cut off the flow, but it came away in his hand with a loud clunk. Raw effluent continued to pour forth.

Clovenhoof shrugged and looked at Nerys.

"Let's go with your plan, and close this door on our way out," he said.

"That's not exactly fixing it, is it?" said Nerys.

"Hey, if nobody can prove I did it, then that's fixed in my book," said Clovenhoof.

They retraced their steps and fastened the steel door across the entrance.

"So, are you saying that this is the Beast of Boldmere, Nerys?" said Ben, as they made their way to the exit.

"I think I'd better get it back to the lab and work out what can be done to contain it," said Michael.

"You'll do no such thing," said Nerys. "The poor little thing is exhausted after all the chasing around. He's coming back with me for a bit of rest and pampering. We'll go and get some of the best butcher's scraps and make him a nice bed."

"You might do better with some crispy pancakes," said Clovenhoof. "Just saying."

Clovenhoof lingered in the rain, once they'd climbed out of the manhole. Much as he relished the foul taint that he'd acquired from his immersion in sewage, he recognised that other people would not appreciate being with him in a confined space. He let the water cascade down his body, and sluiced himself and his clothes down to a level that he judged might be acceptable in the Boldmere Oak. He inhaled deeply to savour the lingering scent, and walked the short distance to the pub.

Lennox raised his eyebrows as he entered.

"Still raining then?"

Clovenhoof demonstrated by wringing out his sleeve on the floor. Lennox offered him a stained beer towel.

"Use that," he said. "I must say, I'm not a fan of your aftershave today."

336

"Lennox, it's probably your beer that makes it smell this way. You should be proud."

He scraped through his pockets and found a five pound note that came with its own little slurry of unidentified stink. He plopped it down onto the bar.

"You do know I'm not touching that, don't you?" said Lennox, looking at the reeking puddle between them.

"You're gonna let me have a drink on the house?" said Clovenhoof, his face lighting up with childlike glee. "You've no idea how I've dreamed of the moment that you'd say you're not taking my money."

"Oh, I'm going to take it, just as soon as you've been through to the gents and given it a rinse," said Lennox.

Clovenhoof complied, using the hand dryer to blow hot air down his trousers as an additional treat.

"Ah, Lennox," he said as he sipped his Lambrini moments later. "There are some days when being soaked to the skin, immersed in sewage, savaged by your mutant offspring, and burned all over is just what you need to make you appreciate a drop of the good stuff."

"I get that a lot," said Lennox as he turned away, polishing a glass.

Chapter 12 – In which protests are made, Nerys gets a lot off her chest, and the alarm is sounded

The Consecr8 church stood at the centre of an area undergoing a transformation. Fifty yards to the south was the leading edge of the Rainbow development, an estate of houses all built in the executive pixie style. Closer, on cleared land, stood the ARC Research Company modules. Earth-movers and a tall static crane stood nearby. On the three other sides of the church were the towerblocks and flats that had once housed hundreds of families but were now almost entirely empty and ready to demolition.

Almost entirely.

Nerys knocked on the door of the only flat that remained occupied in the block nearest to the Consecr8 church.

"Yes?" said the lank-haired old woman who answered the door.

"Jenny?" said Nerys. "We spoke on the phone. My name's Nerys."

Nerys decided not to add, *"We've met before. I was loitering outside the ARC lab, disguised as a prostitute, and you scowled at me so I showed you a bit of thigh."*

"Oh, yes!" said Jenny. "Come in. Watch out for Mr Peppers."

Nerys stepped carefully over the grey cat that was pressing up against the door frame. A powerful pet smell filled the hallway.

"You're earlier than I expected," said Jenny.

"Yes," said Nerys. "I was hoping that I could make a start on the preparations."

A brace of tortoiseshell cats wound themselves around Nerys's legs.

"So, what did you say this thing is you're doing today?" asked Jenny.

"It's a protest event. Local mothers unhappy at the church's attitude to breastfeeding. But it's a family event. You said we could set up on the lawn."

"Absolutely. Happy to help. I refused to move out for that conniving skunk, Malarkey."

339

"I read about you," said Nerys, side-stepping as a ginger kitten swiped at her from a hallway shelf. "Your own protest against an unscrupulous property developer."

Jenny snorted. "Papers made me out to be some sort of crazy cat lady."

"Er, really?" said Nerys. "You did say that you'd make bathroom facilities available?"

"Of course, no problem. This way."

"Well, one of the reasons I've come a bit early is to, er, check things over, and drop off some soap. It won't take long."

"What won't?"

"Bathroom this way?"

Nerys followed Jenny through an obstacle course of house cats and litter trays.

"I'll just be a few minutes. I need to do a risk assessment," said Nerys.

She closed the door on the mildly confused woman and turned to the pristine bathroom with glee. It had been three days since she'd managed to have a shower.

A car transporter lorry stood in the parking area outside the Consecr8 church and, as Michael passed, two men were strapping Chip's battered and savaged stretch transit to the back of it. By the door, a team of men and women were setting up a stall. Boxes, stamped with a smiling baby logo, were being unloaded from a van.

Michael swiped himself into the church. The Consecr8 app on his phone chimed. A jaunty starburst filled the screen. Michael could not hold by a smile of self-congratulation as he took a plush seat in the celebration zone.

"Mrs Bloom," he said, nodding in greeting to the woman next to him.

The look she gave him made Michael immediately reach for his phone to show his authorisation to sit in the superior seats but, before he could do so, Chip spoke from the lectern.

"Welcome, my friends," said Chip.

Michael noted the plaster on Chip's bruised forehead and the grim look in his eyes.

"Our good friend, the very, very Reverend Mario Felipe Gonzalez will be with us shortly, but I have an important message for you all."

The lights lowered. Chip was picked out in a spotlight.

"You've all been working hard in the service of this church. Don't think I haven't seen you scurrying about, doing the Lord's work. And don't think the Lord doesn't see it too!"

"Yeah!" whooped a voice from the congregation.

"Outside, right now, the finest people in baby nutrition are getting ready to distribute free formula samples to local families. We've got bands. We've got face painting."

"And a cake stall!" shouted a woman joyously.

"And a cake stall," agreed Chip with a forced smile. "We're going to have a celebration of our love for each other and our devotion to a wholesome life lived in accordance with God's wishes. We are the embodiment of the perfect religious community, living as the Lord wants all people to live, and we will show the local community what that looks like."

"Amen!" called out a worshipper.

"But, let's not delude ourselves," said Chip.

A slideshow of pictures appeared on the big screen high above him, images of climate change and natural disasters interposed with tabloid newspaper images and TV screenshots of human immorality. Cornish floods, twerking popstars, ice storms in the US, semi-clad nightclubbers, desert sandstorms sweeping through Chinese cities, the latest series of Britain's Got Talent.

"These may seem unconnected," said Chip, "but I wonder if you've analysed it like I have?"

Michael instantly recognised the sermon that Chip had delivered to him in his garage and tuned out the gravy graphs and various inaccurate sex statistics, but saw that the churchgoers all around him were riveted to the onslaught of facts, figures, and lists. There was a hypnotic quality and a seemingly inbuilt authority to Chip's assertions.

"Look around you," said Chip. "Sin and nudity on every street corner."

Several heads turned, checking hopefully for a lack of clothes in their midst. On the screen was the SCUM protest march, Toyah Wilson's nakedness caught on black and white CCTV.

"God is angry," said Chip. "What must he think of mankind? He gave us everything, and we waste our lives with pornography and idleness. He has a plan. He has always had a plan. 'The Lord saw how great the wickedness of the human race had become on the earth, and that every inclination of the thoughts of the human heart was only evil all the time. The Lord regretted that he had made human beings on the earth and his heart was deeply troubled.'"

"Genesis," said Mrs Bloom, nodding approvingly.

"I always think it sounded better in the original language," said Michael.

"Hebrew?"

"The *original* language."

"'So the Lord said, 'I will wipe from the face of the earth the human race I have created','" quoted Chip.

"A flood!" shouted a member of the flock.

"*The* flood, my friends! A deluge! He will purge the earth of all but the most devout and worthy individuals, and I'm helping Him to do that. I have devoted my time to the creation of the Ark. Yes, you heard me right, and you're sitting in it. This church is to be the salvation of the best of us. When the time comes, will you be one of the chosen?"

A hubbub had broken out among the congregation. Questions, disbelief, religious fervour. Chip looked at his people with a savage glee.

"Let's check the leader board, shall we?"

Chip changed the display to a live feed of their piety points. Michael was pleased to see that he was inside the top ten. There were some familiar names up there. Chip Malarkey, Tessa Bloom ... Freddy DeVere? Michael wondered what his receptionist Freddy had done to find himself in such elevated company. Perhaps Chip hadn't been alone in the stretch transit that night, that it hadn't been Chip's hands that had set the fire at Buford's ...

There was a ripple of anxiety around the church as people checked their position.

"If you're in the top one hundred, then you will get the alert when the time comes," said Chip. "Let me demonstrate." He pressed a button and a klaxon sounded in the church for a few seconds.

Michael's phone buzzed. He checked the message. *Alert: It is time. Take your place in the Consecr8 church (test).*

Michael lifted his head and saw that there were people in the other pews getting the same message, but others who clearly weren't. There was an instantaneous rise in the noise level. Michael felt a tap on the shoulder, and turned to the elderly man with a hearing aid across the aisle from him.

"Can you tell me why I didn't get the message?" the old boy asked.

"Where's your name on the leader board?" Michael asked him, pointing.

"There, that's me. Arthur Wilson," said the man, pointing with a grin.

"You're at number two hundred and thirty," said Michael. "You only get the message if you're in the top hundred."

"Get away!" said the old man, incredulous. "So he's going to leave the rest of us behind? Bloody cheek, if you ask me. I pay my taxes."

"I'm sure you do," said Michael.

"Mind you, I'd have given my place to my grandson."

"I'm giving mine to someone special too."

The old man grunted. "Oh, my Spartacus is special, but not in the way you're thinking."

Michael turned fully towards the old man and regarded him curiously. "You'd give your place to Spartacus Wilson?" he asked.

"Course I would."

"But he's not ... not a particularly good person."

"Course he's bloody not. I'm deaf, not blind. But he's still mine, you numpty. Why would you save an old fart like me? In fact, if I was going to end up in a confined space with these people, I think I'd throw myself over the side anyway," said Arthur, and, with that, he got up and left.

Michael looked around and tuned in to some of the animated discussions that had broken out around the church.

"I'm sure some of my points have gone missing."

343

"She's at number nineteen now, but just wait until it gets out about her and that camel."

"All it needs is for five of those people to be in some way, er, incapacitated, and I'm in. Just my little joke, you understand. Ha ha ha."

Michael wondered why Chip wasn't putting a stop to all of this toxic chatter, but, when he looked over towards the lectern, he saw that Chip was in conversation with a man who brandished a microphone and angled the two of them carefully towards his colleague, who was filming them with a television camera.

"Mr Malarkey, is it true that you've swindled vulnerable locals out of millions of pounds?" he asked.

"Who let you in here?" Chip demanded.

"Is it also true that you've funded this bizarre building from your illegal schemes?" asked the reporter.

Freddy appeared and tried to insert himself between Chip and the TV crew.

"If you good people would come with me ..." he suggested smoothly.

"These accusations are utterly groundless," snarled Chip. "That Thomas woman is a liar!"

Urging his cameraman closer, the reporter tried to slide past Freddy. "Our source has uncovered a trail of deceit that criss-crosses the West Midlands."

Michael decided to leave at that point. He glanced up at the leader board on the way out, wondering how much uglier the competition was likely to get in the coming days.

"Do you know where we can find Mr Malarkey?"

A man and a woman had entered the church. They were dressed like police detectives. If they were meant to be undercover, they were rubbish at it, unless they were going undercover as police detectives.

"Sorry, officers," said Michael. "I think he's rather busy at the moment."

The male detective had seen Chip at the lectern and was pushing through the congregation towards him.

The cameraman swung round to capture the new arrivals.

Michael could not hear the conversation that took place, but he managed to lip read the phrases "just after a quiet word" and "pop down to the station, if you like."

Freshly bathed and fragrant, Nerys stepped outside to find Ben setting up a table in Jenny's garden. Across the way, the big formula milk giveaway was under construction. The Consecr8 church was not limiting itself to a simple stall. Around the entrance to the church, various booths and a soundstage were being erected.

"I think our protest event is going to seem a bit pathetic," said Ben.

"What are you talking about?" said Nerys. "We've got badges and brochures and boob-shaped biscuits."

"They're just Hob-Nobs, Nerys."

"And both boobs and Hob-Nobs are ..." Nerys drew a big circle. "... round!"

"Frightening," muttered Ben. "Not got your dog with you?"

"I thought I'd leave Twinklestein at home. He's had a busy couple of days, so he's curled up in his old basket with a couple of chewy dog sticks."

"You know he's not Twinkle, Nerys," said Ben, concerned.

"Not exactly, no."

"And I can't see how that dog is the Beast of Boldmere."

"It's complicated. Isn't that Michael?"

Nerys waved at the man walking away from the church but, apparently lost in thought, Michael didn't notice her.

"Hey, my bookshop's in here!" said Ben, looking at a leaflet showing places in the area that were sympathetic to breast feeding mothers. "Apparently I'll offer a nice cup of tea and a cosy chat."

"There's no mention of terrifying displays of flea-ridden animal carcasses then?" asked Nerys. "You never know, you might get some takers."

"Maybe I should get, you know, a little curtained-off area or something," said Ben.

"Don't even suggest that a woman should hide away when she breastfeeds!" said Nerys. "These SCUM women will tear you apart!"

"I didn't mean for them. I meant for me," said Ben.

A large van reversed up the driveway towards them, beeping as it came. A man got out and approached them.

"Bouncy castle?" he asked.

"Oh, yes, Jeremy said he'd ordered one," said Nerys. "On the lawn here, please."

The man set to work wheeling a large package of bundled-up vinyl down a ramp. Moments later, he had connected up a compressor, and there was a loud buzzing as it started to inflate.

"Kids will love this. It's a nice touch," said Nerys, watching the pink plastic heave into shape. "Now, seriously, Ben, you don't need to get so bashful about women who breastfeed. Just carry on as normal and try to ignore it."

"That's just the problem. It's like that small part of your brain that wants to press a button if it sees a label saying '*do not press this button*'. I know that I wouldn't be able to stop myself thinking about the fact that someone had naked *bosoms* in my shop."

"You worry too much. It's not as if you're going to ..." Nerys gave a little scream and pointed. "Sweet Jesus, it's a giant pair of massive boobs!"

Ben nodded. "Exactly. I'm really afraid I would shout something like that, yes."

"No, look. I mean LOOK!" Nerys grabbed Ben's arm and made him turn to the bouncy castle. She strode over to talk to the man who was closing the back of his van. "Hey, what on earth is this? How could anyone think this is suitable for family fun?"

"This?" he said. "It's exactly what Mr Clovenhoof wanted. We don't get to use it much in this country. Popular at certain types of festivals on the continent, this one. Enjoy it, anyways. I've put the rain cover on it. I'll be back to collect it this evening."

"No, wait!" yelled Nerys, her voice petering to nothing as he climbed into his van and drove away. "Wait! Surely you can swap it for something less ... rude."

Nerys and Ben stood and stared at the castle. The back wall was a woman's face. Framed by blonde hair, she wore a surprised pout as she stared out past the voluminous peaks of her breasts which quivered with the vibration of the pressurised air. The side walls were shaped to resemble the woman's hands, swooping in protectively.

"Well," said Nerys, looking at Ben. "Someone needs to look after it, now it's here."

"What? Not me. I'm the one who's embarrassed to even look at it."

"Call it aversion therapy," said Nerys. "And your first customers have arrived."

Spartacus Wilson appeared around the corner on his bike with a group of boys. They took a moment to stare open-mouthed before dropping their bikes on the grass and launching themselves onto the castle with a series of whoops and hollers.

"No, stop! Take off your shoes first!" shouted Ben, running towards them, waving his arms.

Michael was thoughtful as he arrived back at the flat. Andy greeted him in the kitchen with a cup of tea and a plate of bourbons.

"There's something I want to give to you," said Michael.

"Steady on. We've got time for a cuppa first, surely?" said Andy with a wink.

"This is important."

"If it's his and his matching gimp suits, I might have to tactfully decline."

"Be serious for a second. And that wasn't a gimp suit, not that I know what such things are. Listen, I've got a ... ticket."

"Holiday tickets?" said Andy hopefully.

"Sort of. Sort of," said Michael. "The Consecr8 church have organised a rescue package."

"Right."

"An ark, would you believe, for when the floods come."

Andy gave him a look.

"I think I'm going to need a biscuit. This is simply too exciting."

"I know it sounds crazy. I'm sure it's not going to happen," said Michael, "but what if they're right? Well, if they are right, then I have a ticket, and I want you to have it."

Andy stood there, bourbon in hand, and held Michael's gaze.

"Let me get this straight. We're talking about a biblical flood, as in Noah and his ark and all the animals going in two by two."

"Actually, that's a popular misconception. It was seven pairs of every clean animal – sheep, goats, and the like – and two of every unclean animal."

"Unclean," said Andy hollowly. "So, God, your God, who is a loving and merciful God, I'm sure you've said so, is going to kill nearly every person on earth because ...?"

"Well, the theory is because we have allowed evil to pervade society. Idleness, sin, and evil."

"Right," said Andy, pursing his lips. "Someone has decided that I am more evil than you?"

"Well, I suppose that, given the parameters of this particular enterprise, yes, they have."

"Maybe they're right," said Andy with a shrug. "And the babies?"

"Babies?"

"In what you call the parameters of this enterprise, all of the babies in the whole world are more evil than you as well."

"Nobody's saying that babies are evil," said Michael, feeling that the conversation hadn't gone quite the way he wanted. "You can't go questioning the will of God."

"Can't I?"

"No, he's ineffable."

"He's effing something, I reckon."

"If God wants people to survive the deluge then, in his wisdom, he'd arrange for them to survive. No matter how flawed our systems are, God would have the righteous survive."

"Like people who own boats."

"What?"

"Lots of people live on boats, work on boats, have access to boats. Those people won't die in this flood, so I hope none of them are evil. I wouldn't mind betting that some of those fat cats sitting on giant yachts are polluting the oceans and spoiling the world in the worst ways. Wow, he's a piece of work, your God, isn't he? Did God remember that there are people who've got boats already? Why aren't we trying to save the world from real threats, instead of saying that it's the fault of people who haven't got their gold stars by running around giving away a load of bibles to tramps? Yes, I saw you."

"Perhaps we shouldn't take this so literally," said Michael. "Why couldn't you just accept my gift as a symbol of my love and leave it at that?"

"Good grief, Michael, you could have just bought me a watch or something! Or a ring. Are you trying to propose?"

"I'm not sure that the church agrees with things like that ..." began Michael.

"Things like what, Michael?"

"Like ..."

"Like *us* you mean?" spat Andy. "I never heard crap like this from Reverend Zack at St Michael's."

"But that's it," said Michael, clutching at what little certainty he had. "You don't hear this kind of thing from him. We don't hear anything from him. His faith is so .... so soft, that it might as well not exist. He's the kind of believer who will tolerate anything, will accept anyone. What kind of preacher is he if he accepts anything without argument and doesn't give out rules and doctrine? He's like a bloody sponge, Andy. I couldn't tell you one thing he truly believes in."

"Love."

Michael stared at him.

"Tolerance. Acceptance. Takes everything on the chin and doesn't throw anything back. That's love, you pillock," said Andy.

Michael put down his tea. "I love you, you know."

"I know you do," said Andy. "Doesn't stop you being a daft twat sometimes."

"If you love me, take the ticket."

"Why? You think there's going to be a flood? Torrential rain for 9½ weeks?"

"Um, no. That's a film, Andy. It's forty days and forty nights."

"Are you sure? I think that one's a film too. Frankly, this whole thing is creeping me out. If I took that ticket from you, I'd be scared to death that it might just be for real."

"And I'm scared that it might just be real, and I can't bear the idea of you not being safe."

"Safe. And alone?"

"Don't worry about me," said Michael.

"So, I'm meant to survive you. If there's one thing that I can imagine would be worse than the end of the world, it would be surviving the end of the world with a boatload of scurvy-addled God-botherers."

"Please, Andy."

"Tell those elitist fucks to take a hike. I really don't like what they've done to you."

Andy stormed out the door and slammed the door behind him. A second later, he came back in, put the bourbon biscuit back on the plate, and left once more. A few seconds later the door to the flat slammed shut too.

Michael stared into his tea for a long time.

"Idiot," he said, eventually.

Clovenhoof patrolled the area, clipboard in hand, Gorky perched on his shoulder.

"Information centre, check. Bouncy Boob Play Palace, check. Squadron of SCUM mums prepared for an act of mass civil disobedience, check."

Sandra, baby Jeffny or Jeggings or whatever he was called in her arms, approached with a polite but wavering smile on her face. Gorky spotted Toyah and Beelzebelle amongst the SCUMsters, and scampered down to greet his favourite playmate.

"Jeremy, hello," said Sandra. "This is all very ..."

"Magnificent," he said.

"Unexpected," she said. "I thought we were simply coming down to show our displeasure with Consecr8's attitude to breastfeeding mums."

"We are, Sandra," he assured her. "Displeasure we are going to show."

"But this ..."

She looked at the trampolines and the swings and the bouncy castle – she could barely tear her eyes away from the bouncy castle.

"It's brilliant, isn't it?" said Clovenhoof. "Heinz suggested it to when I called him. They had this bouncy beauty at the BodyLove festival in Germany."

"But do we need it?" said Sandra.

"Need? Sandra, for shame. Do we ask whether we need flowers or baby lambs or male nipples? No, we love them for what they are. But think, that's our enemy over there." He pointed at the fête-like atmosphere around the Consecr8 church. "We stand in opposition to them. We have to fight fire with fire. Now, I can assure you that, when all the coaches get here, we'll be out-gunning them on all levels."

"Coaches?" said Sandra, her voice wavering with worry.

"Friends and well-wishers," Clovenhoof grinned.

"But I thought we would just go over there and, you know, tut a bit, and maybe bare a chest or two to show we weren't going to be cowed by any threats of legal action. Maybe get arrested and get our faces on the news."

"Ooh, yes," said Clovenhoof, remembering. "Best sort that out before Nerys goes off prematurely."

"Pardon?" said Sandra.

"I've already sent in the troops."

He pulled out his phone and called PC Pearson. He had his favourite copper on speed-dial.

Outside Consecr8, immaculate hostesses wore smart blue tunics that hinted vaguely at healthcare credentials and beamed with professional compassion as they handed out leaflets and formula milk samples. Across the way, a calypso band was playing *Banana Boat Song*. The Consecr8 event had drawn folks in from the surrounding housing estates.

Nerys had to admit there was nothing that attracted the average Brit quite as much as the promise of something for nothing.

She went up to one of the hostesses.

"So, you're here to give advice to mothers?" she asked.

"Yes, hun," said the woman with a cherry-red smile and the name Petra on her badge. "How can I help you today? Grab some samples. Don't be shy."

"Are you qualified to give advice?" asked Nerys.

"Oh, you should see my professional qualifications," said Petra, with a dismissive flap of her hand. "They'd fill a wall, but I don't like to show off. Now, what was your question, my darling?"

"It looks to me as if you're promoting formula milk," said Nerys, "and trying to persuade mothers that they should give up breast feeding. Is that what you're advocating?"

"Oh, it's a very personal decision, that one, my darling, and we're simply here to make sure that our local mums are in possession of all the facts. Quite a few are choosing to move on to the bottle, you know, and an estimated eighty-five percent say they wished they'd done it earlier."

"Who estimated that?" asked Nerys.

"I'm sorry?"

"And why would you even quote a figure that's estimated?"

"You're absolutely right, hun," said Petra, touching Nerys's shoulder. "Statistics can be so complicated. Best stick to a mother's instinct. My experience is that, once a mother has seen how satisfied a baby is after a feed of formula, she'll drop a lot of her prejudice. If I've seen it once, I've seen it a hundred times."

Nerys looked up as another hostess came towards the table from the direction of the church. Her eyes narrowed in recognition.

"Tina."

"Nerys," said her former boss. "How nice that you've come to engage with us."

Tina's smile was as bright as it was false.

"I was just enquiring about Petra's healthcare credentials," she said, "but now I know. This lot are all off the *Vacuous but Presentable* register, aren't they? And you're here to make up the numbers."

"I do hope you're not here as a bitter ex-employee, just to cause trouble, Nerys," said Tina loudly.

"I wasn't, to be honest, but now that the opportunity has presented itself, how could I refuse?" said Nerys, squaring up to Tina.

"Excuse me," said Petra, tapping her on the shoulder. "What is the *Vacuous but Presentable* register?"

Nerys was about to reveal some insider secrets from the office of the Helping Hand job agency to Petra and the other hostesses, when Sandra appeared with a group of SCUM mothers.

"There you are, Nerys."

"Are you the back-up?"

"I suppose we are," said Sandra. "Jeremy said, 'could you hold off causing a bit of a brouhaha for the moment?' He's having trouble getting hold of the police."

"Really? I can't quite imagine him using the word 'brouhaha'."

"No," butted in Toyah. "His exact words were, 'don't let the shit go down until the pigs get here.'"

"It's okay. I've got this," said Nerys, turning back to Tina. "They made the mistake of sending the B team. There's literally nothing that this woman here can do that I can't do better."

"Nerys, please," said Tina. "Don't embarrass yourself any further. I think we both know that simply isn't true. Let's think of a small working example, shall we?" She pulled a thoughtful face. "Oh yes, I can keep a job and a roof over my head. I don't believe you can say the same at the moment, can you, Nerys?"

"As a matter of fact, I've moved up in the world regarding my employment status," said Nerys. "I perform the genuinely useful function of finding places for people to live, rather than getting gormless temps to stand around pretending to be midwives."

"Who's she calling gormless?" said Petra.

Nerys ignored her.

"Which, of course, you've failed at, because nobody here believes that the Blue Peter dog here and these women are anything other than wannabe actresses, do we, girls?"

There was a cackle of support from SCUM, and Petra's hand wilted away from offering the free samples to everyone who passed. Tina's eyes narrowed and she gripped Petra's wrist.

"No, the samples need to be distributed. We will not back down because of a tiny band of rabble rousers. Now, do any of you ladies want to take the samples? If you don't, I'll need to ask you to move on so that we can engage with other, more enlightened, mothers."

"I'll take a sample," said Toyah, reaching forward.

"Really?" said Nerys.

"Just being practical," said Toyah.

Sandra turned to the SCUM group.

"Right. Women of SCUM, we came here to make a point. I think we know how to respond to this undisguised hostility. Let's do what we came here to do, shall we?"

She led by example, timorously yet nonetheless determined. She pulled off her top and punched the air. Other women followed suit. The last to disrobe was Toyah, who was delayed by the time it took her to unscrew the top from the ready-mixed bottle of formula she'd just taken and lob it up into the air above the hostesses, adding a careful backspin as she did, so that the bottle wheeled in the air, spraying its contents all over them.

Nerys grinned at her.

"Just being practical," said Toyah, and threw off her top.

Nerys whooped with approval.

"You know what, I wasn't going to join in with this, but, as I'm here and as I'm in a position to show up these shapeless harridans, I think I might."

Nerys pulled off her top. She jiggled up and down and considered her best-loved attributes.

"Well, before I'm too old for this kind of thing," she said.

Tina was trying to smooth her hair into order while formula milk dripped into her face.

"Oh Nerys, you will stop at nothing for attention, will you?" she said with a small shake of her head.

"I told you I'd beat you at anything you like, Tina," said Nerys. She pointed for emphasis "Get a load of these genuine, perky thirty four D puppies."

"Really, is that the best you can do?" asked Tina.

"Come off it, Tina. I know you're basically a big shapeless sausage under the Spanx and the Wonderbra. They don't call you the Great Polony in the office for nothing."

Tina gave a squeak of indignation and pulled her tunic off, thrusting out her chest as she did. Petra looked nervously from side to side, gave a small shrug, and started to unbutton her own tunic.

Nerys was about to launch into a critical tirade when she saw, from the corner of her eye, what Toyah was about to do. She leapt aside just in time, as Toyah unleashed her new formula milk weapon. She had taken one of the larger dispensers from the hostess's table and used it to spray a wide arc across the unfortunate, semi-clad women in the way. Tina took a full blast in the face and squealed loudly. She rubbed the mess from her eyes, and met Nerys with an angry gaze.

354

"I had my hair done this morning. Now look at me," she hissed. She clamped her lips and shoulder barged Nerys, shoving her against the SCUM women.

"Oh no you don't, bitch," yelled Toyah, and she launched herself at Tina, dropping her milk-blasting weapon.

Moments later, Nerys stepped away slightly to see that someone else had picked up the milk-sprayer. Most of the other women were engaged in a violent brawl, and all sense of order had gone.

"Great job, ladies!" said Clovenhoof as he approached the scene. "The fuzz are on the way, so just keep the whole thing simmering!"

He ducked as a baby bottle flew past his ear.

Clovenhoof glanced at the milk-splattered fight and wondered, briefly, whether Belle would be frightened by the ruckus. Her mother was perhaps a little distracted to pay proper attention, so he considered going over to say hi. He was saved the trouble when Belle's buggy appeared from the midst of the chaos, pushed by Gorky, looking enormously pleased with himself.

"Ah, Gorky! Hello, my fine young fiend! Belle seems delighted to see you again."

Belle reached forward, trying to grab the smug monkey, burbling with delight as she did so.

"Well, now that the band's together again for a short while, let's go and welcome the other guests, shall we?"

He crossed to the place where Beechmount Drive met the cleared wasteland in the shadow of the crane at the edge of the Rainbow housing development. A line of coaches had pulled up. A balding man with a velour suit, a considerable paunch, and a heavy bag of photography equipment over his shoulder pumped Clovenhoof's hand.

"So very glad to meet you! You are the organiser, yes? I recognise you from the Tweeting photos."

"Heinz," said Clovenhoof.

"From Helsinki," grinned Heinz.

"D'you know, I thought you'd be ..."

"More Finnish? Like the Father Christmas? Or a Moomin?"

"I thought you'd be naked," said Clovenhoof.

Heinz laughed, loudly and unashamedly, and unzipped his velour jacket to reveal his naked torso.

"I will make your dream come true, Jeremy. I have brought my street team with me to make it so."

"Street team?" asked Clovenhoof.

"A superb group of people who admire my art and help me to create my pieces. My work celebrates the human form, and particularly the impact that can be gained from depictions of mass nudity, so my street team love to get naked with others." He took in the scene and beamed. "We're going to make some wonderful art today. I can feel the potential in the air. If we allow the world to reveal its magic to us, then it inspires constant awe."

"I couldn't agree more," said Clovenhoof. "I think some wonderful art might be happening round the corner, if you want to go and check it out."

He moved onto the next coach, which was a smaller one bearing the logo of Birmingham University.

"You've come to get naked?" asked Clovenhoof, peering through the sliding door. An earnest young woman leaned forward.

"We're the Body Image Empowerment Society," she said.

"Excellent," said Clovenhoof, who had no idea what that meant.

"We are currently clothed."

"I can see that."

"The admin team insisted that we should travel fully clothed, and not sit on the seats with our naked bottoms, but we're about to join you now. We're very conscious that there are people in the world who don't even have any clothes. It makes me choke up just to think about it." She turned to the other students on the minibus. "Shall we show some solidarity?"

There was a polite murmuring of agreement.

"Good," said Clovenhoof. "Well, you get your solid-whatevers out there."

Clovenhoof moved on down the line of traffic, but a line of pedestrians appeared before him. They presented a particularly pleasing sight, Clovenhoof thought. They were all dressed in walking boots, beanie hats and nothing else. There were men and women, all of a similar age, which was a shade older than he'd imagined.

"You'd be the Naturist Rambling Society?" he asked the woman at the head of the line.

"How did you guess?" she asked.

"I am curious how such a group would spring into life," he said. "I approve of it entirely, but it's not something I've encountered before."

"We all attended an evening class together," she said. "There were two classes to begin with. One was *fitness for the over-fifties*, and the other was *sociology in the twenty first century*. There were budget cuts that meant that the two classes had to be combined, and the Naturist Ramblers was the result. We like to think that we're strengthening our bone density and exploring social taboos at the same time."

"You're going to learn so much today, I can just tell," said Clovenhoof. "If you go just round the corner, you'll be able to join in the fun."

At the end of the vehicle line was an articulated truck.

"Just here is perfect," Clovenhoof called to the driver. "Set up the disco, and make sure that there are enough foam guns for everybody who wants one."

"Sure thing. I'll extend the turret from the top of the trailer here so that you, and any other authorised user, can fire the foam rocket launcher when things really get going."

"Sweet. That'll just be me then," said Clovenhoof. "Some things are too much fun to be shared with mortals."

Returning to Consecr8, Michael heard the unfolding chaos before he saw it. The commotion of a large crowd was a buzz in the air but over that were the competing outputs of a calypso band and what sounded like an Ibiza nightclub. He rounded the corner of the last block of flats and beheld the scene before him.

Michael had been present at the first Flood, the Great Deluge, when the Almighty in his ineffable wisdom unlocked the great springs of the earth and opened the floodgates of Heaven. He had been there, too, when the Lord spoke to Noah and, exhibiting that rare Godly wit, told a man living in a treeless region hundreds of miles from the sea to build a great big ship out of gopher wood. Michael had also been there in the final preparatory days, when Noah and his family attempted to round up the local wildlife and the tribesmen came to jeer and scoff, and Michael, warrior archangel, stood as protector of the righteous.

Michael regarded this new ark and considered the general similarities and differences between them.

Well, the basic ark was surprisingly similar. Chip, like Noah, had got his measurements right. The new ark, like its predecessor, nestled in a hollow in the ground, ready to be lifted aloft by the flood waters. And it *was* currently raining. Admittedly, if the second flood was going to be enacted through a persistent but light drizzle, then it might take a little longer to cause global panic. Maybe God might indeed unlock the springs of the earth once more and bring sudden and primordial destruction to even the highest mountaintops.

There were very few further similarities to be noted. Maybe the surrounding tower blocks did superficially remind Michael of the stubby Mesopotamian mountains near Noah's home. Maybe. And, certainly, both arks were surrounded by a high level of industry. Beyond that ...

Michael recalled very little full-body nudity during the first flood. He was fairly sure that bare-breasted women weren't engaged in a milk-squirting war. Nor were various naked people engaged in vocal protests regarding the nature of art, love of one's own body, or the right to wander the countryside without any underpants. And, first time round, Satan (who was nicely locked up in the depths of Hell at the time, thank you!) was definitely not stood atop a disco truck, spraying all and sundry with foam.

With eyes averted, and doing his very best to squeeze through the crowd without actually *touching* anything, Michael made his way towards the church building.

Ben struggled to maintain any control of the bouncy castle situation. Spartacus had declared himself King of the Nipple, and ordered his friends to bring him gifts as he wobbled on top of the left breast like a buckaroo.

"Spartacus Wilson, you shouldn't be eating sweets on there. You'll make a horrible mess," he called.

"It's fine," said Jefri Rehemtula, appearing behind Ben and rushing at the castle. "We can clean it off with this."

He sprayed formula milk from one of the sample bottles and tossed another to Spartacus so that he could retaliate.

"What on earth are you doing? You shouldn't be doing that!" yelled Ben, worried that if he got the breasts all milky, he'd be the one who'd have to clean it off.

"Well, your mate is," shouted Jefri. "That one that Sparts's nan calls a wanton hussy. And so's Sparts's mom. I reckon it's part of the fun day. Some naked guy is taking photos of them all, anyway," said Jefri.

"Proper naked, with his tackle all out?" said Spartacus. "I've always wondered if pubes go grey on old people. Was he old?"

"Well," said Jefri, swelling with importance. "He's really old, like forty or something, but he has no pubes. I think he's shaved them off."

"We should report him to the police for impersonating a woman or something," said Spartacus. "That's just gross."

Ben frowned, unsure how to respond. At that moment, he saw PC Pearson jogging around the corner and talking into his radio.

"Lima Zulu Papa to control. We've got a large public order issue here at the Consecr8 church on Beechmount Drive."

The radio crackled back. "Lima Zulu Papa, are you liaising with the fraud squad?"

"Fraud squad?"

"Yes. We've just had a call from them at the same location. They're requesting backup in order to go in and make an arrest."

"Right. Just one thing, control. Are the fraud squad officers fully clothed?"

"Lima Zulu Papa, repeat the question please."

"I said, are they fully clothed, control? I just want to know how I'll recognise them in this crowd."

Ben watched PC Pearson plunge back into the sea of naked people, looking for his colleagues. Before he could get back to the problem of how to impose some sort of order on the bouncy castle, he heard someone call out to him.

"Ben! Have you seen Michael?"

It was Michael's boyfriend Andy, accompanied by the Reverend Zack.

"Oh, hi. Did you check the disco and the protest?" asked Ben.

"If you mean the fight and the fight then yes, we did. It doesn't look as if he's there."

"Perhaps he's in the church then," said Ben. "Can I interest you in any leaflets? I think your church is listed in here, Reverend."

"No thank you, Ben. To tell you the truth, we're a little bit worried about Michael. Andy came to see me with some concerns about his recent behaviour. Would you say he's been acting strangely?"

Ben gave it a moment's thought.

"No, not especially. The only thing I thought was a bit odd was when we were in the sewers and he said he'd never heard of Scooby Doo. I mean, everyone's heard of Scooby Doo, haven't they?"

A look passed between Andy and Zack, but Ben wasn't at all sure what it signified.

"Thanks, Ben. We'll have another look round, see if we can see him," said Andy.

Michael found Chip in his office.

"Ah, Michael. It's gratifying to see you here at this time," said Chip.

"I came to check on the DNA library. All of the samples are stored, ready for your journey."

"*My* journey?" Chip frowned. "You know, I regard you as a trusted member of the flock."

"Thank you, but I've been thinking about that ..."

"And your place aboard the ark is assured."

"That's very nice but ..."

"And I need a trusted member of the flock to carry out some vital work for me."

"Surely Freddy's your assistant," said Michael, not wanting to get side-tracked with admin tasks.

Chip steepled his hands together.

"While young Freddy's devotion has been exemplary, when things become a little more difficult, the church needs people who are prepared to fight for it, to do what's necessary. The church needs warriors, Michael. I think that you could be a warrior."

Michael couldn't help grinning at that. "You're so right Chip. Tell me what's on your mind."

Chip stood up and started to pace.

"A prophet is without honour in his own country. Jesus said that."

"Or something very much like it," agreed Michael.

"There are people who have made it their business to stand in the way of our vision here at Consecr8. Muck-raking journalists, so-called officers of the law and, most pressingly, certain members of the public who are egging them on. You know who I refer to?"

"I think so."

"I need a warrior to remove them from the situation. Permanently."

"It almost sounds as if you want me to kill them, Chip."

Chip's eyes gleamed. He stopped pacing and placed his hands down flat on the desk, leaning forward for emphasis.

"Yes, mate, that's exactly what I want. There are pressures bearing down upon me from all sides. I have a job to do here, and it's a job that I'm taking very seriously. Now, are you with me for the final push?"

Michael thought carefully about what to say to Chip. The manic fervour that emanated from him was almost tangible, and Michael suspected that a reasoned argument was doomed.

"Chip, did you ever consider that your plan might be wrong?" he asked.

Chip was shocked into silence, as though he had been slapped across the face. "Not for an instant, Michael!"

"Not one?"

"It's like I always say when it comes to faith. You just know. In here." He thumped his chest. "A person can never prove faith to you. We all make our own journey to God. I've seen signs, Michael, signs that this is what I'm meant to do."

"What sort of signs, Chip?"

"Signs that not only is the world drifting blindly towards its own doom – singing as its skirts fill with water – but that this town is the centre of a global pandemic of sinfulness."

"Really? Are you sure that there aren't more Godless places than Sutton Coldfield in the world?" said Michael.

"It's the rate of decline you need to look at. Where we came from and where we're going to. The statistics don't lie. This place here used to be what's known as a nice area. Nothing has changed on the surface of things. We're not at war or anything like that, but this area has changed, mate."

"Changed how?"

Chip counted the local travesties off on his fingers. "The local scout group has been thrown out of the national movement. Did you know that? The sales of alcoholic drinks have trebled in the last three years, and acts of public lewdness have gone up tenfold in the same timeframe. The break-in at our lab. A man peeing on me from next door's balcony. The beast ... *that* beast. Should I go on?"

"There might be a perfectly reasonable explanation for all of those things," said Michael, fully aware of what that was – indeed *who* that was – and knowing that it wasn't all that reasonable.

"No, Michael." Chip walked towards the window. "I look out of here and all I see is – oh. Oh Lord, so soon?"

He staggered slightly, and held onto the windowsill. Michael joined him, and looked down at the scene below. There were many more people there than previously, and nearly all of them were naked. From their elevated position in Chip's top floor office, they could see the ample chest of the bouncy castle woman, with small boys swarming across it. They could see Clovenhoof, naked, high in a crenelated turret, spraying foam into the crowd and playing the role of master of ceremonies, microphone in hand, while a monkey jiggled a baby beside him. A disco ball and a laser show played out beneath, as he co-ordinated a naked dance-off. He came down from the turret and danced amongst them, accompanied by the baby and the monkey. He was clearly encouraging the naked dancers to wiggle their bodies for his amusement.

"Where are my people?" breathed Chip. "The ones I hired to promote modesty and responsibility to the community?"

"From what I can see," said Michael, "it looks as if some of them are over there, engaged in bare-breasted fighting with local mothers, and the rest are doing naked funky chicken dances on the tarmacadam. If it makes you feel any better, they seem to be beating the walking group's naked conga."

At the periphery of the bedlam, police cars approached, their sirens and lights adding to the riotous cacophony. Chip walked away from the window, head in his hands.

"Michael, I thought we had more time, I really did. It's been nice to have this chat, but it's time for action."

Chip woke up the computer on his desk and opened an application.

Michael tried to read over Chip's shoulder as Chip typed in a password and clicked a command.

There was a dialog box on the screen and a question: ARE YOU SURE YOU WISH TO INITIATE THE END OF THE WORLD PROTOCOL?

"Really, Chip?" said Michael, making a show of looking at the sky. "It looks like it's fairing up a bit."

Chip clicked 'Yes'.

Chapter 13 – In which the flood arrives

"All right, all right," sighed Clovenhoof, and leapt down to see what Gorky was making a fuss about.

He lifted Belle up, and was struck at once by a deliciously horrible nasal onslaught.

"Wow, girl!" he said, impressed. "The smells you generate from a limited palette of milk and mushed veg. Pure artistry!"

Beelzebelle said something not unlike "yasfurble fplap" in happy agreement.

"And well spotted, Gorky," said Clovenhoof. "Let's get this bum-bomb sorted."

Jiving and body-popping between the nakedness, Jeremy and his young charge threaded through the bedlam and to the Consecr8 building. He got past the besuited and bewildered wholesome young men on the doors by brazenly ignoring them whilst ensuring they got a right eyeful of his swinging junk.

Gorky had a better memory of the place that his owner, and tugged Clovenhoof's thigh hairs to direct him down to the lower level and the toilets. As he did, a loud and insistent siren wail began issuing from wall-mounted speakers. Belle wailed in shock and confusion. Gorky screeched. Clovenhoof raised his eyebrows at the din, and gave Belle a comforting hug.

"It's okay, baby. That sometimes happens when daddy enters holy buildings. Nothing to worry about."

Gorky pointed and tugged Clovenhoof's ear to get his attention. He saw a young man wielding a mop and retreating through the double doors leading to the toilets.

A pool of dark and wickedly pungent liquid began to seep under the door.

"Dodgy kebab?" asked Clovenhoof with sympathy.

"We should probably make our way out," said the young man, dropping the mop and edging towards them. "Freddy has many talents, underappreciated though they are, but it's just possible that this needs the attention of a qualified plumber."

"Oh?" said Clovenhoof.

"Sewage has completely flooded those cubicles down there."

"Hilarious."

Freddy gave Clovenhoof the grim look of a person who had stood ankle-deep in sewage and could not see any hilarity in the matter.

"And it's rising," said Freddy. "Quite rapidly."

"Well, it smells smashing. But you're right, it might be best to go back upstairs and enjoy the fun," said Clovenhoof. "Come and join the party outside, if you're underappreciated in here. I'll get you a foam gun, if you want."

"I'd settle for clean shoes and fresh socks."

"What's that noise, by the way?"

"That's the alarm to say we're shutting off from the rest of humanity. First time I've known a full drill though."

"Shutting off from humanity? Why would you do that?" asked Clovenhoof.

"Oh, something about isolating ourselves from the pervasive evil of modern society," said Freddy.

"There's only one thing wrong with that plan," said Clovenhoof.

"Oh yes? What's that?"

"What if the evil gets shut inside with you?" said Clovenhoof with a wink.

Ben noticed a steady stream of people heading for the church. Quite unusual in that, apart from himself, they were pretty much the only clothed people around. He wanted to ask one of them if they knew the reason for the annoying siren (which now seemed to have been joined by police sirens), but they all seemed far too absorbed in other matters to pay him any attention. He heard a couple having a particularly loud exchange.

"I do hope we're not all going to be squashed in together. There seems to be quite a crowd here," said the man, pulling a wheeled suitcase behind him.

"You've got your little toilet spray in case you need to share a loo, yes?" said his wife.

"Yes, yes. Now, this is where we need to say goodbye," he said, pulling up and parking his trolley case.

"What do you mean?"

"I only have one ticket."

His wife's face fell.

"I'm afraid you can't come," he said. "Besides, who will feed the cat?"

"The cat? You said that the world is ending!" she replied, anger clearly building.

"So it seems. And it's up to me to be one of the chosen few to repopulate the world. I'll go off and do what I must, and you feed the cat. God, Helen, you wouldn't seriously just leave him, would you? Who knew you could be so callous?"

"Repopulate the world? Repopulate the world?" she yelled. "Is that what this is all about? Have you gone mad and decided to join some sort of free love commune thing just so you can go and shag a load of other women? You make me sick!"

Ben watched as she stormed off in fury.

Clovenhoof wandered thoughtfully through the suddenly crowded church with Belle and Gorky. He followed in the wake of Freddy, who was being pestered from all sides by people wanting to know where to go, whether there was Sky Sports, and how long before they needed to start with the procreation. Freddy's tablet dinged with incoming alerts, but he scrolled furiously and stabbed buttons in an attempt to get help on the plumbing issue.

"Mr Malarkey, sir," he called into his phone. "We've got a situation that needs urgent attention." He paused, listening. "Yes, apart from the obvious one. There's some sort of flood of foul water coming up through the basement."

For some reason, the crowd of mostly self-absorbed individuals gave the naked Clovenhoof, Belle, and Gorky a wide berth. It was almost as though there was a six foot force-field around him, keeping everyone else out. Some of the people whispered to each other and pointed at his nether regions. Clovenhoof looked down at the capuchin squatting on the floor between his hooves.

"It's just my monkey," he told the crowd, reassuringly. "Yes, he may be hairy and ugly, but he's really quite nice. Come on, madam, you can stroke him if you like."

"No, I don't know what caused it," said Freddy into his phone, finger in ear to block out the noise. "It's not just a backed up toilet.

It's pumping in faster than I can clean it up. The whole of the toilet block is inches deep now. I think you need to get all of these people out of here because Freddy really doesn't think we should be at home to visitors."

He paused again, listening for longer.

"Yes, sir. I do understand. It's absolutely the mindset that we should have, yes. I'll get everyone onto the upper floors and see what options we have for bailing. Very good."

Freddy ended the call and, with a small pout, changed gear. He addressed the crowd with a showman's flourish.

"Welcome, everyone! If you'd like to follow me, I'll give you the tour. Expect some fun team-building games in the next few minutes. This way, up the stairs!"

Clovenhoof trotted up with the crowd, and then realised that he knew the woman next to him.

"Mrs Bloom!" he said to the magistrate. "Fancy seeing your worshipfulness here!"

"I'm sure we've never met," she said stiffly, eyes fixed ahead.

"It's because you've never seen me like this," said Clovenhoof. "You'd recognise me if I had my wig on."

Michael could hear the commotion coming from the lower levels, and, from the calls that were coming through to Chip, there was plenty going on. Chip shook his head at the latest call and looked at Michael with that penetrating intensity that worked so well from the pulpit but was now beginning to make Michael believe that the man was really rather unhinged.

"Michael, there are people all around us failing to understand the real crisis here. People who are worrying more about a plumbing issue than the epidemic of evil that stalks our streets. Just look at them!"

Michael looked out of the window to see that many people now seemed to be equipped with guns and were liberally spraying everything in sight with lurid pink foam. Down near the entrance to Consecr8, a bunch of men and women battled their way to the door, looking incredibly conspicuous not only because they were dressed like undercover detectives, but also simply because they were dressed.

"Well, I'll tell you one thing," Chip said. "It's time to shut the doors against that forever. Those people don't know it, but they're about to learn how God feels about their monstrous behaviour."

He pressed a button, and there was the sound of large doors and shutters rolling into place. There were squeals of outrage from somewhere below and the sound of hammering.

"That's it. We're in lockdown now."

Michael looked at a warning flashing on Chip's computer screen.

"The plumbing links haven't disconnected," said Chip, thoughtful rather than worried.

"External pressure over-riding the flow valve in the basement toilets," Michael read.

"Right, let's take a look, eh, mate? I've learned, over the years, that you have to lead from the front. If there's a blocked toilet, then Chip Malarkey can sort it out. When it comes right down to it, I'm a man who can do things with his hands."

Chip rolled up his sleeves, fetched a toolbox from a cupboard, and led the way from the room.

Michael followed and was surprised by the number of people who were inside the church, given the short window of opportunity that Chip had allowed for ticket-holders to enter. They had started marking out their personal territory on the first and second floor by partitioning rooms and corridors with their belongings. A sleeping bag to form the outer cordon, a rucksack to trip up unwanted invaders. People were occupying the maximum amount of space that they thought they could get away with in some bizarre kind of arms race.

Michael was horrified to see that Clovenhoof was inside, accompanied by his monkey, still carrying the baby.

"Jeremy, I'd have thought that you'd be more at home outside, with the foam party," he said.

"Oh, don't you worry, Micky-boy," said Clovenhoof. "I've got it covered." He pulled out his phone and showed Michael the display. "Check it out. Nudycam."

Michael was dismayed to see that there was indeed a webcam positioned, presumably on the turret of the disco lorry, to capture the best of the partying nudity.

"Anyway, don't we have bigger fish to fry?" asked Clovenhoof, with a look of studied innocence. "It looks to me as though the bailing crew isn't quite keeping up."

"Bailing crew?"

Clovenhoof pointed.

A human bucket chain ran from a window on the first floor, snaking down the stairs to ...

It looked to Michael's eyes that the ground level had been replaced by a peat bog. A thick carpet of slick dark brown covered the floor. And, looking over the bannister at the great bowl of the church hall, he saw that the foul tide indeed covered the entire ground floor. It was already at the level of the celebration zone pews.

"Is that sewage?" asked Michael, stunned.

Clovenhoof inhaled deeply.

"Yup. The fragrant contents of the human bowel."

Lazy, fat bubbles formed and popped in the great pool of brown slurry.

"But the basement level ..." said Michael.

"Totally submerged," said Clovenhoof.

"But all the DNA samples. My work ..."

Clovenhoof patted him heartily on the shoulder. "Don't fret, pigeonwings. I'm sure it's all fine. Just, you know, covered in shit."

Freddy was loudly urging the people in the chain to work faster, but it seemed to be having little effect.

Michael gave Clovenhoof a hard stare. "I am certain that you did this," he said quietly, through gritted teeth. "I don't know how, but I'm certain that you did."

He turned away and sought out Chip.

"Well, this is a turn up," said Chip, with an unfazed bafflement.

Michael was sure that, if this was someone else's building, someone else's problem, Chip would have been doing one of those backward whistles builders do when preparing to deliver a massive quote for repairs and saying something like 'you've had some cowboys in 'ere, mate.'

Instead, he simply said, "I think I'll head upstairs to have a think about how we sort this out."

"Well, the very first thing you need to do is re-open the doors," said Michael.

Chip clasped Michael's shoulder and gave it a squeeze. "It's not that simple, Michael. This was always designed to be a one way ticket for the faithful, and so I built in certain safeguards to make sure that we wouldn't waver. Those doors cannot be opened for forty days. Also, mate, we can't be sure that there isn't a flood situation on the outside as well."

"Oh pur-lease!" laughed Clovenhoof. "Have you listened to yourself? Check out Nudycam. There's no flood."

"Michael! What is this man doing in here? He's .... he's *unclothed*."

"If we could open the doors, I'd gladly throw him out," said Michael.

"I can't be near such filthy nakedness," said Chip, and backed away. "Michael, sort this out!"

Clovenhoof snapped a picture of Chip's retreating form and typed with a small flourish. "There we go, hashtag batshitcrazy. Michael, you do know that your new friend's going to kill everyone? I suggest you apply your knowledge of technology to the problem of how to override the doors and get us all out of here."

Michael glanced at Chip, but knew that Clovenhoof had a point. He tapped his earpiece.

"Little A?"

There was silence. He tapped it again, but there was only an empty hiss.

"Oh no!" gasped Michael. "The server room is in the basement too. The computers will be under ten feet of water. How can I override the door controls now?"

"I've seen the films," said Clovenhoof. "This is the bit where you hold your breath, swim down through to the bottom levels, cut through the red wire or whatever, and fix the computer system before your air runs out."

"I saw that film too," said Michael coldly. "I don't seem to recall Tom Cruise having to swim through corridors filled with human effluent."

"Details," tutted Clovenhoof. "Another case of scientologists rushing in where angels fear to tread."

The bubbling cauldron of foul-smelling slop crested the stairs and washed across the first floor carpets. Gorky climbed up Clovenhoof's leg to get out of its way.

There was shouting from the stairwell, and they all looked across to see the members of Freddy's human chain staging a mutiny. Tessa Bloom, local councillor and Justice of the Peace, hurled her bucket across the room and shrilled in frustration. The bucket sank without trace into the rising gloop as she scurried away up the stairs, while Freddy looked on in exasperation. Freddy turned to Chip and Michael, gave a small shrug, and climbed the stairs himself.

"Freddy imagines this isn't going to end well," he said to no one in particular.

With the reeking tide of human poo-water on their heels, Clovenhoof and the increasingly squashed crowd of people climbed up through the levels of the church. Everyone was attempting to find a way out, and elbows jostled roughly as they climbed. Gorky kept Belle safe in his arms, and snarled if anyone came too close.

"Oh my God, it's a monkey!" declared a woman. "An actual monkey."

"Well, it is an ark, madam," someone replied.

"Yes, but I didn't expect to actually have share space with the animals."

"Move it!" yelled someone towards the back. "Ugh! It's seeping into my sandals!"

"Surely it must start escaping through the walls or windows or something," said a man with more hope than confidence.

"But surely this place is waterproof," someone replied. "Nothing in. Nothing out."

They emerged onto a crowded roof, the upper deck of the ark. A hardwood rail ran around the sides, and people were hanging off every edge, hollering to the crowds below.

Clovenhoof peered over. With a swell of pride, he surveyed the riotous pandemonium he had helped orchestrate. Milk, foam, laughs, cries, screams, all sewn together with acres of naked human flesh, from the palest freckly white to the richest black. It was like a bare-bottomed United Nations, and it was beautiful.

He realised his phone was ringing.

"Good morning, king of the world here. How can I help you?"

"Tell me you've got my daughter," said Toyah.

Clovenhoof picked out Toyah among the SCUM ladies in the crowd and gave her a wave.

"Certainly have. She's right here with me and Gorky."

Gorky dangled Belle over the side to show her.

"Okay, Bubbles. No need for us to go completely Wacko Jacko," said Clovenhoof. "She's perfectly safe up here with us. Well, when I say safe ..."

"Something seems to be the matter in the church," said Toyah.

"Yes, I think it's fair to say that something's the matter. The church is a giant boat."

"What?"

"Well, an ark really."

"Say what?"

"It's been sealed off from the outside world, and now it's filling up with sewage, which has nothing at all to do with me messing about with the sewage pipes in the drains under the church."

Down below, Sandra leaned in toward Toyah to speak into her phone.

"An ark? Like Noah's ark?" said Sandra.

"Noah didn't have wifi and a coffee bar in his," said Clovenhoof. "Actually, I think the coffee bar's gone now, so, to be fair, neither do we. Anyway, there are people here that would like to escape."

"Leave it with me," said Sandra.

Nerys was beginning to think that things were getting a bit out of hand. She'd given in to some base urges, and it had been enormously satisfying to thump Tina and kick over that stupid display stand that she'd set up, but she had seen someone taking pictures, and there was no saying who might see those pictures. Invariably, if Jeremy Clovenhoof was around, embarrassing pictures would end up in social media. She wondered how much more internet notoriety would be tolerated by her new employer.

A crowd of topless SCUM women moved off with a sudden sense of urgency, like an Amazon raiding party.

"What's going on?" called Nerys.

"The church!" said one.

"It's full of trapped people and it's flooding from the inside!" said another.

"We have to try and help them get out!" said a third, and ran off.

Nerys tried to process this bizarre new piece of information. On a day when so much else had happened that defied reason or logic, it didn't seem so unusual.

"Did Jeremy do this?" she shouted after them, but they were gone.

She looked up at the Consecr8 building. People crowded around the rooftop railing. Clovenhoof grinned down at her, waving. Some distance along from him, and looking far less happy, was Michael.

She cupped her hands to her mouth and shouted. "What's going on?"

"A lot, I'd say," said Andy, next to her.

Andy and the Reverend Zack had returned. Andy had a phone to his ear.

"Oh, you two are a sight for sore eyes!" said Nerys. "It seems as though things have got a bit out of hand."

Zack coughed gently, and Nerys remembered that she was naked from the waist up.

"Yes," she said. "Not this. This isn't what it looks like. Well, I suppose it is, but there's a really good explanation. Possibly. *Anyway*, more importantly, there are people in trouble up there. I'm not sure what's going on."

"The church is full of shit," said Andy.

"I think that's a bit strong," said Nerys, her eyes flicking nervously to the vicar.

"No," said Andy. "Literally. I've just spoken to Michael. Some sort of plumbing catastrophe."

"What can we do?" said Nerys.

Andy studied the scene, his hands on his hips.

374

"Those walls look solid. If we had a wrecking ball, we could force a hole and ..."

He was cut off as the bouncy bosom castle slid past them, pushed and pulled by many semi-clad women.

"Surely it's too far for them to jump," said Zack, "even onto something soft."

"What we need," said Andy, swivelling his gaze around until he found what he wanted, "is ... that. That over there. Come on, Zack. Let's go."

Zack seemed unsure. "Really?"

"Trust me," said Andy. "I used to work in the building trade."

From below deck came the most intriguing of sounds: groans, creaks, and squirts. In his mind's eye, Clovenhoof could picture the viscous tide of sewage breaking through doors, slipping into every crevice, compressing every last air pocket, stress-testing every wall, door, and window. The stairway to the roof was brimming with stinky brown sauce. It gurgled and shifted like the world's crappiest tar pit. The whole sensory experience was like Clovenhoof's intestinal tract after a post-pub kebab, but on a much grander scale. If it wasn't for the actual life-threatening emergency going on around him, Clovenhoof would have pulled up a deckchair and taken the time to savour it.

As it was, he had to make do with watching Sandra gesturing emphatically and issuing instructions to the other naked women. Clovenhoof took photos of the naked women clustered around the inflatable breasts.

"It's like a hive," he said. "They're like the worker boobs all swarming about the queen boob. Nature is truly a wondrous thing."

His phone rang.

"Jeremy, you'd better get Bea out of there safely," said Toyah, a helpless desperation in her voice. "I don't know what sort of crap is going on in there ..."

"We've got all kinds of crap, let me tell you. Light ones, dark ones, firm ones, sloppy ones, those dark nuggety ones that means someone's been drinking Guinness. I could open a crap emporium and everyo..."

"Jeremy!" she snapped, her voice cracking. "Please!"

Clovenhoof stopped.

There was a new voice on the phone. It was Spartacus. "Do not be a complete cock, Mr Clovenhoof. You need to take care of my sister, hear me?"

He looked down at Belle, who reached out and grabbed his horn, laughing. He was suddenly keenly aware of the mortality of the tiny person in his arms, and he was worried. Worrying about humans wasn't really his *thing*, not really his forte. He was much better at the other thing – what was it? – that's right, the complete opposite of worry about people. But this little one was different. He'd put time and effort into her upbringing and education. He'd shared in her nappy-based triumphs. He'd invested in her. With a shudder of repugnance, he realised he actually cared.

"Yes, yes," he said testily. "I'll take care of her."

Gorky screeched at him.

"The 'I' includes you too," he told the monkey. "It's implied. You're part of the Clovenhoof team. Don't hassle me. Nobody likes a monkey on their back, okay?" Into the phone, he said, "We're going to be fine. I think the bouncy castle's in position now."

"No!" said Spartacus. "Just no. Don't even think about it with my sister! It must be a hundred feet!"

"Only a hundred feet," said Clovenhoof reasonably. "Trust me, I've fallen much further in the past."

Michael could see that the semi-clad women had dragged the huge bouncy castle over to the edge of the church. The giant breasts wobbled as it settled into place. The leader of the shameless ladies looked up and gestured to the crowd at the handrail. It was a gesture that said, '*come on, jump! It'll be fun!*', but there was no movement whatsoever from the crowd.

"What is that ridiculous woman up to?" said Chip.

"Well, it's looking like our best option at the moment," said Michael. "If you're waiting for a convenient *deus ex machina* to save us, you'll be waiting a long time."

"Yuck, I hate it when that happens," said Clovenhoof. "The bloody Big Guy being winched out of the Heavens to put everything right."

"The Lord moves in mysterious ways."

376

"Right. And I suppose he's currently moving a pair of gas-filled norks into place for us to jump onto?"

"Look, there are fire engines over there," said Mrs Bloom, pointing off towards the main road.

"But how will they get through this crowd?" said Michael. "The bouncy ... cushion is our only choice."

"Hmmm, well, let someone else try it first," said Mrs Bloom.

Chip harrumped. "I don't think anyone up here is so foolhardy as to ju... Oh."

Freddy DeVere, laboratory receptionist, church helper, and unsuccessful poop-cleaner, climbed over the handrail, gave a little wave to everyone else on the roof, and leapt away from the building. His plummet was marked by a thin scream that was quickly muffled by one of the mammoth breasts. He gave a little whoop of relief, and then rebounded from the steeply angled cleavage and bounced off sideways onto the pavement, landing on his head.

"First aider!" yelled one of the naked women.

"What's Freddy thinking of, joining that *orgy* down there?" said Chip. "Look, a naked first-aider tending to him, with her breasts on show. If Freddy gets complications from his lustful thoughts, then it will serve them all right."

"I doubt that's going to happen," said Michael.

"The devil snares the faithless in all manner of ways."

Michael sighed in the manner of one who had just had quite enough. "Chip – Mr Malarkey – putting aside the facts that, one, the devil isn't snaring anyone down there because he's up here with us ..."

"Hello!" said Clovenhoof, and gave them a cheery thumbs-up.

"... And, two, that your argument isn't even the slightest bit sensible and true. Freddy's not going to swoon from lustful thoughts about breasts. Freddy's gay, Chip."

"Gay?" said Chip, his forehead wrinkling. He gave a small laugh. "No, I don't think so. Homosexuality's not something that you get in a group of decent people. You're mistaken, Michael."

Michael was about to reply when there was movement that made them all turn their heads.

The boom of the building site crane was swinging towards them. All heads on the roof turned to look as the huge hook on the end trailed across in its own, slightly slower arc.

"Oh my good God," said Michael, in quiet surprise and admiration.

"Do you see who's behind the controls?" Clovenhoof grinned.

"I certainly do," yelled Michael, delighted. He turned to Chip. "For your information, Chip, that's my boyfriend."

"What?"

"And the vicar of Saint Michael's church. And they've come to rescue us."

In the glass control cab, Andy stuck his tongue out of the side of his mouth in concentration, and swung levers with a certain devil-may-care attitude. Squashed in behind him, Zack gripped the back of Andy's chair and offered unheard advice (although, given that Zack's eyes were mostly screwed shut in fear, it was debatable how useful that advice was).

Chip shook his head. "Oh dear, Michael. I thought better of you, I really did. It sounds very much to me as if that other church is one of those trendy liberal ones that encourages all this sort of filth. It takes a bit more backbone than that to be a proper Christian."

"This is all very educational," said Clovenhoof. "I always like a nice incoherent rant, Chip, and you seem to me as if you could be a major player if there was ever a TV show called *Britain's got Lots to Shout About*, but I wanted to ask a question of Michael here, who likes to think he's the sensible one."

"Go ahead, Jeremy," said Michael.

"How is your toy boy going to ..."

"Excuse me? Toy boy?"

"Yes. How old is he?"

"Twenty-nine."

"And you are ...?"

"Older than creation, but that doesn't make him my toy boy."

"Makes you a pervert. Anyway, how is he going to get people down with that thing? There are dozens of us, and it's just a hook. Sadly, everyone's not conveniently wearing dungarees so we can hang them up by their straps."

Gorky screeched loudly and beat his chest, then he scampered over the handrail and disappeared from view.

"That was strange," said Michael.

"Did I mention that he's really smart?" said Clovenhoof.

"If he's trying to tell us that we're all in trouble," said Michael, "then that's old news. Look!"

Michael pointed at the burping, seething mess that filled the opening to the stairs they had all just climbed a few minutes ago. It bulged for a second, forming a fat shitty meniscus, and then the bulge burst and began to spread out across the roof-deck.

A massive chorus of "Ewww!" – entirely unique in all human history – swept across the roof.

Clovenhoof focussed on where Gorky had gone. He leaned over the rail to get a better view, jiggling Belle on his opposite hip.

Michael was on the phone to Andy. "... Any thought to how we're going to get everyone down, my love? Wrecking ball? No. This is solid gopher wood – treated cedar wood. You'd kill us all before you made a hole."

Clovenhoof watched as Gorky reached the ground, scampered over to the small parking yard, and climbed up on top of the battered remains of Chip's stretch transit van strapped to the back of a car transporter. He capered on the roof and gave Clovenhoof vigorous arm signals.

"What is that monkey doing on my van?" said Chip.

"Michael! Tell Andy and Zack to see if they can get the crane to lift that," said Clovenhoof pointing at the van. "We'd get loads of people inside."

"It looks somewhat damaged to me," said Michael.

"It's not going to need wheels and a bumper for this job," said Clovenhoof, "and that hole in the roof is hardly going to matter."

"It's not a terrible idea. I take it the monkey thought of it, not you?" said Michael.

"I taught him everything that he knows," said Clovenhoof proudly, as Gorky bent over and showed them his bottom.

Nerys watched the crane swing round and the hook descend. She was mildly jealous that she hadn't thought of it first. She quite liked the idea of wielding power and control on such a massive scale.

"I wonder how he knows what the controls all do?" said Ben.

"Didn't Andy used to work in the building trade?" she replied.

"Yes, as a plasterer's mate, not a bloody crane driver."

As if to confirm this statement, the giant hook swung over the roof of the church, stopped moving sideways, went briefly upwards, and then came crashing down into the centre of the roof, people scattering to either side. Moments later, the hook came up again and swung sideways, further round.

"What the Hell are they doing?" said Ben.

Nerys's phone buzzed.

"It's Andy," she said.

In fact, it was Reverend Zack on Andy's phone.

"Help. Attach. Hook to van," panted Zack. "Straps. Move the people out."

Nerys tugged at Ben's sleeve, pulling him towards the car transporter and van.

"Are you all right, Reverend?" she said.

"Scary," stammered Zack. "Very scary. Heights. Mmmm. Not good."

The exact location of the stairway was lost now, somewhere near the centre of a still-growing pool of poo. The scores of faithful (some regretting their faith at this very moment) pressed up against the railing and stood on tiptoes and tried not to breathe in the stink.

"Hold fast!" yelled Chip. "Hold true to the Lord and he will provide salvation."

"I'd settle for some hand sanitiser," said one woman, miserably.

Down below, Ben and Nerys were busy removing the ratchet straps that held the van to the car transporter and using them to suspend the chassis from the crane's hook. They took the straps under each end, assisted by Gorky, who scrambled underneath without difficulty. Nerys climbed awkwardly onto the top of the van to fasten the straps onto the hook.

"What's she doing with my van?" shouted Chip.

Nerys turned to the cab of the crane and gave a big OK signal to Andy and Zack.

"Is Nerys known for her abilities with knots?" Michael asked Clovenhoof.

"Her party trick is tying a knot in a cherry stem with her tongue."

"Why?"

"It's a transferable skill, Mickey-boy."

"Transferable to this situation?"

"Probably not."

From the bowels of the building beneath them came a deep rending sound like a mighty tree falling.

"You reckon that was something important and structural?" said Clovenhoof.

"This was designed to be an ocean-going vessel," said Michael confidently.

"But not the world's biggest septic tank."

Nerys clambered down, and the crane took up the slack and lifted the stretch transit up into the air.

"That woman is a complete disgrace," said Chip, disparagingly. "She has no shame about her breasts. No shame. And that is *my* van."

Nerys stood on the transporter back and waved directional instructions to the crane cab.

"Look, there's a man taking pictures of her, and she's not even covering herself up!" snorted Chip.

Michael watched the van rise, and elbowed Clovenhoof excitedly.

"Not quite a *deus ex machina*, I admit."

"More of a *transit ex machina*," said Clovenhoof. "Hardly divine intervention, is it?"

Michael shrugged. "I don't know. A Reverend and the sexiest little man in Boldmere. Sounds pretty divine to me."

The van swung towards the roof, where eager hands reached out to steady it so that people could climb aboard.

"Don't be fools!" yelled Chip.

"Man with a baby coming through," said Clovenhoof, and elbowed his way to the front of the crowd.

"That is false hope!" cried Chip. "It's been stolen and misused, and this foolishness is just a symptom of the sickness of this world."

"It's clean," said a woman as she scrambled inside.

With half of the ark passengers stuffed inside and the van doors closed, Michael waved to the crane.

Ben helped form a cordon as the van descended.

"Is my Bea in there?" said Toyah, distraught. "Is she all right? Oh, Christ on a bike, this is doing my head in!"

"It'll be all right," said Spartacus, squeezing his mum's hand.

"I'm sure Jeremy got her in there," said Ben. "We just need them to get it down to the ground now."

"You are stunning, like Amazon women! Your naked forms add so much beauty to the drama of the moment!"

Ben and Toyah looked at the odd little man clicking away with his camera.

"Oi, perv, you can pack that right in!" said Toyah.

"Oh, please, do not misunderstand," said the man, holding up his hands. "I am the conceptual artist, Heinz Takala. I work so often with nudity, but it is rare to capture beautiful women showing their naked breasts in a life or death struggle."

"Have you ever captured a naked woman about to punch your lights out?" asked Toyah.

"No," said Heinz, lifting his camera again. "What would ...?"

Toyah blew on her bruised knuckles. "Well, now you have."

Ben waved frantically as the van touched down, and pulled the doors open.

"Is she there?" demanded Toyah. "Is she there?"

Men and women, young and old, staggered from the van. They were shaken, had unbelievably stinky feet, but were otherwise unharmed. Last of all was Clovenhoof, leaping out with a giggling girl in his arms.

"That was fun! Again! Again!" sang Clovenhoof.

"Not bloody likely," said Toyah, and tearfully threw her arms around her baby and the least ideal father-figure in history.

"Still think I'm a complete cock?" Clovenhoof said to Spartacus.

"Course I do," he said, but hugged Clovenhoof and his family all the same.

Michael watched the crane hoist the transit away from the ground and begin a slow second ascent towards the roof of the flooded ark. He tried not to think about the stuff pooling about his ankles.

"We'll all get aboard this one, won't we?" said the worried and very Reverend Mario Felipe Gonzalez.

"I suppose so," said another man. "Though my wife's going to give me Hell when I get down there. I only wanted her to stay behind to feed the cat, and I didn't even get to do any repopulating of the earth."

"No one's leaving," said Chip. "The cowards may flee, but the faithful must stay strong."

Michael was shaking his head before Chip had even finished speaking.

"Chip, why don't you take a deep breath and look around you? The ark thing just didn't work out. Give it up."

Chip thumped the hand rail angrily. "Chip Malarkey never gives up and he never backs down! That's the only reason I got where I am today."

"Where you are today isn't looking all that great just now," said Michael. "You're trapped in your own ark. Everything in it has been destroyed and, even if the deluge comes, which doesn't seem so likely since the sun's coming out now, this thing won't float."

"Have faith!" said Chip doggedly.

The van was level with the deck. The Reverend Mario Felipe Gonzalez hauled on the bumper to bring it closer and Mrs Bloom, the thwarted procreator, and the dozen or so remaining members of the Consecr8 flock, pulled their legs out of the knee-deep mire and crawled into the van. All except Chip. He remained in position by the ark's railing, as though glued there by something deeper and more profound than a foetid swamp of human filth.

"We need to go, Chip," said Michael from the doorway.

Chip shook his head. "I will not accept any so-called rescue from these tainted sinners! I look down there and I see Sodom and Gomorrah. If I walk amongst them, then they've won."

"It's not about winning, Chip! It's about surviving."

"No, Michael. It's about doing the right thing."

"Like these people, then," he said, gesturing to the crane, the SCUM mums, and the rescue operation going on around them. "These people doing the right thing and helping each other."

"Sinners," said Chip softly.

Michael closed his eyes and shook his head at the man's stubbornness. He shut the rear door on his fellow churchgoers, stepped back, and waved to Andy to lower it.

"You're not going with them?" said Chip.

"No," said Michael.

Chip smiled. "You believe in the ark."

"I believe in giving people one last chance."

Ben had trouble hearing Zack over the sound of the crowds. Around him, people hugged each other in relief at their rescue. Toyah, clasping her baby daughter to her side, had climbed up the turret on the party lorry from where Spartacus and his friends were dropping milk-filled balloons on people. Clovenhoof was deep in discussion with the odd little photographer with the black eye who had regained his composure somewhat.

"There's someone still up there?" he said.

"Michael. And some other guy. Two of them."

"Then we'll get the van back up to them as soon as we can."

Clovenhoof started to adopt various heroic poses while Heinz took photos. Clovenhoof handed Heinz his phone to take a photo.

"I want to post them as hashtag sexy devil, OK?"

"Thank God I am a miracle worker," said Heinz.

From within the Consecr8 building came a whale-like moan.

"That does not sound good," said Nerys.

The van touched down on the ground for a second time, and the rescued church members disembarked.

Michael stood next to Chip and leaned on the railing.

"Do you know why God chose to destroy the world with water?" he asked conversationally.

"Why?" said Chip.

"First line of the Good Book – *one* of the Good Books, 'In the beginning, God created the Heavens and the earth. Now the earth was formless and empty, darkness was over the surface of the deep and the spirit of God hovered over the waters.'" Michael looked at Chip. "It started with water and the Almighty erased it with water. He rebooted His creation. World 2.0."

"He saw that he'd made a mistake," agreed Chip.

Michael's mouth twisted and he shook his head. "The Almighty doesn't make mistakes. He's God, after all."

Michael scoured the crowd below and saw Clovenhoof posing for a photographer. It looked like Clovenhoof was pretending to ride an invisible horse while slapping his own backside.

"There was one individual in Heaven who thought the Almighty had made a mistake in creating man."

"Lucifer. The devil."

"People tend to call him Jeremy these days. But the Almighty always had faith in His creation. Sometimes, I struggle to share God's faith in humanity, but not today."

"But look at them!" said Chip. "Fornicators! Idolators!"

"I know! And these aren't the worst of them. Trust me."

"Surely this world needs to be cleansed, mate? You can sense it, you can almost taste it."

"Maybe, but the Almighty has already done that. He did it once. Aeons ago. He created the world and, as soon as humanity's capacity for evil shone through, He pressed the reset."

"He showed His true power."

"Exactly," said Michael. "He showed what He was capable of and then, afterwards, He made a promise to Noah that He would never do it again. Do you see?"

The van swung precariously as it rose up the side of the ark.

"No," said Chip. "What?"

"The Almighty took His ability to destroy mankind and placed it beyond His own reach. The Almighty has placed His complete trust in humanity. However stupid and shallow and selfish and cruel they might be – and they are – the Lord believes that they will live up to that trust He placed in them."

The van crested the edge of the deck. The flood of sewage was thigh-deep, and Michael waded with difficulty over to the van. He reached for the door.

"Let's just get inside and away from this horrible mess, shall we?"

Chip looked up at the groaning straps and the battered shell of his own transit van.

"You want to abandon this ark for that?" he scoffed. "You're putting your faith in some wire and fabric."

"Right now, I'm putting my faith in the two men at the controls of the crane," said Michael.

He held out a hand to Chip.

The deep and unhappy groans and creaks coming from within the Consecr8 building were a constant noise now but, when there was a sharp crack and the 'pe-yow!' ricochet of bolts or nails or something flying out of the wall, Ben looked round in panic.

"Nerys!" he called. "Did you hear that?"

"Yes," said Nerys. "I really hope it wasn't what I think it might have been."

"Which is what?" asked Ben.

The wall of the church by the side of them suddenly groaned like a wounded animal. Something shifted, and water began to spurt from a gap that had appeared between the hardwood planking. A fine, high-pressure spray of human effluent jetted from the edges of the ground floor doorway.

"That!" yelled Nerys. "Run! Everybody, run!"

The world shifted beneath Michael's feet. Or, to be precise, the waist-deep bog of eternal stench shifted about him. He managed to maintain his grip on the van door and hold himself in place. Just. He made a grab for Chip but, caught unawares, Chip Malarkey was pulled under the surface as though he had been grabbed by a tentacled horror from the deep.

"Chip!"

Michael clung to the van door and fought the pull of the ooze, the forces dragging the crane line several degrees away from the vertical. His arm muscles screamed in agony. If he could just lift his legs out …

Above him, cables snapped loose, and the van swung free to hang solely by the straps wrapped around its front axle.

The deck beneath him suddenly gave way and, within the church building below, walls imploded and Michael was no longer stood on the flooded deck on an ark but mired in the walls of a rapidly emptying bowl. At what had been the centre of the deck, a whirlpool-like vortex appeared, and Michael found himself not dragged directly towards it but off to the left, drawn into its sucking gyre.

He let go of the door handle, rolled in the muck, and looked up to the distant crane cab.

"Andy …" he called, and then the foul soup closed over him.

Nerys had grabbed Ben's hand and pulled him away, but they got no more than a few yards before the Consecr8 doors exploded outwards, and then the wave bore down upon them. Ben had never been in a washing machine, but he imagined it would be a similar experience, if the washing machine was the size of Boldmere and it was filled with human crud. For long, terrifying moments, he had no idea which way was up, and was convinced that he was going to drown in the tumbling blackness, but then he found the pavement. He found it by being slammed upon it painfully, but he clung to it, wondering if he might possibly be able to stand and break the surface of the water. He tried, but then a huge, unseen current dragged him sideways, and he tumbled over and over in a different direction. Panic turned to despair, but then he felt a hand grab his waistband and haul him above the surface. He gasped for air and sucked it in so greedily that he started to cough.

"Put some effort in, Kitchen!" shouted Clovenhoof.

"What?"

"Get on board my inflatable tits, man!"

Ben flailed and felt the touch of slippery plastic. Scrabbling with his hands and with Clovenhoof hoisting him up by his belt, Ben managed to flop onto the sanctuary of the bouncy castle that was now afloat in the vile flood.

Looming above him, Clovenhoof's grinning face was like something out of a nightmare, as Ben spat out the unspeakable detritus from his mouth. Nerys was there already, panting and spluttering. All around them, people were crawling from the filthy water.

"Come one, come all!" bellowed Clovenhoof. "Everyone, come on my tits!"

Ben sat up and took in the scene.

Their inflatable raft drifted on the wave, away from the remains of the church, picking up bedraggled and confused people on its way. The church was gone. Splintered wood and oddments of furniture bobbed in the water. All signs of the formula milk display were gone too, although the sewage in that area had a thick, porridgey look that suggested it was forming part of the flood. Cars had been washed down the street but, miraculously, the disco lorry was still standing, with Toyah, Belle, several boys, and a capuchin monkey gazing down upon the flood.

Ben crawled over to Nerys and gave her a nudge.

"You all right?"

Nerys gave him a look.

"Define *all right*? I think I'm physically unharmed, until the typhoid from the sewage kicks in anyway."

The water level quickly dropped as the dark water spread out across Beechmount Drive and the Rainbow housing estate. The bouncy castle, a score of flood survivors clinging to its lewd surfaces, washed up in Jenny's front garden, where it had been originally placed.

A thought occurred to Ben. "Jeremy, did Michael get out?" he called.

Clovenhoof shrugged. "Michael's a survivor, but I'm not sure exactly where he – ah, there!"

Two figures rose from the swampy remains of the Consecr8 church. Initially, it was hard to determine that they were even human, but, as the sludge slid off them, it became clear that it was Chip and Michael.

"Michael!" shouted Ben. "You're all right!"

Ben slipped off the bouncy castle, rolled in the shallow muck, and picked himself up. Clovenhoof and Nerys managed to make a more graceful exit, and they walked over. Around them, hundreds of people, some clothed, many not, some shit-spattered, many coated in filth, staggered and stared in bewilderment, horror, and revulsion.

"I bet you're loving this," Nerys said to Clovenhoof.

"Don't think I've ever been happier," he agreed.

"Get back!" yelled Chip, flinging his arms and flecks of sewage at the approaching people. "Stay away from me, you filth!"

"It's all right," said Michael, soothingly. "It's over."

"But look at them! Filthy, depraved, sordid, and base!"

He flung out an accusatory finger which seemed to pin this accusation on Nerys's breasts, although Ben couldn't necessarily say which one specifically.

"You ridiculous shit-gobbler!" she snapped. "You're the one who's ripped off hundreds of local people. You're the one who's corrupted local politicians. And you're the one who ran over my dog!"

"Dog?" Chip's fury reduced his voice to an exasperated and breathless squeak. "Who gives a damn about your dog?"

Ben heard a groan (or was it a growl?) from the crane overhead. He looked up at the dangling transit van, then to the empty cab.

Down on ground level, Andy and Zack were approaching through the slurry from the opposite direction. Andy broke into a run.

"You're the animals!" Chip ranted. "Yes! You! All of you! I'd rather be drowning in human waste – yes, you heard me – I'll take any amount of sewage, but you people are rotten to the core!"

"The Almighty has faith in them," said Michael, and placed a hand on Chip's shoulder.

Chip shrugged it off angrily. "Don't try and force feed me that drivel." He looked up to where the top of his ark had once been. "Up there, you almost had me convinced. But now I'm down here with them, up close ..." He gave the crowd an ugly scowl of hatred.

"I admit I struggled with that too," said Michael. "I loved them more the further away from them I was but, down here on earth, eventually ..."

"Michael!" shouted Andy, waving.

Michael grinned and made towards his boyfriend.

"Go!" screamed Chip to the crowd. "Go, all of you! Run to your homes, your pits of sin. The day of cleansing is yet to come, but it will come!"

"The van!" shouted Andy.

"I know!" Michael shouted back. "Ingenious!"

"No!" yelled Andy. "The van!"

Michael frowned.

"You will see God's power in action," snarled Chip. "You will see it come down and wipe the evil from the face of the earth."

"The van," said Michael.

Ben squinted. He felt it might have been a trick of the light but, for an instant, he saw something dark and beastly moving on top of the precariously hung van. There was another growl (or was it a groan?).

Chip looked up at the van – his van – directly above him.

The stretch transit van slipped its final bonds and nose-dived to earth.

"Oh," said Chip.

The van crumpled into the ground, end on, and then stayed there, upright, like a battered white monument to the man it had just squished. Stunned silence held sway over the on-lookers.

"Do you think he's dead?" said Reverend Zack, eventually.

"What?" said Ben.

"Are we sure he's dead?" he said. "I mean, should we try and get him out, give him first aid?"

Clovenhoof clapped Zack on the shoulder. "He's currently taking up a space that looks to me to be about two inches high. I've got a much better idea. Let's order deep pan pizza and then we can make sure we'll have a coffin that's the right size."

"You are a sick, sick man," said Michael.

Zack pulled a face as Clovenhoof cackled at his own joke.

The foam guns of the disco lorry and the hoses of the local fire service were employed to clean off the crowd. An orderly queue formed (because the British – even in an apocalyptic toilet-themed disaster – understood the importance of a good queue).

As they emerged from the human-washing process, Ben took off his jumper and gave it to Nerys to cover her naked upper body.

"Is that your dog?" he said.

"Twinklestein? No, he's at home with a chewy ..."

The Yorkshire terrier yipped at her from the roof of a nearby car.

"Twinkle!" she said sternly. "Come here now!"

The tiny dog stepped from foot to foot nervously, apparently unable to get down from the car. Nerys went over to pick him up.

"Good boy! Who's my beautiful boy, then?"

She tickled him under the chin.

"You know," said Ben, "I had wondered where your dog was because, just before that van came down, I thought I saw something up there and ..."

He stopped, derailed by the ludicrousness of the idea. He looked away.

Andy approached with a pile of fresh clothes.

"Thank you, Andy, my man," said Clovenhoof, reaching for them.

Michael slapped his hand away. "They're not for you," he said, and took the T-shirt from the top. "You were magnificent."

"Thank you, dearest," said Clovenhoof.

"Again, not for you," said Michael.

"I *was* quite magnificent," agreed Andy.

"I don't know how I can ever show you how grateful I am."

"May I suggest sorting your friends out with somewhere to stay, for starters. You know, now that we're nearly done with 'the decorating'. I heard they've been living in utter squalor."

Toyah stepped down from the truck, holding Belle, Spartacus behind her, sploshing experimentally through the muck on the floor.

"Do most protest events end like this?" she asked.

"Jeremy specialises in death and destruction," said Nerys. "This one more than most."

"I'm thinking how we could commemorate this astonishing event," said Ben thoughtfully.

Nerys narrowed her eyes. "Are you about to say something about recreating it as a scale model using stuffed gerbils or something?"

"Um, maybe."

"Naked mole rats would be better," said Clovenhoof.

"Not sure the SCUM mothers would like to be represented as naked mole rats," said Nerys.

"Speaking of which," said Clovenhoof. "Where are they all?"

"They went straight to the Boldmere Oak," said Toyah. "I saw from up there. Lennox has a hose outside to wash them down. I'll join them in a mo."

"I told you you'd enjoy joining a mother's group."

"I've offered to run a self-defence class for them." Toyah beamed with pride. "Anyways, you did all right in there. You got my Bea out safe, although I think your monkey's the one with the brains, to be honest."

"He *is* an amazing monkey."

Gorky back-flipped. Belle clapped her hands in joy.

"And a show off," Clovenhoof added. "You know, you really ought to take him on as your live-in nanny."

Toyah gave him a look. "Has he got some monkey disease or something?" she said suspiciously.

"No, but he really, *really* loves to care for babies. And you can pay him in oranges."

Gorky jumped up and down in approval, while Toyah considered the plan.

"I suppose I'm used to the strange animal smells and things that aren't necessarily house-trained," she said.

"Was it that bad when you were with Animal Ed?" asked Clovenhoof.

"No, I'm talking about Spartacus."

"Mom!" moaned the pre-teen menace.

"And I hope you're still okay with me helping out from time to time?" said Clovenhoof.

"Sure, long as you put some clothes on, that is."

"Hmmmm," said Clovenhoof, regarding his own lack of clothes. "I reckon Heinz would have got some superb shots of me. Wonder what happened to them?"

"You might want to check out hashtag Sutton Sausage," said Toyah, pulling out her phone. "It looks as if Heinz is in the pub as well."

"Come on then, gang," said Clovenhoof to the rest of them. "If Lennox has been kind enough to get his hose out, we really shouldn't ignore the man. To the pub!"

Acknowledgements

As John Donne said, no man is an island, and no book is a solo effort. I mean, obviously, this isn't a solo effort because there are two of us, but even if we had been just one person or were like two people squashed together to make a single author, this still wouldn't be a solo effort.

We'd like to offer a big thank you to Tracy Fenton, Laura Pontin, Sarah Hardy, Karina Garrick, Tracy Karet and Lindsay Stone from *THE Book Club* who read early drafts and gave us feedback and advice and all round support when we needed it.

Thanks also to Keith Lindsay (for some skilful edits and more than a couple of gags in this volume), to Christina Philippou (for proofing this work and helping us see the errors of our ways here and there) and to Mike Watts (for yet another cracking cover).

And, always (and not just because we have to), an enormous thank you to our better halves, Simon and Amanda, who put up with our stupidity on a daily basis.

Seriously. Daily.

About the authors

Heide and Iain are married, but not to each other.
Heide lives in North Warwickshire with her husband and children.
Iain lives in south Birmingham with his wife and two daughters.

Made in the USA
Monee, IL
10 August 2020

37879936R00236